TEMPEST'S LEGACY

I had a brief, intensely detailed fantasy of springing up and hovering, like Keanu Reeves in *The Matrix*, only to land straddling the barghest. After a second I registered how ridiculous that was, and I had a secondary, equally vivid fantasy of my short-assed legs hopping awkwardly across the floor toward Anyan while he stared with a mixture of confusion and horror.

Shaking my head to clear it of my daymare, I ruefully smiled at nothing in particular just as Nell yelled for me from the yard.

'Training time!' I sang, awkwardly and too loudly, before plastering on a grin and pivoting on my heel to flee to the front side of the cabin.

What the hell is wrong with me? I wondered. *Could I be any more of a spaz?*

Luckily, my self-recriminations were short-lived. Mostly because the second I turned the corner I was diving to the ground as Nell tried to take my face off with a mage ball.

Motherfucking gnomes, I thought as I struggled to maintain shields, scramble to my feet, and create a mage ball all at the same time. Nell loved what she called surprises. And by 'surprise', Nell meant trying to maim you when you least expected it.

BY NICOLE PEELER

Jane True novels
Tempest Rising
Tracking the Tempest
Tempest's Legacy
Eye of the Tempest

TEMPEST'S LEGACY

Book Three of the Jane True novels

NICOLE PEELER

www.orbitbooks.net

ORBIT

First published in Great Britain in 2011 by Orbit

A CIP catalogue record for this book
is available from the British Library.

ISBN 978-1-84149-968-0

Typeset in Times by Palimpsest Book Production Limited, Falkirk, Stirlingshire
Printed and bound in Great Britain by CPI Mackays, Chatham ME5 8TD

Papers used by Sphere are from well-managed forests
and other responsible sources.

MIX
Paper from
responsible sources
FSC® C104740

Orbit
An imprint of
Little, Brown Book Group
100 Victoria Embankment
London EC4Y 0DY

An Hachette UK Company
www.hachette.co.uk

www.orbitbooks.net

To Abby and Wyatt
Keep reading,
and eventually you'll be allowed to read
one of your aunt's books.
I love you both so very much.

Chapter One

I love it when people pre-laugh at their own jokes. And whatever Marcus was about to say, he obviously found *very* funny, since he had started chuckling as soon as he'd told us he'd heard 'a good one'.

'A god gives a selkie, an Alfar, and a nahual each a free wish. The selkie asks for an ocean full of fish.' With that, Marcus paused to give me a Look, as if it were my cue to pull a halibut out of my bra and start gnawing on it, before continuing: 'The Alfar pushes the selkie aside and asks for a walled city for only the Alfar to live in.' We all pushed our drinks around as Marcus stopped again, silently revving his engines for the punch line. He also indulged in one more self-congratulatory chortle. 'The nahual thinks about his options. Then he looks at the god, looks at the Alfar, and asks how high the wall will be. When the Alfar says he'd want it to be very high, the nahual tells the god . . .

'. . . to fill the wall with water!'

Iris giggled, tossing back her honeyed mane of hair. Marcus was laughing so hard he was doubled over, as his partner, Sarah, gave him the long-suffering grimace of a woman who'd heard the same joke fifteen times in a row. Marcus and Sarah were one of those couples who, like dogs and their owners, had come to look exactly the same. They were both short and very lean but muscular, with similarly cropped haircuts and almost identical outfits of jeans and college sweatshirts. In other words, they looked like twins, except he appeared to be African-American and she Caucasian. In reality, however, they were both nahuals – or shape-shifters – and not really human at all.

Not that you would know by hearing their punch lines, I thought as I shook my head, articulating my biggest complaint about supernatural jokes in general and Marcus's in particular.

'Dude, all your jokes are just human jokes in which you take out the ethnic slurs and replace them with faction slurs. You're like Cartman, from *South Park*, when he switches "baby" with "Jesus" in popular songs and calls himself a Christian rocker.'

'So not true,' Marcus replied again. We'd had this argument just about every time Marcus told me a 'new' joke. 'Humans stole *our* jokes and replaced our factions with human religious leaders.'

I snorted. Fat chance of that happening, what with the way the supes jealously guarded their secret existence. But again, this was an old argument that neither of us was going to win. Not to mention, Iris was still giggling and she was too pretty to ignore.

'Oh, Marcus, you're so funny,' she tittered as Sarah and I rolled our eyes.

'Don't encourage him,' Sarah muttered beside me.

'We know he's got more where that came from,' I added for her ears only, just as Marcus turned to Iris and said, 'Well, I've got more where that came from.'

Sarah and I threw up our hands at the same time, yelling

out a triumphant, 'Ohhhh!' Then we sealed our collective brilliance by high-fiving each other and collapsing into laughter.

'You two are hilarious,' Marcus said drily as he stood to get us all another round from his stand-in at the bar. He and Sarah had the night off, but the Sty was the only place in Rockabill to drink, so they often ended up spending their free time at their place of work.

Sarah and I were still chuckling as Iris's blue eyes started to glow in that telltale succubus manner. Sure enough, when I turned around, it was our local minister and his wife. They were paragons of conservative propriety in public, but in private they swung like piñatas. Iris gave them a small wave, which they returned benevolently as they went and sat down in the restaurant portion of the Sty.

Iris watched them, her eyes all aglow. Her succubus mojo rolled against my shields and I gave her a warning look. No matter what, Iris received a lot of attention: she always sent out little waves of attraction compulsion, plus – with her Playboy-model figure and girl-next-door features – she was drop-dead gorgeous. But she sometimes got excited and let her shields slip, unleashing the full power of her succutastic self. Unfortunately, when Iris lost control, *everybody* lost control.

The last thing we needed was for Iris to start an orgy here in Rockabill . . . Our puritan ancestors would rise up from their graves and spit us on their razor-sharp rod of approbation.

My friend gave me an apologetic smile, and I felt her tone down her magic. I was just about to make a joke, since Iris always felt bad when she slipped, when the cell phone in my purse buzzed. After fishing it out, I saw Ryu's name blinking at me from the caller ID. While I debated whether or not to take it, he hung up. I frowned at my phone until, finally, I excused myself. Iris gave me a knowing look as I walked toward the Sty's exit, pulling Ryu's number up on my phone once outside. Then I proceeded to stare at the phone, again, trying to decide what to do.

My former lover and I were still on the outs after he'd made a big scene demanding that I move to Boston to be with him. We'd never stopped talking entirely, and we were talking a bit more nowadays. But I was still unsure about what I wanted. On the one hand, I did care for Ryu a whole hell of a lot. He was beautiful, and generous, and he knew how to *live*. He'd also saved my life, in more ways than one. When we'd first met, during an investigation into a murder here in Rockabill, Ryu had stuck around to sleep with me. He could have wrapped up his portion of the investigation in a few days without my help, but he'd drawn it out and schlepped me about with him because of our mutual attraction. Which I later realized had saved my skin, as there'd been a killer waiting in the wings to murder me who'd been thwarted by Ryu's presence.

Ryu had also brought me out of the long torpor to which I'd succumbed after my first love, Jason, had died so many years ago. I'd been only half-alive till Ryu came along. That said, meeting him had inaugurated my plunge into my current position, floundering in the supernatural world. But I couldn't blame him for that. I'd been the one to find Peter Jakes's body, and, anyway, I was too strong in my powers. Nell the gnome, along with the other supernatural folk who lived in or around Rockabill, would eventually have brought me into the fold anyway.

So, on the one hand, I did care for Ryu. On the other hand, however, the baobhan sith had some strange priorities, especially when it came to love. I couldn't shake the feeling that, while I knew my vampire lover did genuinely care for me and we were definitely attracted to each other, the real reason he wanted me so much was because I was the halfling equivalent of a bento box. For whatever reason, my mixed blood had combined into a very rare cocktail: I was both supernaturally magical and sanguinely human. In other words, I was a rarity in that I could be a complete partner to him. He could feed off my essence-rich blood, and yet I was able to keep up with him both magically and in terms of longevity.

While I couldn't blame him for wanting a true partner, neither was I comfortable with living my life as a walking, talking sack lunch.

Another major factor that made my falling back into Ryu's life awkward was that I had a serious high school crush on someone who was probably the most inappropriate person in the world for me to crush on. Anyan Barghest was a badass warrior, an internationally renowned artist (throughout many human lifetimes of name changes), a stud muffin, and someone who had known me since I was a toothless, drooling infant. In other words, he was so out of my league it was ridiculous. But somewhere along the way I'd not only fallen for him, I'd fallen like a seventh grader. I wanted to pass Iris notes signed Jane Barghest. I wanted to write ANYAN LOVES JANE on my geography notebook, if I were still in geography classes. I wanted to play MASH with him as my only 'husband' option. That said, I wanted to do a whole hell of a lot of things to him that were *not* seventh grade, many involving various forms of slathery foodstuffs, but it was all hopeless. Not least because I hadn't seen Anyan once, and I mean once, since I'd fallen asleep next to his doggie-form after I'd returned from Boston two months ago.

I'd been assiduously ignoring my true feelings for the barghest, until that night when I dreamed we did the pokey-pokey. After Boston, those first days back in Rockabill had been brutal. I hadn't slept at all, until I'd gone to my cove to rest next to the safety of my ocean. I'd started to have the same nightmare that kept waking me up, when Anyan had found me tossing in my sleep. He'd let my sleeping body know he was there to protect me, and my sleeping brain had thanked him by making him the star of one of the most explicit erotic dreams I'd ever had. And I'm someone who dreams dirty.

Unable to deny what my subconscious had thrown in my face, I'd woken up overly excited and chagrined and completely alone. All of which meant that I had mixed feelings about Ryu, who wanted me, and very solid feelings for a man who'd never feel the same.

Awesome.

Giving my bottom lip one last, fortifying chew as I stared at Ryu's name and number glowing from my phone's screen, I steeled myself and pressed Call. It was no mean feat to ring that number. After all, whenever we spoke, there was one part of me (namely, my libido) that wanted to demand Ryu come to Rockabill, *right now*. But another part argued that I should make our separation permanent. In other words, our relationship was as complicated as ever.

'Jane?' Ryu answered on the fourth ring.

'Hey, Ryu. What's up?'

'Nothing, I just wanted to hear your voice.'

My libido purred in response, even as I rolled my eyes at Ryu's line. The baobhan sith had graduated magna cum laude with a degree in Romance Schmomance, something I found both endearing and irritating.

'Jane, did you hear me?'

'Yes. Sorry, Ryu. It's been a long week. Thanks, I miss you, too.'

Liar, my virtue thought petulantly.

No you're not, my ever-irrepressible libido grumbled.

'What are you doing?'

'I'm out for drinks at the Sty with Iris, Sarah, and Marcus. Grizzie and Tracy are on their way.'

'How is everybody?'

'Fine. Tracy's pregnant!' I said, remembering I hadn't yet told him the news.

'Really?'

'Yup! Three months. They're doing great. Tracy's freaking out because she's already starting to show, but that's just because—'

'That's great news, Jane,' Ryu interrupted rather rudely, considering I was telling him something so important. 'But how are you?'

I paused before answering, knowing something was up. Whatever his flaws, Ryu usually had impeccable social grace. So not only was it weird that he interrupted me like that, but his voice was odd and really intense.

'I'm doing good,' I replied cautiously. 'Work's the same. Training-wise, I managed to crack that magical probe I've been stuck on, finally. And I trounced Trill in a duel the other day.' I'd been working my ass off on offensive magics, and I was doing pretty well. Getting kidnapped by Con and having the crap kicked out of me by Graeme had been pretty good motivation, plus the lessons I'd learned from Anyan about manifesting my power had stood me in good stead. I'd discovered I had surprisingly aggressive magic at my disposal, considering I was half-selkie. I just had to get comfortable with the idea of Jane True: Offensive Hybrid.

'Turns out,' I joked, using my sassy voice, 'I'm the kind of seal who clubs back.'

'That's great,' Ryu replied, his voice still distracted.

He paused, and when he spoke again he sounded even more intense.

'You know I'm always here for you, right?'

What the fuck? I thought.

'Okay,' I said.

'I mean that. I'll always be here for you, baby.'

Ryu was being more than a little dramatic, but drama and Ryu went together like cheese and . . . Well, cheese goes with everything.

'Thanks. I'm here for you, too,' I added lamely.

'I'll let you get back to your friends.'

'Um, okay. Thanks for calling.'

Ryu didn't respond for a second, and then when he did, his voice was resoundingly portentous.

'Remember what I said, Jane. We'll talk again soon.'

With those cryptic words, he hung up. I blinked at my phone, wondering what the hell he was up to, until I heard a car door slam from the parking lot in front of me.

It was my old arch-nemesis, Linda Allen, and her current boyfriend, Mark, the postal worker I'd nearly dated a while ago until he'd learned of my sordid, suicidal history and dumped me like a hot potato.

Things were different nowadays, and Linda and Mark merely smiled politely at me as they passed. Granted, I'd nudged them with a little glamour a few weeks ago, which had made them want to be polite to Jane. But somewhere along the line, I'd also stopped being someone who took shit.

I watched Mark open the Sty's door for Linda, and I felt a twinge of sadness. I'd been so used to being alone after Jason died, but then Ryu had shaken up my world as if it were a snow globe. He'd reminded me of what it was like to have someone, and I missed that connection. I also really missed the nookie, but at least I had a drawerful of sex toys from Grizzie to make up for it. That said, pocket rockets didn't open doors for you or hold your hand, nor were they great conversationalists.

Then again, sex toys are rarely, if ever, complicated, I thought, jumping as someone grabbed my ass.

I calmed my breathing and dropped the magical shields I'd thrown up the minute I was touched. *I know that pinch*, I thought, turning to find Grizzie behind me, leering. 'Think of the devil,' I said drily, 'and she gooses you.'

'You were obviously thinking about something,' my tall friend said, laughing as she hugged me. 'I was stomping away in my big-girl boots, and you didn't bat an eyelash.'

'Off in my own world again.' I shrugged, watching as Tracy waddled up next to her life partner.

'I'm getting fat,' she wheezed.

'You're not fat,' I chided as I went to hug her. 'You're pregnant.'

When I released her, Tracy pointedly looked down at her belly.

'With twins,' I conceded, giving her already bulging stomach a little pat.

'Twin sumo wrestlers.' Grizzie chortled, for which I shot her the evil eye.

'Never again,' Tracy mumbled as I held the door open for her. 'Next time, Ms Montague, *you* get turkey basted and *I* point and laugh.'

I smiled as they bickered over who would next get knocked-up. Grizzie kept arguing about her 'girlish figure', but I knew she was being blasé and was actually looking forward to her turn at being up the duff.

We chitchatted a bit before walking inside. Bars in Maine had been smoke-free forever, which was great as it meant we could hang out at the Sty despite Tracy's being pregnant.

My two human friends had integrated pretty seamlessly with Rockabill's little supernatural contingent. Granted, they knew nothing about our 'real' identities, but it didn't matter so much with this crowd, who had highly developed human personas and were happy to have Grizzie and Tracy around. Not least because Grizzie took the pressure off. If anyone looked like some creature out of mythology, it was Grizelda Montague. While Tracy was dressed in her usual long-sleeved polo shirt and carpenter-cut jeans, her life partner was wearing a skintight PVC jumpsuit, and had braided her long black hair up into a Princess Leia bun on each side of her head. For a Wednesday night out at the Pig Sty in Rockabill, Maine, population 1,003.

Grizzie rocked.

Marcus helped the mother-to-be into the booth he'd just vacated, next to Iris, and then went to get another round of drinks and an orange juice for Tracy. Grizzie pulled up a chair to sit at the end of the table, next to Tracy, as Sarah slid out of the booth to go help Marcus with the drinks. I listened to Grizzie squelch around in her PVC, then slid back in to sit across from the succubus. Everyone started talking at once, but, as good friends do, we turned it all into a great conversation.

Soon enough, Sarah came back with drinks and started talking with Tracy and Grizzie about their pregnancy. Iris took her opportunity to lean across the table and gossip.

'Was it Ryu?' she asked, her voice honeysuckle-sweet.

'Yeah.'

'I could tell by your face. What did he want?'

'I don't know, actually. He was being typically cryptic.'

'Are you going to see him?'

'He said something about seeing me, but he didn't seem to have any particular plans. Girl, what the fuck am I going to do with him?' I groaned, dropping my forehead down onto the table in defeat.

'Well, first I'd tie him up. Then I'd start with a feather and a Dustbuster—'

'Iris! I meant . . . not that. I meant what am I going to do about him and me.'

'Oh. I don't know. I'm only good with the sex stuff. Relationships are another matter entirely.'

I blanched, feeling inconsiderate. I'd only very recently learned that Iris had been in love with a human, ages ago, with whom she'd borne a child. The child had been entirely nonmagical, and both her son and her husband had died of old age while she remained young and strong. Iris had been gutted and hadn't had a real relationship since.

'I'm sorry, Iris.'

'Oh, don't be. It's fine. But we were talking about you and Ryu.'

I knew Iris didn't like talking about her past, so I let her change the subject.

'I just hate that we're tiptoeing around each other like this. And I do care about him, but it's so complicated.'

'And there's Anyan,' Iris whispered, dropping her voice so only I could hear.

I snorted. Don't get me wrong: I wanted to do things to Anyan that would make Casanova blush. But for every fantasy I had about the barghest involving handcuffs and drizzled honey, I had an equally vivid fantasy about slapping him across the face. I felt we'd really connected when we were in Boston, and he'd said he felt bad about not being there for me. Then he'd gone MIA the minute I was back in Rockabill. I felt rejected. And stupid for feeling that way, since I had no right to such emotions. We'd never really been more to each other than acquaintances. But I still felt angry at him, even though I knew it was irrational. It was the illogical ire of unrequited love, and I wasn't strong enough to resist its temptation.

'There's *no* Anyan,' I replied heatedly. 'And I'm stupid if I think there is. Anyan is never *here*, first of all. Plus, he's out of my league. And he's *never* seen me as anything other than something to take care of. I may have issues, Iris, but they're not daddy issues; I don't want to be with a man who thinks he needs to babysit me. Besides, I have to deal with how I feel about Ryu without taking Anyan into consideration. I owe Ryu more than that.'

'Do you? Owe Ryu more than that? And would you feel this way about Anyan,' she continued, 'if you already felt what Ryu wants you to feel for him?'

I made a face at Iris. 'I don't know what I feel. And I certainly can't base my feelings for the bloodsucker based on my feelings for the hellhound who apparently doesn't even know I exist. Besides, there's no issue. Not yet, at least. Ryu's in Boston; I'm in Rockabill; Anyan is in absentia. So I'll just keep ignoring everything till I get walloped with it. Then I'll panic and run to you.'

Iris laughed. 'Your plans always suck, Jane. But you know I'll be there when you need me.'

And I did. Unlike Ryu's cryptic statement, I knew exactly what Iris meant. She meant she was my friend and would be there when I needed her, just as she had been every day for months. I smiled at her and reached over to touch her hand.

'Thanks, lady. You know I love you.'

The succubus laughed. 'I know. You tell me every time you get drunk.'

'To drunken declarations of affection,' I said, holding my drink up to her. We clinked glasses, bringing everyone into the toast.

I smiled at my friends, knowing how lucky I was to have them. We all talked for another hour, until the pregnant lady called it quits and we went our separate ways. Tracy and Grizzie left first, then Iris trailed off after our swinging minister and his wife. When Sarah and Marcus said good night, I did, too. Then I went to the only other thing I loved as much as my friends and family.

My ocean.

Chapter Two

The next day found me basking on my favorite flat rock, soaking up the rays of a late-afternoon sun draped in plump repose across the horizon.

It was only in the past month that I'd really mastered my invisibility glamour and could swim during the day. Now that I could be in my ocean at any time without fear of discovery, I'd found that there was no heaven so pleasurable as lying on a warm rock jutting up from the shallows, the sea foam frothing at arm's reach.

That said, I may have looked peaceful – but I was secretly working. Today was my official 'day off', both from my job and from my magical training. But after going out the night before I wasn't going to waste another big chunk of time. So while I lay, outwardly quiescent, I practiced manifesting little bursts of power that scooped and released small handfuls of water near my head. It took a lot of control and a very dense power weave to hold fluid, so the exercise was actually very demanding.

'You're supposed to be *resting*, Jane,' came an oil-slick voice from somewhere near my feet. I raised my head petulantly, frowning toward my unwanted visitor. It was my kelpie friend Trill. Kelpies were two-formed, like selkies, only instead of turning into a seal like my mom had, Trill turned into a weird little underwater pony. She was currently in her humanoid form, all the better to bask with me.

'I *am* resting,' I said. 'I'm horizontal, ain't I?'

'From what I've heard, you do a lot of things horizontally that aren't resting.'

'Ha-ha, very funny. Move over, Ricky Gervais . . . here comes Kelpie Trill!'

Trill emitted a strange grating sound it had taken me forever to realize was actually her version of a girlish giggle.

'Everything "pony" is better. Especially pony-style.'

I laid my head back down, squeezing my eyes shut. 'Ohmigod, are you talking about pony sex? 'Cause if you are, I think you may have ruined me for life.'

Just thinking about two little kelpies going at it made me shudder.

Trill grated her harsh giggle at me again, then I heard her haul herself out of the water. I meeped my protest when she dripped cold droplets over my sun-warmed flesh. The kelpie's pearl-gray skin gleamed dully in the sunlight, her black-nailed hands – cold from the sea – prodding me like frozen brands to move over and make room. For a moment, too comfortable to budge, I refused. Until she threatened to wring her green seaweed hair out on my belly and I finally made way so Trill could share my rock.

We lay in companionable silence, drowsing together for at least a half hour. But I knew such peace couldn't last, and soon enough Trill's slippery voice eeled its way through my respite.

'How are you feeling this week?'

From the time I'd met Trill, she'd been my friend and my swimming buddy. After everything that had happened in

Boston, however, she'd also taken it upon herself to be my therapist.

I wish I could say I didn't need her help, but I knew better.

If I was honest, after Boston I'd been pretty fucked up. Don't get me wrong, I knew that I was really lucky. Unlike the two women we'd been searching for, Edie and Felicia, I was alive. I didn't bear a single physical scar from the beating Graeme, the rapist incubus, had dealt me. I looked like the exact same Jane True who'd gone off for a romantic Valentine's Day weekend with her boyfriend.

But I wasn't that Jane True, not anymore.

There were moments, especially when I was with my friends or when I was training, that I remembered how to feel without feeling guilty. But when alone, my thoughts could be heavy.

I'd always known life wasn't fair. Losing my mom and Jason had taught me early that bad things happened to decent people not because they deserved it, but because life was arbitrary and death capricious. But I hadn't thought of the universe as *cruel* until last February. Seeing the look in Graeme's eyes as he bit through my lip, the lack of emotion on Phaedra's face as she'd hacked off Conleth's head, and Conleth's own expression as he'd pleaded with me for help just before he died... All these things had done a number on me. I hadn't been able to help anyone, not even myself, and certainly not the two women who'd died at Graeme's hands because we weren't smart or fast enough to save them.

And then all the various players – except the dead, of course – had just gone back to their normal lives. Ryu had returned to Boston, I'd returned to Rockabill, and Phaedra and her lot had returned to their Compound. Phaedra was Alfar, and her lies about Conleth being responsible for all the murders – both in Boston and in the Borderland city of

Chicago – had been believed. Ryu hadn't even attempted to tell the truth, knowing that Alfar would side with Alfar; that the king and queen would never turn against Jarl and his crony Phaedra.

And so my understanding of a capricious universe had transformed itself into something darker, more sinister. Life wasn't just unfair . . . it was cruel. The weak *would* fall to the strong, and no one – no higher power – stood in judgment.

And I'd finally realized that I was one of the weak.

It's not like I'd ever been powerful. As a human I was small and physically vulnerable. I'd never been a fighter, not in the physical sense. Therefore, learning of my selkie blood had meant I'd gained strengths I'd never dreamed of having. But I'd also been thrown into a world that had no laws, no conscience. Power was all that was understood. I was learning, gradually, that I had far more elemental force at my disposal than I could easily conceive of, but what did having power matter when I was afraid to use it?

In other words, I had been raised a law-abiding member of human society, used to thinking in terms of social contracts, the greater good, and 'if it harm none'. All of which were values that made me weak in a supernatural society that took pleasure indulging in lashings of the old ultraviolence.

So now I'm stuck talking about my 'feelings', I thought. *As if they ever change . . .*

As if on cue, Trill turned on her side to face me. 'How are you feeling this week?' she repeated.

I nearly sighed, but stopped myself. Time to put on my game face. Sitting up only to squint in the sun, I fiddled with my toes – painted a now rather chipped shade of bright blue.

'I'm good, actually. This week was really good. Quiet,

and . . . normal. I'm superexcited about Grizzie and Tracy. And we got some books in that I've been excited about . . .'

Trill didn't respond. She just listened, impassively, as I babbled nervously.

'. . . Um, and I feel good about what I learned this week, in training. I feel like I'm getting stronger, which is awesome.'

'Stronger?'

'Yeah, stronger. No offense, but it felt good when I won our duel. I felt . . . badass.'

Trill's flat nose wrinkled and her mouth gaped in her kelpie version of a grin. 'You did win, certainly. But soon we'll take your training to the water, and you'll *really* see what I can do.'

'Yea!' I squeaked, like a little kid just told she got to go to the circus. I really wanted to start training in the water. But because my greatest threats were coming from the land, they wanted me strong there first.

'That said, I'm concerned about what you're saying about yourself. I've always thought you were strong, Jane.'

I snorted. 'Are you serious? I mean, thanks. But I definitely need to be more kick-butt. You know that.'

Trill frowned at me. 'You just said yourself that I'm not strong on land. You're already kicking *my* butt all over Rockabill.'

'Yeah, but you're not strong on *land*. You'd trounce me in the ocean.'

'And don't you forget it,' Trill said, her flat nose wrinkling at me teasingly again. 'I just think you should concentrate more on what you *are* good at, and the strengths you already have, instead of worrying about changing yourself into something you're not.'

I thought about Trill's words for a moment. 'But sometimes it's not about you changing yourself, it's about circumstances changing you. And trying to make the best of those changes,' I replied eventually.

'Eep. Think about what you just said for a second, Jane. You're basically saying that you think, on some level, that you should let Jarl have control over you and your life.'

I grimaced at Trill's harsh words. They stung, although I did appreciate that Trill had no problem pointing fingers at the Alfar. The sea folk, like Trill and my mother, were a breed apart from the land folk. Those creatures who lived in the ocean rarely came onto land and almost never had any dealings with the Alfar power structure. Which explained why the pool at the Alfar Compound was so overcharged: very, very few water-elementals ever used it. After all, the oceans were so vast, and the Alfar weren't interested in ruling great swaths of seaweed. So they stayed out of ocean life, for the most part. That, coupled with the fact there weren't many water-elementals left, meant the ocean folk ruled themselves, and had developed their own code of justice, fair play, and general ethics. The Sea Code, as they called it, was complicated when it came to dealing with one another, but very simple when it came to dealing with landlubbers. When it came to the Alfar and their cronies, the Sea Code said, 'Never, ever take the side of a non-water-elemental over other ocean folk.' Even a being like Trill, who really enjoyed being on land and had a lot of land friends, would, realistically, have dropped us like a hot potato in a toss-up between water politics and land politics.

The ocean was a harsh mistress, but she bred loyalty, and you had to do something *really* dramatic – like attack another water-being with no just cause – for the sea folk to act against one another.

I'd been absolutely enchanted when I learned about the Sea Code and, even more excitedly, discovered that it applied to me, too, even though I couldn't shape-shift. I'd been so delighted, I took the Code as carte blanche to punch Amy

Nahual in the arm every time I saw her, calling out, 'Sea Code!' as my excuse. Up until she punched me in the stomach, hard, yelling, 'Asshat!' at me in response.

'How is the rest of your life?' the kelpie asked, changing gears and letting me recover.

'Oh, good,' I said. 'My dad's still doing well. Training is great, as you know. Work is fine.' I smiled at that. 'Better than fine, actually. Tracy's pregnant.'

Trill grinned her mad, jack-o'-lantern smile. 'Really?'

'Yeah. They were very crafty about it; we had no idea this was even in the works. They weren't entirely confident, as both of them are in their late thirties, so they kept everything on the DL. But yeah, Tracy's three months gone.'

'Who's the father?'

I shrugged. 'A donor. He's anonymous, but they do know he's an Irish astrophysics student. I refer to him as "Guinness McRocket Scientist", in order to be as offensive as possible.'

'Well, that is great news,' the kelpie said, longing in her voice.

The supes had trouble conceiving. They didn't know why, but I was pretty sure it had something to do with the purgative powers of their magic. Using magic meant we aged much slower than humans: the more magic used, the longer and healthier the life. In my own experience, since I'd started really training I hadn't had a single cold, or even a pimple. I was no doctor, but I knew there had to be a connection between that purgative force and supernatural infertility.

But whatever the cause, the effect was that there were a lot of supes running around who would do pretty much anything to have a child. Like my mother, many would turn to a human partner. For some reason, it was much easier to create a new life with a human, especially for supernatural males with human females. But even for supernatural females, they had a better chance of having a baby with a human male.

So my mother, a selkie whose home was the sea, had come onto land to meet my father. I'd been born after their union and she'd left when I was six.

'It is great,' I replied to Trill. 'Tracy and Grizzie are going to be awesome parents.'

Trill nodded. 'And you will be a marvelous Auntie Jane.'

I smiled at that, genuinely pleased. I did plan on being the babies' swimming instructor . . . and I could introduce them to the finer points of obscenitizing while I was at it. The secret to truly creative swearing, I'd been speculating, was to use a combination of established swearwords in conjunction with words you made up for yourself . . .

'Everyone else?' asked the kelpie, interrupting my reverie.

'Oh, fine. Iris is great. We all had dinner yesterday at the Sty.'

Trill grinned again, poking a black-nailed finger into my hip in approbation. 'Everything is always so great, Jane. And yet you look so sad.'

I frowned at her. What was I supposed to do? Complain all the time?

'Never mind.' She sighed, shifting back around to lie on her back. 'Anything new in the love life? Ryu making any inroads yet?'

I paused until Trill made another inquisitive noise. So I did what I did every time the subject of Ryu came up. I frowned, shrugged, and shook my head.

'I dunno, Trill. It's complicated.'

The kelpie chuckled. 'Love is a many-splendored thing,' she said, and I was terrified she'd start singing. I adored Trill, but her voice could crumble Sheetrock.

'Yes, well, I'm sure it is. But right now it's a pain in my

ass,' I said, lying back down only to groan in pleasure. Bared to the sun from my having sat up, my rock had gotten deliciously hot again.

The kelpie allowed me to maintain my silence, and we basked together for another hour. She didn't even comment when, about ten minutes into our basking, I started practicing my water trick again. Finally, as the sun began to set, we took one last swim in the Old Sow, taunting the ancient whirlpool, who obliged us by swirling her power through both Trill and me till we practically glowed with magic.

It was power I accepted gratefully, knowing I'd need it to keep me strong.

Chapter Three

A few hours later I was drying myself off with the beach towel I kept hanging in a rock cranny and shielded from the elements by a little umbrella of magic. The best part of all the mojo I'd learned pertained to my swimming. I could swim whenever I wanted now, and I could also do things like keep a towel and an extra set of clothes in the cove, under shields that kept them dry.

I had just finished pressing the water out of my hair when I heard something rustle behind me. Figuring it was Trill, I went ahead and hung up my towel before turning around.

Only to find Anyan the man standing in the little break between the cove walls that led to the forest near my house. He turned around so fast he scraped his long, crooked nose on the rough stone.

'Gods, Jane, I'm sorry. I should have shouted,' he said as I dove for my clothes, pulling on my jeans with my back to him. It took me forever to get them buttoned because my hands had started trembling the second I saw him. My heart was thumping in my chest and I prayed he couldn't sense my nervousness. When I finally had my drawers buttoned and my shirt on, I turned toward him.

'Yeah, well. Let a lady get dressed next time,' I grumbled, trying to cover for my nervousness by acting tough.

The fact was, I couldn't have been more thrilled to see the barghest. I tried not to stare as he came forward, his huge frame dwarfing me. But when I met Anyan's eyes and smiled, he didn't return it. He looked haggard, and none too pleased to see me. I straightened my spine. Magical shields weren't the only sort of armor I had at my beck and call.

He was about to say something when he finally really looked at me. He paused. 'Your hair's all grown out.'

'It's been months, Anyan,' I replied, trying not to sound miffed. I'd had a big chunk of hair singed off in Boston, precipitating a hairstyle a few inches shorter than I'd previously worn. But now it was even longer than it had been originally. It flowed to my waist in swirling dark waves, as I knew my mother's had when she'd first arrived in Rockabill.

'Many?' the barghest growled, and he looked grieved.

'Three. Well, more like two,' I admitted, annoyed at how petulant my voice sounded.

Anyan ran his hands through his poofy black curls, then ran one hand over his jaw. I'd never seen him so discombobulated, and suddenly I started to worry.

'Jane, I'm no good at these things.'

I blinked at him, confused, as my anxiety spiked.

'At what?' I began, but he interrupted me.

'I'm so sorry, Jane. Someone else should be here to tell you. I don't know how to do this, I don't know what to say . . .'

'Anyan,' I said sharply, growing concerned. 'What's going on? What happened? Is it my father?'

'No,' the big man rumbled, coming toward me. 'Not your father.'

'Then what?' I said, relieved. That relief was short-lived.

'Your mother.'

My breathing hitched. 'My mother? Have you seen her?'

'Oh, gods, I'm so sorry to tell you this.' Anyan took another step, reaching out a large hand. 'Your mother's dead.'

I stared at him, then looked down at his outstretched hand. It was grimy, like he hadn't had time to wash. Meanwhile, I couldn't hear what he was saying. I wouldn't hear it. I shook my head.

'No,' was all I said. It was impossible. She'd only just come alive for me again in the past year, when I'd learned my true heritage. How could she be dead?

'Jane,' Anyan said, his voice breaking, 'I'm sorry.'

His hand moved to take mine, a movement that up until now I'd fantasized about. But this was no dream, and instead of letting him touch me, I drew back.

'No.'

'Please,' he said, taking another step forward.

'Anyan, *no*,' I said, walking away from him across the cove. I'd never heard my own voice so hard, so cold. He didn't follow me.

I stood, facing the rough stone of my cove wall, my back to him. It felt as if my brain were stuttering like a car engine. It would start to turn over, then it would stop. I couldn't think past the feeling that my entire universe had wrenched to a halt.

'Why are you telling me this?'

'I hate having to. I'm so sorry.'

'How?' I asked eventually.

He paused and I finally turned to face him. 'Tell me *how*, Anyan.'

The barghest looked down at his feet, raising his eyes to meet mine only in the last second before saying, 'She was murdered.'

I felt my legs drop out from underneath me, and suddenly I was kneeling on the soft sand of my cove.

'Murdered? How?'

'Jane, we can talk about this later. Let me get you somewhere warm. Safe.'

'*Fuck you, Anyan.* Tell me how.'

Visibly startled by the vehemence of my tone, the barghest knelt down in front of me.

'Jane, please, let me take you somewhere . . .'

'Tell. Me. *Now.*' My voice, at this point, wasn't even my own.

The barghest wrung his hands – actually wrung his hands! As if he were the one who had just been told he'd never know his own mother. I gritted my teeth, suddenly hating him with a ferocity that astounded me.

'You know I have contacts in the Borderlands?'

I nodded sharply. How could I forget? During the Boston debacle, Anyan's contacts in the Chicago area had been both controversial and priceless. The information they'd gathered for us had been vital, especially considering no one, and I mean no one, who had anything to do with the Alfar power structure was supposed to know anything about what happened in the Borderlands.

Ryu had nearly popped a blood vessel when he found out Anyan had been keeping something so big a secret.

The barghest continued. 'When I asked for help with the investigation in Boston, some stuff was uncovered in Chicago. In looking into that stuff, they found a thread connecting a bunch of halfling females who'd gone missing. Eventually, that thread led to an abandoned laboratory. It was a human fertility clinic once, just like where Conleth was kept. But this one was only recently destroyed, on purpose, to hide evidence. My friends in the Borderlands have far more access to human technology than we do, however, and they took DNA samples. Some of the DNA belonged to the missing women. So they dug up the ground behind the laboratory, and found the bodies.'

I shuddered, suddenly feeling deathly cold. But my voice was surprisingly calm.

'Was my mother one of them?'

'No. This was right at the beginning of the investigation, days after we got back from Boston. I went to the Borderlands to help, since I owed my friends a favor. When I was there, we found a connection between that lab and some purebred females from inside the Territory who'd disappeared in the past year. At that point, I was brought in officially by Orin and Morrigan to investigate. Ryu was kind enough to tell them about my contacts, and I've been dodging that bullet since. But once they needed me, I knew I was safe enough. I told them I'd work with my contacts, but they couldn't interfere. If I did this, I wanted no one else knowing where I was or what I was doing. Not even Jarl. Surprisingly, they agreed. Well, almost—'

This was all very interesting, but not what I wanted to know.

'Anyan?' I interrupted, with a growl that sounded vaguely barghestian. He had the good sense to look sheepish.

'Friday night, we raided a laboratory outside of Chicago. Or at least we tried. By the time we got there, the staff had cleared out and the patients had been . . . disposed of. That's when we found your mother. I came as soon as I could, to tell you.'

I let the full weight of what Anyan had said settle on my shoulders. Or at least I tried to. But I didn't want to hear it. So I focused on everything else rather than what really mattered: the fact that my mother was dead.

'So you've known for almost two days, and I'm only finding out now?'

Anyan's fists clenched on his knees. 'I'm sorry, Jane. After we verified your mother's identity, I got right on my bike and rode straight through. I got here as quickly as I could.'

I glared at him, unable to speak through my rage.

Anyan sat back on his heels. 'Maybe we should have called. It just didn't seem right to tell you like that, after everything you've been through—'

I stood up, cutting him off with a strangled sound that emitted from my throat without conscious thought.

'Don't you dare presume to know what I have been through, and don't you dare presume to know what I can and cannot handle.'

Anyan watched me, obviously upset. 'Jane, I . . .'

'No, Anyan. You don't get to come out of nowhere and tell me these things. You don't get to do that.'

'Please, I want to—'

'It doesn't matter what you want, Anyan. I don't want my mother to be . . . I don't want any of this. Get away from me.'

But the barghest didn't move. His long face was sad, and it was the pity in his eyes that pushed me over the edge.

'Fuck you,' I said, starting to pull off my jeans, much to his evident consternation. 'You're not some hero riding in to save me from myself. You come here telling me my mother is dead, and act like I should be grateful? Who the fuck do you think you are?' I was garbling, but it was all I had. My anger was keeping me from breaking down. Part of me recognized that what I said was unfair, that what I was doing to Anyan was cruel and that he didn't deserve it. But I didn't know how else to keep from losing my tenuous grip on . . . on everything. On my emotions, my sanity, my reason. I was losing me at that moment. And Anyan caught the brunt of my loss.

I stripped off my shirt and threw it at him. He let it drop into his hands and stood holding it, not knowing where to look as I stood naked in front of him.

'You don't know me, Anyan Barghest,' was my parting shot as I ran into the ocean and to one of the only people who did.

'Jane, what are you doing here?' Iris asked. She sounded concerned, as she should, considering the state I was in. I was still naked, shivering as if I were freezing, but more from shock than from the cold. I'd swum to Eastport then walked to her boutique, dripping wet, down Main Street. I only just remembered to keep myself invisible to the mortals.

Iris pushed open the door and ushered me upstairs into the lush little apartment over her shop. She stood me in the front hall until she'd retrieved a towel and a blanket. The towel she wrapped around my dripping hair; the blanket she wrapped around me. Only then did I start sobbing.

I was so hysterical it took me a while to get out what happened. After I'd finally managed to articulate that Anyan had shown up to tell me my mother had been murdered, Iris and I were cuddled together on her little sofa. She'd made me a steaming hot mug of chamomile tea, but I wasn't drinking it. I just held it in my hands, letting it warm them, as I cried.

'Oh, Jane,' Iris murmured, stroking my hair. 'Not that.'

Tears were still streaming down my face, but I'd stopped sobbing, finally, and could talk.

'I've been so stupid, Iris. This whole time, since I found out about all of you, I thought everything was just a matter of time.'

Iris cuddled against me, surrounding me with her warmth.

'As a child, after I got over the shock of her leaving and after I accepted that it was for real, I'd always assumed my mother was totally gone,' I explained, tipping my cheek against her shoulder.

'Mm-hm,' Iris encouraged, her honeydew voice washing over me.

'Then I learned the truth about everything and suddenly I knew I would see my mother again. I just assumed, you know? That one day I would be able to find her. I knew she was out there, and would live a long time, and so would I. So it was all just a matter of time . . .'

My voice trailed off as a fresh wave of grief hit me. Iris took my hand and held it, occasionally leaning forward to kiss away my tears.

'I was so stupid to assume. I just thought I'd finally get a chance to know her. To tell her everything I wanted to tell her.'

'What did you want to say to her, Jane? Tell me.'

'I wanted to tell her what she missed. I wanted to tell her what I was like and to ask her so much stuff about her life, and the decisions she'd made.' I sat up just long enough to put my mug on the coffee table and blow my running nose before returning to Iris's arms.

'And the worst part is, I wanted to tell her how mad I am at her. How much she hurt me. I was thinking of all the things I could say that would really zing her, really make her feel my pain. What the fuck was wrong with me? I thought I'd see her and all I wanted was revenge?'

'You have every right to be angry, Jane.'

'But it's not about rights. It's about opportunities, and I fucked mine up. I didn't take the opportunities I was given. Shit, I dreamed about all the ways I could waste my opportunities. What was I thinking?'

'You weren't thinking, honey. You were reacting. When it comes to your mother, you're still that little girl who feels abandoned. And your mother did that to you, so don't beat yourself up.'

'But now what? How am I going to get over this, Iris? Is that all I have to look forward to, continually being that little fucking girl?' I finally admitted what I'd always feared: 'What if I can't get over her, ever? I thought I'd see her and we'd hash things out and she'd help me conquer what she did to me. What if that's impossible now?'

Iris shook her head. 'No, Jane, that's not what I meant. You are strong, and you are *not* damaged goods because of what happened to you. I simply meant that when it comes to your mother, your reactions are tempered by your loss. But your whole life isn't affected. You've proven that.'

'Have I? I've never left Rockabill. I've never committed to anything or anyone besides Jason, and he was dead when we were so young. I went completely crazy when he died, yet I flicked Ryu aside because he wants commitment. What if I'm just . . . damaged? And what if now there's no cure?'

'Oh, honey, it's not like that. You've committed yourself to so many things. To your father, to Grizzie and Tracy, to me. You've committed yourself to school, and then to your training. You're only focusing on the negative and not seeing the good.'

I listened to what Iris said, but it didn't make me feel any better.

'I just thought I had time,' I said. 'And how am I going to tell my father?' I begged, starting to sob again.

'Oh, baby,' Iris murmured, rocking me gently. 'You'll figure out what to do about your dad. And I know you're sad you won't ever hear your mother's side of things, but I have no doubt that she missed you every day she was away from you.'

I choked on my tears, and Iris ran a soothing hand down my back.

'You know I don't like to talk about my son, or his father. They were both human, even my son. It was like I'd given birth to a pureblooded mortal. And they grew old, and they died. I was with them till the end, but that's not the whole story. I had other choices, Jane, and I was too cowardly to take them.'

I peered up into Iris's beautiful blue eyes. They were still and sad, and in all the time I'd known her I'd never seen her so serious.

'Other choices?'

'We are only long-lived because of our access to the elements. Which means that I could have cut myself off from my magic. Doing so would have let me age normally. I would have had to learn to live as a mortal, but I would have died with my husband, and I would never have had to see the look of betrayal in my son's eyes when he lost his battle with death, as a decrepit old man, while his own mother sat next to him, young and healthy.'

'Oh, Iris,' I breathed.

'But I didn't, Jane. I was too afraid of dying and of living without my power. I was too weak. And I've lived with that decision every day of my life. I don't envy your mother. She wanted two things that were diametrically opposed. She tried to have both and she failed, and I have no doubt that she suffered, just as much as she made you suffer, for her choices.'

'But I still loved her,' I said, trying to forgive Iris in the place of her son and knowing it was impossible.

'And I know she loved you.'

I scrubbed my hands over my face, trying to get my head around everything I was feeling, just as there was a determined knock at the door.

Iris went to answer it, and, dehydrated from all the crying, I drank long and deep from my cooled tea.

When I put my mug down and looked toward the figure in Iris's doorway, I felt the little modicum of control I'd gained collapse. My face crumpled and, without even thinking about it, I held out my salt-streaked arms.

'Jane,' Ryu choked, coming to me and gathering me up in his arms.

'My mother.' I sobbed as he held me tighter.

'I know, baby. I know. I'm here now. I'll take care of you.'

Through tear-blurred vision I looked into Ryu's face. I knew I was being selfish, and that I was taking from him with no guarantee I'd be able to give anything back. But at that moment I didn't care.

I buried my face in his neck and let him carry me away, Iris watching us depart with tears in her own eyes.

Chapter Four

The bed-and-breakfast where Ryu was staying was one we'd used often when we were together. He'd even gotten our usual room. Under a heavy glamour he'd carried me up the stairs, setting me down on the edge of the bed before locking out the world behind us.

He disappeared into the bathroom and I heard him turn on the shower. When steam started pouring out the open door, he reappeared, naked, then came back to where I huddled.

'Where are your clothes, baby?' he asked as he unwrapped me from my sea-salty blanket.

'I left them in the cove,' I mumbled. 'I swam here.'

Ryu stroked his strong hand down my tearstained cheeks as I studied his lovely, sharp-boned face. His chin was pointed, fey, and his lips were small yet succulent, almost feminine. He wore his bright chestnut hair, usually short-cropped, slightly longer than usual. At this length, I could see just how unusual the color was, with blond and black hair twining with red and brown to make that bold, brassy chestnut. The color fit Ryu's personality, and he looked younger, and cheekier, with this slightly longer style.

I met his hazel eyes, almost pure gold with only the

thinnest edging of green at their center, knowing I looked a mess but refusing to flinch under his scrutiny.

'Let's get you cleaned up,' Ryu said after a moment.

He led me into the bathroom. We'd always liked this room because it had a large, two-person shower and a separate whirlpool bath, also big enough for two. I thought of everything we'd done in this random bathroom, and I suppressed the cruel question that popped, unbidden, into my consciousness.

Had Ryu and I ever done anything but fuck?

Once I was installed in the shower, under the water, Ryu opened his shampoo and began to wash my hair, very gently.

'I can't believe how long your hair has gotten, baby.'

I didn't do what I'd done to Anyan and remind Ryu how long it had been since we'd last seen each other.

'I may have nudged it a bit, with magic,' I admitted instead.

'You look absolutely gorgeous,' he murmured in my ear as he massaged my scalp. I relaxed back against him, letting his fingers soothe and settle me.

Ryu rinsed the shampoo from my hair, then repeated everything, including the massage, with conditioner. I just let him go at it; let myself be putty in his hands. I'd cried the entire short walk to the B and B, but now I just felt . . . empty.

Ryu soaped up a soft washcloth and ran it down my arm from my shoulder to my fingertips. Then he lifted each arm, gently swabbing underneath before lifting my heavy hair to run the cloth over my neck and back. He did the same thing to my front, dabbing gently at my breasts but not touching with his hands. Then he crouched down to clean my legs and feet, before standing up to rinse off the washcloth and apply more soap.

Ryu kissed me, very gently, as he ran the cloth between my legs. Nudging my knees apart with his own, he pressed the soft fabric between my folds, cleaning me thoroughly. Maybe I should have felt embarrassed or shocked by his touching me so intimately after so long, but it was like I was in a trance. His hands on me were comforting, in an animal-like way, as if I were a startled horse in need of soothing. That said, my body was also reacting to him sexually. He knew everything that turned me on, after all – every nook and cranny that responded to the touch of lips, tongue, and teeth. But my head wasn't in it. It was like I was watching our entwined bodies from a great distance.

He cleaned my backside, just as thoroughly and gently, before setting aside the washcloth. Cupping his hands, he sluiced water first down my front and then down my back, washing all the soap away. Finally, he lathered his favorite, expensive face wash between his hands to clean away the final evidence of my grief. I shivered; his deft fingers felt more invasive on my face than they had between my legs. When he'd rinsed the soap away, he kissed me very gently, wrapping me up in his arms.

'Better?' he asked.

I buried my face in his chest, unable to respond. I wasn't sure when or how I would be better, after tonight. I couldn't imagine what 'better' would entail.

'I've missed you so much,' he whispered, letting his fingers trail down my spine before he pulled my hips tighter against his. The hot water still ran down our bodies, comforting me with its steady force. I didn't know if it was fair to Ryu, or if I deserved it, but his arms around me felt good. He was warm, and solid, and I knew that he did care for me. For a moment, I desperately wanted that to be enough.

I lapped at the water running down his chest, moving my mouth across his chest to his flat pink nipple. Stroking my tongue across his smooth flesh, I heard him moan as his hands cupped my bottom.

'That's it, baby,' he sighed. 'Come back to me.'

I raised my lips to his for a kiss before he turned off the water then pulled me from the shower. We dried each other off and I wound my long hair up in a towel before following my lover into the bedroom. Ryu was waiting, standing beside the bed. When I joined him, he pulled the towel from my hair and, ever practical, he draped it to cover the pillows at the top of the bed. I sat down, scooting back toward the center of the bed, and he followed me. Inserting his hands under my hair at the nape of my neck, Ryu fanned its wet, dark length against the white towel as he lowered me down to lie before him.

'Beautiful,' he murmured, coiling a long, black strand in his fingers, which he raised to his lips as his golden eyes met mine. It was lovely, but I felt entirely unmoved. Ryu had a stockpile of such poignant gestures, and after everything that had happened tonight, I felt . . . past gestures.

Ryu stretched his muscular frame alongside mine, finding my lips with his. He tasted so familiar, so safe, that I nearly started crying again. Ryu's body was linked in my memories with so many important moments that feeling him against me was almost like going back in time.

'Stay with me, Jane,' he whispered, kissing my eyelids before moving down my body. And I tried. I wanted, so badly at that moment, to be with him the way he wanted me. To love him the way he expected. I certainly loved what he did to my body, and a moan escaped my lips as he took my nipple between his teeth. But the moan came from far away. I had a bizarre sensation that made me feel, at that moment, less like I was making love to him and more as if I were flipping through an old photo album where I'd once been happy.

I cried out when he pushed my legs apart and licked me with those long, lazy strokes that he knew drove me crazy. But the pleasure was hazy, unfocused, and I bit my own tongue to try to force myself back into my body. He toyed with my clit, bringing me to the verge of climax, again and again, before finally kissing his way back up to my lips. I reached down between us to rub him against me, all the while licking, gently, at his lips. He loved it when I did these things. We played each other's bodies like maestros, but my heart was stone in my chest.

When he moved inside me, shifting himself to hit all the right spots, I felt a physical pleasure wash over me that only made the void in my chest all the more obvious. Tears came to my eyes as unbidden thoughts sprang forward to plague me.

Maybe I just can't love, I thought as Ryu's unhappy face kissed away my tears.

'Not your fault,' I murmured to him guiltily as I hid my expression in his neck under cover of gentle bites. He stroked me harder, reaching between us with seeking fingers to precipitate the orgasm that shattered over me moments later. My head fell back with my cries, and Ryu's fangs found my throat as he came with me. Momentarily quieted by my body's pleasure, my mind gave me a blessed, if short-lived, respite.

After he'd fed, Ryu stayed inside me. His weight grounded me as I cradled him with my cupped pelvis, enjoying the heavy pressure of his body on mine. It felt as if he were holding me to the earth.

'You taste of sorrow,' Ryu said softly, feathering my lips with kisses.

'I'm sorry,' I murmured, unsure of what else to say.

'It wasn't an accusation.'

He shifted off me and we went into the bathroom to clean up. As usual I took longer, and when I returned to the bedroom Ryu was huddled up in bed waiting for me. I yawned as I joined him under the covers.

'Sleep, baby. I'll be here when you wake.'

My mind was already shutting down, lulled by my body's demands for rest.

'Thank you, Ryu. For being here.'

I felt his lips brush my eyelids. The last thing I remembered was his purring voice in my ear, telling me that he meant it when he said he'd always be there for me.

I was dreaming of my mother.

She was in front of me, perpetually one step ahead, as I tried to follow her through our house. Her voice echoed, laughing, from the kitchen. But when I crossed the hallway and pushed open the door, she was gone. Then I heard her upstairs, in her bedroom . . . but, again, by the time I'd thundered up the stairs, the room was empty.

This happened again and again, until finally I saw her pinning laundry on the line that stretched from our small back porch to the back corner of our shabby detached garage. Keeping my eyes on her, for I knew she'd disappear if I so much as blinked, I pushed open the screen door.

I crept forward, wanting so much to reach her. And yet my steps were hesitant, as if I feared what I might find when I turned that Mari-shaped figure around.

And that's when the buzzing started. Like a fly but louder, echoing through our backyard. And each time it buzzed, something fell away. First the trees that bordered the very back of our lot disappeared, as if they'd fallen into the maw of some world-devouring goddess. Then, with each buzz, the darkness took another bite, until my mother was the only solid thing in front of me and I knew she would be next to fall. In my dream I lunged forward, screaming, as that deathly buzzing reverbrated again . . .

In reality, I jolted awake as Ryu's BlackBerry thundered out another loud ring and Ryu finally answered it.

I lay in the bed, my heart pounding, trying to shake off the horror of my dream.

'What do you want?' Ryu said, his voice curt.

'She's fine,' he responded after a second. Then he listened.

'Well, she's safe now. I've got her.' I kept an ear tuned to his conversation as I peeled the sweaty sheets away from me and glanced at the clock. I'd been asleep only an hour and a half.

'I told you I'd take care of her, and I did. She was sleeping before you woke us up.' I knew Ryu was talking about me, but he didn't sound concerned. He sounded . . . smug.

'Why don't we leave the day after? Fine, tomorrow. Whatever. I'll be there.' Then he turned off his phone, without saying goodbye.

He smiled when he saw me curled up under the covers, then he joined me.

'Gods, I've missed you in my bed,' he said, gathering me close. I was still disoriented by the dream, but I was also confused by Ryu's telephone conversation.

'I've missed your bed, too,' I echoed carefully as I tried to pin down what it was that was bothering me about our present situation.

His lips found mine and his hands stroked my sides. He was very obviously ready for round two, but I realized I needed to know who was on the phone.

'Were you talking to Iris?' I asked as he nipped at my neck.

'Hmm?'

'Iris. Were you talking to her on the phone just now?'

Ryu pulled away, glancing up at me with an unreadable expression.

'No, it wasn't Iris,' he said, taking my nipple between his fingers and rolling it gently. But I was not so easily distracted.

'Then who was it?' I asked. 'You were talking about me. Unless you have another woman stashed about here somewhere.'

'Jane, let's just enjoy our time together.'

I didn't understand why he was being sketchy. Then again, now that I was fully awake and had had some time to recover from the shock of learning about my mother, I didn't understand a few things. How had he known to come to Iris's? Why had he been in Maine at all? How had he known about my mother's death?

Grimly, my mind racing, I pulled away to sit facing him with the sheet in my lap.

'Yeah, Ryu. We do have to talk. Who was on the phone? And how did you know what happened?'

'Anyan. It was Anyan on the phone,' he finally replied begrudgingly.

'Oh,' I said. 'What did he want?'

'He was checking to see if I was with you.'

'Right. Why did he think to do that?'

'You weren't anywhere else so he checked with me.'

'But why would he assume I'd be with you? You live in Boston.'

Ryu leaned back against the headboard, sighing. He didn't respond. A cold flash of realization went off in my head and everything fell into place.

'Ryu, how did you know about my mother? How did you know to come looking for me? What aren't you telling me?'

'Do we have to talk about this now? I haven't seen you in forever; I just want to enjoy being with you.' Ryu leaned forward to run his hand under the sheet, up my thigh, toward my sex.

My hand snapped down to his wrist to stop his forward advance.

'Tell me,' I ground out between clenched teeth.

'You weren't at Grizzie and Tracy's, and you weren't home, so I figured you were with Iris.'

'Yeah, but why were you even here?'

His jaw clenched, and suddenly I knew everything. But I wanted him to say it.

'Ryu?'

'I've been helping Anyan with his investigation,' he said eventually.

My breath faltered. I had thought as much, but hearing him say it shook me to the core.

'So you knew my mother was dead.'

His only answer was a silence that screamed in response.

'Were you there when they found her?'

Again, only that telling silence.

'That's what you meant on the phone yesterday. When you said you'd be there for me. It's because you knew my mother was dead.'

He reached for me. 'Jane . . .'

'You bastard,' I hissed, springing away from his touch. 'Tell me you were going to say something but you chickened out. Tell me you didn't just say those things, knowing the truth.'

'Jane, Anyan and I had already talked. We thought it was best . . .'

'You asshole,' I breathed, seeing the truth about his actions, and realizing how perfectly they'd played out . . . and what a stupid bitch I'd been.

'So you let Anyan take one for the team,' I said, my voice cold. 'You let him come and tell me this awful thing, and then you swooped in to pick up the goddamned pieces. My goddamned pieces. And I fucking fell for it.'

'Jane, it's not like that. He wanted to tell you. I didn't

think you needed to hear it from both of us, but I knew you'd need me after you heard.'

'Bullshit, Ryu.' Anger seethed within me, but it was aimed mostly at myself. I could see the entire scenario with brutal clarity. The fact is, I knew that Ryu could not have helped his actions. Everything he'd done was quintessentially Ryu.

'I know you didn't mean to hurt me,' I said finally. His face brightened, but what followed wiped away his smile, as did my angry tone. 'I know you probably believe the shit you're telling yourself. But deep down inside, you have to realize that you treated my mother's death and my grief as just one more ace up your sleeve. You can't help but manipulate people, Ryu.'

He blinked at me, his face expressing his shock, hurt, and outrage. And that's when it all fell into place for me: all that *stuff* he was always trying to give me, even when I told him I didn't want it; his little spats of jealousy, some joking but some not; his harping on about my moving to Boston . . .

He has no idea who I am, what I want, or what I need.

'Jane,' came Ryu's voice, breaking through my epiphany. 'That's not fair. I . . .'

'I know you don't get it, Ryu,' I said, suddenly tired but also suddenly clear, suddenly sure and confident. My voice soft yet firm, I met his hazel eyes with my black, feeling that gulf that had always been there – the gulf that had been bridged by sex and mutual attraction, but now was too cavernous to ignore. 'And I understand you never meant to be cruel or hurtful. But *you* can't seem to understand that I'm not something to be won or lost. I'm not a pawn, or a prize, and our being together isn't a game. *It's not a game,*' I repeated firmly, seeing his face flash anger, 'and I'm not playing anymore.'

I got up from the bed.

'I'm leaving. You can take me home or not.'

'Jane,' he said, his voice strained, 'please, just let me explain.'

'Save it, Ryu,' I said as I walked toward the door.

Swimming home sounded like a much better idea anyway.

Chapter Five

Right after work the next day, I was at the door of Anyan's cabin. It was twilight, and the cabin looked cozy and welcoming in the encroaching gloom. My heart was in my throat, however. I hadn't slept for shit the night before, so physically I was exhausted. Magically, my two long swims had left me glowing like an overcharged reactor. After what had happened in Boston, not only was my control over my power much stronger, but I also had more access to the elements. Yet, despite that energy, my body felt gritty and heavy with exhaustion, especially mentally. And on top of everything, pressing down on my mind was the issue of what I was going to tell my father.

Regardless of the years that had passed, he was still waiting for my mother to come home to him. He'd never gotten rid of her stuff, not even packed it away. Her raincoat still hung in our hallway closet; her boots still sat with ours by the door. Sometimes he talked about her as if she were merely on vacation and had a return ticket, the date of which we knew. Except for one ugly scene, when I was thirteen and so tired of him loving a woman who had abandoned us, I'd never confronted him on the issue.

When he talked about her returning, I held my tongue and ignored him.

Now I knew that she was dead. I knew she would never be able to come home. But how could I tell that to my dad?

It would kill him, and not just metaphorically. What with his bad heart, death was a definite possibility. Besides which, how could I explain how I knew she'd been murdered? I'd lain twisted up in bed all night, trying to imagine that conversation.

Well, Dad, Mom was a seal and I'm magic! Another magic dude, who's a hellhound in his other life, told me that he found Mom's dead body. She was probably murdered by the evil elf who's tried to kill me at least twice. Oops, I forgot to mention any of this? Sorry about that! Oh well, now you have more closet space. Can I make you a sandwich?

Granted, that speech was the extra-callous version, but how could I tell him in a way that *wasn't* callous? I'd have to destroy all his hope, and I would inevitably have to lie to him at the same time. I'd have to lie to him about my mother's real identity and my own, in order to cover for all those other lies. In other words, it was either lie to him or he'd find out that the wife who'd abandoned him had done so because he'd never really known her at all, and, to top it off, his daughter had been living a secret life for the past year and a half as well.

It ended up being a pretty textbook definition of betrayal, no matter how it was approached. Not least because there was no doubt in my mind that I was the reason my mother was dead.

On the long swim back to Rockabill from Eastport, I'd finally consciously made the connection I'd been pushing to the back of my brain. I'd known, the second Anyan had said my mother was killed in a laboratory, who was responsible.

It had to be Jarl. And I knew damned well that he'd murdered my mother to get back at me.

Anger welled up inside me as I touched lightly upon the subject I planned on addressing *after* I apologized. It was time for me to get my own back. Not to mention I had to keep what little family I had left safe from Jarl. If that meant I had to stop being Jane True, sidekick, and become Jane True, superhero, so be it. I hadn't worked this hard just to lie down and take another beating.

But first I had to make things right. Finally gathering my courage, I knocked, stiffening my spine as I heard footsteps. I was here to apologize, but after the way I'd behaved the night before I wouldn't be surprised if Anyan slammed the door in my face before I had the chance.

To my surprise, however, it was Julian who opened the door.

My fellow halfling blinked his sea-green eyes at me from behind his glasses as his slender face broke into a huge grin.

'Jane!' he practically shouted, throwing open his arms.

I launched myself forward gladly. I'd really liked all of Ryu's Boston deputies, but Julian was my absolute favorite.

'What are you *doing* here!' I laughed as Julian set me back down on my feet.

'I'm here with—' Julian began, right before he was muscled aside.

'Ryu,' Julian finished, as I came face-to-face with my former lover.

We blinked at each other until he reached a hand toward me that I stepped back to avoid.

'Where's Anyan?' I blurted out. I could not deal with the sith right now, not after the night I'd had.

Ryu's face hardened. He didn't answer me.

'Where is Anyan?' I repeated, gritting my teeth.

'Why?'

'I have to talk to him.'

'Jane, please,' Ryu replied. 'We need to talk.'

'No,' was my response. 'We really don't. Where's Anyan?'

Ryu watched me, his eyes hooded. Finally he jerked his head back.

'He's in his workshop. Go talk to him then come back. We're not finished.'

I wanted to tell him that we were most certainly finished, in all the ways that mattered, but I knew he wouldn't let me leave if I did. *And you've got bigger fish to fry*, I reminded myself, striding around to the back of Anyan's wraparound porch, smiling at the mental image of a fuzzy-haired, glowering, iron-eyed fish that consequently popped into my brain.

I knew Anyan had a workshop behind the cabin, but it had always been padlocked. Or I would have snooped like nobody's business. I loved the barghest's art and had always wanted to see his creative space—which was why I'd once brought out my step stool to peer in all the windows. There were curtains involved, unfortunately.

This time, however, there was no padlock on the door and the workshop stood open. I tiptoed toward the entrance, once again extremely nervous. Peering in, my eyes swept the room until they landed on the big form of the man I'd come to see.

Anyan sat on a bale of hay, his powerful legs drawn up. Between his knees he cradled a wooden statue. It was a sinuous representation, the curves of which settled into a stylized female form. He was sanding those curves gently, bringing out the hue and grain of the wood he polished.

I watched him, gathering my nerve. He looked weary, sad, distracted. His big hands moved gently over the figurine, and my tired body rallied itself for an almost painful shudder of lust. I tamped it down, clearing my throat at the same time.

Anyan's eyes snapped up to meet mine. We stared at each other for an uncomfortable minute before my own gaze dropped to my new purple Converse.

All day at work I'd rehearsed a very good apology speech. It was elegant, eloquent, and, I now realized, totally inappropriate.

I forced myself to raise my eyes, stepping forward into the workshop as I did so.

'I shot the messenger,' was all I said, my voice thick with shame.

A strange look passed over his face. It appeared mostly composed of relief, but combined with something I couldn't identify. He gently placed the figurine down at his feet.

'I'm sorry, Anyan.'

'I'm sorry, too. Sorry I had to tell you like that. That it happened.'

'Yeah, but those things weren't your fault. I was a bitch.'

He smiled ruefully. 'No worries, Jane. I'm used to bitches.'

It took my tired brain a few seconds to get his joke. When I did, I gave one of my unladylike snorts. Then cringed.

'How are you holding up?' he asked.

'I dunno. I'm so tired right now, I'm on autopilot.'

'You didn't work today, did you?'

'It was good. A distraction. Got me away from the house.'

Anyan frowned. 'What are you going to tell your father?'

I shook my head, tears springing to my eyes. I blinked furiously, feeling my nose start to run. I was on the brink of a major meltdown.

Suddenly Anyan was standing in front of me, his big hands grasping my elbows. For a second my imagination ran wild. I saw myself burying my face in his abdomen, sobbing long and hard. I imagined Anyan's hands stroking my hair; Anyan's hands smoothing down my back. But I wasn't going to use my grief the way Ryu had, to get something I wanted. Anyan, for all intents and purposes, was virtually a stranger to me, and crying on him wasn't appropriate.

'No more weeping on people,' I choked out. 'Do you have some Kleenex or something?'

Anyan cupped my jaw gently, and for a second the look on his face nearly broke me. Until I realized I was about to drip snot on his hand and I sniffled, noisily. Saved by the booger, Anyan withdrew to grab a rag from the top of one of his workbenches.

'It's clean,' he said, handing it to me.

I noisily blew my nose, then held the rag, unsure of what to do with it.

'You can keep that,' he said, as if reading my mind. I smiled at him tentatively, then he smiled back. I knew I was forgiven, and I was glad. Furthermore, I now felt free to ask everything I should have been asking the night before, instead of freaking out.

'First of all, I need to know what happened to . . . to my mother's body.'

Anyan nodded. 'Of course. She was given back to her people, who laid her to rest in the sea. A traditional selkie burial.'

I closed my eyes, a sudden pain gripping my heart. I would have appreciated the chance to see her again, to say goodbye . . . and yet, I knew Anyan had done the right thing. My mother may have loved us, but she'd loved the sea more. The sea was where she belonged. Taking a deep breath, I opened my eyes again to meet Anyan's.

'I need to know what happened.'

The barghest's open face shuttered as he returned to sit on his bale of hay. He picked up the statue and his sandpaper and went back to work. 'We still don't know that much. Whoever is running this show is careful to stay hidden.'

'Well,' I said, trying to sound reasonable, 'tell me what you do know. How do you think she was captured?'

'She had to have been taken on land. Your mother was strong, and only another water-elemental could have taken her in the ocean. The Sea Code would have prevented that from happening.'

'So she was taken on land, then brought to one of these labs. What are they for?'

'All we've found are abandoned labs that have been cleaned out. The few times there've been real leads, the labs in question have been . . . liquidated.'

Along with my mother, I thought, and at the same time I stomped down on my emotional response before it could overwhelm me.

'He may have covered his tracks, but we know who's behind this, Anyan.'

The barghest shook his head. 'We can't jump to conclusions. We can't make assumptions. This is huge, and we need more pieces of the puzzle.'

'Oh, get off it, Anyan,' I replied heatedly. I was so tired of this pussyfooting around the subject of the Alfar. 'You sound like that one back there,' I said, jerking my head toward Anyan's cabin where Ryu, presumably, sat stewing. 'He was saying right up till Conleth fingered Phaedra that Jarl's involvement in that fertility lab was impossible. No one wants to point fingers at the Alfar. But I know how you feel about them, and I know you know the truth. Jarl did this. Jarl is behind these labs, just like he was behind Jimmu's killing spree and Conleth's imprisonment. Yeah Jarl's gotta have tons of help, but the buck stops with him. Unless you think Orin and Morrigan are involved, which I doubt. Taking my mother was personal, and Orin doesn't work like that. He's too cold.'

'You can't know that your mother was a victim because

of you, Jane,' the barghest responded, his voice softening sympathetically.

Damn him, I thought, feeling tears needle my eyes again. *Why does he always know what I'm thinking?*

'Whatever,' was my terse response. 'But the lab thing is all Jarl. You said yourself that it was like where Conleth was kept. If we assume Jarl's involvement from the beginning, and don't waste time acting like that's an impossibility, we'll be a hell of a lot closer to catching him.'

Any softening of Anyan's hawkish features hardened the minute he heard the word 'we'. He stood up before placing the statue on one of the workbenches. Then he strode to the door.

'Yes, you heard me right,' I shouted after him, scrambling to keep up with his long strides. 'Don't you ignore me, Anyan Barghest!'

He was already inside his cabin, the screen door slamming in my face. I wrenched it open only to see he was already halfway through his living room. Hustling after him, I darted past a surprised-looking Julian and a sulking Ryu, both sitting on the sofa, just as the barghest gathered up a couple of bulging saddlebags and headed out his front door.

'Anyan, you shitball, you stop right now!'

Within the arc of the porch lights, he was calmly attaching his saddlebags to his gorgeous, refurbished Indian motorcycle. But now was not the time for admiring; now was the time for whooping a little man-dog keister.

'Anyan!' I shouted, demanding he acknowledge my request.

'There is no way in heaven or hell that you are involving yourself in this investigation, Jane. So don't even start.'

I'd never been one to contain my emotions, but I don't think I'd ever felt this sort of fury before. I'd grieved; I'd loved; I'd felt overwhelming sadness. But never real *fury*. Until now.

The anger started in my toes, then pushed up my body in a wave of rage so fierce I trembled. Already overcharged, my power fizzed and whizbanged right alongside my emotions. I'd always been told that emotional control was vital to magical control, but ever since I'd reached out to my ocean a year ago, I'd found that shunting off my feelings actually weakened me. Maybe it was because I was a halfling and my humanity tempered the demands of my supernatural heritage. Whatever the case, I felt a heady combination of power and anger beating through me, looking for release.

'He killed my mother,' I responded in a hoarse voice, but the barghest ignored me. And that's when I felt something snap inside me. Fury ignited in my soul like a puddle of gasoline flaming to life.

'You cannot deny me this, Anyan,' I raged at the barghest's retreating form. I moved to confront him when Ryu's voice came from behind me.

'Jane, Anyan's right. Your coming is a bad idea.'

I ignored Ryu. I wasn't talking to him, yet.

'You know I have to do this,' I demanded, spearing Anyan with my gaze.

The barghest shook his shaggy head. 'Which is exactly why you're not coming, woman. You're furious and this isn't a vengeance quest. This is bigger than any of us, and I'm not going to waste time chasing after you chasing shadows.'

'Anyan, I swear to the gods that if you treat me like a fucking child I am going to take that saddlebag and shove it up your . . .'

From behind me, my rant was interrupted by an unwelcome hand on my shoulder.

'Jane, listen to me, I know you're upset . . .'

Suddenly, it was as if something broke and all the feelings of shame, hurt and anger that had been roiling around impotently inside me for the past two months lashed out. I was so tired of playing these games; so tired of being underestimated, and overlooked, and manipulated. What happened in Boston had changed me, and although I still looked like mild-mannered Jane True, the selkie-halfling, backing up my comfortable little body was a whole fuck-load of thuggishly brutal elemental force and pure, un-Jane-like venom.

Still in control enough that I didn't actually hurt him, I allowed my power to flatten Ryu. One minute he was standing behind me, hand on my shoulder, and the next he was sprawled on the ground. I let my force sit on his chest like a lolling mastiff, effectively pinning him and keeping him quiet at the same time.

Anyan's eyes widened, staring behind me to where Ryu lay prostrate. Before the barghest could snap up his own powerful shields, I was on him.

I surrounded Anyan with a ball of my own energy, keeping him open, exposed, and vulnerable. I narrowed my power into a rough imitation of two fingers that poked him squarely in the chest. The big man grunted, taking a small step backward.

'Now you listen to me, dog breath. I am *not* a child. I am *not* weak.'

To emphasize my point, I gave him another hard jab to the sternum. He took another startled step back.

'I know when to stay out of shit, and I know I've been weak in the past. But I'm not that girl any longer.' One more poke and Anyan gave more ground.

'You have two choices. You say this isn't personal; I say that's bullshit. So either you take me with you on your official investigation or I'll come anyway. You can't keep me from following you.' I shoved him again, much harder than before, hard enough to make him stagger. I stalked toward him, using my power to punctuate my points.

'You can't keep me from being one step behind you, the entire way.'

Shove.

'You can't stop me from going into the Borderlands and meeting these contacts of yours.'

Shove.

'You aren't my father.' Shove. 'You don't control me.' Shove. 'You don't tell me what to do.' Shove. 'I'm strong now, and you can't stop me from coming with you.'

With those words, I let the wodge of power that I used to hold down Ryu spread out, pressing him harder into the earth. I knew the baobhan sith wasn't the issue, however; the one who stood between me and my goal was standing in front of me. But not for long.

'I'm coming with you, Anyan,' I said as I pulled a Gladiator and unleashed hell.

I let my Atlantic's power manifest itself forward, blasting out of me to lift the barghest off his feet. It took him up, up, and then flipped him over onto his back. Anyan hung there, in midair, for a split second. And then I drilled him back down into the earth. Feeling him call to his element, I knew the ground helped to cushion him from the brunt of the impact. But he still landed hard enough to create an Anyan-shaped crater. He lay spread-eagled, the wind undoubtedly knocked out of him. When he didn't breathe for a long handful of seconds, I began to worry. But finally the barghest exhaled with a whoosh, and I saw the big man blink a few times. Probably clearing the stars from his eyes.

I reined my power back in, stepping to the side so I could keep both men in my line of sight as I released them. Ryu was up first.

He stared at me like I'd grown a handlebar mustache. I resisted the temptation to flick him off.

I was just about to snap at the vampire to close his mouth and stop gaping when I heard a bruised-sounding wheeze emit from Anyan's prone form.

He sat up slowly and carefully. For a second, I thought he was gasping for breath before I realized he was actually . . . chuckling? Was he laughing at me?

Anyan leaned back on his hands, letting his head fall back as his slightly breathless chuckles became full-on guffaws.

I frowned, unable to figure out why he was laughing. If it was because he thought I was joking, I'd happily expand the Anyan-crater he was currently lying in by pile-driving him once more . . .

But when his laughter finally slowed a bit, and his eyes met mine, he wasn't angry. Nor was he mocking me. He glowed with pride, and he was smiling like I'd just brought home a trophy.

'Dear gods, Jane, I've been waiting for you to do something like that.' Laughter bubbled up in him again as he carefully lay back down.

'Fuck, that hurt.' The barghest groaned as he gathered power from the earth to heal himself. 'But it was worth it to see your mettle. And Ryu . . .' Anyan chortled again, enjoying his joke. 'I thought Ryu was going to piss himself.'

Ryu's face was still slack, so shocked by my aggression that he didn't even blink when the barghest needled him. Normally Ryu would have flipped.

Anyan stood slowly, stretching his big frame as if to make sure everything still worked.

'I knew you'd be strong,' he said, finally growing serious, although his eyes still twinkled. 'I figured you'd be stronger than me. But you beat all my expectations. And I'm glad, Jane. I hated seeing you vulnerable.'

I blushed, looking down. Why was he being nice? If he was trying to butter me up only to tell me to stay home, I'd give him a buttering . . .

'And you've made it clear that we can't stand in your way, if you really want to come.'

My eyes met his, which were suddenly fierce and hard.

'But if you do this, Jane, you know the drill. You have to follow *my* orders. I'm in charge of this little outfit, and I grant no quarter. If you're with me, you do what I say. And just because you're strong doesn't mean you're invulnerable. I know Nell has given you good defensive training, because I told her to. And as you've just illustrated, you can muscle your way around. But you're not trained offensively, nor have you any finesse. So if I say you stay behind on a particular mission, you stay behind. It won't be because you're weak,' he said before I could protest. 'It'll be because I'm your general and you're my soldier, my weapon. I deploy you where I think you can do the most damage. Or I hold you back so I don't lose you before the next fight. Do you understand me?'

I wrinkled my nose at him. 'You don't actually want me to call you "General", do you? 'Cause that's creepy.'

'Jane.'

'Fine. I'm in. What you say goes. General.'

He shook his head at me. 'Don't make me regret this by getting yourself killed. I told Nell to make you strong, and you both succeeded. Now don't fuck it up. We leave in an hour.'

Anyan walked off, leaving me to watch his retreating backside. I was stunned. And more than a little appreciative of the view . . .

I heard a throat clearing behind me. I turned around.

It's like he's never seen me before, I realized. Strangely enough, the thought made me smile. I also noticed, for the first time, that Julian was watching us from the back porch. He had a way of blending in with the background that wasn't magical, as I would have felt the glamour, but was equally effective. For despite the fact I'd been unaware of his presence, there stood my fellow halfling, his whole body somehow exuding excitement and amusement, even though he wasn't smiling or anything. Julian did love it when I stuck it to the Man.

So he was certain to love *this* . . .

'Ryu Baobhan Sith,' I said, smiling at my former lover sweetly, drawing out my next words, caressing them with my tongue and lips. 'Meet Jane True.'

Then I used my mojo to wallop Ryu back to the ground with one more healthy blast of my Atlantic's power. He came up spluttering as I swished off in the direction of my house, sighing happily. Julian gave me a furtive low-five as I walked past him, and I could tell he was trying very, very hard not to laugh at his boss. Ryu probably hadn't strictly deserved that last wallop, but, I have to admit, showing off my magical muscles – both to him and to Anyan – had felt so good, on so many levels.

Turns out my former lover wasn't the only one with a little suntin' suntin' up his sleeve.

Chapter Six

I stood in front of my closet, completely at a loss. What do you pack for a vengeance quest? I didn't have time to re-watch my Tarantino, and from what I remembered, Uma's wardrobe wasn't going to work on me. Imagine yellow pleather on a girl who was half-seal rather than pure Viking. *Not* pretty.

I sat down on my bed, feeling nauseous as I realized what I'd gotten myself into. I was determined to help find my mother's killer, but I hadn't really thought this through. First of all, my mother was dead. She was dead and I was . . . packing. Furthermore, I didn't want to go anywhere with Ryu; I wanted to pull out his toenails and poke them into his eyeballs. That said, I kept thinking of the look of horror on his face when Ryu realized I was no longer just a walking, talking snack bar. It felt good. Less good, however, was the fact that, despite how Anyan had reacted, I knew he had to feel the same way, on some level.

So, running off like this probably wasn't the best idea. It meant that I wasn't dealing with my grief, I was launching myself into imminent danger, and I was about to embark on a trip for who knows how long with my ex *and* the man I had a crush on.

Which brought me back to packing. Should I pack my safety razor and nice panties? Or the kitchen knives and a balaclava?

I sighed, glancing at the clock. Which informed me I now had but thirty-five minutes to figure out how to pack for revenge, tell my father that I was disappearing with three random dudes, and find someone to cover for me at work. Keeping in mind that I was already helping to cover for my pregnant boss.

Well, Jane, I thought, *you were just complaining about being bored. You've read your Mercedes Lackey. She warned you about wanting to live in interesting times.*

I yanked open my old duffel bag and shoved in a few shirts, a zip-up hoodie, two pairs of jeans, and about eighteen pairs of underwear. I was terrified of running out of clean panties, which I realized was completely ridiculous. So I unpacked ten pairs and threw in a small bottle of Woolite for handwashing instead. Then I reconsidered, pulled out the Woolite, and put back in the undies. I repeated this process about eight times before I nearly pulled my own hair out.

Get a grip, Jane True! I threatened myself. *Your underwear is not the priority!*

I sighed and added the Woolite, removed five pairs of panties, and packed some bras. And what the hell was I going to sleep in? I had flannel pajamas, a couple of T-shirt nighties, and some hoochtastic sexiness. My libido, ever irrepressible, suggested the black teddy for Anyan, while my temper, still simmering over Ryu's behavior, suggested I go naked and bring a taser, just to torture the vampire.

I went with a long T-shirt.

Finally, I packed socks to wear with my Converse, a toothbrush and toothpaste, my face wash and lotion, and a pack of travel razors. For makeup I brought my concealer, blush, and some mascara. I didn't know if makeup was appropriate for vengeance quests, but I decided to file it under 'war paint' and let it go at that.

Everything ended up being a ton of shit, and my old duffel was bulging. I couldn't think of anything to unpack, so I just forced shut the zippers and prayed it would hold. Now I had to deal with my dad. I had fifteen minutes to explain to him that I was leaving and that I wasn't sure where I was going or when I would be back. I also had to articulate to him how much I loved him and how much he meant to me, just in case I died while I was gone. All without making it seem like I was scared that I might, indeed, die. Fuck.

I took a deep breath and walked downstairs, clutching my backpack. My dad was in his old recliner, watching the Food Network. I laid my pack by the door and went in to talk to him.

'Dad?'

'Yeah, honey?'

I paused, stricken. What the hell was I going to tell him? I imagined myself blurting out the truth: that Mom was dead and that I was going to help find who killed her. Because I was magical, and stuff.

That'd go down well.

'Jane, what's going on? What's wrong?'

'Daddy . . .' I breathed, my voice in my throat.

Just then the doorbell rang. Watching me with concern, my dad stood to answer it. I was rooted to the spot, incapable of figuring out how to get out of that door without breaking my father's heart.

'Mr True,' Ryu's smooth voice echoed from the doorway.

Shitpissbugger, I swore. Why was he early? He was never early.

'Ryu. Well, that's a surprise. How are you?'

The men shook hands and I felt my own palms begin to sweat.

'I'm fine, sir. Just here to pick up Jane.'

I groaned inwardly as my dad's face crinkled in confusion.

'Pick up Jane? Where are you two going?'

I shot Ryu a dirty look as I went to talk to my dad.

'Dad, I have to go somewhere. With Ryu and some other friends. I'll be gone . . . a few weeks,' I hazarded. My dad looked as suspicious as I sounded. 'It's last-minute, I know, but something has come up. It's important and I . . . I have to go, Dad. I'm sorry. I love you. Remember Nurse Ratched?' During the Boston debacle, Nell the gnome had guarded my dad for me. Anyan had roped her in, again, for while I was away. She'd make sure my dad was safe from Jarl.

My father blinked at me. 'The short one?'

'Yup, that one. She'll be staying here again. And there's tons of food in the freezer, plus I'll call the guys and make sure they come by for poker. You'll be fine and I'll be home soon . . .'

'Honey, where are you going? Are you in trouble?'

If my father had been pissed, I would have been okay. If he'd been angry, I would have muscled through my emotions and just gone for bluster as a way to cover my emotion. But he just sounded worried, and that hurt.

'Dad, I'm fine. Really. I just have something I need to do. But I will come back, I swear. I'll come back and we'll talk.'

'Honey, what's going on? I don't understand. I've never seen you like this . . .'

To my horror, I felt hot tears run down my cheeks. I was furious with myself for reacting this way, but I couldn't help it. I wasn't strong enough to keep it together around my dad, not after everything that had happened. I wanted to cry with him about my mom, not lie to him and leave him like this.

'I'm fine, Dad, really. I'll be in touch, and I have my phone. I have to go now, but I'll see you soon, I swear.'

I hugged him to me fiercely.

'I love you, Dad,' I whispered in his ear before I released him. Then I went and picked up my bag. I had to get out of there before I broke entirely.

'I'll call you when we get to where we're going. Or tomorrow morning.'

Ryu took my stuff and headed out to his rented SUV. I waved to my dad and ran to the car, then I changed my mind and ran back to give him one more hug and a kiss on the cheek before rushing back to the passenger's seat.

'Drive,' I said before I'd even buckled myself in.

Ryu did as I asked, and I watched my father in my side mirror. He looked confused, lost, and lonely.

'No matter what happens to me, you tell him the truth,' I growled at Ryu, choking back tears.

'Baby, everything is going to be fine, you'll—'

'Shut up, Ryu,' I snarled, turning to stare him down. 'Just promise me that whatever happens, you'll tell him the truth. He can't just be left again.'

Ryu was silent, his face hard.

'I can't promise that, Jane. He's a human.'

'He's my father.'

'And he's human. We can't risk exposing our kind. You know that.'

'Fuck your kind. And fuck you. Anyan will tell him, or Julian.' And I knew they would, at that.

Ryu just shook his head. He was angry now, but I didn't care. I dug out my cell phone to start dealing with the fallout of my leaving.

'Jane, I don't know what I did . . .'

'Yes, you do. Now be quiet while I deal with my responsibilities.'

As I searched through my list of contacts, I took one last look out the back window as we pulled out of my long drive and onto the main road. My father was still standing there, looking small and lost. My heart breaking for him, and for the family we'd once had, I dialed Grizzie and Tracy.

Ryu, smart for once, kept silent.

I woke with a start as we bumped to the ground at O'Hare. Our trip was on the Alfar, so we were in first class. At any other time I would have enjoyed the experience. But after staking out the seat next to Julian, to Ryu's obvious consternation, I simply settled myself in, waited until the captain turned off the 'Fasten Seat Belts' sign, then reclined my seat as far as it would go and forced myself to rest. That I fell asleep was a shock, but I guess I was even more tired than I thought.

I yawned, made a face at the taste of my own mouth, and pulled a piece of gum out of my pocket. It was rather linty, but it would do. I stretched, letting my brain shift into autopilot, something I'd learned to do long ago, after Jason's death. I'd have tons of time to think later. For now, I just needed to keep it together and get through these next few weeks.

After we'd coasted to the gate and were allowed to stand up, Anyan handed me my duffel from the overhead carrier then pulled out his own bags. From which he dug out his cell phone and made a call. He made no attempt to hide his half of the conversation.

'Hello, Carl? It's Anyan . . . Yes, I've brought three others with me. A pureblood, whom I trust,' Anyan said, giving

Ryu a look that clearly challenged the baobhan sith to be anything but trustworthy. 'And the one I told you about, Julian, as well as Jane. Yes, Mari's daughter.' I felt a stab of pain at the mention of my mother's name, but I kept it under control.

'We're heading straight to Borealis. We'll check in with you and Cappie when we get to the hotel. Will she be at the site? . . . Okay . . . Thanks, Carl. Bye.'

I perked up, wondering if we'd meet this Capitola woman. She'd helped us during our last investigation, and I had all sorts of questions for her. Like where she got that name.

And who she is to the barghest, my libido thought petulantly. I ignored it.

Anyan flipped shut his cell and slipped it into his back pocket. 'Okay, we're good to go. We're here officially. That said, remember not to show off, Ryu. Alfar lackeys aren't popular here.'

'I'm no one's lackey,' Ryu replied huffily.

'Whatever you say, Chief. Just don't go flashing your powers.'

'What about me?' I interrupted. 'Am I an Alfar lackey?'

'You're fine, Jane. They know about you already.'

I am the 'victim's daughter', after all, I thought sadly.

We headed to the rental car place to pick up our wheels. Ryu had, of course, ordered something luxury, another large SUV. Anyan was driving, since he knew the terrain. Ryu, the little shit, took stock of Anyan in the driver's seat and therefore opened the door to the backseat for me. I ignored him, however, and hoisted myself up into that passenger seat, next to the barghest. Ryu watched me with dark eyes that only got angrier when Anyan yelled from the front for him to stop lollygagging and get in the car.

The drive from Chicago to Borealis, the far western suburb

where my mother's body had been found, was about fifty minutes. There was tons of construction – apparently a normal occurrence – on the tollway, but we'd arrived with the last of the flights, around midnight, so traffic was light.

None of us made much conversation on the way. O'Hare was well outside Chicago, so there wasn't much to sightsee. Just a string of strip malls, with all the same stores, repeated over and over again. Occasionally the strip malls mixed it up by being an outlet strip mall, but those, too, contained the exact same stores as the full-priced versions.

One thing there wasn't, at all, was water. I'd never been this entirely inland before. Even when Ryu and I had gone to Quebec, it hadn't felt landlocked because the Territory was infested with streams, rivers, and lakes. Illinois, however, felt like a desert to my selkie blood. And the farther west we went away from Chicago and Lake Michigan, the more I felt the absence of real water. I kept peering out the window and shifting about, growing increasingly uncomfortable with the idea of being landlocked.

'You'll be fine,' Anyan rumbled beside me. 'We'll find you water. The Fox River runs through Borealis, and Lake Michigan isn't too far away.'

'Sorry?'

'You're twitchy. I figured you could feel the lack of water. But don't worry, we'll find you something wet.'

'Thank you,' I said. 'It does feel . . . weird.'

Anyan smiled. He hadn't shaved in a few days, and the scruff made his tanned skin even darker. His teeth gleamed white in the darkness.

'That's the trouble with water, as an element. On the one hand, it's strong as hell, yet water-elementals get so tied down geographically. But we have Julian, as well, as a backup. We'll make sure you stay strong.' I turned my head slightly to catch Julian smiling at me. He gave me a friendly wink and I felt myself relax.

Shutting my eyes entirely, I rested for the remainder of the trip to Borealis, until I felt us exiting the tollway. We drove just a few miles through a rough-looking strip of dive bars and long-closed businesses before we hit downtown Borealis. There were a few short streets of tawdry glitz – Borealis housed a riverboat casino – and then we were at a nondescript chain hotel, right next to the train station.

After having insisted there was no way we'd need reservations, Anyan looked decidedly sheepish when we arrived at the hotel to find it was almost entirely booked. Especially because I'd immediately demanded four rooms, cutting Ryu off before he could ask to share with me.

I'd been just as promptly denied.

Apparently, there was a wedding reception at the giant brewhouse/comedy club/bar and nightclub complex next door to the hotel. Everything, even the suites, was taken except for two rooms. Ryu looked like he'd won the lottery as the receptionist handed over the two sets of keys. But I had other plans.

'Halflings bunk together!' I sang, grabbing Julian's wrist and pulling him toward me. He looked a bit startled, casting Ryu a slightly panicked look. I know it wasn't fair to Julian to use him as a buffer between me and Ryu, but I didn't really care. Plus, to be honest, I wanted to get to know my fellow halfling better. We'd spent so much time together, but none of it alone. I was curious about Julian, not least because I wanted to know what kind of life he led as a halfling surrounded at all times by purebloods.

Anyan shrugged, quickly handing me the keys to one of the rooms. 'Whatever you want, Jane.' Ryu looked like he wanted to protest, but Anyan kept talking. 'We have two choices: hit the hay, or head over to the site. Cappie's gang's been hired to clean it, so they'll be there all night. It's up to you what we do, Jane.'

Part of me wanted to crawl into the hotel bed and act like none of this had ever happened. But I knew that wouldn't work.

'Let's get this over with,' I said finally. 'Just let me drop off my stuff and brush my teeth.'

Anyan nodded and headed into his room, while Julian headed into ours. But Ryu lingered.

'Jane,' he said. 'Please.'

I stopped and turned.

'I'm sorry,' he said, although the begrudging way he said it made it sound less than apologetic.

I sighed. 'I'm sorry, too, Ryu.' I meant I was sorry it was over, sorry it had to end this way, sorry he didn't get any of that . . .

'Can't we talk this through?' I knew what he really meant was could we share a room.

'No, Ryu. And we need to go.' I met his eyes, letting the force of my resolve show through in my own black gaze.

He didn't look happy, but he acquiesced. We walked away from each other to our separate habitations.

Julian was already using the bathroom, so I set my bag down on one of the beds, immediately stooping to dig out my toiletry bag without pausing to rest. If I rested, I'd think, and if I thought, I'd lose my nerve.

I really didn't want to see the place where my mother had died.

Chapter Seven

It was after two in the morning when we arrived outside the same sort of nondescript strip-mall clinic that Conleth had been kept in for so many years. This one, however, wasn't burned. As Anyan had explained again in the car, by the time the halflings of Borealis had raided the lab, the staff had cleared out. They'd murdered all their test subjects, but hadn't bothered to hide any of the evidence except for paperwork. Everything else was left intact. Whoever was in charge was taunting us.

There was a battered old Ford Explorer in the parking lot, covered in bumper stickers and with a vanity plate that read 'TRPTICH'. Anyan smiled when he saw the car, and I figured it had to be his friend Capitola's. I had to blink a few times at the bumper stickers on her car, because they kept . . . shifting. Then I realized they were glamoured. At first, they'd said things like 'Keep Illinois Clean', but when I exerted a wee bit of force I could see messages like 'Halflings Do It Wholeheartedly'. I couldn't help but laugh, despite the circumstances. It wasn't that the stickers were very witty, but more that I was shocked to see anybody proud to be a halfling. My time at the Compound had made it very clear halflings weren't making the Alfar A-list anytime soon.

Anyan parked our rental car next to the Explorer before turning to me. 'You ready, Jane? We don't have to do this now,' he added when I paused. Ryu kept silent, as he had been since we left the hotel. Julian was always quiet, and tonight was no exception. I sometimes forgot he was there, to be honest.

'No,' I answered Anyan, trying to add some steel to my voice. 'Let's get it over with.'

We got out of the car and headed toward the door.

Again, just as we'd found at Conleth's lab, there was a small entryway that looked like any other clinic's reception area. But through the doors, all pretense of a proper clinic had been dropped entirely. There were Perspex-looking cells with gurneys inside them. Horrifying-looking surgical tools were lying around willy-nilly alongside more serious medical equipment.

And there was a lot of blood.

Blood was everywhere: on the walls, on the ceilings. Newer-looking blood, older blood, and lots of . . . other substances. The place stank to high heaven, a horrifying combination of fear, sweat, blood, excrement, and death.

Ryu put a protective hand on the small of my back, and I didn't resent his touch. I took a series of short, shallow breaths through my mouth, concentrating on not getting sick.

Suddenly, a tremendous groaning sound echoed through the space. Anyan, Ryu, and I backed up hastily toward the safety of the doorframe. The clear plastic cells all shuddered as one, straining at whatever anchored them before they ripped off the floor. The panes of plastic hovered, rotating slowly onto their sides, then stacked themselves up midair.

A dark-skinned figure, lovely and elegant, strode into the center of the room. Power, Alfar power, swirled about us, and I felt confused.

I also felt horrified that this must be Capitola. The woman was *beautiful*. She was long and lean, with a catwalk model's body. Her face was carved from jet-black ebony; an artist's rendering of the perfect female. She was a queen, a Nefertiti, and I knew the barghest must be in love with her. *I* was a little bit in love with her.

Julian and I exchanged wide-eyed looks, wondering at this woman and her magic. Her dark braids slithering around her shoulders, she calmly stacked the panes of Perspex against a side wall.

'C'mon, Moo-Cow! Let's get rolling! That took you ten whole seconds!'

Out of the shadows from the other side of the lab came a short, voluptuous woman. Her long brown hair bobbed in a ponytail, and her succubus juju was prominent and powerful. Unfortunately, she, too, was beautiful, in a polar-opposite way from the other woman in the center of the room. The newcomer's lush shape promised naughty evenings and naughtier afternoons, her beautiful almond eyes framed by thick liquid eyeliner and even thicker black lashes. She was like Aladdin's Jasmine, only chubbier and sexier. And definitely not G-rated.

The smaller woman saw us standing in the doorway and she waved. 'Hey, Anyan!' she called, before turning toward the back of the radically refurbished clinic. 'Capitola!' she hollered. 'Anyan is here!'

'Why must you be so loud all the time, Shar?' the tall woman asked, her voice Alfar-calm.

''Cause somebody has to put a fire in your belly, Moo-Cow,' the shorter woman said, giving her friend a vicious grin before turning to us. 'Excuse Moo-Cow,' she said to me. 'She lacks social skills.'

I blinked at the woman who seemed to be named Shar,

unable to believe that the statuesque beauty beside her was called 'Moo-Cow'. I was also very pleased to find out that neither of these two luscious ladies was Capitola. Hopefully this Capitola was ungainly, maybe wart-ridden, perhaps wall-eyed or hunchbacked . . .

Or she was the goddess striding forward out of the darkness.

Seriously? She was one of the most beautiful women I'd ever seen. And she was everything, and I mean *everything*, I wanted to be. Exuding strength and capability, no one would ever take this woman anything but seriously.

She looked to be of mixed race. Unlike my own pale pallor, her skin was a perfect, healthy café au lait. And instead of my weak softness, she was all hard athleticism . . . with curves. Basically, she looked like the heroine on the cover of one of those urban fantasy novels. She was terrifying *and* sexy, with six-pack abs *and* Victoria's Secret-model boobs, bulging biceps, *and* a big juicy ass.

I hated her, and I wanted to be her, and I knew I could never compete, in anything, ever, with the perfection that was Capitola.

At least she has a stupid name, I tried to comfort myself.

As if in response, she ran a hand through the kinky chestnut Afro that stuck out proud and gorgeous around her perfectly sensual features, her green eyes shining, and the name 'Capitola' sang in my heart.

She made it beautiful.

Dammit.

'Uncle Anyan!' she called, smiling a huge, brilliant smile.

Uncle? I thought, even as I felt myself growing smaller and shabbier with every step she took toward us.

'Hey, Cappie,' he said, beaming with affection and pride as he strode forward to give her a hug. I realized, then, just how tall Capitola was. She must have been a good six feet tall, and she and the barghest fit together perfectly.

I only fit with oompa-loompas, I thought sadly. Even Ryu had forgotten he was currently trying to win me back, his gaze going from beautiful woman to beautiful woman – excluding me – as if he couldn't decide which Baskin-Robbins flavor to choose from.

To be honest, I couldn't blame him. All three women were seriously hot.

Only Julian appeared unfazed by the attractiveness of the ladies. If anything, he was looking at them with a face full of . . . hope? He was standing there, peering at the women like a nerdy little kid watching the cool clique from afar.

He wants to play, I thought, *but not* play, *like Ryu*.

I filed that thought away, fully intending to have that long talk with Julian about what sort of life he'd lived, growing up halfling in the Territory. His reactions to everything in the Borderlands so far suggested to me it was going to be a fairly bleak tale.

It must be something to go from viewing halflings as tolerated to seeing them so free here. Not to mention wicked strong, I thought as I felt another blast of power, and all the gurneys that had littered the cells suddenly crunched together to make a massive, twisted ball of steel. The Moo-Cow woman floated the ball of steel to rest next to the Perspex, and suddenly the middle part of the room was nearly empty.

Her friend Shar snorted and rolled her eyes. 'How are we supposed to get that out of here now? It needs to fit in a *Dumpster*, Moo.'

Moo's dark eyes flashed again, but her voice was still calm when she spoke. 'I can make it fit into a Dumpster. And still leave room for a fat succubus-halfling,' she added, causing Shar to do a double take.

The two started arguing, and Capitola shook her head.

'Sorry about them,' she said, acknowledging Ryu with a wary nod. 'Ryu Baoban Sith,' she intoned, before turning toward Julian.

'It's a pleasure to meet you, brother.' Capitola grinned, all wariness gone, as she clasped both of Julian's hands in hers. 'Welcome to the Borderlands. We hope you feel at home here. You are among friends.' Her words were richly laced with portent, her large green eyes locked on Julian's, whose gaze flicked uncomfortably between Ryu and Capitola.

'And you must be Jane,' she said, turning to give me a warm smile as she let go of Julian's hands to extend her own to me. 'It's such a pleasure to meet you. I'm sorry it had to be under such circumstances. Please accept our condolences.' She shook my hand, her grip firm but gentle, and I hated myself for ever having criticized her. I started to thank her, when there was a roar from behind us.

The short woman had the tall woman in a headlock. Capitola sighed.

'Goddammit, quit it! What the hell is wrong with you two?' She strode off to referee the wrestling match as Anyan chuckled.

'So that's Capitola?' I asked the barghest rhetorically.

'Yup. Everyone calls her Cap or Cappie, though. You should ask her about her name. You'll like the story; it involves books.' Anyan nodded toward the other two women whom Capitola was physically separating.

'The other two are Emuishere, or Moo; and Shar. As you probably felt, Emuishere is an Alfar-halfling. Her father set himself up as an Egyptian deity and forced her to serve as his daughter-consort.' I made a face and Anyan nodded. 'Yeah, they did things differently back then. The other is Shar. She's half succubus. And all trouble.'

I smiled, liking all three already. Julian cleared his throat. 'So they really are halflings?' he asked. Anyan nodded.

'And everyone here in the Borderlands is halfling?' Julian continued when he saw Anyan nod.

'No, there are purebloods aplenty. Here in Borealis there are quite a few who followed halfling or human partners away from critical parties in the Territory. But they're all registered. That's what I was doing when I called Carl as soon as we landed. There's a lot of infighting in the Borderlands, but one thing everyone agrees with is that they want to keep Alfar intervention nonexistent. So they pool resources.'

'Resources?' I asked.

'There are a slew of halflings like Peter Jakes out here, only far, far more powerful. They're called Sensors, and they monitor power, even unused power, reporting any unregistered power signatures they come across. If we hadn't reported to Carl, who cleared our presence, we would have been greeted by quite the welcome wagon.'

'I take it they'd be bearing less-friendly gifts than muffin baskets?' I quipped.

The barghest's lips twitched. 'Far less friendly than muffins, yes.'

'But that would mean—' Julian started to say, just as Capitola finally separated her two friends and they all three came forward. I registered Julian's protest, knowing he was probably about to raise the same questions I had. But right now we had to meet the rest of Tryptich . . . now that they weren't trying to kill each other, that is.

Even the Alfar-halfling looked contrite, and both women mumbled their apologies for their behavior and for my loss. After we'd been introduced and exchanged pleasantries, Capitola shooed the other two to continue their cleaning before turning back toward us.

'Ready to talk?' she asked me.

I thought about that for a second. On the one hand, I felt almost mesmerized by the sight of the laboratory and all its gore before me. But another part of me felt unmoved. I didn't associate this terrible place with my mother, even though I knew it was where she died. I felt anger at knowing that last fact, but it was still a strangely disjointed feeling, like I wasn't really making any emotional connection to the place. So I stood and stared at where my mother had spent her final moments, and part of me still felt . . . nothing.

When Capitola interrupted my reverie by giving my shoulder a gentle squeeze, I nodded, and she led the way to the doors.

Peering over my shoulder, I took a last look at the now cavernous lab space. A fierce sense of satisfaction washed through me as Moo let rip with another blast of Alfar power. This time all the various instruments of torture, in their medical disguises, were collected into another compact ball of twisted metal and plastic. It felt right to me that these three women would expunge all signs that this evil place had ever existed.

Julian stayed in the main room to help the women clean up, a strangely vexed expression blanketing his normally sedate features, as the rest of us returned to the relatively clean reception area. Anyan, Ryu, Capitola, and I pulled four chairs together and sat down. After a moment in which we all shuffled about trying to get comfortable, Cappie turned toward me.

'First of all, Jane, is there anything you want to ask me about what was . . . found? Here in the lab?'

She meant did I want to know how my mother had died. But I'd seen the blood, and I'd seen the instruments. I knew for what purposes this place had been built. The questions one normally asked when a loved one died suddenly – 'Did he feel any pain?'; 'Did she suffer?' – were moot.

'No. I don't think that's necessary. But thank you.'

'Okay. If you change your mind, I can talk whenever,' Cap replied, and she meant it. I realized that behind that strong body lay a very warm heart.

'Our people have already done a thorough investigation of the premises,' she said, moving on. 'We were brought in to clean, but don't worry, we won't be destroying any evidence.'

'That's great,' Ryu said, giving Capitola his most winning smile. 'We really appreciate all your help. I hope you're getting something for all of your hard work.'

Cap laughed. 'Thanks, Ryu. But we're still not telling you who's signing our paychecks, so you can stop right now.'

Ryu frowned even as Capitola breezed along. 'Speaking of who we work for, TPTB want to see you tonight, Anyan. And they want to meet Jane and Julian.'

The barghest nodded, and Ryu's frown grew deeper. The Powers That Be must not trust Ryu, which made sense. Anyan was obviously Capitola's friend, even though he *was* technically working for the Alfar, and she obviously trusted him not to share everything he saw with the Alfar. I was a little surprised at their including Julian, but from what I was seeing, there was obviously a lot of Halfling Power going on in the Borderlands. But as for Ryu, there wasn't anything 'technical' about his loyalties – he was definitely his monarchs' man. For the first time I realized how odd this whole situation was, and questioned why the hell the baobhan sith was even here. I hadn't thought about how weird it was till now, as it had seemed natural he'd be with us: when things went kablooey in my life, Ryu was always around. But Anyan and Ryu didn't like each other, and Ryu was clearly the odd man out here in the Borderlands.

So why *was* he here?

I stored that question away for when we were alone and focused back on Cap.

'We've found two other abandoned labs in the area. Both have evidence of body disposal in the vicinity, but neither had the sort of wholesale slaughter that went down in this one. One seems to have been abandoned quite a while ago, the other more recently. We're finished with the first one; we're still working on the other, gathering evidence. But you're more than welcome to go check them out tomorrow. I'll text you the addresses, Anyan.

'We've also got a few leads we're working on now. I don't want to say too much' – at this, Cap glanced at Ryu – 'but one looks really promising. We want to find a working lab, not only so that we can liberate the subjects but also because we really want to capture some of the staff.'

As she said the last bit, her smile became distinctly predatory and I shivered. Despite her size and strength, Capitola had been as warm and fuzzy as a teddy bear up until that moment. Then I saw her mettle, and I went back to being in awe.

I wondered if it would be inappropriate to start up a Capitola fan club.

Just as Anyan started to ask Cap a question, there was an enormous bang from the other room. Suddenly, Shar came flying – and I mean flying – through the doorway from the lab. She whacked against the wall opposite us, her shields absorbing most of the impact, but she still collapsed with an audible groan.

Capitola shook her head as the succubus drew in a few ragged breaths. Finally, Shar peered up at us. Giving Ryu a bawdy wink, which he instinctively returned with his own side of sauce, she smiled sweetly at Cap.

'I'm fucking killing her this time, Cappie. I don't care what you say. I'm killing her. After I shave off her eyebrows . . .'

The 'her' in question strode through the doorway at that moment. Moo looked elegant and unruffled, although I saw her lips twitch at the sight of Shar still sitting, propped against the wall.

'Capitola, you *did* instruct me to take out the trash,' the halfling's chilly Alfar voice said as Shar began sputtering in rage.

Capitola hung her head, visibly gathering her patience. 'For the love of Pete, can't you two stop fighting for fifteen seconds? Seriously?'

'I can stop fighting,' Shar said, standing up. 'As long as I have the proper motivation.' She took a long, lascivious look at me, then Ryu, and finally the barghest.

'Can *I* call you Uncle Anyan?' the succubus-halfling queried as she did a little shimmy that was supposed to be about brushing herself off, but was really about feeling herself up.

Anyan laughed. 'Nope. Sorry, Shar.'

'Damn.' With that she strode forward and put an affectionate arm around Moo, who, moments before, Shar had genuinely appeared to want to murder.

'C'mon, Moo-Cow. You get the fire hose, I'll get the bleach. Julian, you gonna help us?'

For the first time, I realized that Julian was, once again, watching from the doorway. I was beginning to think we needed to put a bell on him to know where he was at all times.

He nodded, breaking into that sweet smile I adored, as Shar slung an arm around his waist and pulled him back into the other room. He peered down at her, his face glowing, like he'd just been asked to the birthday party of the coolest girl in school.

Moo followed, her Alfar-calm expression betraying just a hint of pleasure at the sight of Shar with their newest halfling friend. When they were gone, Capitola shook her head, smiling at us ruefully.

'I love them, but they're nuts. Sorry about that,' she said, checking her watch and rising from her chair. 'It's nearly three-thirty. You guys go get some rest and you can check out the other labs tomorrow. And Anyan, see you, Julian, and Jane at the house tomorrow night, around eight?'

We all stood as Anyan nodded, Ryu grumbled, and I waved goodbye at Capitola. She came over to give Anyan an affectionate hug. I enviously watched their ease with each other, before Capitola suddenly turned to sweep me up in her arms. Her hug was hard and generous and warm.

'You'll find who did it, Jane. I promise,' she whispered fiercely in my ear before letting me go. For the first time since arriving at the place my mother had died, I blinked back tears.

'Thank you,' I told her as Anyan put a hand on my shoulder to steer me toward the door.

Hearing Capitola say those words made me believe it. We *were* going to find my mother's killer. And this time, Jarl wasn't going to worm his way out of the justice he was due.

Chapter Eight

'You all right?' Anyan asked. He must have seen me shiver.

'Yeah,' I said. 'It's just . . .'

When I trailed off he let me be for a minute, then cocked his head.

'It's nothing,' I finished finally.

We were in Plano, a little town outside Borealis. It was home to a big plastics factory and little else. Except for the small fertility lab, tucked into the corner of an abandoned strip mall. Behind the tiny waiting room, it had once held five halfling women in plastic cages. Those women were now dead, their bodies returned to their families if there was family; or burned, and their ashes scattered, if there wasn't. The people responsible for their deaths had murdered them and disappeared, leaving the local halfling community to clean up the mess.

But that's not why I'd shivered. Off and on all day, I'd had this feeling that I was being watched. I knew I was being paranoid, not least because the two men I was with made 'paranoid' into a competitive sport. They'd been sending out so many competing probes and shields and glamours that only very old and very purebred Alfar could have kept themselves concealed.

'You sure?' Anyan asked, his deep voice concerned. Right at that moment, the feeling of being watched suddenly ceased. It had to be my imagination.

So I smiled, nodding. 'Yeah, really. I'm fine.'

And I should have been fine, knowing – from what Anyan had told us the night before about the Sensors – that there was *supposed* to be no chance such a very old, very powerful purebred Alfar could ever be in Borealis.

That said, Anyan's words had raised more concerns than they answered, and Julian and I had stayed up late the night before talking everything through. On the one hand, everything Anyan had said explained why the Alfar hadn't succeeded in spying here; why the Borderlands were invisible to them. And why they *should* be relatively safe for our team.

In reality, however, we were now left with a whole slew of unsettling issues. After all, if unregistered, visiting purebloods were sure to give themselves away, then serious questions had to be asked about how my mother had been brought here to be killed. And about who was running these labs and doing the actual killing.

As soon as we were alone last night, Julian and I had started asking such questions, turning to good old Sherlock Holmes for help. Holmes, after all, was famous for using Occam's razor to help him solve crime. It was a theory urging that the simplest, most sufficient explanation of a particular problem was usually the correct one. If I applied Occam's razor to the problem that was my mother, a strange pureblood dying in a territory that was supposed to be guarded against unregistered pureblood or halfling entry, there was only one obvious explanation: some of the registered halflings in the Borderlands couldn't be trusted.

There had to be people on the ground working as guards,

or some of the Sensors had to be covering up for unregistered power signatures, or both.

We knew better than to ask Anyan whether or not that person was one of his friends and contacts here. Anyan wasn't a man who trusted easily, nor was he stupid or naive. The man was a warrior, through and through, and the fact that he genuinely appeared to believe in Capitola and whomever she worked for spoke volumes.

But Julian and I both knew something didn't add up about my mother dying in Borealis, and Anyan, earlier, had admitted as much. Before saying good night to Julian and me the previous evening, Anyan had told us to sleep tight, that we should be safe here in Borealis. I'd started to understand that Anyan communicated more through what he didn't say than what he did. And the barghest never said we *were* safe here, just that we *should* be safe.

So neither Julian nor I had slept very well, and I watched Anyan and Ryu interact with the local team processing the crime scene through bleary eyes. Being an official Alfar employee, Ryu was undoubtedly unwelcome, and he'd been treated with distrust when we first arrived. But he was also damned good at his job, and he'd quickly ingratiated himself with the other investigators.

Meanwhile, Anyan was wandering around sniffing things, in what I assumed was his own barghestian style of detective work.

So Julian and I tucked ourselves away in a corner. I knew I wasn't of any use in this place, and I think my fellow half-ling was just trying to be supportive. That said, I was glad I was here. Being part of this investigation, in whatever way I could, felt right. The safety of my father and all my other loved ones rested on this investigation.

I can't let Jarl run around trying to get back at me through my friends and family, I thought, just as Julian interrupted my dark reverie.

'How're you holding up?' he asked, his tone careful. 'How was the lab this morning?'

'Just like Anyan said,' I replied. 'There was nothing there. But I did call home while he poked around.'

That morning, Anyan and I had driven south to Kankakee and the other abandoned laboratory while Ryu and Julian slept through their weird vampire comas. Ryu had been pissed when he found out we'd gone without him, but Kankakee was about two and a half hours away from Borealis, and if we ever wanted to wrap things up here, we couldn't wait for sleeping beauties.

Plus, that lab had been the long-abandoned one, and it had already been cleaned out. Anyan had sniffed around while I used the opportunity to make phone calls.

'That's good. How's your dad?' Julian asked.

'Oh, fine. Nell must've glamoured him. He's convinced I'm on a Caribbean cruise.'

'Well, that's okay, I guess?'

'Yeah, I guess. I'm rather annoyed Nell's futzing with my father's brains again. But I also know I made a total shambles of my leaving, so at least my dad isn't worried about me the way he would be otherwise.'

'How's everyone else?'

'Fine. Rockabill never changes, thank the gods.'

After I'd spoken with my dad and Nell, I'd called Grizzie and Tracy. Things at the store were slow and I wasn't needed, although I still felt guilty for abandoning them. But I didn't detail that for Julian, knowing that Julian didn't need to know every facet of my oh-so-exciting life in Maine. And I also left out the part where, after my phone calls were made, I had almost eagerly gone back to watching the barghest sniff around. Indeed, when I'd walked back into the abandoned lab, I'd found Anyan sniffing at the corner I'd just left. Walking toward him, I had indulged in a wild fantasy of him taking a moment to sniff *me*.

I didn't think Julian wanted to know *that* information any more than he did the boring facts of my day-to-day life. *Although*, I figured, *this is as good a time as any . . .*

'So how are *you* doing?' I asked, turning the tables on my fellow halfling.

Julian blinked. 'Me? I'm fine. Why wouldn't I be fine?'

'Well, I think this must be a lot for you. Going from the Territory, where halflings are treated pretty shitty, to here, where they rule.'

Julian looked away from me, then took off his glasses, nervously cleaning them with the bottom of his T-shirt.

'It's interesting, that's certain.'

'Interesting?' I asked incredulously, giving him my best gimlet eye.

'All right,' he acceded very quietly. 'It's fucking *awesome*.'

I giggled. 'I know.'

'I mean, those women last night . . .'

'So foxy!'

'Huh?'

'They're *so* foxy!'

Julian blinked at me. 'I meant how strong they were. And confident.'

'Oh,' I said. 'Yes. They are strong and confident. For sure. And they're so *foxy*!'

'I suppose,' he said, frowning at me.

'You're not much into the females, are you?' I asked, grinning up at him.

'No, not so much,' he replied with a laugh. 'What gave it away?'

'Julian, those women last night were seriously hot. Even *I* was a little turned on. You? Couldn't care less. But I've noticed that when a hot male is around . . .' I waggled my eyebrows as Julian blushed shyly. 'Especially one male in particular,' I teased, letting my eyes slide across the room to where Anyan stood talking with a local technician. I'd already noticed that the barghest was filling out his jeans particularly well that day. I'd also noticed Julian noticing earlier.

My fellow halfling's eyes widened and I thought he was going to protest, but instead he shook his head ruefully.

'Well, I'm not the only one who enjoys the view,' he said, eyeing me pointedly. Just like him, I was about to protest, when I realized it would do no good.

'It's true. You've got me.' I giggled. 'I can't help it.'

'I know. Those thighs.'

'Oh, the thighs.' I groaned in agreement. 'And that keister.'

'Oh, yes,' Julian murmured as we both turned to stare with appreciative eyes at Anyan. 'And let's not forget that . . .'

'Package!' came a loud shout from the doorway, causing Julian and me nearly to jump out of our skins. We looked at each other with wild eyes.

'Package! I'm here to collect a package?' the voice shouted again, revealing a woman standing in the doorway and wearing some sort of delivery-service uniform.

Julian and I looked from her, to each other, to Anyan, before bursting into hysterical laughter.

'Brilliant,' I said, wiping the tears from my eyes as our giggles finally subsided. 'Just brilliant. Package,' I said again, snorting my unladylike snort of amusement one last time.

'Too good,' Julian agreed, chuckling still. 'Almost as good as the man himself.'

'Almost as good as powerful halflings?' I queried.

Julian's face fell at that comment, and my own heart missed

a beat at the look in his eyes. He looked so heartsore and despondent, even as I thought I saw a glimmer of something hopeful.

'No, nothing's that good,' he replied, his voice urgent, his expression beseeching. 'Jane, I really don't know what I . . .'

'Hey, Julian?' Ryu called from the other side of the room.

I watched with sadness as Julian wiped all emotion from his face, replacing it with the sedate, bland expression I now realized was the mask with which he confronted his existence.

'Yes, sir?' he called, turning toward Ryu.

'Can you come help us with this?'

Julian nodded at me, then headed to where a knot of technicians surrounded a dead computer. I frowned at his retreating back, wondering what he would have said had he the chance. It was enough to keep me musing for the next few hours.

By the time everyone was finished collecting evidence, it was already six o'clock and I, for one, was ready for dinner. And so was my stomach, as it made clear with a very loud, very angry roar followed by a series of petulant gurgles. Of course it waited until the room was almost cleared out, and everyone remaining was quietly packing up their things. I stared down at my belly, vowing revenge, as everyone turned to stare.

No doubt wondering where I've hidden the rabid Tasmanian devil, I thought, blushing at the attention and cursing my prodigious appetite.

'Hungry?' Ryu called from the other side of the room.

I gave an apologetic shrug, resisting the urge to shout, 'No shit, Sherlock.' After all, Anyan and Ryu should have known by now that only two things could be depended upon in this investigation: Jarl was the culprit and Jane was hungry.

Ryu excused himself and walked toward me. When he

came closer, I could smell balsam with that very faint, delicious undertone of musky cumin.

He may be a dick, but he's still hot, my libido whispered regretfully. That said, my body didn't stir at Ryu's approach.

We're done, I suddenly realized. *Ryu and I are over, at least for me*. At that thought, I felt an uncomfortable combination of relief and sadness sweep through me. Not least because, from the look in Ryu's eyes, he hadn't come anywhere near that conclusion.

'We should get you something to eat, Jane. Maybe I can take you to dinner? Whatever you want . . . we can talk.'

'I don't think so, Ryu. Besides, I think I have to do that thing with Anyan and Julian . . .'

Ryu frowned. 'I'm really not thrilled with the idea of you going off alone into Borealis. Who knows what those people want—'

'"Those people" are our hosts, and they're letting you participate in this investigation against their better judgment,' growled Anyan's rough voice as he put in his own two cents from where he was standing. Then he joined our little huddle, forcing Ryu to take a step away from me.

Anyan's leather jacket smelled like lemon wax, and underneath that was the smell of cardamom I'd come to associate with the barghest.

'I know you trust these people, but I'm not comfortable allowing Jane to meet them by herself. Who knows what they want from her? Either you leave her with me or you take me with you.'

That sent Anyan off on a tirade about how 'those people' only wanted to meet me and Julian, and I wasn't Ryu's to control, and Ryu was here only as a courtesy to begin with. Ryu replied by telling the barghest that if he thought representing the king and queen was a courtesy, Ryu would be happy to pass that message on to Orin and Morrigan. It all went downhill from there.

I listened to the two men argue, feeling more and more irritated. Part of it was simply because, truth be told, I hated conflict. I hated being around people who were arguing; I hated being around people who were stressed out. Why couldn't we all just get along?

The scents of lemon wax and balsam, cumin and cardamom washed over me and my stomach rumbled again. I suddenly fancied a curry, and I was tired of, quite literally, being argued over. The two men were giving me a crick in the neck as I peered up at them while they fought.

'Anyan, Ryu, shut it!' I snapped. 'I'm hungry and this is pointless. Ryu, you just want to come along so you can spy. Anyan, why are you arguing? You know that's what he wants, and you already know that despite what Ryu says, both Julian and I are going with you to this meeting.'

Both men stared down at me for a moment, surprised. Finally, Anyan nodded. 'Sorry, Jane. Let's get you something to eat. Julian?' He called to the other halfling, jerking his head to the door to tell Julian it was time to leave. 'Ryu, you can get a ride back to the hotel with Enrique; he lives near Borealis. That okay, Enrique?'

The short, stocky man Anyan hollered at nodded his head, causing Ryu's scowl to grow darker. I shrugged when he glared at me. Ryu should've known he wasn't going to win this battle and left well enough alone.

Julian, Anyan, and I walked toward the exit and out into the parking lot, and this time there was no question about whose eyes were on us.

Just as we were getting into the car, Anyan's cell rang. I got in the passenger's side and belted myself in as I listened to his half of the conversation.

'Hello? . . . Hey, Cap . . . Yeah, we're on our way . . . Cool, thanks for calling . . . See you in about forty minutes.'

Anyan grinned at me as we pulled out of the parking lot and took off down the main drag that led out of Plano. 'That was Cappie; we'll have dinner over there.'

I thought about the dinners at the Alfar Compound. They ran a short, intense gauntlet between formal and very, very formal.

'Do we need to change?' I asked Anyan, looking down at my black T-shirt, gray hoodie, jeans, and purple Converse. None of which were particularly clean after a long day in abandoned torture facilities.

Anyan eyeballed me from the driver's seat. 'Nope, you look perfect, Jane.'

I snorted at the word 'perfect', and his big mouth creased in a slight smile.

'I look perfect for running to the grocery store, Anyan. A really ghetto grocery store. Maybe a dollar store. I didn't bring anything fancy, but I could still clean up . . .'

'I can take you to the hotel if you want, but honestly, you look fine.'

I studied the barghest's stark profile, giving him my best skeptical look from the darkness of the passenger seat. He ignored me.

'This from the man wearing the Eukanuba shirt?'

Anyan chuckled. 'I left the tux in my saddlebag, sorry.'

When I laughed, his iron-gray eyes flicked toward me, and I felt his gaze like a caress. My laughter stilled and tension sprang up in me like a small dog.

Anyan's big hands also tensed on the wheel, and I wondered if he felt it, too, whatever was between us . . . and then he swore. Then laughed.

Confused, I finally noticed he was watching the rearview

mirror. I turned in my seat but saw only headlights, and Julian, who was blinking at us in the dark.

Once again, I'd completely fucking forgotten he was there. I thought of my own life after Jason, and how I'd hidden in plain sight for so many years. We were both people used to hiding, it seemed, and that made me unaccountably sad.

'Oh, Ryu.' The barghest chuckled, bringing me back into the moment. 'So predictable. Hold on, Jane, Julian. We've got to lose an Alfar spy . . .'

And with that, Anyan floored the SUV. The colossal car might have looked staid and decorous, but it kicked like a pissed-off mule.

We were darting down country roads that had grown dark, going way too fast. Anyan would turn the SUV on a dime, sending me crashing into either his big bulk or the car door to my right.

'Sorry,' he'd mumble each time I banged into him. But the barghest didn't sound apologetic, he sounded gleeful.

At one point, I realized that Anyan was playing with Ryu. The engine wasn't roaring like it had been, and I could see Anyan watching in the rearview as the car slowed.

'Oh, Ryu . . . of all the cars there, why'd you steal Enrique's piece of shit?' The barghest laughed.

I couldn't believe it.

'Would you stop taunting him?' I chastised, using my best mom voice. 'We have a dinner party. With important people. And you're playing tag.'

Anyan attempted to look suitably chastened, although it didn't reach his eyes.

'All right,' he grumbled. 'I'll put him out of his misery.'

Wrenching the wheel to the left, I smacked into him again as we made a series of complicated hairpin turns on an insanely curvy road. The next thing I knew, we were parked behind a barn, both the car and the lights off. The engine ticked, ticked, then fell silent just as another car whizzed past us on the dark road.

Anyan put a finger to his lips and waited a full minute before restarting the car. Leaving his lights off, he went back the other way on the curvy road before turning down another side lane.

We drove in silence for a while before hitting a real highway. At that point, Anyan turned his lights back on and joined the thin trickle of traffic.

'You enjoyed that, didn't you?' I asked the barghest. He grinned at me, chuckling.

'Sorry, Jane. It's immature. But yeah, I enjoyed that.'

'Poor Ryu,' I mused, knowing that, wherever he was, he must be *pissed*.

'Yes, poor Ryu,' Julian echoed, laughingly. I turned around in my seat to wink at my fellow halfling, a gesture he returned with a grin.

'Why is he here, anyway?' I finally remembered to ask.

Anyan snorted. 'Ryu was my devil's bargain,' he said. I waited for him to continue. He didn't.

'And what does that mean?'

'Orin and Morrigan were more than a little miffed that I hadn't told them I had contacts in the Borderlands. They didn't try to kill me once we'd learned about the pure-bloods disappearing, since I was the only one who could investigate. I'd made myself valuable, but not trusted.'

I nodded, suddenly understanding his cryptic words.

'So Orin and Morrigan let you investigate, and they agreed they wouldn't tell anyone else. But they insisted you take Ryu.'

'Exactly. They trust him. Not me.'

'That's not true. They trust your power.'

'But not my loyalty.'

I thought about that.

'Are they right to distrust you?'

'What do you mean?'

I thought of the barghest and his quiet ways. He'd once fought and killed for his people. Then he'd hid himself in the boondocks and dropped out of politics.

'Who *are* you loyal to now?'

The big man drove in silence for a while, and I thought he was going to ignore me. We turned off the highway, then drove a short ways on a smaller road before turning into a neighborhood I recognized as near downtown Borealis.

The houses were small and nondescript, really rather shabbily middle-class. I figured the mansions must be up ahead.

'I'm loyal to those I care about,' Anyan eventually replied as we pulled up at a stop sign. He stared out the windshield at the empty street, and when he finally spoke again his voice was dark. 'I'm loyal to my friends, and the people I love. Not anyone else. Not anymore.'

I didn't know how to respond to that admission, so I stayed quiet. I looked to my right, out the window, only to find Julian watching me in the side mirror. He raised an eyebrow at the barghest's words, and I matched his expression with pursed lips.

'We're almost there,' Anyan said, and his voice had an apologetic note. I think he was ashamed of his outburst.

I looked around for the place that would hold Borealis's seat of power. The Alfar Compound, after all, was this fairy-tale creation of Escher and Disney World, melded into a massive, if whimsical and haunting, structure. I wasn't expecting such grandeur, but neither was I expecting what I saw when we finally pulled into a driveway on our right.

The driveway ended in a carport attached to a small,

dark-brown ranch-style house. It had a chain-link fence around the small backyard, which housed a rather arthritic-looking golden retriever that panted at us with his black nose pressed through the chain-link. A purple glass globe sat on top of a cement pedestal in the middle of the front yard, and I think I even saw a garden gnome – the plastic kind, not the kind currently babysitting my dad – peeking at me from underneath a ferny-looking plant in the small garden under the front picture window.

We got out of the car, and Anyan laughed at the expression on my face. In my defense, Julian looked equally nonplussed.

'Is there . . . more?' I asked. 'Like at the Compound?'

When I'd first pulled up to the Alfar Compound, I'd seen only a giant McMansion. It was covered in glamours so powerful, I hadn't had the slightest inclination something was off until Ryu had cleansed my sight.

Anyan chuckled, putting a hand on my lower back and steering me toward the front door.

'Nope. This is it. Welcome to the seat of power here in Borealis, Illinois.'

Chapter Nine

'Anyan,' said a tall, slender woman with silver hair as she pushed open the screen door. 'So good to see you.'

She wrapped the barghest in an affectionate hug, then let him enter the house.

'Julian?' she asked my fellow halfling, smiling at him as he nodded, startled. 'Welcome to Borealis, and to my home. It's wonderful to have you here. Make yourself comfortable, please.'

'And you must be Jane,' she said once Julian had passed. To my surprise, she then stooped down to give me my own hug. She held me tight, telling me, 'I'm Paige. It's such a pleasure to meet you. I'm sorry it had to be under these circumstances.'

I blinked over her shoulder toward where Anyan watched us, smiling. Paige and I were standing in a tiny entryway that was part of a small combination living and dining room. Anyan had moved across the short room to a doorway that appeared to lead into the kitchen/family room. Next to him stood a man who, like the woman, appeared to be in his mid-fifties. He was shorter than both Anyan and the woman, but very strong and handsome. African-American, his skin was a lovely chocolate brown made even handsomer by his salt-and-pepper hair and goatee. And yet, there was something . . . other about him. Like Paige, he wasn't using any power, but I was pretty sure this had to be Capitola's supernatural parent. His large dark eyes were much older than his apparent age.

The woman let me go, leading me toward Anyan and the other man.

'This is my husband, Carl. You've met our daughter, Capitola.'

I grinned as everything fell into place. 'Of course,' I said, extending my hand toward Carl. 'Capitola's lovely. It's so nice to meet you.'

Carl took my hand in a firm grip and pulled me in to give me his own hug.

'It's shitty circumstances, no denying that. But it's a pleasure to finally meet Jane True,' he said, grinning. 'We know a certain someone who won't stop talking about you . . .'

His voice trailed off and he and his wife laughed heartily. I blushed, looking between them.

Who's been talking about me? I thought, confused. *Certainly not Anyan*, I wondered, peeking up at the barghest. But he looked just as lost as I did.

I had just opened my mouth to ask what they were talking about when I heard a *pop*. Floating in front of me was a beautiful bouquet of wildflowers.

Eyes wide, I reached forward. Then I nearly jumped out of my skin when, from the other side of the bouquet, something grabbed my fingers.

Actually, six things grabbed me. Rather than freaking me out, however, the touch of six little hands made me smile.

'Terk?' I asked, as six solid-black eyes peered around the bouquet at me. He blinked a random smattering of eyelids, and gave me a friendly wave with the three hands on his right side.

I pulled the bouquet away from him, laughing at the sight of the brownie floating in midair. Terk looked like a miniature Ewok would if he'd been spliced with Kali, the six-armed Hindu goddess of destruction, and a wolf spider. His shaggy fur was long and thick, capped by tiny fluffy ears. The little creature was adorable.

And very strong, I thought, feeling its First Magic battering at my shields.

Terk had acted as a courier ferrying information between Anyan and his contacts here in the Borderlands, and I'd met him in Boston. I'd been more than a little surprised to see the bit creature, but not nearly as surprised as my supernatural cohorts. Brownies had served the purebloods, then they'd served only the Alfar, and now they were supposed to be extinct. But as it turned out, they were still very much alive, living in the Borderlands, and serving whoever was in power here.

They were from a race of creatures older than the Alfar; creatures who used something known as First Magic. It felt different, certainly, than our own, elemental power: immensely strong and not entirely . . . natural, in the way our elemental force did.

I laughed as the little being hovered to me, and I let it settle against my bosom. It cuddled against me like a little puppy, blinking its black eyes up at me innocently. Unable to resist, I stroked the little creature's ears, giggling when he purred in my arms.

'Um, Jane, I don't know if you should—' Anyan was interrupted by the door opening behind us.

'Hey, Mom! Dad!' Capitola said, pushing through the screen door. She was still lovely, despite being laden down with groceries, which she handed over to her father and to Anyan, who retreated to the kitchen behind them.

'Hey, lady,' she said, turning toward me. She stopped when she saw me cuddling Terk, her eyebrows rising. 'Um, Jane . . .'

'It is not my fault that your backside has gotten so large that you cannot easily extricate yourself from vehicles,' Moo's cool voice said from the doorway as she let herself in.

From behind her, a mage ball whizzed past Moo, clipping her ear as it flew into the room. Terk had perked up at Moo's voice, and when he saw the mage ball one little hand shot forward. I felt a cold rush of power blast out of the brownie's small form, and the mage ball fizzled out as if it had never existed.

He settled back against me, his little hands using my breasts for leverage as he made himself comfortable, cooing like a wee, hairy, six-eyed baby.

'No shooting people in the house, Shar,' Capitola's mother chastised gently. 'You two troublemakers go set the table. Julian will help; show him where everything is. Terk?' She intoned, last, to the little being in my arms. One eye glared open at her; the other five flicked open to blink sweetly at me.

'A little help, if you don't mind?'

Terk sighed, then *poofed* out of my arms. A second later, I heard another *poof* in the kitchen.

'Beer?' Anyan asked me as everyone walked next door into the living room. I nodded, pulling a few brown strands of hair off my black T-shirt.

After Anyan, Cappie, Carl, and I were settled with drinks, we got down to business.

'First of all, Jane, welcome to Borealis,' Carl said. 'I know that after what happened to your mother, you probably won't ever want to return. But Borealis is, and always has been, a safe place for halflings, and those purebloods who, like me, want to live more . . . democratically.'

I knew Capitola was a halfling, according to Anyan, but except for that sense of age around Carl, I wouldn't have been able to guess who her supernatural parent was. They both appeared entirely human, and they were both aged in a way that humans aged. Supes didn't grow old like humans; rather, they looked young but worn out. And although Carl was admitting he was both supernatural and a pureblood, I still couldn't feel any power coming off him. Now that I thought about it, in fact, while I could feel power throughout the house, I recognized that power as Terk's.

Capitola was watching her father with a resigned expression that brightened when she realized I was peering at her. She smiled at me, raising her beer in a salute that I returned.

'Are all the Borderlands so friendly?' I asked curiously after sipping my beer.

Carl frowned. 'In a word, no. The northern suburbs are ruled by powerful halflings who do things Mafia-style. Chicago is a free-for-all of competing gangs. Borealis, however, has a powerful patron who likes to keep his surroundings peaceful.'

'Patron?' I asked.

'The Grim,' Capitola said, waving her fingers and making an 'ooooooh' noise as if she were telling a ghost story.

Carl made a face at his daughter. 'Not *the* Grim, just Grim. His name is Grimauld. He's . . . a force.'

Anyan grunted next to me. It was the grunt that meant, 'You're telling me.'

'He doesn't interfere with things, ever. But if anyone comes in, trying to *make* an interference, they get the Grim,' Cappie explained.

'What is he?' I asked, my mind filled with images of a

killer fog, like in Stephen King's novel. I am from Maine, after all.

'Nobody knows, except for Anyan,' Cappie answered. 'And he won't squeal.'

I looked at the barghest and he shrugged. 'Grim keeps to himself,' was all he said, meaning that if that's how Grim wanted it, Anyan wasn't going to ruin things for him.

'Why didn't he stop the laboratory if he's so strong?'

'I don't know,' Carl replied. 'I don't think he knew about it. Like I said, he doesn't interfere with things. But something like that . . . I can't believe he'd ignore it.'

'Could he have been running the labs?' I asked. It seemed an obvious question.

'Not Grim. No way,' was Anyan's only response. I didn't bother to ask Anyan if he was sure. He only ever said something if he was sure.

'But I'm sure you'd have put together what I have,' I said, choosing my words carefully. 'If purebloods can't enter Borealis without you knowing, then whoever was running those labs had to be other halflings. Even if Jarl was paying them, there had to be halflings on the ground.'

Carl sighed and took a swig of his beer. Capitola nodded sadly.

'That's why they asked me to help, Jane. And why, when we found the bodies of the purebloods, they allowed me to contact Orin and Morrigan.' Anyan's voice was gentle and I realized he was afraid I'd tar his friends with our enemy's dirty brush. He obviously cared for Capitola and her family a great deal, and he hated the idea that I would associate them, and their city, with my mother's death.

'This is big, and people are dying,' Carl confirmed. 'We can't let our feelings for the Alfar get in the way of the facts. Or we're monsters just like they are.'

'True dat!' Shar yelled from the kitchen area, where she was folding napkins into complicated shapes. Moo, slicing cucumbers at the counter, shook her head at her fellow halfling as if wondering when Shar had killed her last brain cell. Julian stood grating a carrot next to Moo, looking as at-home and comfortable as I'd ever seen him.

'Anyway,' Carl said, giving his daughter's friends an indulgent smile. 'We have more mysteries here than we can handle. Who's running these labs? How were they recruited? Who do they work for? And it was bad enough when halflings were the victims, but how are they getting purebloods into the Territory? The only way for that to happen is to completely knock out their powers. There hasn't been an Alfar with that kind of ability in thousands of years, and he was killed by his own people when they realized what he could do.

'So we need help. These people need to be shut down, and we can't do it alone. And, as much as we hate bringing anyone associated with the Alfar into our lands, we'll do what needs to be done.'

I set my beer down, blinking back tears. For the first time since I'd gotten to Borealis, I stopped thinking only of myself and thought about everything these people had done for me and for my mother, neither of whom they'd ever known.

'Thank you so much for letting us in,' I said. 'You're taking so many risks, when you don't have to. Thank you.'

Anyan's hand was warm and large on the small of my back, and a box of tissues apparated with a *poof* next to my elbow. I blew my nose as Carl made soothing noises.

'No, hon, our women are dying, too. We had to do something. These murders should never have happened. But we're going to find out who did it.'

Capitola nodded fiercely at her father's words, then nodded at me. Again, I felt a wave of confidence shoot through me.

We *would* find out who did this and we *would* bring them to justice.

Now if only they would fucking feed me, my stomach piped up, just as Terk popped in, right in front of us. He was wearing a tiny chef's hat and apron, and he was carrying a little wooden rolling pin. I giggled at the sight.

Terk offered me one of his six little hands, while prodding at the barghest's knee with his rolling pin. I laughed, taking the tiny hand in mine. Just like that, I heard a tremendous cracking noise, everything went black, then we *popped* the short distance into the kitchen. My head swam as I reeled, only to be caught by cool, dark hands.

'Little brownie,' Moo chastised, 'stop apparating people without warning. Are you all right, Jane?'

Moo's beautiful dark eyes met mine, and I saw concern behind her Alfar calm. I thought of her long life and wondered.

What an incredible, dreadful story she must have, I thought as my world slowly stopped spinning.

'Yes, thanks,' I said after another few seconds. 'That was . . . intense.'

'The first time he apparated Moo she puked all over herself. It was *so* gross,' Shar said as she plopped down at the round kitchen table that had been extended to fit us all.

I took a seat beside the succubus-halfling, and Moo sat to my right, with Julian next to the Alfar-halfling. Cappie sat next to Julian, scrunching his shoulders affectionately in her hands before sitting down, with Anyan next to her. Carl placed a lovely looking salad and a cutting board that held two warmed loaves of soda bread in the middle of the table, and was about to sit down next to Anyan when he snapped his fingers and headed back into the kitchen.

Please tell me there's butter and honey, my stomach prayed as I eyed the soda bread covetously, just as Carl appeared with a dish of butter and a plastic teddy bear full of honey.

Score!

A moment later, Paige walked over and placed a bubbling Pyrex dish full of shepherd's pie on the trivet that sat in the center of the table.

She took a seat next to her husband, placing her napkin in her lap. She touched his hand gently with her own and gave him a look of such tender affection, I felt my own heart flutter in response.

I thought of my own father and mother, and everything they'd had for such a brief moment in time. And I thought about how any chance for their reunion was over now.

My mother was dead.

But I was alive, and these kind people had invited me into their home. They'd comforted me and prepared a delicious meal.

So I forced down my emotions, and when Shar nudged me with the salad bowl I held it while she filled her own plate, then passed it to my right so Moo could do the same.

I'd get through dinner. I could figure out how to get through the rest of my life sometime after dessert.

'Will you be totally offended if I undo my pants?'

Anyan laughed. 'Nope, have at it, Jane. With the way you ate, I'm surprised you didn't just bust out of them at the table.'

We were driving back to the hotel, just the barghest and me. Julian had stayed behind with the girls. If I hadn't known his sexual preferences, I'd have high-fived him. As it was, I didn't know what scheme he was cooking up, but I sincerely hoped it was a good one. In the meantime, I might have felt a bit squishy on the inside about being alone with Anyan, but my insides were too full of shepherd's pie to go squishy at anything, unfortunately.

'Hardy har. You're hilarious, Anyan Barghest. Wait a minute,' I said, putting on a speculative face. 'There's another film I've seen that talks about people like you . . . now what was it . . . there was a man, who was also a dog . . . I believe they called him a Mog . . . Ahhh, yes, *Spaceballs*! You're a Mog! Are you related to Barf? I do see the resemblance.'

'Once again, your grasp of classic cinema floors me, Jane.'

'You're just jealous, you Mog. You wish you could have a giant fire hydrant all to yourself, just like Barf . . .'

'And the ejector seat is right around here somewhere,' the barghest replied, reaching for the buttons on the dashboard. I giggled.

'Seriously, though. Thanks for inviting me to Carl and Paige's. They're amazing.'

'Yeah, they're a great couple.'

'How long have they been together?'

'Carl met Paige when she was twenty-two. They've been together ever since.'

'Wow. When'd they have Capitola?'

'Cappie just turned thirty-five, and they had her about five years after they got together.'

'Well, they're a stunning family.'

'Yeah, Carl and Paige are totally dedicated to one another.'

Anyan's voice almost sounded sad when he said that, and I was confused. 'Is that a bad thing?' I asked. The barghest only frowned.

Then it hit me.

'He's cut himself off from his power, hasn't he?' It made sense. The fact that Carl looked older than most supes, the way I hadn't felt him use one iota of power the entire night.

'That's why the brownie's there. Terk protects the two of them because Carl's stopped using his magic.'

Anyan nodded. 'He did it right before they had Cappie. He cut himself off so they could get pregnant, and then never started again. He wants to die with his wife.'

'Wow,' was all I could say.

'Yup.'

'That's intense.'

'Yup.'

'It must be really hard not to use your powers, ever, at all. What is Carl, anyway?'

'Nahual.'

'How old is he?'

'A few hundred years. About 225, I think.'

'So he's old-ish?'

'Yeah.'

'But still. To choose to die with someone . . .'

Anyan stayed silent.

'That must be hard for you, as his friend.'

Anyan shrugged. The barghest shrugged a lot.

'It's his choice, Jane. And I care for Paige, as well.'

'But still . . .'

Anyan smiled a sad smile. 'But still, it is difficult to see him age.'

We sat in silence for a while.

'I'm surprised you think Carl's choice is so radical, after how you reacted to losing Jason,' Anyan said eventually and very carefully.

I thought about that. There was no point in trying to downplay my rather dramatic actions after Jason's death. Anyan, after all, had visited me in the hospital. He'd seen me strung out and tied up and bearing the bruises and stitches of all my various suicide attempts.

'I was crazy, first of all,' I replied. Anyan frowned, but I didn't let him interrupt. 'Seriously, Anyan, I was *crazy*. I think Jason's death was like a dam breaking. His death was bad enough, but Jason had helped me hold everything else together. My feelings for my mom, and about my dad's illness, and always feeling so out of place, and . . . everything else. He wasn't just my friend or my lover, he was like my Prozac. Without him I just . . . fell.

'So the good thing about everything that's happened,' I continued, trying to be practical Jane. She was much more fun than 'drown yourself in the toilet' Jane. 'The good thing is that in spite of everything that's happened, recently, I haven't flipped my biscuit. I mean, I did beat up you and Ryu.' The barghest grunted his agreement, causing my lips to quirk up in a smile. 'But I didn't go totally gaga. So that's good.'

Anyan smiled at me, the streetlights letting me see his strong, crooked profile in detail. His face had so much character that I could watch him watching other things for hours.

'You have been remarkably non-gaga, Jane,' he rumbled eventually. 'You have so much strength, you should give yourself more credit.'

I snorted. 'Strength is what Carl's doing. I reacted. He's making a choice: this big, difficult, all-consuming choice that affects every aspect of his life. That's strength.'

Anyan didn't reply for a bit. And when he did, his always rough voice sounded rougher.

'No, that's what love does. Some of us, it drops from a great height. The rest of us, it merely crushes.'

And with that, he was silent.

I sat there, the admittedly rather-beer-greased wheels of my mind spinning.

What the hell happened to Anyan? I wondered. *And what does he have against love?*

And why do I suddenly want another drink?

I was pondering those mysteries when my phone rang. I pulled it out of my pocket and checked to see who was calling. It was Amy, our local nahual waitress.

'Hey, Amy,' I said, but I was cut off before I could ask her anything else.

'Jane? Iris is missing.'

'What?' I said, sitting up in my seat as a cold blast filtered through my system.

'Iris is missing. She hasn't been answering her phone for a few days, and so I went out to her apartment. It's been broken into, and there's been a fight. And she's gone.'

'Oh my gods . . .'

'Can you come home now? Bring Ryu and Anyan?'

'Of course. We'll come as soon as possible.'

'Good. Jane, I'm so scared . . .'

'We'll be there soon. Go to my place. Stay with Nell and my dad.'

'I will. Get here quickly, please.'

'We will. Bye.'

I closed my phone, knowing that Anyan had heard every word with his sharp hearing. His face, when I turned to him, was dark with rage.

I started to shake as I sat there clutching my phone. Anyan's only response was to put one big hand on the back of my neck and pull me closer. I cuddled against his solid bulk, unable to comprehend the fact that Iris was missing.

All I could feel was terror.

Chapter Ten

Iris's usually neat, cozy apartment was a shambles. The furniture was overturned, the upholstery shredded. Mage balls had scorched the creamy walls, blackening her large, framed prints of somnolent Pre-Raphaelite women. Dishes had been smashed, trinkets crushed, and houseplants overturned.

I'd seen such wanton destruction only once before: at Edie's place in Boston. The monsters responsible for the violence done to both the apartment and, later, to the women were Jarl's lackeys: Graeme, the rapist-incubus; and Fugwat, the spriggan.

Anyan and Ryu were carefully picking over the evidence. Ryu seemed to be cataloging things and making little notations in the small moleskin notebook he carried everywhere. Anyan, however, was employing his long, crooked nose. His snuffling was the only sound to be heard in the silent apartment, although I was trapped in the cacophony created by my racing heart and the sound of the blood it sent whizzing through my system and beating against my eardrums.

'This is entirely different from the other kidnappings,' Ryu noted eventually, half to himself.

The barghest snuffled into a corner, grunted either at what he'd smelled or at the baobhan sith, then snuffled again.

'The other women were all taken without a struggle. Either off the street or from work. Very few were taken from their homes, and when they were, there was no sign of forced entry or a fight.'

My heart beat more frenetically as I came to understand what people meant when they said someone's 'blood was boiling'. Because that's what I felt at that moment. Like my blood was simmering through my system, faster and faster, ready to blow out my ears and eyeballs and eventually out the top of my head.

'Jane, you all right?' Ryu asked.

'I'm fine, Ryu. It's Iris who's missing.'

Ryu frowned at me, walking over to where I stood, fists clenched.

'Jane, it's going to be all right. We'll get Iris back.'

'I know we will. And then I am going to neuter Jarl. I'll do it with a spoon. Or dental floss. Something that will make it a slow, tedious process. Maybe chopsticks . . .'

Ryu blinked at me. 'Um, Jane . . .'

'What, Ryu?' I demanded, rounding on my former lover. 'Please don't start the bit about Jarl's possible innocence again. Taking Iris was done to *provoke* us. You said it yourselves: they didn't take her quietly and carefully like they did the other women because they *want* us to know how powerful they are. They killed my mother, but that wasn't enough. Now they're going after everyone I care about.'

Ryu frowned. I didn't let him start.

'Don't even begin telling me I'm wrong. You know that this apartment looks exactly like Edie's did, except for the mage balls. Fugwat and Graeme aren't bothering to hide the fact magic was used this time. So don't try comforting me.

I don't want comfort; I want action.' My voice was starting to rise and I could feel my power pushing to the surface. The air shimmered and prickled with magic as my control wobbled when Anyan interrupted.

'That's enough, Jane,' the barghest said calmly from the other side of the room. 'Get it together so we can work.'

I stood there with my mouth hanging open, blinking in surprise. Worn out and anxious, I briefly considered throwing a good old-fashioned temper tantrum, but Anyan was right. My wigging out didn't get us any closer to Iris. So I tamped down my anger and my frustration and strode out to sit on the stairs that led up from Iris's boutique to her apartment. Breathing deeply, I got myself sorted out and then called my house to talk to Nell. I'd been in almost constant contact with the gnome since hearing of Iris's disappearance – first to tell her what had happened and then to make sure that she was keeping an eye on everybody – but I needed to touch base again and know all was still well.

'True residence, how may I direct your call?' answered a voice dripping with a sugary, Southern coating. It was Miss Carol, Nell's niece. An immature gnome, Miss Carol had yet to stake out her own territory and bind with the earth. The process would not only wizen her up to Nell's size, but also give her access to the First Magics, a force not even Alfar would challenge willingly. Until then, however, she lived in Rockabill under the protection of her aunt and posing as an eccentric old Southern lady, resplendent in pastel suits with matching gloves and hats. The only thing that broke character, however, was her obsession with filthy literature and her inability to keep a rein on her sharp tongue. Behind that ladylike drawl lurked verbal razors.

'Hey, Miss Carol, it's Jane. How're you?'

'I'm fine, sugar. You in Eastport?'

'Yes, just got in. We're wrapping up here and will come straight back to Rockabill.'

'Good. Your daddy misses you.'

'How is he?'

'Oh, fine. I think he's enjoying all the hubbub.'

My house had become ground zero for what I'd dubbed Operation Keep Supes Un-Kidnapped. As soon as Amy had discovered Iris's kidnapping, she'd gotten everyone moved in under Nell's watchful eye.

'Good. Is Nell there?'

'No, she's at Read It and Weep, keeping watch on Grizzie and Tracy. But if anything happens here, she'll be back, quick as a wink.'

I knew that was, quite literally, the truth. Like Terk the brownie, Nell could apparate herself within the boundaries of her territory using First Magic. Apparently, the two creatures were really very similar, only gnomes bound themselves to large tracts of land, while brownies bound themselves to domiciles and the people who lived there. Within their given territories, they were strong. Outside their territories, however, gnomes were weak as kittens. Brownies, since they were naturally of the First Magics to begin with, had a lot more oomph outside their homes. That said, nothing compared to what they had when safely ensconced on their own turf.

'Did you get Grizzie and Tracy into the house?'

'Yes. They think there's a gas leak at theirs and that they have to sleep here till it's fixed. Your dad gave them his room; he's in the guest bedroom. I'm in your room, and the nahuals, including Amy, are staying in Sarah and Marcus's trailer, parked in the driveway. It's like hillbilly heaven here. We'll have to reshuffle when you come home.'

'We'll sort it out, but you can stay in my room.

I'll take the couch or something. And thanks for watching out for everybody. I'm sorry I brought this down on you . . .'

'Oh, fiddlesticks, girl. You haven't brought anything down on anybody. You're as much a victim in all of this as anybody else. So don't start moping or I'll have to turn you over my knee.'

I smiled despite myself. 'Yes, ma'am.'

'Good. Now get yourself home and don't let those two males bully you. You're not letting them bully you, are you?'

I thought of all my recent, very un-Jane-like behavior.

'No. I think I might be bullying them, actually.'

There was a short, sharp guffaw from Miss Carol's end. 'Good! That's how it should be. We'll see you soon, honey.'

'Bye, Miss Carol.'

'Goodbye, sugar.'

When I got off the phone, I leaned my forehead against the cool wall of the stairwell. I felt entirely useless at that moment. I didn't know how we'd go about finding Iris, or what we would find if we did locate her. I felt like total deadweight as far as this investigation was concerned. I shut my eyes, trying to quiet my thoughts.

A minute later I smelled lemon wax and cardamom as a big hand wrapped itself around my hair at the nape of my neck. The hand rolled around, gently twisting my hair into a rough queue before giving a gentle tug.

As if conditioned to do so, my body immediately relaxed. The barghest's gesture sent my fevered thoughts spiraling into calm as my body reacted with a warm flush of sensuality that spread out from my spine, infusing my limbs with a heavy lassitude.

I knew Anyan was crouched behind me. I could feel the heat of his body and hear the rough sound of his be-denimed thighs rubbing against his calves. I would have given anything at that moment to lean back into the embrace of his strong legs, to shape myself into a little ball that the big man could engulf and protect. But I held myself still, my only concession to his touch a small sigh that escaped my lips unbidden.

His fingertips grazed my neck just as we heard the shrill sound of Ryu's BlackBerry ringing from inside Iris's apartment.

I heard Anyan stand and I realized my heart was again beating fast, but for an entirely different reason than anger. Before I could stop and consider what had just happened, however, I homed in on Ryu's voice.

'Yes, my queen . . . No, my queen . . . Of course, my queen. I will leave immediately.'

Ryu clattered out onto the stairway, and I turned to face him. I avoided looking at Anyan, unsure of how to interpret what had just occurred between us.

'That was Morrigan. She demands my presence.'

Anyan frowned. 'She wants your report on the Borderlands.'

'And I will give it to her, barghest. You knew that was my purpose. This information is important to our people.'

'No, it's important to the Alfar. There is a difference.'

Anyan and Ryu squared off, staring daggers at each other as the barghest blocked the baobhan sith from leaving.

'Ryu, go do what you have to do,' I said wearily. 'Anyan, let him go. He has to do this, you know that.'

My voice was sad. I knew Anyan, and everyone else, had made sure Ryu hadn't seen anything important in Borealis, but I also knew that anything was too much for a people who had guarded their privacy so assiduously.

Ryu nodded his appreciation at me. 'Julian, get ready to go. We're leaving in five.'

For a second I saw a mutinous look cross over Julian's face, and I wondered what he would do. But instead of refusing, my fellow halfling only nodded, turning on his heel to go collect his things.

Then Ryu turned to me. 'Jane? Can I talk to you for a minute?'

I nodded, sighing as he headed down the stairs and outside. This wasn't going to be fun.

When we were standing in front of Iris's shop, Ryu turned to face me.

'Jane, I want you to give me a second chance.'

I frowned, then shook my head. 'Ryu, it's not that simple.'

'Why not? I made one mistake and you're just giving up on us?'

'It wasn't just what you did, Ryu . . .'

'Then what is it, Jane?'

The fact was, it *wasn't* one big thing. What had happened surrounding my mother's murder just represented a bunch of problems we had; it wasn't *the* problem. But Ryu obviously thought it was, for when I didn't respond immediately, he shook his head furiously.

Staring me down, his voice angry, he started in: 'If we're going to talk about mistakes and forgiveness, I'd like to point out that I'm not the only one who kept important information from someone, information they knew would hurt that person. How do you think I felt when I learned that you'd lied to me about Jarl's attack?'

Caught off guard by the vehemence of Ryu's tone, I did the one thing I should not have done: I engaged.

'That isn't the same thing,' I protested, knowing I was making a mistake even as I said those words.

'Isn't it? You kept a secret from me, and with Anyan of all people. But I forgave you, Jane. Right away. Because I understood that you didn't mean to hurt me. And yet, I do this one thing, and it's like we're strangers.'

'It wasn't this one thing, Ryu. It was . . . a bunch of things. It was . . .'

'What, Jane? What was it exactly?'

I stood, mute, unable to articulate what I'd first felt sitting on Ryu's floor in Boston all those months ago, and what I'd known was the truth staring into his eyes in that B and B room in Eastport.

But words eluded me and I flinched. Which Ryu read as acquiescence to his point.

'See, you can't even answer me. And that's what I want you to think about. While I'm gone at the Compound, I want you to think long and hard about why you're doing what you're doing. You're shutting me out. I know you have every reason to be angry with me, but you've gone beyond anger. You're just quitting on us and closing me out.'

'That's not . . .'

'Don't make excuses, just think about what I've said. Because I think you're using what I did to get rid of me for reasons that have nothing to do with what actually happened. You say I play games. Fine, I know I do; it's who I am. But I think you do, too. You're just not aware of them.

'So think about that. And for once, be honest with yourself. Even if you can't be honest with me.'

And with that, Ryu turned on his heel and walked toward his parked car, Julian appearing as if on cue to follow Ryu and get in the passenger seat. I watched as Ryu peeled out, driving angrily into the last vestiges of dusk: a thin line of light clinging to the horizon, soon to be snuffed by the encroaching darkness.

I stood there, my muscles clenched and my mind racing.

Is he right? I wondered. *Am I using what happened with my mother's death as an excuse?*

But an excuse for what?

I shook my head, physically trying to dislodge all the doubts rattling through me when I heard Anyan exit Iris's boutique and lock the door behind him with his magic.

'Ryu gone?'

I nodded, still facing the street. Anyan walked toward me, but paused when he saw my face.

'You okay?'

I thought about that. 'I need a swim,' I said eventually.

'Yikes. Did he do something?'

'No, we just . . . talked.'

'Oh.'

We stood together without speaking, watching as the darkness pressed the last glimmer of sunshine from the horizon, leaving the night sky a brightly bruised purple. When Anyan broke the silence, his voice was rougher than usual.

'Well, Ryu took the car. So you'll have to ride with me on the bike.'

I sighed, then stared off at the ocean. The thought of being on a motorcycle with Anyan, with everything that was swirling through my head, was . . . intense.

Mistaking the cause of my reticence, Anyan shuffled his big feet.

'Or swim, I guess,' he said. 'If you wanted. You probably need to recharge and we need you at full throttle. I can drive you to the seashore. Sea Code means you're safe in the water, but I'll still phone ahead to Trill and have her meet you.'

I contemplated my choices. On the one hand, I could use the long swim home to think about everything Ryu had just said.

On the other hand, if you choose the bike, you'll finally have the barghest right where you want him . . .

I looked down at my thighs. They did look lonely.

Then again, I thought, *perhaps they should stay that way, at least for now*.

I sighed. 'I think I should just swim and recharge. Kill two birds with one stone.'

Anyan nodded. 'Okay, but I want to drive you to the water, and I'll meet you at the cove. Nell has it booby-trapped so anyone outside of her jurisdiction won't be able to enter it without getting zapped. You're safe in the water, and Trill will meet you halfway. But I'm worried about you on land, so don't make any pit stops.'

I nodded, and we walked to his bike. 'Can you carry my clothes home with you?'

The barghest nodded again.

'Thanks.'

Anyan pulled out his helmet and a spare. They were both German half-helmets, and he handed me the one that was plain but for a spike right at the top. Anyan's was decorated with flames and looked very cool. I watched as he settled his own helmet over his wiry, unkempt curls and then smoothly mounted the bike. He waved me to him, where he helped me buckle on mine. It felt heavy and strange, and I doubted I looked very cool. Standing next to him, I also realized the Indian was a lot bigger than it looked from a distance. There was no way I was hopping onto that thing while maintaining even the slightest shred of dignity.

Before I could ask Anyan for help, however, his big hands were around my waist, using a combination of his physical strength and a burst of his magic. I held back a squawk as he lifted me up behind him.

'You can put your arms around my waist, or you can reach back and hang on to the seat from behind you,' he instructed, starting the engine.

That's really not much of a choice, I thought, but I was

still hesitant as I wrapped my arms around his muscular torso. He moved my hands tighter across his stomach, pulling me in close.

'Just hang on, Jane. Don't lean in with the curves; sit like you would in a chair.'

I nodded, then said, 'Okay,' when I remembered he couldn't see me as I was sitting behind him.

We took off down the main street of Eastport, and I felt my heart lurch. I'd never been on a motorcycle before, but, after a moment or two of fear, I decided I liked it. *Really* liked it.

We like it, too, my thighs purred from where they lay alongside the barghest's hips.

We purred slowly down the street toward the harbor. For a second I fantasized about yelling over the rumbling engine for Anyan to drive us all the way back to Rockabill.

He'd pull my arms even closer around him. Then he'd veer away from the docks, punching the engine and racing toward 190 to get to Rockabill. I'd be forced to give a girlie squeal and tighten myself against his body . . .

Do eeeeeet, my libido demanded. The rest of my body, tingling against Anyan's, could only agree.

But I didn't do it. Instead, Anyan drove me to the docks. He turned his back as I stripped down and folded up my clothes. I left them lying there as I turned and ran hell for leather to the water, gracefully swan-diving into the freezing-cold Atlantic – and nearly crashing into an unmoored fishing dinghy.

The shock of the water hitting my Anyan-heated skin brought me back to earth, so to speak.

I thought about the barghest: his age, and his experience, and the fact of his very Anyanocity.

He just isn't for you, Jane. And you know it. But a girl could dream . . .

And, despite the cold water, dream I did.

Chapter Eleven

Punching through the water toward Rockabill, I took my frustration out on the waves. I'd always been a freakishly powerful swimmer, capable of doing just about anything I wanted in the water. But now that I knew I wasn't entirely normal – now that I was extra-normal, so to speak – I'd stopped hampering myself by thinking of what I should or shouldn't be able to do.

In other words, when I still thought I was entirely human, I swam, more or less, like a human. I came up for air quite often, and I muscled my way through tough spots. Of course, I was really muscling through using arms and legs charged with magic, but I hadn't realized that.

Now, however, I didn't bother. One day, soon after I'd returned from the Alfar Compound to Rockabill all those months ago, I'd decided to see what I was really capable of in the water. It had been eye-opening.

Take breathing, I thought, even as I dove deeper into the sea to escape a pesky current that was dragging on me. *I used to think I needed to breathe. Now . . . I just go.*

Not breathing had been a huge revelation. Don't get me wrong, I don't think I was *really* not breathing. Instead, just like some sea creature with enormous lungs, my magic allowed me to pull in more air, or to make that air last longer. To be honest, I had no idea what I did. All I knew was that my muscles were clearly still oxygenated – after all, they flexed and pulled and powered me through the water. But I didn't need to rise to the surface except very occasionally.

The other cool thing I could do was see underwater. I'd always had really good 'night vision', but now that I wasn't constraining myself, I could see in the darkest water as if it were daytime. That revelation had put a whole new spin on my big black eyes. I'd always hated them growing up. They marked me as different; as an outsider. Now I knew they had a purpose, and that purpose was to allow me access to the astonishingly beautiful world underneath the waves. I loved my black eyes now, and I kept my bangs trimmed so that they showcased rather than hid.

Nowadays, I also did something that was more like *flying* through the water than it was like swimming. It sort of felt like I pulled myself along by the elements around me. Meanwhile, pulsing around me at all times was the power of the ocean. She'd fill me with her magic as quickly as I expended any, giving me almost perfect stamina in the water.

So I motored along, quite happily, figuring I'd beat Anyan to Rockabill.

He has to obey traffic signs, after all, while I can bend the water to my will, I thought in my faux-superhero voice. I was so busy faking omnipotence, in fact, that I nearly missed my turn. Veering sharply to continue northwest along the coast-line, I finally escaped that hindering current and could swim closer to the surface.

Wrapping my glamour around me so that humans would see but a small porpoise, I allowed myself a little playtime. Breaching into the black sky only to dive back down into my sea, I reveled in the freedom and security I felt in the water.

Except for when I swam with Trill, this was my turf, my territory . . . Besides the kelpie, I was the only supernatural swimmer in the waters surrounding Rockabill.

Which was why, when I felt the skittering of a foreign power on the very edges of my perception, my shields were up and ready. That said, because of the Sea Code I didn't expect to have to need them. So the blast of magic and water that came at me was deflected easily, although I couldn't have been more startled.

What the hell? I wondered, even as another blast – stronger this time – buffeted my shields.

I'd stopped dead in the water, floating about two feet from the surface. Peering around the darkness, I scanned for my attacker while trying to figure out what to do.

The fact was, I'd never really fought besides in practice, and I certainly hadn't fought in water. We'd always assumed I was safe in the water, as I was accepted as a water-being despite being, more accurately, amphibious. Therefore, the one genuinely offensive thing I knew how to do – besides belch the alphabet – was throw mage balls, but they worked only on dry land . . . *Don't they?* I wondered, as I realized I had a few Boeing jet–sized holes in my training . . .

So I did what Jane does best. I fled.

The ocean helped me along, speeding me through her waters as if she wanted me to escape. But I could feel my attacker behind me, using that same power to propel himself as I remembered Anyan's words about my mother's kidnapping . . .

'Sea Code', my foot, I thought as an ominous blast of dark water shot past my ear.

Apparently there does exist the water version of mage balls.

Too bad I don't freaking know how to make one . . .

Really panicked now, I opened myself even further to the ocean and put on the speed. I also began a weaving maneuver as I felt at least two blasts of energy hit against the shields protecting my feet. Those blasts were strong, and I needed to put as much energy I could into escape.

I was swimming as fast as I could, but I knew the creature behind me was gaining. I could feel the presence of powerful magics more than anything else. We were close to Rockabill now, but not that close . . .

Where the fuck is Trill? I thought, suddenly remembering Anyan had said he would contact her just as one of those dark water balls clipped the tail end of my shield.

It didn't blast through. But it was strong enough, and I was going fast enough, that it sent me into the aqueous version of a tailspin.

I stopped only when I slammed against the seafloor. The wind was knocked out of me, and in my panicked state I nearly took in a deep breath, a *real* breath, that would have drowned me.

Get it fucking together, girl! I screamed at myself, even as I skittered away as one of those black balls of magic came piercing through the water toward me.

I forced my heart to slow as I raised my shields. Then I tried to calm my racing brain and focus.

You know how to make mage balls. It can't be too different to make the water version . . . Think, Jane.

As if to give me an example, two powerful magical strikes hit my shields inches from my face. My attacker was obviously close. Had I been above water, I would have screamed for him to show himself. Limited, however, in my ability to express frustration, I shook my fist good and hard at the surrounding darkness.

The water around me started to heave as a shape began to

coalesce just outside the range of my vision. It was small – not as small as Nell but a good foot shorter than me – and vaguely humanoid, although it appeared to be hunchbacked.

As it came closer, and the swirling sand settled back to the ocean floor, I saw it clearly.

Oh, shit, I groaned. *It's a fucking kappa . . .*

I'd heard of kappas from Trill, who'd explained to me that the Japanese legend of the dreaded water sprite was based on the cousin to the kelpie, the kappa. Kappas and kelpies had probably started out the same evolutionarily, but when kelpies veered off to become shape-shifters, the kappas had stayed humanoid with modifications.

Holy shit, Trill was right. It does *look just like a goddamned Teenage Mutant Ninja Turtle.*

I'd scoffed when my friend told me that kappas resembled those surfer-dude-voiced reptiles. Or were they amphibians? Whatever, this little guy was very green, with a strange, slightly beaked face, and a definite shell on his back.

If he's got nunchakus, I am so screwed.

The water around me increased its buffeting, and I beefed up my shields in response. But even though I could feel what the kappa was doing, when I tried to emulate him, I was stumped.

Not least because of how my ocean had decided to play me. Granted, people had been writing the same type of sea shanties ever since that first ancient sailor had learned to shant: the songs about how the ocean was a fickle mistress who would grace you with bounty one minute and take your life the next. But it was hard to take that message to heart, when every night I swam in her and loved her and she loved me back.

So I was more than a little surprised to find *my ocean*

practically ignoring me. Don't get me wrong, she was still responsive, but not nearly as responsive as she was being for the kappa. For the ocean was answering *his* call at the moment.

How is he doing that? I wondered, panicked, as he continued to brusquely cut me off each time I reached out to the water.

I pulled hard, sending out my own probing magics to figure out how he was managing to pull my own element away from me.

There it is, I thought, as I could suddenly 'see' what he was doing with his power: where I asked politely, he forced; where I pleaded, he demanded. And the ocean ignored me to fall over herself doing his bidding.

Fickle bitch, I swore as I felt the side of one of my shields bow under the strain of the attacking water. I couldn't believe I was sitting here, being defeated by my own element like I was some landlubber, especially after the virtual miracle I'd performed when caught in Phaedra's Alfar trap months ago.

Hmmm . . . speaking of what happened months ago, I thought, suddenly inspired by remembering Conleth's own tactics. In a desperate bid to escape, I tried waiting till the kappa was between attacks and then shooting away as Conleth used to do using his fire. To be fair, I did a pretty good job. I was rocketing up through the water, until the power of the kappa batted me down to the seabed like he was a badminton player and I was his shuttlecock.

This time when I hit sand, I hit hard. And the kappa's power was there immediately, taking advantage of my dis-orientation to press in with his power. If he breached my shields, I was a goner.

That's when I heard the cavalry approaching, sweet music to my ears.

Tiny hoofbeats, weirdly booming underwater, struck the

ground ever more loudly. I knew I just had to hold on a little while longer . . .

Throwing the last of my power into my shields, I nearly wept when Trill's little pony shape came hurtling past me. Trumpeting a weird underwater war cry, she made straight for the kappa, sending out pummeling blasts of water like thick, liquid laser beams.

I sat, catching my breath, pulling power from the water around me as the kelpie and the kappa squared off. Baring his teeth at Trill, the turtle-man began a complicated barrage of attacks. In response, Trill weaved through the water like a maned eel, lobbing her own spheres of power.

In that moment I realized two things. The first was that the unassuming My Little Pony whose ass I continually kicked on land was like My Little Ninja Pony underwater. The second thing I realized was that if the kappa had attacked me the way he was attacking Trill, I'd be a goner right now.

He didn't want to kill me, I realized. *He wanted to capture me.*

And then it hit me.

We were wrong. Everyone assumed that my mother was captured on land, but I bet she wasn't . . . I bet this little motherfucker took my mother.

With an admittedly rather watery roar, I leaped to my feet and swam toward Trill. Joining my shields with her own, I watched until I figured out what she was doing. First of all, I realized where I went wrong with the ocean herself. Having used my element only to recharge, or to play, I was used to doing something akin to sort of *vacuuming up* the power I needed. In other words, being in the water meant I was surrounded by power that I could just suck up as I needed it. But what the kappa and the kelpie were doing was pulling from their power in a way that made it as much offensive as defensive. They were putting power into their pulling; effectively dueling each other for access to the ocean even as they recharged themselves. I could see how effective a strategy it was, and how cunning. A truly powerful water-elemental could put so much force into their own gathering that the enemy would end up draining themselves trying to recharge, making them extremely vulnerable.

Shit, I have a lot to learn, I thought. *My new daily mantra . . .* But now was not the time for contemplating life lessons.

Now is the time for putting a cap in that kappa's ass, I thought as I put all my own power into forcing the ocean's strength to flow toward Trill and me. Once the Atlantic was firmly back on our side, and the kappa was starting to look a little panicked, I began lobbing my own modified mage balls at our attacker. The first few fizzled before they hit their target, but soon they were hitting home.

Okay, fine, they were hitting *near* home, as my throwing arm isn't everything it could be. But, whatever: Jane True was on the attack.

I've no doubt that my forcing the ocean's favor so firmly back to us helped win the day, but I also have no doubt it was Trill's ferocity that finally made the kappa turn tail and flee. With an almighty roar of power, the murderous little turtle shot away after sending out a fierce barrage as cover.

While the sand settled in the water around us, I turned to Trill. She raised a shaggy eyebrow, her pony features expressing a great deal of concern. I smiled, mouthed, 'I'm fine. You?' as I stroked a hand down her flank. She'd totally pulled my fat out of the fire on that one . . . or my cellulite out of the whirlpool, whichever was more accurate.

She nodded, turning so that we could swim together the rest of the way to Rockabill and my cove. We went fast, but not so fast we couldn't stay aware of our surroundings. For the first time in my life, I couldn't wait to get out of the water. Sensing the pull of the Sow and her piglets, which meant we were nearly home, I suddenly craved dry land and the safety of my cove. So I ran straight out of the water and up the beach without thinking or looking, only to trip in a wet, naked heap over Anyan's sprawled-out legs.

'Jane, what the hell?'

'Mmph,' I mumbled, my face full of sand. I was trying to say, 'Sea Code,' as in, 'That Code that's obviously fucking broken.'

I felt Anyan extricate his legs from mine, but I stayed facedown in the sand. For I knew that, this way, I was (a) less likely to die of humiliation when I saw Anyan's face and (b) only showing off my bare patootie, as opposed to a little full-frontal action, to the undoubtedly horrified barghest.

'We were attacked by a kappa,' came Trill's oil-slick voice behind me. 'Why's Jane on the ground?'

'She doesn't always walk so good,' the barghest muttered as I felt the towel I kept in the cove fall over my naked haunches. 'Did you hurt yourself?' he asked me, his hot hand branding the ocean-cold flesh of my shoulder.

I shook my head, finally lifting my face from the beach. I was now wearing a mask of powdery white sand, but I didn't care.

I sat up slowly, careful to pull the towel around with me to cover my nakedness. But Anyan wasn't paying any attention anyway.

'Did you recognize him?' he was demanding of the kelpie.

'No, and I know all the water folk for miles. He was a stranger. And fierce. The way he just attacked, like that, on my territory . . . it disobeyed *all* of our laws.' I could hear the rage in Trill's voice. To betray his own people like that, the kappa had pooped on every tradition the ocean folk held sacred.

'Can you track him?'

The pony grinned her eerie equine smile. I loved Trill, and even more after she'd just saved my ass. But gods, I hated when she smiled.

'You couldn't stop me. I'll find out where he goes. If whoever is behind this attack knows anything about us, however, they'll know I'll follow. So it could be a trap, to lure me away. Jane needs to be careful in the water. She'll have to be watched.'

I frowned, hating the idea of having to be watched – again. In response, fine white sand fell from my crinkled-up face onto the towel, as if to remind me I was a disaster.

'Okay. We'll keep her safe. Happy hunting.'

The pony grinned one more fierce grin before she turned tail and bolted for the water. I watched as she plunged into the ocean, wishing I could go with her.

Anyan came back to where I sat wrapped up in my towel. I hurriedly began to brush the sand from my face.

He sat down next to me and we watched my heretofore peaceful waves, which I'd thought were my second home, rush up and down the beach.

'You okay?' the big man asked eventually.

I grunted. Anyan always brought the grunter out in me.

We sat in silence as I pondered what the hell this would mean for me. I *needed* to swim, and not just for power. It was also my great love, my life . . . and now Jarl had taken even that away from me.

'It'll be okay, Jane. We'll make sure you can swim and recharge.'

I grunted eloquently again. To be honest, I really wanted to cry. And when I thought about the fact I wanted to cry, I felt tears well up. I snuffled noisily, trying desperately to keep back the waterworks.

'C'mon, Jane,' Anyan said, clearly not wanting to have anything to do with another Patented Jane True Emotional Breakdown, either. 'Let's get you home.'

He stood and helped me to my feet. Then he took a corner of his T-shirt and used it to wipe the last of the sand off my face.

He wrapped his big hand around the nape of my neck and pulled me to where I could see my clothes piled up on the old driftwood log that decorated a corner of the cove.

'Get changed, and I'll meet you outside. We'll walk to your place together.'

I nodded, still feeling miserable, as he sidled through the break in the cove walls. Once he was outside, I shook out my towel, then quickly changed.

As I was lacing up my Converse, I heard Anyan muttering to himself. I froze, listening closely, unsure whether he was talking to me. Then I shook my head. He was repeating, in various sotto voce impersonations of a television presenter, a single line:

'Just when you thought it was safe to go back in the water . . .'

I guessed that passed as humor to a barghest.

Chapter Twelve

Between Iris's abduction and not being able to have a proper swim, the following week was pure, unadulterated hell. I'd learned from the investigation in Boston that real-life detective work consisted mostly of sitting around, sorting through things you'd sorted through a thousand times before, and hoping that some new detail would pop up to catch your eye. In the meantime, you sent out feelers so that other people would sort through their stuff, looking for something, anything, new on their end. While all this paper shuffling was going on, the only thing you could do was sit and stew.

Stewing had been bad enough when the victims were merely names on files. Stewing when I knew it was Iris's life at stake was a torture unlike any I'd ever known.

Anyan, luckily, had more feelers than a millipede. He'd called everyone, and I mean everyone, he'd ever known. He'd even borrowed Terk to send messages to beings so old and powerful they eschewed modern technology. He mustered the forces of both the Alfar power structure and the networks of halflings that stretched across the Borderlands.

Finally, however, even he had to sit down and wait like the rest of us. And I couldn't even blow off steam with my usual, stress-reducing swims. Instead, I had to scamper about in the shallows like a child under the watchful eye of Nell or Anyan. It was humiliating. Other than that, I spent the week calling Anyan every five minutes to see if there was news about Iris; thinking around all the issues that went along with my mother's death, including how I was going to tell my father and trying to figure out how to deal with my own, strange grief; and worrying about everything and everyone till I would physically panic and then force myself to come down from that panic . . . usually by lobbing badly aimed mage balls at things.

The one thing I wasn't doing, however, was sleeping. And so, eight days after Iris was kidnapped, I stood like a zombie behind the counter of Read It and Weep. I wasn't, yet, trying to eat people's brains, but I did look like the walking dead. There were huge bags under my eyes from over a week spent half sleeping on our crappy couch. Between my nightmares about Iris, my lack of a good swim, and the lumpy cushions, I hadn't had a decent night's rest since returning to Rockabill.

Tracy was back at my house, still believing they'd been exiled from their own home due to a really difficult-to-fix gas leak. Grizzie, meanwhile, was puttering around the shop behind me, singing Lady Gaga. My tall friend was wearing pink skintight jeans that were dusted with glitter, a purple tube top, and a long-sleeved, fake-fur Bandolero jacket a slightly darker pink than the jeans. So her current soundtrack fit her wardrobe, really.

'You look like shit, honey,' Griz said, for the fifth time that day, as she moved me aside to dust the counter in front of me.

'Thanks. 'Preciate it.'

'It's only true. You look like you haven't slept since you got back. We should get you a blow-up mattress or something.

Miss Carol can fill it with all her hot air, and you can finally get some shut-eye.'

I grinned. Having Miss Carol and Grizzie in the same house was like unleashing Archie Bunker on Al Bundy. I thought our walls were going to turn indigo from the blue streaks the two women swore.

'Yeah, well, I'm glad you're all here. I'll have lots of time to sleep soon.'

'I just wish they'd fix that gas leak . . . It seems like it's taking an awfully long time.'

With a sigh, I nudged the glamour that Nell had put in place in both Grizzie's and Tracy's minds. Grizzie's words trailed off, then she shook her head as if remembering something.

'I'll go make us coffee,' she said, wearing the dazed smile of the recently glamoured.

I'd already had about six coffees, the most I could drink in one day before experiencing heart palpitations, but I didn't stop her. For some reason, Grizzie balanced out the interference of glamouring by making coffee.

And that's how I waited out the rest of my workday, till, at five o'clock, we shut up shop and went back to my house. I ate dinner, changed out of my work uniform, then took the shortcut through the woods to Anyan's cabin for my nightly training.

Normally when I walked up, Nell would be waiting for me on the porch, rocking in her little chair. But this time no one was around. After beefing up my shields, just to be on the safe side, I followed the sound of sandpaper around the cabin toward Anyan's workshop.

The big man was sitting just where I'd found him the day I'd come to apologize, again sanding smooth the curves of that same statue. In the darkness, the workshop glowed warm and cozy while the soft rasping of sandpaper stroked against wood lulled my tired brain. I closed my eyes, leaning against the lintel of the workshop door, as the gentle susurrating sounds along with the smell of freshly cut wood and lemon wax washed over me.

'You're going to fall asleep standing there,' Anyan rumbled, causing me to jerk upright and blink hazily in the suddenly overbright room. As my eyes adjusted to their opened state, I saw that Anyan had put his statue down and was leaning back on his bale of hay, long legs stretched out before him.

I had a brief, intensely detailed fantasy of springing up and hovering, like Keanu Reeves in *The Matrix*, only to land straddling the barghest. After a second I registered how ridiculous that was, and I had a secondary, equally vivid fantasy of my short-assed legs hopping awkwardly across the floor toward Anyan while he stared with a mixture of confusion and horror.

Shaking my head to clear it of my daymare, I ruefully smiled at nothing in particular just as Nell yelled for me from the yard.

'Training time!' I sang, awkwardly and too loudly, before plastering on a grin and pivoting on my heel to flee to the front side of the cabin.

What the hell is wrong with me? I wondered. *Could I be any more of a spaz?*

Luckily, my self-recriminations were short-lived. Mostly because the second I turned the corner I was diving to the ground as Nell tried to take my face off with a mage ball.

Motherfucking gnomes, I thought as I struggled to maintain shields, scramble to my feet, and create a mage ball all at the same time. Nell loved what she called surprises. And by 'surprise', Nell meant trying to maim you when you least expected it. She was like Cato from the fucking *Pink Panther*, only more destructive.

So, for the next hour and a half she chased me around the pasture, then the woods, and finally to my cove, lobbing mage balls at me the whole time while she flew through the air like a hovercraft, laughing maniacally. I did manage to squeeze off a shot or two, but my aim was pants and I inevitably missed her entirely.

We called a truce when we got to the cove, and Nell watched my back as I splashed in the shallows. After I'd dried off and put my clothes back on, we went back to the cabin so she could 'assess my progress'. Which, in Code Nell, meant going into great detail about how much I suck.

The night had turned chilly and damp by the time we made it back to Anyan's. This meant that, since he was around and his cabin open, I got my dressing-down inside the cabin instead of shivering on the front stairs as usual.

When we walked inside, Anyan was sitting at the enormous butcher-block island that dominated the center of his kitchen, reading over the reports he'd gotten that day. But when I dragged my straggly wet-haired self inside, he frowned.

'Nell, she looks like death warmed over.'

The gnome shrugged. 'She has to train.'

'I know, but . . . look at her.'

'Hello, I'm here,' I reminded both of them. 'Can we not discuss how shitty I look?'

'Sorry, Jane,' Anyan said. 'But you do look like crap.'

I shot him my best gimlet eye.

'Can I make you some tea?' he added apologetically.

'Do you have chamomile?'

'Yup.'

'Sure, that'd be nice. Thanks.'

The gnome accepted Anyan's offer of tea as well, and we

walked toward the cabin's seating area. Nell levitated her little rocking chair inside, next to the warm fire blazing in Anyan's fireplace. She settled down in it comfortably as I took the place nearest the fire on Anyan's giant, overstuffed sofa.

His sofa isn't lumpy, my exhausted body whined petulantly as I curled up contentedly against the armrest.

Yes, well, I reminded myself, *Anyan isn't supporting two people on government disability and a job at a bookstore. So quit yer whining.*

And speaking of Anyan . . . I watched, a little too appreciatively, as the barghest moved about his kitchen. I tried to keep my attention on Nell, but I was failing miserably. Part of the problem was that I'd heard everything I did wrong with mage balls a thousand times already. And hearing what I did wrong obviously wasn't connecting, for me, with what I needed to do in order to improve.

I watched as Anyan's big hands deftly unwrapped two comparatively minuscule tea packets, one of which he dropped into a normal mug and one of which he dropped into a wee, gnome-sized mug. Then, from a stack of dishes on his draining board, he pulled out an enormous mug, a barghest-sized mug, and placed it next to the other two.

Mama mug, daddy mug, and baby mug, my tired brain chortled, and I felt myself smiling.

'Jane, are you paying *any* attention to what I'm saying?'

I turned to the gnome, unable even to appear contrite. I tried to look sorry, I really did. But all I could do was blink stupidly.

'I'm sorry, Nell,' I said as Anyan brought over the three steaming mugs. He placed Nell's on the floor by her feet, and mine he set on the side table next to me. Then he joined me on the sofa.

'. . . you keep *throwing* the mage ball. But you want to *send* the mage ball,' Nell was saying for the fiftieth time. But I was too busy sniffing the air.

Following my nose, I sat up and leaned toward Anyan. Floating in his enormous mug of tea were about six little seedpods, bobbing about and emitting their heavenly aroma.

'Cardamom,' I said happily. 'That's why you always smell of cardamom.'

The barghest blinked at me, and I realized that my nostril quest had sent me traipsing into his personal couch space. So I backed off, sheepishly settling down into my own little corner.

'. . . once you stop thinking of physical distance as a space to be *crossed*, you'll shoot more accurately and forcefully . . .'

'I smell like cardamom?' the big man rumbled his basso profundo underneath Nell's lecture.

'Yes. And lemon wax,' I added, blushing when his wide mouth quirked in a small smile.

'. . . and if you two would stop whispering to each other like hundred-year-olds, we might actually get Jane to a point where she can defend herself!' Nell yelled from her chair, causing us both to startle.

'Sorry, Nell,' we mumbled as the gnome took an annoyed sip from her mug, grumbling under her breath the entire time. We sat in shamed silence, till the barghest spoke.

'Nell, may I?'

'Since you'll just pass notes or something otherwise, why *don't* you go ahead and take this one?'

Anyan had more self-control than I did, and he looked very contrite as he nodded to Nell. But when he turned to me, his eyes were sparkling with amusement.

'Okay, Jane, here's the deal. You throw like a girl.'

Before I could even begin to think, I was spouting off. 'First of all, I am a girl, shit for brains. And second of all, girls throw hard nowadays. Haven't you seen a girls' softball team? That is gender equality in kinetic energy, so don't tell me I throw like a girl.'

Anyan sighed. 'But you do throw like a girl.'

'Anyan!'

'The whole point is, you don't have to be throwing at all. All you have to imagine is your mage ball going from point A to point B and then make it go that way. Stop physically throwing it. Because you really do throw like a girl.'

I glowered at him, even as I felt that little tingle that I get when I finally understand something.

'The fact that you're an unreconstructed male chauvinist aside, you're telling me that when Nell says, "Send, don't throw," what she means is that I should . . . *zing* the mage ball with my mind? Instead of trying to manually lob it with what is, admittedly, very little force or accuracy?'

'Yup.'

'Huh,' I grunted. 'That's sort of how I swim . . . and that should make mage balls a hell of a lot easier.'

Nell was looking between the two of us like she wasn't sure whom to kill first.

'Really? Is that all it took?'

I wanted to tell her that it wasn't her fault, that Anyan understood how my brain worked. But even as I thought it, I was so struck by that idea that I clammed up and my mind went all numb.

I noisily sucked down some of my tea.

'Well, if that's all, I guess I'll just go home,' Nell said, her voice still irritated. 'Since Anyan's finished clarifying for Jane, in one sentence, what I've failed to explain in three weeks, I'm obviously no good here.'

Anyan laughed, then made soothing gestures toward Nell's wounded pride. I also made some concessionary noises from my corner of the couch, but my heart wasn't in it. Not least of all because, while a corner of my brain was still mulling over what I'd just thought about Anyan, the rest of my body was doing its best to fall asleep in the nest of warmth and comfort that was my corner of the sofa.

'Jane, are you coming?' Nell barked from the doorway. I started to struggle to my feet when I felt Anyan, from the other side of the room, push me gently back down onto the couch. I'd let my shields down when we walked inside, a luxury I allowed myself only around Nell or the barghest, so it took me a confused second to figure out how he'd gotten past my guard.

He didn't, my brain worked out as I saw Anyan say something quietly to Nell, who looked at me, nodded, looked at the barghest, scolded, and then apparated both herself and her rocking chair with an audible *pop*.

'Anyan, I should—'

'Shush, Jane,' he said as he walked back to the couch. 'You're spending the night here. Remember what I said about being a soldier? Well, soldiers need sleep. So you're here for the night.'

'Um, but where will you . . .'

'No worries, I can take the couch. You can have all the upstairs to yourself. There's clean towels for the shower up in the little cabinet outside the bathroom door. If you need any . . . girlie stuff, I can have Nell send it over.'

'Um, as long as you have shampoo to get the salt out of my hair, I'm pretty low-maintenance.'

'Yup, and I think it even has conditioner in it,' the barghest replied. 'It was on sale,' he added hastily, as if the addition of conditioner to his shampoo might make me doubt his masculinity.

'Great,' I said as I yawned so hard my jaw popped. 'But I don't have anything to sleep in . . .'

'You can borrow something of mine.'

Anyan's response was immediate and forceful. For some reason, it made me smile.

'Unless you want me to call Nell?' he amended.

'No, that's fine. I just need a T-shirt or something,' I said as I stood up from the couch.

Anyan smiled down at me, the skin at the corners of his iron-gray eyes crinkling. But before I could return his grin, he'd turned to walk toward the stairway to the loft. I followed, hustling to keep up with his long strides.

I took a deep breath as we walked upstairs. The idea of encroaching on the barghest's man space was both terrifying and . . . my idea of heaven, really. So I was in full snoop when we finally got to his loft bedroom. The space was large, about half the size of the whole downstairs, with a small en suite bathroom. Big canvases hung about the room or were propped up against walls, with smaller works of art dotted around here and there. None of them were done by Anyan up here, and some looked suspiciously similar to very famous pieces I remembered from my art history classes.

Besides art, there were books everywhere. Piled up on tables, set into bookcases, towering precariously in stacks well over barghest-high. Many of them were jumbled around the huge, rumpled bed standing in the corner. The bed was the barghest's sole concession to his own identity as an artist, as he'd very obviously done the ironwork; it looked like the bedstead version of the cartoon in the bathroom.

Only those *little figures are engaged in an epic battle*, *while* these *little figures are diddling one another*, I thought, blushing as I realized that this piece of art was decidedly more Kama Sutra than Bhagavad Gita.

Tearing my eyes from Anyan's raunchy, raunchy bed (*Delightful!* my libido purred), I watched as the barghest pulled a T-shirt from a low chest of drawers in the corner.

'Let me guess, it says Purina,' I joked as he handed it over.

He paused, still holding the shirt, and actually blushed. 'Beggin' Strips, actually. I can get you another . . .'

I laughed. 'No, that's fine. Anything is fine.'

There fell an awkward silence as we stood in his bedroom, me holding his shirt and looking down at Anyan's big feet shuffling nervously in front of me.

'Well, everything in the bathroom should be self-explanatory. If you need anything, just holler. Otherwise, I'll see you in the morning. Do try to sleep as much as you can,' he chided gently.

'Yes, sir,' I responded impudently. 'And thanks,' I added, meaning it.

'You're welcome. Sleep tight, Jane.'

'You, too.'

I watched as Anyan walked downstairs, then made short work of a very hot shower. Before I knew it, I'd thrown on the T-shirt – it fell to well below my knees – and was slipping in between Anyan's soft, hunter-green flannel sheets.

I lay back, listening to Anyan putter around downstairs as my eyes took in the circus of metal flesh dancing before me, upside down, from Anyan's headboard. Soon enough, however, I heard the creaking of the sofa. Then the light shut off downstairs and I was alone, in the dark, in Anyan's room. His sheets smelled like cardamom, as well as another scent I realized, after a moment, must be his body. That thought brought me back to full wakefulness, and I lay in the dark, eyes wide, before turning on my stomach and burying my face in the pillow. Which also, of course, smelled like Anyan. I sighed, then began counting down from one hundred as I traced my finger over the intricate curlicues of iron in front of me.

Soon enough my fatigue won out and sleep stole over me, but that meant I began to dream. I dreamed of Iris being attacked and myself, standing like a statue, unable to help her and unable to look away. As the nightmare took hold, my brain screamed at me to wake up. Swimming to the surface, my consciousness struggled, wanting so desperately to rest but unable to face the nightmares that lurked—

The bed dipped as the heavy form of a giant dog leaped up next to me, made three tight circles, then lay down with its head cradled in the small of my back.

'Anyan,' I mumbled, my mouth curving in a smile. I knew I was safe then, and I let the darkness swallow me.

This time, when dreams came of Iris's attack, at my side was a wolfhound made of white light, who snapped and bit at my friend's tormenters till they fled and I held Iris safe and close and close and safe . . .

Chapter Thirteen

I pressed the side of my face into the pillow, snuggling back into the heavy arms blanketing my midriff, but the humming wouldn't stop . . .

The warm arms holding me withdrew and suddenly I was cold. At least the noise had quieted. Then I heard a door click shut, then a muffled voice, and then I realized I wasn't in my own bed or on my own couch.

Arms? I thought, realizing I was at Anyan's and remembering my dream. *Arms? Doggies don't have arms . . .*

Before I could think through the fact I'd apparently just woken up with the barghest of my dreams wrapped around me like a big, hairy man-girdle, the big, hairy man in question emerged from the bathroom to stand in front of me, with a towel wrapped around his waist and his cell phone pressed against his ear.

Clothes don't shift with the shape, I remembered, swallowing nervously.

'Jane, get up,' Anyan barked, not exactly using the tone of voice I expected from anyone with whom I had just non-euphemistically slept.

'Ummmm,' I said intelligently, suddenly needing coffee,

and a cold shower, and, if I was entirely honest, a wank. Although I knew that was not at all appropriate given that I was in someone else's bed.

Maybe you and the barghest can wank together, my irrepressible libido suggested, even as Anyan picked my clothes up from where I'd stacked them on his dresser and threw them at me.

'Trill tracked the kappa all over the place, till he finally returned to Rhode Island and what looked to be another lab. So she contacted the local investigator. They did, indeed, find a dockyard lab nearby, and they're getting ready to raid. We gotta hustle!' he yelled, already running down the stairs.

Iris, I thought, all thoughts quashed other than fear for my friend. *Please don't let them botch this raid.*

We hit the road just twenty minutes later, and within the hour we met Orin and Morrigan's private jet – it was good to be Alfar – at Eastport's little municipal airport. They flew us directly to Providence, where we were met by two of the local supernatural investigator's deputies.

The half-hour ride to the site nearly killed me as I kept wondering about Iris. Luckily, Anyan kept me distracted.

'This is going to be a raid, just like you've seen in the movies. I want you to participate.'

I blinked across the backseat at the barghest sitting next to me.

'Sorry?'

'I want you to take part in this raid, Jane. You need offensive training, and we might as well start now.'

My eyes went wide in surprise and I frowned, my thoughts swirling. On the one hand, I knew I'd asked for this. I wanted to be involved and the barghest was willing to involve me. That said, I hadn't thought of 'involvement' as including fighting. I guess I just thought I'd do research and try to make connections, like I'd done with Ryu at the Compound and then, later, in Boston.

While I thought, Anyan patiently waited me out till I'd figured out my major concerns.

'It's not that I'm scared . . . okay, the thought of doing this scares the shit out of me. But above that, what if I fuck it up? And someone dies?'

Anyan nodded, letting me know he was listening.

'If there's any chance that you could, actually, fuck anything up, I wouldn't let you do this. From what I've been told of the situation, everything should be well in hand. You'd just be along for the ride. But if the situation has changed and the hostages would be at risk if you were involved, then, obviously, the hostages' lives trump your gaining experience.'

I nodded, but I knew my eyes were still like saucers.

'And I know you're afraid. I was terrified the first time I took part in real military action. But this is how you learn to overcome the fear. It's not about being fearless, Jane. It's about being brave despite your fear. And I know you're brave already.'

The car had gone quiet, the two deputies driving us had ceased chattering to each other, and Anyan's voice seemed suddenly overly loud.

He called me brave, I thought, even as I nodded again.

'Thanks. I don't feel brave.'

'Well, you act it. And that's what counts.'

I looked ahead just as we turned off the highway. The silence had grown heavy and I knew it was up to me to break it.

'So, um, how will this work?'

Anyan nodded sharply, as if he were putting on his official badass persona, then launched into a detailed explanation.

Apparently, the supes did their police work based on the human model, so this was exactly like a human SWAT raid. As I didn't actually have any clue what that meant, he also filled in the details.

We were currently driving to the command post, which was set up well away from the action, where the overall mission commander; high-ranking officers; intel people; 'commo,' or communications, people; and other support personnel planned everything. Just like the lab Conleth had been held in, our target was located in a run-down, abandoned strip mall on the edge of an ugly set of equally abandoned piers, warehouses, and dockyards. The local supes had commandeered an empty office building about a mile away from the lab. Closer to the site of the raid – but still well out of sight – was the tactical command post, where the tactical team, healers, and assault force commander checked in and prepped their kit. We were using another abandoned warehouse about a block away from the strip mall. It was perfect because not only was it well out of sight, it also had its own access road so our forces could loop around and never get anywhere near our target until we wanted to. Finally, there was the FAP, or final assault point, where everyone 'stacked up', ready on their primary breach point. From there, our team would 'bring the pain' . . . and hopefully rescue the hostages held inside the lab.

'I was with you right up until you said, "Bring the pain." I've only ever brought cookies, or the occasional casserole.'

Anyan's big nose twitched. 'Well, for your first time, you can just bring a minor irritant.'

I giggled. 'I'm good at the minor irritants.'

'Yes,' was his only response. 'You are, at that.'

I was about to snark back at him when I was distracted by the view out the window. We were pulling up to the

warehouse that obviously housed our command post. Big
black sedans that resembled those driven by Ryu's deputies
in Boston were pulled up outside, as were a few vans, and
the huge garage doors of the warehouses were raised to show
a bunch of tables covered with maps, papers, laptops, and
cell phones. Harried-looking supes milled about everywhere,
some dressed in civilian clothes (or just fur and a smile) and
some dressed in black SWAT gear.

I watched the chaos unfold as the deputies driving us parked
the car. Anyan had made me feel like I could do this, like I
could go ahead and bring somebody some pain. But seeing
everyone in action, seeing how professional it was, I seriously
doubted my own role in all of this.

What the hell am I doing here?

'I'm sorry about last night,' Anyan said, interrupting my
self-doubts a second after the deputies had stepped out of the
car.

'What?' I blinked at him, caught completely off guard.

'I'm sorry about last night. Sometimes I shift in my sleep.
I didn't mean to, and I'm sorry if it was invasive.'

My face flushed. I'd nearly managed to forget the way
we'd woken up. I wanted to tell him that it'd been anything
but invasive, that waking up in his arms was a dream come
true. But instead I said, 'No, it's fine. Don't sweat it.'

The very tip of his nose twitched once, hard, and he got
out of the car.

Don't sweat it? I thought, sad that he felt he needed to
apologize. *Yeah, he doesn't have to sweat it . . . I'm the one
who's sweating this nonrelationship.*

I sighed as I, too, exited our vehicle, then followed in
Anyan's wake to where the two deputies who'd driven us
were waiting to introduce us to their leader.

The chief investigator for Rhode Island – and the overall

mission commander for this raid – was a baobhan sith named Isolde. She was a formidable-looking woman, tall and strong with equally harsh features and an obviously iron will. After a perfunctory greeting to me and Anyan, whom she obviously knew well, she briefed us on their plans.

'There's five women being kept in the lab. It's small, with only a few people on staff. The kappa didn't appear to know he was followed, but they aren't taking any chances. They are preparing to clear out, but they're taking their time. There don't seem to be any plans to . . . dispose of their patients, so we waited for you to arrive. But if there's any sign of violence, we're ready to roll.'

I couldn't begin to guess how they knew so much about what was going on inside the lab, but I'd learned early on in my experience with the supernatural world not to look a gift horse in the mouth. So I just went ahead and asked what I wanted to know.

'Is Iris in there?'

Isolde looked up at me, frowning. 'Sorry?'

'Our friend, who was taken. Iris Succubus . . . is she in that lab?'

The woman shrugged. 'I don't think so, but . . .' She eyed me with her steely, assessing gaze.

'She cool?' Isolde asked Anyan eventually, her eyes not leaving mine. I looked over toward Anyan to escape their intensity.

Only to find the barghest smiling one of his big smiles that always caught me by surprise. He was always so broody; when he grinned like that he looked absolutely joyous.

And edible, my libido reminded me rather unhelpfully.

'Yeah,' Anyan said. 'Jane is definitely cool.'

Without thinking about it, I stuck my tongue out at him before I remembered Isolde was there. I carefully pulled my wayward appendage back in my mouth and turned back to her. She had an eyebrow cocked at Anyan, a look of surprise on her face she wiped away when she realized I was looking at her.

'All right then,' she replied. 'Let's go ask our intel. Come with me.'

Isolde stalked off toward a large van behind us. She opened it to reveal what looked like the inside of a movie SWAT van, with computer equipment lining the walls and captain's chairs facing the equipment. The central space was empty, but for a small woman who sat cross-legged on the floor, her eyes closed.

'Frida, quick question.'

The woman cracked open an eyelid. 'Sure. But make it snappy.'

'Can you describe the civilians?'

'Sure. They're all female and purebred. Two selkies, a very weak kelpie, a kappa, and a havsrå. I still can't believe a water-elemental turned against his own like that, by the way. I wouldn't want to be him if his own kind catch up with him. He'd better pray we get him first. I don't think anything the Alfar would do to him could be as bad as what he'd get back in the ocean.'

I nodded at Frida's words, although I was listening to my own thoughts. All water-beings . . . the kappa that attacked me must be supplying this lab with victims. That said, he was certainly connected to Jarl's stunt and he'd obviously been sent to Rockabill by someone for some reason, so maybe Iris had been held here for a night or two, or maybe there was some information on other labs where Iris could be held.

And in the meantime, my virtue reminded me with an angry note of censure, *there are five females in that lab who need rescue. Let's not forget what's at stake here.*

I hung my head, ashamed at my focus on Iris although I was, even then, focusing on Iris. I couldn't help it. I loved that succubus, and I wanted her home, safe.

'Thanks. You can pull back now. We're about to go in.'

The woman sitting on the floor shut her eyes as I wondered what Isolde meant by 'pulling back'. Soon enough, however, my question was answered as I watched another woman just like the one sitting in front of us, only incorporeal and ghostly, float through the top of the van and sink into the solid, breathing Frida. Upon joining her two halves, Frida grew exponentially until there sat in front of us a plump, round-faced woman who was exactly twice the size of the former Frida.

'Wow,' I breathed. What the hell was she?

Frida gave me a small smile, then rose creakily to her feet. She shooed us away, mumbling, 'Nap time,' as she shut the van door in our faces.

I gave Anyan a quizzical look as we headed back to the main table.

'Frida is a drude,' he explained as we walked. 'They can separate themselves into two halves – one earthly and one incorporeal. The incorporeal half can spy, or run messages, or possess humans for short periods of time. It's where the myth of demonic possession came into being. But Frida's existence on the Alfar payroll is top secret, so don't advertise.'

I nodded, marveling at what I'd just seen. Every time I thought I was getting used to supernatural surprises, I met a new creature, or saw a new power, that completely floored me.

Suddenly realizing that Anyan and Isolde had walked well away from me, I trotted after them and listened as Isolde continued to brief Anyan on the mission. They were using a lot of jargon, but the plan seemed to boil down to capturing the bad guys and freeing the women. I approved.

After we collected a few more of the people dressed all

in black – a female satyr and an incubus – from the command post, we headed toward the tactical command post. When we arrived, we saw about fifteen supernaturals milling about wearing SWAT gear. I was surprised at that, especially at the fact they had the usual guns and big black shields I'd seen in the movies.

Guns? I thought. *Nobody said anything about guns.*

The assault force commander was Isolde's second, an ifrit named Ezekiel. I couldn't help but shiver when I saw his flaming figure, causing Anyan to cock an eyebrow at me. Trying to reassure myself as well as him, I gave him a tight smile and reminded myself that Conleth was dead, and this ifrit had nothing to do with what had happened in the past.

Anyan and Ezekiel shook hands, once the ifrit had pulled the fire back from his arms.

'Anyan, sir, it's an honor to have you with us. Will you be participating?'

Anyan nodded. 'Yes, we'll need gear.'

'Is the halfling participating as well?' the ifrit inquired, giving me a rather dismissive once-over.

'Ezekiel, you know damned well that this is Jane True, and that she is with me. So, as I said, we'll need gear.' At Anyan's obvious irritation, the ifrit looked suitably chagrined. And I had to clamp down on the smile that was pulling at my lips.

I don't think I've ever, once, heard Anyan use that word, I realized. *He always says half-human, or half-supernatural, but never 'halfling'.*

When we were led toward an equipment van, I again asked Anyan whether my taking part in the raid was the best idea.

'You have to learn. We were all green once, and at some point we all had to take part in something like this for the first time. You'll be with me the whole time, and we'll be embedded in the middle of the assault force. There's only a few perps to deal with and rather too many of us, to be honest. You probably won't even have time to make a mage ball, let alone shoot one at anybody. So all you have to do is help us hold the line and secure the women. You're strong, Jane, but what you need is confidence in yourself and your abilities. You're only going to gain that through experience.'

I gulped, trying my best to look competent as Anyan paused to think.

'That said, we won't be giving you a gun. You'd probably shoot yourself in the foot.'

I nodded; he was right. But that did remind me of the question I'd been itching to ask: 'Yeah, what is up with that? Why are you guys using guns and not mojo?'

' 'Cause we're going in human. Otherwise, they'll feel our magic and know we're coming.'

To punctuate his point, Anyan let a tiny thread of his power shiver over my skin, giving me goose bumps.

I gulped. I'd been scared enough when I thought everything was just gonna be magical, but the sight of all those assault rifles had totally freaked me out. I really didn't like guns.

There was no time to sift through my antigun feelings, however, as we were already at the van with all the gear. The barghest led the way, sorting through everything till he found things that would fit us. We were both already wearing dark clothes, so we didn't worry about those, thank goodness. He was so big and I was so small we would never have found anything that fit. But the barghest did strap me into an overly large bulletproof vest (in case of friendly fire, he explained) and a helmet that kept slipping over my eyes. I felt like a little kid playing dress-up, but I let him have his way.

Anyan was, after all, the badass of our little operation, while I was part seal. I knew when to smile and nod.

Chapter Fourteen

The next half hour was this bizarre combination of the longest and shortest moments of my life. The lead-up to the assault itself felt like it was happening in fast-forward. We went from dressing ourselves in the van to hightailing it to the final assault point. Everyone fanned out into position.

The laboratory was in the end building of the strip mall, and it had two entries: one in the back, and one in the front. Each of these areas had two teams ready to move: the first was a two-supe breaching team that would take down the door, and the second was an entry team that would sweep past the first team and secure the premises. We were in stealth mode and not using any magics, so the breaching team had the same kind of combined battering ram and shield jobbies they use on TV. One person rammed while the other person covered him with a rifle. As for the entry teams, Anyan and I were on the team going in the front door. Both entry teams were going in using a 'stick' formation – which just meant a single-file line. I was sandwiched, toward the end, between Anyan and another experienced operative, a small woman who handled her assault rifle with the familiarity of a lover.

The breaching teams were hitting both entry points

simultaneously, as neither of the doors were booby-trapped, according to Frida. Not happy with using only two points of entry, however, the supes were creating a third: a 'porthole' between the building we were attacking and the empty shop with which it shared a wall. Earlier that day, two of our team had climbed up the far side of the strip mall, crawled to the empty shop neighboring the lab, and entered through a skylight. One of the supes, a nahual, was an explosives expert, and he'd set a detonating cord – a superthin tubing filled with powdered plastic explosives – into a small circle that he'd blow when the breaching teams struck. The hole wouldn't be anywhere near big enough to crawl through, but it was big enough for the other supe – a stone spirit whose calm nature made her an excellent sniper – to shoot through.

As for what we'd do when we were inside, that was simple. Our rules of engagement, or ROE, in this scenario were what was called 'direct to threat', meaning we had to neutralize the perps first to minimize the danger to the hostages. In other scenarios, without civilians at risk, we'd put our own safety first and go in slower. But because of the threat to the women contained inside the lab, Anyan explained to me that we had to think in terms of speed, surprise, and violence of action.

As I was used to thinking in terms of going slowly and carefully, always calling ahead first, and avoiding violence at all costs, the barghest's calmly stated goals were anything but comforting.

Not that I had a lot of time to ponder my situation, for one minute I was walking with Anyan from the van, and the next I found myself standing in a single-file line with a bunch of people carrying guns. Every time I looked at one of the assault rifles, I physically cringed. As if to hammer home to me just how much I wasn't meant to be there, my helmet kept slipping down over my eyes, and I really, really needed to pee. While I knew it was just my nerves, that didn't matter.

If I pee my pants I am going to be so pissed, I thought, just as time stopped.

Seriously, time just – stopped. It was like everything up to our getting into that line was moving at three times the normal speed, but as soon as we were standing there it felt like some great thumb, a la Martin Amis, came from nowhere and turned off time.

All the silence helped contribute to that feeling. The windows of the former shopfront-turned-lab were all bricked in, and the glass doors had been replaced with large steel ones. Unlike the labs we'd come across in Boston or in Borealis, this laboratory was so far off the beaten track that the creatures running it hadn't even tried to camouflage it as a clinic. In other words, we didn't have to worry about being seen, but we did need to worry about being heard. So the entire trip from the FAP to the doors, everyone was communicating only with hand and eye signals while tiptoeing as quietly as possible.

Even more eerily, however, was that everyone was *magically* silent. I'd become so accustomed to a constant undertone of power humming through me, my friends, and the supes around me that to be suddenly without that hum was startling. It was like I'd had a slight case of tinnitus that had miraculously cleared up, leaving me marveling at how quiet the world could be. I was also struck by how – without their flaming mage balls or blue-flamed swords – the supes around me, even the ones who were physically so different, like the satyr, looked so very *human*. Clutching their weapons, their bodies tense and their eyes bright with anticipation, but without that slight sheen of supernatural power gleaming around them, they could have been any SWAT team about to start a raid.

Granted, some of them were slightly more furry and hornier, in a nonmetaphorical sense.

As that tension rose, time slowed, and slowed, and slowed . . . and my helmet kept slipping. I kept pushing it back. Then it would slip again. I could feel a bead of sweat leaking out from under my hair to trail down my cheek, where it trembled on my chin before falling. It felt like it traveled for eons, and while I knew my heart was thudding out of control, because of the trick time was playing it sounded, in my ears, like a slow bass drum beating ominously in the background. And still time continued to slow, until I thought it might stop again. Then, just as suddenly, the great thumb moved again to press another button and kick everything into hyperspeed.

All at once, the breach teams were shouting and pounding through the door with their battering rams, and I could hear an explosion from inside the building. Before I could even register that it was, apparently, the time for bringing pain, the breach team had stepped aside, making way for the first members of our entry team. I could already hear gunfire from the front members of the line, and I could feel the shots reverberating down my spine.

Anyan's hand met that tingle on my back as he pushed me forward with the rest of our stick. The woman in front of me had her rifle raised and ready, till we heard the cold, clear call of the ifrit commander's voice shouting, 'Magic!' She smoothly sheathed her weapon into a holster she wore on her back, even as she raised a mage ball with her other hand. The supernatural silence ended just as the physical one had, with a sudden cacophony of blasts and hums as an onslaught of magic was unleashed: mage balls let rip, shields went up, and the raid suddenly went from normal to paranormal.

Everyone seemed to be everywhere, shouting at once.

Our stated ROE had required we try to catch the bad guys alive, so we could pump them for information. That said, Isolde had declared that hostage safety came first, and the sniper had been instructed to take out the 'doctor' whose desk had been set up right between two of the hostages' cells. He'd been a little too close to the females for comfort, considering the predilection for offing their prisoners demonstrated by other guards.

Sure enough, when I looked to my left, I saw a male in a lab coat slumped back in his office chair, a neat hole between his eyes and a lot of blood and brain-goop spattering the wall behind him. Our sniper had done her job and that part of the raid, at least, had gone according to plan.

Unfortunately, the rest of the raid had not gone quite so well. By the time we'd all gotten into the lab, all three of the bad guys were dead, and only two by our own hand. For the kappa, as soon as he'd realized what was happening, had taken out the other doctor himself. Then he'd tried to start in on his hostages. He'd blasted a hole in the poor havsrå, but before he could finish her off, the first members of our entry team took him down. A rifle blast from one side of the room, coupled with a mage ball from the other, had been the end of the evil mutant turtle, and our only chance of finally getting some real, insider information on what was happening in these labs.

That said, the havsrå would live, and her life was more important.

I learned all these details afterward, however. For what I can actually remember of the raid goes something like this:

loud noises, shouting, hand on back – Anyan's – moving forward moving forward moving forward oh my god I really don't want to be moving forward shit I'm moving

*forward, shit we're inside, maybe Iris is in here? lots
of smoke, eyes burning, ohmigod I'm gonna pee in my
pants, dude that's blood, what if it's one of us, what if
it's Iris, lab coat, oh good it's a bad guy, the women,
the poor women, I don't see Iris, I knew she wasn't in
here but what if drude-lady was wrong and she was
hidden, there's that fucking kappa, he's dead too, Sea
Code, biatch! oh no he got one of the hostages, but he's
dead and so are the other two, WHERE IS IRIS, I didn't
even do anything, is that it?*

And that was, indeed, it. For after all that chaos and that
fear, the great thumb pressed another button and time went
back to normal. I was left standing in the center of the room,
one of Anyan's big hands still at the base of my spine, while
his other hand cupped an unnecessary mage ball.

After a moment, I realized I was shaking. Everything was
done and over, but I was still trembling like a medieval virgin
on her wedding night. I was shaking so hard, in fact, that the
damned helmet fell down over my eyes. But this time I let
it stay there, blocking everything else out, till Anyan gently
moved it back away from my face.

'You okay?'

I looked at him, mute. A mixture of fear and adrenaline
had captured my tongue.

'Jane?'

I searched for and finally found my ability to speak. 'Is
that it?' I reiterated, still unable to think past the idea that it
was all over.

'Yeah, honey. That was it. And you did great.'

I stood there, blinking. 'So everything's over? We're safe?'

'Yeah, honey,' Anyan said gently. 'It's all over and we're
safe. And all the women are safe now, too. But are you okay?'

My heart was still beating in my throat, my limbs were still shaking with adrenaline, and I could feel the blood surging through my brain as if I were about to have a stroke. But despite all of this, I felt . . . to be honest, and despite the chaos around me, I felt . . . awesome.

'That was so fucking cool,' I said finally. 'I mean, I didn't do anything, but it was still so fucking cool. This must be how people who jump out of planes feel . . .'

Anyan laughed, his crooked nose wrinkling with pleasure.

'Honey, you were awesome. And you *did* do something. When I told you, "Move forward," you moved forward. Do you know how many newbies bolt on their first raid? And besides, this was never about you taking somebody out. There were only a few bad guys, but a lot of hostages. This was about getting enough firepower in that door as quickly as possible, so that we could get those females out alive. And you were part of that.'

I grinned at Anyan's words, suddenly seeing some truth in what the barghest had said. For I'd ended up standing directly between the spot where the kappa had made his stand and one of the cells with a hostage.

I was a human shield, I thought rather proudly. *Well, a halfling shield . . . but speaking of shields, why didn't the havsrå shield herself from the kappa's attack? And how could three creatures hold five to begin with?*

I'd been standing there, dumbly staring about the room, for long enough that the supes brought in to search the place for clues were already making inroads. Various beings were pawing through the desks and the filing cabinets, while others bagged and labeled the various medical instruments strewn higgledy-piggledy around the room.

I saw Isolde stride in with two of the other high-ranking officers, stopping to congratulate various members of her team.

'So you did good, Jane,' Anyan was concluding, and I couldn't help but grin.

'It was kind of fun,' I admitted. 'But I was terrified. I don't know how much good I would have been if I'd had to fight.'

I watched as Isolde approached Ezekiel, who was going through some filing cabinets near one of the desks. She stopped to talk to him, and then he was digging through the cabinet again.

'Well,' Anyan said, 'that's what we're going to work on next. I wish I could tell you that fighting didn't matter, that you wouldn't have to duke it out with anybody. But with everything that's been happening, that's not realistic. Now that your shields are strong—' he began, reminding me of what I'd been thinking. Before he could continue with his master plans for me, I interrupted.

'Anyan, why didn't the women just bust out of here? Where were their powers? And . . .'

Before I could continue, I saw Isolde approaching from the corner of my eye. Ezekiel was with her, and she was holding a file folder.

'Zeke just found this,' the baobhan sith said, her expression grim. She passed the folder over to Anyan but studiously avoided my own eyes.

Anyan read the writing on the folder, then opened it. I watched his big features fall, and I knew. I held out my hands, and he looked at them for a moment before balancing the file in my outstretched palms.

The tab at the top of the file folder read 'Succubus, Iris'. Inside was a bundle of half-completed forms, but they weren't important to me. What was important was the word stamped on the front of the top paper.

That word was 'Terminated'.

Chapter Fifteen

When I heard the scratching at my door, I was lying on my belly, half under my bed, trying to flush out my deodorant. I'd dropped it and it had rolled away like a captured thing finally offered release.

It was only a few hours since I'd read about Iris's death in that file folder. Anyan had checked us into a hotel in downtown Providence, where we'd be staying for a few days. There were witnesses to question, and Ryu's team was meeting us tomorrow. So I'd focused on what we had coming, rather than what had happened. I'd deal with Iris's death later, when Jarl had been brought down.

In the meantime, to keep busy, I figured I'd do some hand washing. I had a little pile of dirty things that I'd taken out of my duffel, and I felt as if the world would be a slightly better place if I made those soiled clothes clean.

But then my deodorant escaped and I'd had to recapture it. Which brings me back to the scratching . . .

What the hell? I thought as I froze, still half under the bed. The scratching was repeated, a bit louder this time.

I stood cautiously, then padded over to the hotel door so I could peer out. There was nothing to be seen at eye level, but when I looked down I could see the flashing tip of a wagging tail.

I thought we were past the hiding in plain sight as a dog thing, I thought as I unlocked my door to let Anyan in.

'Jane,' he rumbled, his big doggie face peering up into mine.

'Anyan,' I replied cautiously. What did he want?

'Can we talk?'

I sighed. Anyan had kept trying to engage me in a heart-to-heart earlier, but I was totally not in the mood.

'I was just sort of getting organized,' I explained, pointing at my piles of clean and dirty clothes. 'I thought I'd do some hand washing . . .'

'That's great. I can keep you company,' the big dog replied, pushing his enormous head through the door and padding past me.

'Great,' I said, my voice sarcastic.

Anyan came in, sniffing around. I looked around for a newspaper or magazine to whack him with if he took a sniff at my laundry. Finally, he jumped up on the king-sized bed, twisting about in a few tight circles until he settled down.

I closed the door and locked it, leaning back against it as I watched the barghest speculatively.

'Go ahead and take care of your stuff; I'll just hang out.'

I narrowed my eyes at Anyan. 'You just want to hang out?'

'Iris was my friend, too, Jane. If you must know, I don't really want to be alone right now.'

I felt my spine stiffen, and a wave of grief threatened to wash over me.

No time, I reprimanded myself harshly, clenching my fists and heading over to my pile of dirty laundry.

I scrabbled at the pile, realizing my hands were shaking as I kept dropping things. But I persevered, unwilling to let my sadness get the best of me. When everything was collected, I headed into the bathroom where the sink and my Woolite awaited.

When I was finished, and my few pairs of dirty panties and bras were hanging, clean and wrung out, over the shower curtain railing, I took a second to collect myself. Staring into my own black eyes reflected in the bathroom mirror, I took a few calming breaths before going into the main room to confront Anyan.

'All done?' the big dog asked. He was lying on his stomach, his front paws hanging off the side of the bed, his back legs stretched out behind him. I couldn't help but smile at his position, and his tail wagged in response.

'Can we talk?' he asked again, causing all smiles to cease.

'About what?'

'About what we found today. About Iris. About how you're feeling.'

I sighed. I didn't want to talk. And I really didn't want to feel.

'Please?' he asked.

'I don't really want to,' I said. 'I just . . . don't.'

'Okay. I just want to know what you're thinking.'

'I'm not thinking about anything.'

Anyan's muzzle split into a doggie grin, his tongue lolling. 'Jane, you're always thinking. Please, just talk to me. A little. For my sake?'

Those oddly human iron-gray eyes staring at me from that fuzzy face broke me.

'Fine,' I said. 'The truth is, I've been thinking about the book of Job.'

'Job?'

'Job,' I confirmed unhelpfully.

'Well, what have you been thinking about, when you think

of Job?' the barghest replied, his voice oozing patience, warning me he wasn't a dog that gave up.

I rolled my shoulders, trying to work the knot of tension that had formed sometime between looking at that file folder and sitting here with Anyan.

'Sit by me,' he urged. 'Tell me.'

I sat down on the end of the bed, my butt near the end of his tail. I didn't want to be too close and I definitely didn't want to see those gray eyes.

'You know I wasn't raised with religion,' I said, 'except the vague pseudopaganism of Jason's grandparents Nick and Nan.'

Anyan's tail thwapped gently against my lower back in affirmation.

'So when we were about thirteen, Jason and I decided to read the Bible together, mostly to see what all the hubbub was about. Both of us became slightly obsessed with the book of Job. Jason thought it was a great story, and he liked how it highlighted the character of Jehovah: He of the sound and the fury. But I'd never understood how anyone, at any historical time period, could ever have found comfort in such a myth.'

I paused, trying to figure out what I was going to say next. Anyan responded by scooching around the bed so his big front paws draped next to my thighs. He wasn't going to make this easy.

'And now?' he prompted.

'And now . . . now I get it. I get what it feels like to cry out like that . . . into oblivion.'

'Well, you've lost a lot, Jane. Asking why is natural.'

'Yeah, but what's the point, Anyan?' I demanded, my voice suddenly heated. 'Job, at least, got something. It was a distinctly unsatisfying nonanswer to his question, but it was *something*. The whirlwind's response to him might have sucked, but it *spoke*. The very act of speech implied that this tempest that had brought such tragedy to Job's life had *something* behind it. In other words, that voice spoke of intent, cementing the idea that things happened for a reason, even if those reasons were incomprehensible to Job.

'But when I rage into the whirlwind? I get bubkes, Anyan. When I grieve, my tears are met with silence; and when I rage, apparently Jarl merely laughs and plans a new set of atrocities.'

'So what do you want to do?'

'I need to stop questioning. I need to stop *thinking*. I need to *act*.'

'What do you mean, act?'

'I need to take down Jarl,' I replied. Before Anyan could contradict me, I spoke again. 'I know Jarl's Alfar, and one of the most powerful Alfar at that. I know that besides all of the power at his fingertips, he also has the backing of the king and queen and every other Alfar in their court.

'But none of that matters. He *has* to be stopped. And if that means being Jane True isn't good enough, that's fine. I can change – until I'm smart enough, strong enough, and ruthless enough to stop that bastard.'

My voice, gone loud, rolled through the hotel room, a little vehement and strained even to my own ears. But I meant every word.

I'm so tired of being weak, I thought, feeling my fists clench as a wave of pain and anger threatened my cool facade.

Instead of confronting me as I expected, Anyan responded by shifting onto his side so that the top of his head was pressed against my hip.

'Can you scratch right behind my shoulder blade?' he asked, to my surprise.

'What?'

'Can you scratch behind my shoulder blade. It's been itching for a while, even before I shifted. I was hoping you could scratch it for me.'

I stared down at the barghest, confused. Normally he was the first to yell at me when I tried to go all Battle Jane. Then I shrugged and started scratching, my nails digging harder into his side as he growled and panted. I smiled, then blushed as I remembered this was *Anyan*, not just a black dog. My fingers slowed, then stopped. He reacted to my cessation of scratching with an ear flicked toward me and a gray eye rolled back to give me a 'oh hell no' look, so I started scratching again.

Finally, he grunted, 'Stop.'

He stood up and shook himself, a cloud of black fur falling onto my previously pristine bedspread. 'That was great. Now, we talk for real.'

I frowned. I'd really thought he was going to let me be . . .

'You're angry,' he said.

A loud snort was my only reply.

'But you can't just be feeling anger?' Anyan prodded.

'No,' I replied. 'I'm not. In fact, I'm pushing the anger away. I just want to act, Anyan. Rage and grief have never gotten me anywhere. They didn't bring my mother back when she'd disappeared all those years ago, nor did they resurrect Jason. And they aren't going to revenge either Iris's or my mother's murder.'

'So is that what you want? Revenge?'

I laughed, but it was a dry, pained sound.

'Yes, Anyan! I really, *really* want revenge,' I whispered finally, in a voice so cold and intent it could have been Jarl himself speaking.

Anyan moved around so that he was facing me, one leg

hanging off the bed awkwardly so that he was far enough forward to look me in the face.

'What's going on, Jane?' he asked, as if I hadn't just said exactly what I felt.

'I told you,' I replied petulantly.

'No, you're talking about what you want, but you haven't said anything about how you really feel. That's what worries me.'

I kept staring straight ahead at the flat-screen TV across from me, refusing to meet Anyan's eyes. But I could feel the soft pant of his breath swirling the hair hanging about my face.

I knew he wasn't going to stop, not until he'd gotten whatever it was he wanted from me.

'I just feel . . . like I'm past feeling,' was what I finally came up with.

'Hmm,' was the barghest's only response.

'"Hmm" what?' I demanded, when I realized that was all I was getting.

'I don't like the idea of you not feeling.'

'Well, it makes sense to me, Anyan. Since all I get to feel recently seems to be bad things. So I'd rather just work. Be active. Stop thinking and do stuff.'

Anyan took his time thinking through what I'd said.

'Is it working?' he asked finally.

'Is what working?'

'Not feeling.'

'Yes. I think so. I don't know. I feel numb. Numb is good.'

'But numb's a feeling. You've had a lot of shocks recently, Jane. You can't expect yourself to recover quickly—'

'This isn't about me, Anyan. It's about my mother, and Iris. I tried grieving, and I tried getting angry, but nothing works. They're still dead, and whoever killed them is still out there. My hurting is just . . . weak. And I need to be strong.'

'Is feeling hurt weak?'

'Of course it is, Anyan. I don't see you running around crying. And people fear you; do what you tell them to do.'

'And is that what you want? People to fear you?'

'Yes. No. I don't know!' At this point, I was nearly shouting, I was so frustrated. Why couldn't he just understand me, and leave me be?

'The Jane True I knew wouldn't want people to fear her,' was all Anyan said, calm in the face of my frustration.

'Well, I let grief get the best of me before. When my mom left, and again when Jason died. And look what it got me. That Jane gets stomped on. A lot. It's not much fun being that Jane.'

'So what would the new Jane be like?'

'She wouldn't take shit. She'd strike first. She'd have the strength to do what needed to be done, and her friends wouldn't die because of her.'

'That sounds like quite an extreme Jane.'

'Stop mocking me, Anyan.'

'I'm not mocking you. I just want you to hear yourself; hear what you're saying.'

'What's wrong with it? It's true.'

'It's a version of the truth, yes. But it's not the whole truth, or the only truth. You're forgetting that there are all types of strengths, and when we embrace new ways of being, we have to let other ways of being go.'

'Well, I really want to embrace some strength, Anyan. I'm tired of being powerless.'

'Who says you're powerless?'

'Jarl. Nyx. Phaedra. Graeme . . .'

'So, the bad guys think you're powerless.'

'Exactly.'

'But how do they define power?'

'I know what you're doing, Anyan. Stop trying to Dr Phil me.'

'I'm not, Jane. Like I said, I want you to think through what you're saying. Tell me what Jarl defines as power.'

'Ruthlessness. Cunning. Strength of magic . . .'

'And you want to become all these things?'

'Yes, Anyan! I do! Jesus, what do you want from me? Do you want me to be somebody who keeps getting her ass kicked, and her friends killed?'

'Is that all that's happened in these past months?'

'I swear to the gods that if you answer one more of my questions with a question, I am going to go all Tyson and bite your damned ear off . . .'

Frustration was welling up inside as the pinpricks of angry tears stung the corners of my eyes.

'What would your father have to say to your becoming ruthless, and cunning, and—'

My head whipped around toward Anyan as I felt the tears overflow my eyes. 'Don't you dare bring up my father, you bastard!' I choked, as hot rivulets ran down my cheeks.

Anyan's only response was to lean forward and gently lap the tears from my face. And, just as he knew it would, his gentle touch broke me. After all, I always fucking cried on dog-Anyan, as the manipulative little shit knew full well.

Within seconds I found myself sobbing, almost hysterically, as all the pent-up anger and sadness and frustration came pouring out of me. Anyan dragged himself forward a bit, the leg hanging off the bed following him like a dead thing, so that I could bury my head in his ruff.

'That's it,' his gruff dog-voice murmured. 'Let it out.'

I buried my face deeper into his wiry fur, beginning to

shake as an overwhelming sense of loneliness crashed over me.

Your mother is dead and your father is sick, came an insidious whisper through my head. *Soon you will be all alone . . . more alone than you ever thought possible.*

Suddenly and overwhelmingly terrified, I began to shake, as the faces of every loved one I could lose began to flash before me.

'Jane? Honey?' Anyan asked, his voice gentle but also betraying a whisper of worry. I don't think he'd intended for me to let go *quite* so much.

'They're all going to leave,' I said through my sobs, although I was so snotty and incoherent it came out sounding like, 'Der ah gonna leab,' and Anyan shook his doggie-head.

'Sorry?' he asked. My shaking increased, alarming even to myself, and I asked for the one thing I knew would comfort me, not worrying about the fact this was Anyan. I just needed to know I wasn't alone.

Hold me, I thought.

'Hoad be,' is what I asked.

But this time the barghest was able to translate my Boogerian. Before I could repeat myself, the air around me shimmered with Anyan's power until strong arms encircled me. Then my tears were wetting the crinkly chest hair of Anyan-the-Man, rather than dog-Anyan's coarse ruff.

Shock ran through my system as Anyan pulled me closer. I'd wanted to feel comforted, wanted a hug, but my body surprised me by reacting with a whole passel of other sensations above and beyond comfort. As if I'd depressed a button my crying stopped, but Anyan wasn't going to let up on me. I felt his large hand wrap itself around my hair, again knotting it roughly at the nape of my neck. He tugged my head back to meet my black eyes with his iron-gray gaze.

'I know it hurts, honey. I know you want to bury everything. But you have to keep feeling, Jane. This is important. *You have to keep feeling.*'

I stared into his strong face, trembling not only at the closeness and the heat of his body but at the depth of emotion I saw swirling in his eyes.

I thought of his long life, and the terrible things I knew he'd seen, and done.

'Do you still feel?' I managed to choke out finally around the knot that had developed in my throat.

Anyan's hand in my hair tightened – not enough to hurt, but enough to emphasize his next words, which rumbled through his chest into my own. It would be years later that I fully understand everything he was telling me. But, at that moment, I understood enough.

'Of course, Jane. It's the only thing that keeps us human.'

I thought of the inhuman calm of the Alfar, and the cold viciousness of Jarl and Phaedra, and tears welled anew in my eyes.

Anyan pulled me against his chest again gently, and I relaxed in his hold, letting the tears flow. I cried for Iris, and for my mother. I cried for my father, and I cried for myself. And I cried because I could – because to do other than feel under such circumstances would mean I'd become something other than Jane True.

The grieving hurt, yes. But it was real, and it was right, and I knew Anyan would keep me safe while I let myself go.

Which is exactly what he did until, finally, my pain subsided and those other feelings again surfaced. For Anyan's skin was hot against my cheek, and I knew there was a lot of skin to be had.

All together now: 'Clothes don't shift with the shape,' my virtue commented drily. *You really need to start remembering that fact.*

I remembered, my libido purred, willing me to look downward.

Feeling myself blush, I finally pulled away from Anyan while carefully avoiding looking anywhere but into his eyes.

'Um . . .' I started, unsure of how to thank him. Or how to extricate myself from him without seeing his junk.

'Ice cream?' he interrupted before I could continue.

'Sorry?'

'Do you wanna go for ice cream? I would take you to White Castle, but there isn't one in Rhode Island.'

I couldn't help but laugh. 'Um, I think I'd take ice cream over onion-burps anyway.'

Anyan grinned as the very tip of his nose twitched. 'Philistine.'

'Whatever.'

'Okay, my clothes are in my room. No shoes, no shirt, no service, and all . . .'

I blushed even redder and looked down at my own lap – the better to avoid looking at his.

'Um, sure. Right. I'll be here.'

Anyan rose from the bed next to me and padded away on bare feet. I squeezed my eyes shut, mustering every ounce of self-control I had. Until I heard him pause at the door, opening it slowly to check for safe passage, and I imagined him standing there . . .

Don't do it, Jane . . . Don't you dare . . .

Luckily, I've never had any willpower. After about one whole second of being good, my eyes were latched onto

Anyan's ass. I sighed contentedly as the barghest flexed his way around the corner and out of sight.

The girl behind the counter at the local Ben & Jerry's Scoop Shop was your typical slightly overskinny but otherwise adorable skater chick. She had amazing tattooed sleeves peeking out of her uniform, and a cheeky smile I couldn't help but return.

It helped that she was currently scooping out copious amounts of Mint Chocolate Cookie ice cream into a steel cup to make me a milkshake. I automatically liked pretty much anyone who fed me, and feeding me ice cream bought even strangers pure adoration.

I watched with avid eyes as she finished scooping my choice, then began scooping Chubby Hubby for Anyan. I was so distracted by watching her cut a swath through a particularly thick vein of peanut butter that I barely registered when Anyan excused himself to use the bathroom.

Anyan had just left the room and the pretty, blonde skater girl was just setting both steel cups into their blenders when, all of a sudden, everything went black.

I don't mean the lights went off, I mean my *world* went black. And quiet. I couldn't hear the telltale buzz of power from anywhere, but I still automatically raised my shields as I called forth a swirling, iron-gray orb of energy into my palm.

'Who's there?' I called into the darkness tremulously.

No answer.

'Come on! Who's there?'

Around me in the darkness, light flared as patterns began to appear in the black.

Dark purple vines began to snake around me, growing in a random pattern. Turquoise flowers sprouted from the ends of some of the vines, their stamens a lurid, fluorescent pink.

Pouring power into my shields, I searched the darkness for an enemy even as I searched for any ping of power. But I felt and heard nothing.

'Who is *out there*!' I shouted, my calm cracking underneath the oppressive hush. I made a circle, starting to panic as the vines began to float toward me, closing in on me like Briar Rose in the grip of her curse.

I kept circling till my eyes caught a glimmer of white light that appeared in the purple ivy. The glimmer grew to a crack, which grew into a sliver, which grew into a door large enough for a skinny girl.

And Blondie is exactly who came through, only the Ben & Jerry's Scoop Shop uniform was gone and she was naked. Her lithe frame was entirely tattooed, and hoops gleamed in her nipples. She came toward me, that cheeky grin still cutting across her features.

I raised the hand with the mage ball, only to find it suddenly empty.

'Who the fuck are you?' I shouted, just as she reached up to me.

I flinched back, shielding my face with my arms, but nothing happened. I could hear her chuckling, and I finally peeked around my hands to find her standing there, holding out two milkshakes, with napkins and straws.

I blinked at her, and her smile grew bigger. Eventually I dropped my arms, and she came forward with our ice cream.

The unnatural foliage around us finally began to shake as power – but none I recognized – began to swirl around us. As I raised my own hands to take the milkshakes, she nodded.

Then, with a bawdy wink, everything went black again.

I blinked once . . . twice . . .

Then found myself standing in the middle of the Providence, Rhode Island, Scoop Shop, holding two milkshakes while, next to me, Anyan stared at me like I'd lost my marbles.

I looked from him to the girl on the other side of the counter. She was short and chubby, with a bad complexion and lank brown hair.

I looked at her, then at the shakes, then back to Anyan.

'Uhh . . . weren't you . . . blonde?' I asked hesitantly.

'Huh?' she asked, looking at me like I was extra loony.

I sighed, then handed Anyan his milkshake. He raised an eyebrow and twitched his nose at me, hard.

'Here's your milkshake. And while you were in the bathroom, everything went black, then purple shit grew out of the dark, and then I was approached by a hot, naked, tattoo-advert chick. Who used to be her,' I said, pointing at the brown-haired girl across the counter. 'But she was blonde and made us milkshakes. Then she disappeared and changed into that one.'

The girl behind the counter backed away slowly as Anyan sucked on his straw, staring at me curiously.

Finally, he shrugged and held out his milkshake toward me, straw first, so I could taste.

'Well, it seems simple enough. Either someone is fucking with you, or you're having a nervous breakdown. Want a sip?'

I blinked at him. *The joy of comforting words. Barghest-style.*

Chapter Sixteen

'So everything went black, purple ivy grew, and then she gave you a milkshake?' came Ryu's dry voice from the backseat, where he sat beside Caleb. Daoud and Julian were wedged into the small seats in the very, very back of the enormous gas-guzzler we'd rented.

My former lover made what I'd said sound even crazier, and it already sounded pretty batpants. Ryu had talents, after all.

'Yup,' I replied from the front seat, watching Anyan's hands on the steering wheel of our rented SUV.

'And there was no power signature?' Ryu prodded.

'Nope, nothing. Only at the very end did I feel . . . something.'

'But not elemental magics?'

'No.'

'First Magics?'

'If First Magic feels like what Terk does, then no. It didn't feel like that at all.'

I could see, in my side mirror, Ryu frowning, his handsome features scrunching up as he sucked on his bottom lip. My libido, ever clueless, made a hesitant suggestion, which I immediately and firmly quashed.

'Anyan?' the baobhan sith asked, after a few seconds more of petulant lip-sucking.

'No clue,' the barghest grunted from beside me, his nose twitching.

We were driving to the safe house right outside Providence where the local Powers That Be had stashed the females rescued from the laboratory. In the wee hours of the morning, Ryu, Caleb, Daoud, and Julian had arrived to begin officially questioning the freed hostages. I had been very happy to see everyone from Boston again, although I did miss Julian's baobhan-sith mother, Camille. She was serving as Ryu's replacement while he traveled.

'Could it have been a really powerful glamour?' Caleb rumbled forth.

'Anyan would have felt the magic,' Daoud replied. 'Unless the person was so powerful they could mask all trace of their power.'

'And there hasn't been anyone, even Alfar, that strong since before the Third Great War,' Ryu cut in, clearly frustrated.

'Was that a long time ago?' I queried the barghest sotto voce.

'Yup. About eight hundred years.'

'What was that?' Ryu's voice cut in from behind us.

'Nothing!' Anyan and I both responded, too quickly and as one.

The car went silent. Ryu's irritation was palpable.

Caleb, bless him, was the first to stick his neck out. 'I think the obvious question, Jane, is whether you think this could have been some sort of . . . episode.'

I couldn't help but smile.

'Like a nervous breakdown?'

'Well . . . yes.'

'I have been rather stressed,' I said, wryly. 'But you're

right, Caleb. I think it's a distinct possibility. After all, I saw Blondie, when Anyan saw only the dark-haired girl. And neither of us felt any magic, except for that one moment, but it wasn't . . . normal magic.'

'Could it have been drugs?' called out Julian from the very back of the SUV. 'When, exactly, were you given the milk-shakes?'

'We don't *use* drugs,' Ryu broke in snippily.

Caleb's calm voice overrode Ryu's, to my surprise. 'True, it is not our nature to use science or its by-products, but these are not normal times. Perhaps Daoud has a point. Jane?'

'Sorry,' I said. 'I wasn't given my ice cream until after my psychic break from reality.'

Anyan shook his head once sharply. 'Jane, you didn't have a psychic break. You were fine. Something's going on; we just have to figure out what it is.'

'And pray that whoever has that kind of power, to make you see shit that's not there without exposing themselves at all, isn't working for the bad guys,' said Daoud, his voice grim.

We all processed that information in silence, the only sound the computer-calm voice of our GPS telling us where to turn on our way to our destination. When we finally arrived at the safe house, it revealed itself to be a large, very baronial mansion in a wealthy suburb. Gathering our things we headed inside, pushing through various layers of magical shieldings as Ryu 'knocked' with his own power and was allowed through.

Inside the house everything was clean, expensive, and vaguely institutional. Healers and guards wandered around, increasing the hospital feel of the otherwise beautiful surroundings. The women were being housed on the second floor, in separate bedrooms. They'd all been in various states of serious disrepair and had needed quite a bit of medical attention.

And after what they'd been through, I could only imagine what sort of help they'd need to begin to recover from the trauma of their incarceration and torture.

We'd been ushered into a small reception room to the right of the landing to wait for the Rhode Island investigators to meet us. Ryu had been given carte-blanche authority in the region, but ever the political animal, he didn't want to step on any toes unless he had to. So we waited for Isolde, but it was Ezekiel who arrived, his ifrit fire banked to only a glow of flames surrounding his wiry figure.

'Sorry I'm late. I was . . . detained.'

'It's no trouble,' Ryu said smoothly. 'But where's Isolde?'

A look of barely contained fury crossed the ifrit's face as his fire flared up like a geyser until he regained his control.

'She's been pulled from duty,' he said, his voice tight.

'What?' Anyan barked, his growly voice extra-growly.

'She's been fired, Anyan. For not capturing the kappa.'

'But he was going to kill that female,' I interjected. 'She did the right thing.'

The ifrit gave me a short, dismissive look. 'Not according to the Alfar. According to the Alfar, we are all expendable, and the knowledge contained in the kappa was more important than any of our lives . . .'

Ezekiel's voice trailed off as he glanced at Ryu. 'I'm sure they have their reasons, of course,' he concluded begrudgingly. 'But Isolde is a good investigator and a damned fine female. She didn't deserve to be dismissed like that.'

Ryu's expression went blank, like it did when he was machinating. 'You're right, Zeke. Isolde was a good investigator. But we all have our orders —'

'Orders, my hairy ass,' Anyan interrupted from behind me.

Ryu turned, his expression furious, but the ever-calming Caleb intervened.

'Let's remember why we're here, gentlemen. Upstairs are females who don't need to see any more violence.'

I could have licked Caleb for his ever-present good sense.

Both Anyan and Ryu frowned at each other but nodded at Caleb.

We were taken upstairs, to another, smaller room that was set up like a small informal therapy area with a few chairs and a couch. Caleb, Julian, and Daoud stayed outside, but I was allowed in with Anyan and Ryu.

The first woman to come in was the kappa female. She was even shorter than the male kappa had been, and her skin was the same, wrinkled-green flesh of a sea turtle. She, too, wore a shell, and I wondered if she could take it on and off, like a coat, or if it was fused onto her. Her human eyes peered nervously around the room from her turtle face.

Meanwhile, healthwise she looked terrible. Physically she'd been healed, but she still looked terribly frail. I could also tell she was suffering being outside the sea. More to the point, however, her haunted eyes testified more eloquently than mere words to the horrors she'd endured.

'Ula Kappa,' she introduced herself quietly when she'd taken a seat.

'Hello, Ula,' Ryu said, his voice saturated with warmth and friendliness. But the kappa ignored him, flinching down into her shell and avoiding looking at either Ryu or Anyan. Instead, she kept her eyes focused on me.

I tried to smile at her but failed. Instead, I met her eyes with mine, trying silently to acknowledge her pain without implying I could ever understand it.

She met my gaze for what felt like minutes but could only have been seconds. Then she nodded, and, when she spoke, the voice emitted from her beaklike protrusion was as soft and breathy as a young girl's.

'You're of the sea,' she said.

I nodded. 'My mother is . . . was . . . a selkie.'

I realized that was the first time I'd referred to my mother in the past tense, and I shivered.

'I want to go back to the water,' Ula said. It wasn't a demand, just a statement.

'I know. And you will. Soon.'

'Yes. Now that he's dead. I would never have been safe with my cousin still alive.'

Forgetting what I knew of the sea folk and interpreting her words literally, I nearly choked.

'That was . . . that was your *cousin*?' I asked, horror infusing my voice.

Her smile was small and bitter. 'We are all cousins, those of us who live for the sea.'

Of course, I remembered, thinking of the Sea Code . . . and reminded again of just how thoroughly that damned kappa had shat upon it. 'But he . . .'

'Yes,' was all she said, but her soft voice reverberated with her feelings of betrayal. 'He captured us, which is not our way. But he was wrong – twisted inside. As well as very powerful.'

I recalled vividly how well the kappa manipulated my own ocean against me, and I nodded.

'He's gone now,' Anyan said gently.

Ula shrank even lower into her shell, her eyes flicking toward the barghest.

'Ula,' I said, beginning to see what was going on. She was okay with me, as I was another female. Her prison guards had all been men, and I was beginning to understand the nature of some of the 'experiments' they had undoubtedly performed.

'Ula, we need to know everything you can tell us about who captured you, what they did, and who else you might have seen coming and going in that laboratory. We need to know all of these things because we want to capture the people responsible and make sure this can't happen again. Okay?'

The kappa nodded, although her face bespoke her agony.

'You can tell us anything. Please . . .'

She nodded, shifting around in her shell and knotting her small green hands in her lap.

'I was captured about one month ago. I thought the male was interested in mating, and that I was protected by the Code. So the fight was not much of a fight.'

The kappa's small voice was carefully controlled, but I knew how much it hurt her to admit her weakness. She coughed slightly, and I went to fetch her water from a side table that held a pitcher and glasses. When I returned, I sat down next to her on the sofa rather than returning to my own chair. She took the water, drank, then turned toward me as if we were the only two in the room.

'I was in the laboratory the longest. The other females have only been there a week or two, at most. The havsrå was only just captured. Others were there before me, and others came after. They didn't . . . they didn't survive.' Her breath caught and I placed a hand on her wrinkly green knee for comfort.

'I only survived because I was considered less . . . inter-esting than the other females.' Her small, gray-nailed hand scrabbled at my own, and I grasped it.

'I don't know anything about human science,' she said. 'But what they did, it wasn't *anything*. It wasn't . . . it couldn't have . . .'

'There was no point to it?' I suggested, trying to keep my shit together when what I wanted to do was curl myself around this little female and soak up some of her pain. Not that I could. Not that anybody could.

'No,' she whispered fiercely. 'There was no *point*. Some of the things were made to look like there was a purpose, and a few of the males seemed to think there was a purpose. But most of them were just enjoying hurting us . . . No, they were *all* enjoying hurting us, but some of them were better at acting like they weren't. They called themselves "doctors", like humans do, and they made us call them that as well.'

Her hand was hot and damp in mine and she was nearly crushing my fingers. But I wouldn't have complained under pain of death.

'You saw what became of your captors from the lab, Ula. They can't hurt you anymore. But we have to know, were there others?'

'There was. Or there were. One of the doctors that was there when I was first captured, he snapped and killed himself. He killed one of the prisoners first, then blew his own head off with a mage ball when the other guards came back in the room.'

I gulped. The things this poor female had witnessed . . .

'But for the most part, it was the two doctors you killed, the kappa, and . . . and the Healer.' Ula said the last bit in a whisper so breathy I could barely hear her.

'A healer? As opposed to the doctors?'

'No, *the* Healer. That's what he was called.'

Listening to Ula, my memory started to ping like crazy as déjà vu's pattering little footsteps ran up and down my spine.

'What did the Healer look like, Ula?'

'He was a goblin-halfling. Tall and green-scaled, like a goblin, but with human hands and face.'

As if he were sitting with me in the room, Conleth's voice from so many weeks ago rang in my ears.

'. . . *he looked half lizard. His nose was sort of flat and snakelike, and he was mostly sort of scaly. But his face had human flesh and his eyes were human. And his hands looked human . . . but for his claws . . .*'

'Did the Healer have claws, Ula? Human hands but for claws?'

'Yes,' she gasped. 'His claws . . . How did you know?'

'I've met someone who told me about him,' I said, hearing Ryu and Anyan shift in their chairs on the other side of the room. 'He sounds like a nasty piece of work.'

'He called himself a Healer, but the things he did . . . He just tore through our bodies . . .' For the first time since we'd started talking, Ula's eyes filled with tears. I extricated one of my hands from her grip, squeezing the other to let her know I wasn't letting her go, then passed her a tissue I had stashed in my hoodie's pocket. I glanced quickly at Anyan, and he nodded. Ula had done everything she could for now. Except for one, last question . . .

'Ula? Honey? I understand how you were captured. But how could . . . how could they keep you? Why didn't you use your magic?'

'They gave us shots. Two the day we were captured, then every morning. Something in them made it so we couldn't feel our elements.' Ula let go of my hands in order to grasp the cushions she sat on. I could hear fabric ripping as she tensed. 'And I still can't feel them. I can't feel . . . anything. What if I can never use my magic again?' Her eyes searched mine, her expression pleading, and I could feel her rising panic so palpably it made my flight-or-fight response start to kick off in reaction.

'What if I'm ruined?' she asked finally, her small green face creasing with agony.

'We'll figure out what they did to you,' I hissed,

suddenly furious. 'We will figure out what they did, and then we will fix you. You're not ruined, Ula. Never ruined.'

She sobbed once, hard, and I reached for her. She cried in my arms, and I told her, over and over again, that we would find out what had happened to her.

And I prayed to every god I'd ever heard of, including that of Job, that I was telling the broken little kappa the truth.

Chapter Seventeen

'Do they make something stronger than whisky?' I asked numbly from my corner of the booth.

'Nope. Unless they have moonshine,' was Anyan's only response.

'Then I'll take whisky, too. Make it a double. If they won't sell you the bottle.'

The barghest gave me a grim smile then went to get our drinks, leaving me with Caleb, Daoud, Ryu, and Julian.

We were spread out in one of our fancy hotel's giant, cushy booths, but we all looked like we'd just come from a funeral.

Each of the women had told a similar story of horror, and the healers who attended them had been able to fill in blanks that they were as yet incapable of revealing. Besides rapes and beatings, each of the women had endured different series of bizarre, Dr Mengele-type experiments. One woman had her ovaries replaced with a human's; one had her womb removed and replaced with a bizarre balloonlike contraption; yet another had a human fetus implanted inside her. We didn't even bother to conjecture about what had happened to the pregnant human. By the time they were rescued, most of the women's 'surgeries' were so infected that they'd basically had to be hollowed out, losing any of the female reproductive organs that the 'Healer' and his monstrous cohorts hadn't gotten to first.

And I'd been the one to talk to all of the victims. They'd clammed up, and understandably so, whenever a male spoke to them. Even Ryu – who, for all his flaws, was a master at getting people to trust him – couldn't make a dent. Anyan, with his huge size and intimidating features, didn't stand a chance.

But they'd all talked to me. I was small, and a woman, and the havsrå – an absolutely beautiful creature with perfect female features, except for a strange, hollowed-out back – had commented that she could see I'd been hurt as well. When I told her that the people who captured her were responsible for the deaths of my mother and my close friend, she'd actually tried to comfort me. Her kindness had nearly broken through my attempts at professionalism, considering that her beauty and grace had made her a particular favorite of her captors.

And yet, despite the horrors she'd endured, there was still kindness in her soul.

'Those bastards tried to break those women,' I said rather randomly. 'But they didn't succeed. The females, they're going to be okay.' I nodded my head firmly, as if by saying it I could make it so.

The boys just looked down glumly. I think the fact that they'd had to sit on their hands and be quiet through the women's stories made it all even worse, for them. Especially for Ryu, who was used to being in the center of things. And despite their violent histories, both baobhan sith and the barghest had been horrified by what they'd heard from the women and from what we'd been told in our own healer's reports. My compatriots may have been accustomed to war and certain forms of brutality. But there was a big difference between what happened on a battlefield and the shit some sadist could dream up given time, a female captive, and a lot of pointy medical equipment.

Ryu sidled closer to me in the booth. I was too weary, at that point, to sidle myself away.

'You were amazing today, Jane.'

'Thanks, Ryu. But I just did what I had to do.'

'No, it was incredible how you talked to those women. You were so brave.'

'Somebody has to talk to them. They have to tell their stories. And somebody has to listen.'

Ryu frowned, clearly at a loss for how to talk to me. But after everything we'd heard today, the last thing on earth I wanted was flattery. I wasn't being brave or strong, I was simply in the same position that we *all* were in: doing the best we could to get through the next five minutes.

And to stay human while we do it. That thought managed to bring a small smile to my lips, and my eyes sought out Anyan's big figure at the bar. He was hard at work negotiating with the waitress as I think he was really trying to buy the whole bottle. I'd noticed, over the course of our various adventures, that he never glamoured any humans unless he absolutely had to, and she appeared to be giving him a hard time.

'Jane?' Ryu interrupted my barghest-ogling.

'Sorry, what?'

'I was asking about how you were doing. With Iris and everything.'

'I'm doing okay, actually. I think.'

'I'm very sorry for her loss. And for yours.'

'Thanks,' I said, wishing we could talk about something – anything – else.

'Whisky,' Anyan's gruff voice interrupted as he plonked down a bottle of Black Label and five glasses. 'She wanted a kidney for the Balvenie, so this'll have to do,' he apologized, quite unapologetically.

'Thanks, Anyan,' I said, already reaching for the bottle. 'I am gonna have some booze, and then go to bed. I feel like we've been running a gauntlet all day, I'm so exhausted . . .'

Before I could finish, I felt that familiar, yet ever strange tingle of First Magic, just as Terk apparated in, directly onto my lap.

Fuck, I thought, knowing that whatever the brownie was here for, it would probably mean an end to my early-to-bed fantasies.

The little creature in my lap waved at me, then threw open its arms for a hug. I couldn't help but smile as I leaned forward, wrapping my arms gingerly around its little shape. Terk was so small that I was practically smothering the poor little brownie in my bosom, when Anyan coughed.

'Um, Jane, I really wouldn't . . .'

Before he could finish, Terk pulled back to give Anyan an angry squint with his right three eyes. Then he made a gesture and there was a loud *pop* as a letter apparated onto the low tabletop in front of us.

Terk gave me one last sweet smile, chittered something that sounded rather miffed in Anyan's direction, and then *popped* himself out. After which we all sat, staring at the letter like it might be a bomb.

Finally, Anyan reached forward with a small sigh and opened it. After a few seconds, he read to us its contents.

'It's from Cap. In the last few days they discovered another laboratory in Wisconsin, but still in Borderland territory. Terk flashed everyone in for a raid, right away, and they captured a doctor. The rest of the staff were killed or killed themselves.

The rescued vics were all halflings this time, so they don't want to talk to us. But we can have the doctor now that they're done with their questioning. Cap and the girls are gonna start toward us tonight; we'll meet her halfway and she'll give him to us. There are maps, everything else we need. Bad news is, we need to leave in an hour.'

'Fuck.' Daoud moaned, scrubbing a hand over his face.

We all nodded agreement as Anyan corked the whisky back up. Standing wearily, we made our separate ways to our rooms so we could pack. I was so tired, in fact, that it took me a second to process anything past the fact of my exhaustion. But then I finally realized what we'd just been told: we were finally getting our mitts on one of the doctors. We would finally get some answers; maybe get some proof as to who was really behind these laboratories.

My power crackled about me, the ocean's power surging through me at the thought of getting answers. And of getting our hands on one of the monsters responsible for all the pain to which we'd been witness today.

For a brief moment I fantasized about the doctor in question not talking, and about ways we could loosen his tongue. Then I shuddered, feeling my power and my anger drain away as the havsrå's lovely, gentle face rose in my memory.

Strength doesn't equal violence, I realized suddenly. But then I thought about how good it would feel to kick that damned Healer-monster in the goolies. While wearing a pair of Iris's very pointy designer shoes.

Strength doesn't have to equal violence, I amended. *But sometimes a little violence can go a long way, too.*

'Jane, Anyan . . . Good to see you both,' Capitola said as she gave us each a hug in turn. The tall woman was wearing a simple outfit of jeans, boots, white T-shirt, and leather jacket, but that just made her look all the more like she'd just stepped off the cover of an action-adventure novel. That said, when she got closer, I could see her eyes were shadowed and tired.

We were in Pittsburgh, which we'd settled on as the halfway point between our two parties, and it was about ten hours after we'd gotten the original call from Capitola. I'd slept about four hours as Anyan drove, then we'd switched and he'd stretched out in the backseat while I drove the rest of the way. He'd snored away – and occasionally barked, to my consternation – while I thought about the case, and about what I'd like to do to this 'doctor' when we laid hands on him.

'Sorry we had to make you come all this way,' she apologized, as I watched Moo and Shar emerge from the back of the unmarked white van Cappie had been driving.

'Terk totally exhausted his mojo taking all of us in for the raid. He barely made it back from getting you that last message, but I didn't want to use phones . . . None of us know who to trust anymore.'

'No worries, Cap,' Anyan rumbled. 'How's the prisoner?'

'Alive. Squealed like a pig when first captured, but has since clammed up. No doubt you'll be able to get through, but just in case, I've brought you the tapes and the transcripts . . .'

Capitola kept talking to us, but all my attention was riveted as Ryu, Julian, Daoud, and Caleb stepped up to the white van. Moo and Shar each took a moment to greet Julian warmly. He looked thrilled to see the two women. So thrilled, in fact, that he was like a whole new Julian.

Julian wasn't the show, however – the main attraction was waiting for us in the back of the van. The prisoner was about to emerge, and we were finally going to have our hands on one of the murderous bastards who'd caused so much pain.

Fury beat through my system as I thought of finally coming face-to-face with the kind of shit who could take away a woman's power and then abuse her, as if he were some monstrous god from Greek mythology. There was commotion from the van when something Capitola was saying recaptured my attention.

'. . . and this one's a halfling, like everybody in this lab was, including doctors. A decent fighter, and definitely a damned zealot. Somebody known as the Healer, also a halfling, is recruiting from the Borderlands. That's why we never sensed anything. This batch of vics was all halflings, like I'd said, but they were a new crop. Former "patients" were apparently all purebloods, captured inside the Territory and brought to the border by their fellow purebloods, but then they're given over to halflings. So that's why nobody ever raised any alarms: purebloods never enter, unless they're prisoners.' Capitola sighed, running her hand over her raucous chestnut Afro.

'And this is where it gets extra freaky. We don't sense the pureblood prisoners who enter because they've been given some kind of—'

'Injection,' Anyan grunted. 'We rescued some hostages this side of the border who told us the same thing. Hopefully, whatever it is they've been given probably just needs to wear off, but, in the meantime, they're still cut off from their power.'

Both Anyan and Capitola fell silent, as if processing the horror of something that could steal a creature's magic.

'Does your doctor know who's behind everything? And why are the halflings participating?' I interrupted. After all, if Jarl was running the show and he wanted to purge the world of halflings, it made no sense for creatures like me to participate in his mad schemes.

Capitola shook her head. 'The only person the good doctor

ever met was this "Healer" character. He's apparently a goblin-halfling—'

'Yeah, we know about him,' I interrupted, wanting Cap to get to my question.

'We're gonna have to have a powwow before you leave, Anyan. Looks like you guys have learned as much as we have in the past few days.' Anyan nodded as I cleared my throat, causing Capitola to smile.

'To answer Jane's questions: our prisoner was singing like Pavarotti right up until we asked about the higher-ups. Said the worst we could do wouldn't compare to what they would do, they're scarier than we are, the usual. We couldn't get anything more after that; I'll leave that up to your king and queen.

'As for why someone would be willing to turn on their fellow halflings like that, the shit the Healer promised all his minions is crazy. Basically, despite being a halfling, he hates halflings and wants to be a pureblood. Which ain't gonna happen, obviously, but I guess he thinks he can make up for it somehow . . . probably for the same reasons Hitler worshipped a race that looked the polar opposite of him. Talk about self-loathing. Anyway, as for the "doctor" back there—' Cap jerked a thumb roughly back at the van, which was rocking as Daoud and Caleb tried to clamber into the back. Nobody's fool, Julian watched from the sidelines, cleaning his glasses with the bottom of his shirtfront. 'The Healer apparently promised everyone who worked for him a place in the new world they're "building". And that once they solve the fertility crisis for the purebloods, they'll get to breed with them so their children will be nearly pureblooded . . . Then their children's children can breed with purebloods, etcetera. They're told they'll contribute to a new race. Of course that's not how genetics works, but who needs reason and logic when you get to torture people?'

I nodded. 'I'm sure some of these halflings are fucked up enough, like Conleth was, to believe in crazy-assed ideologies like that. But I'm sure a lot of them just want to cause pain.'

Capitola nodded her own agreement. 'Exactly. The one we captured I think really believes in all the Healer's philosophies. But from what we know they did to their captives, I think it was as much about hurting people as anything else.'

Our philosophical discussion was interrupted, however, as Daoud and Caleb both came stumbling out of the van to land with a thump on their asses. Moo shook her head, stepped forward, and calmly raised an arm. Alfar power bloomed forth, that distinctive blending of all four elements that rushed through the air toward the van.

I moved forward, knowing that our enemy – or one of them, at least – was finally to be revealed.

Only to gasp as what floated out of the van, surrounded by a sparkling nimbus of Moo's power, turned out to be . . .

A female.

She was middling height and weight, and wearing scrubs. Her hair was sandy brown; her eyes brown as well. She looked unutterably average.

And yet she'd been willing to sell out her own people, and to stand by as other women were raped and abused, because she'd been lured by the Healer's promise of (maybe, someday) having children that were more 'pure' than her?

I knew my jaw had dropped, but neither Anyan nor Ryu seemed bothered that the 'doctor' was a woman. Then again, I supposed it made sense. I'd been raised human, in a world where a little extra upper-body strength, a few inches of average height, and some extra pounds of average weight meant men were, for the most part, physically stronger than women. That left us vulnerable in certain situations, no matter how much we hated to admit it.

But in the supe world, who cared if you couldn't bench-press a couple hundred pounds using your muscles when you could loft a thousand using your magic? Tiny females like Phaedra could, quite literally, rip apart the most muscle-bound human male without even blinking. So power and mastery, I realized, weren't tied up with gender for the supes as they were for humans.

Moo lowered the struggling prisoner to her feet, and then, to my surprise, the Alfar-halfling exerted enough pressure to force the woman to her knees. My gaze flicked to Moo's face, and I saw that behind her calm, Alfar exterior lurked menace and anger. As if sensing her friend's mood, both Cap and Shar strode forward to each place a gentle hand on Moo's shoulder. The statuesque woman blinked once, her power gathering, before she blinked again and it dispersed, leaving Daoud, Ryu, and Caleb responsible for the 'doctor' at their feet.

Cap stroked a hand across Moo's shoulders as Shar put an arm around Moo's waist. She blinked again in response, and for a second I wondered if she was forcing back tears. Then it hit me.

Anyan said her father was a god-king who made her his consort . . . In modern times, we call that child abuse. I shivered, my heart going out to the beautiful woman before me who was busy burying her pain behind her pride.

And maybe supernatural society isn't so different from human. 'Cause the minute a female is vulnerable, she's not used to play tiddlywinks.

Shaking my head to dislodge unwelcome thoughts, I saw Caleb reach forward to pull the woman to her feet. Even the satyr, who was always so calm and kind, looked like he only barely managed to keep his actions from becoming violent. Then he frog-marched her to the SUV in which the Boston crew had arrived, placing her in the back, where he joined her. Ryu turned to thank Capitola, then nodded at Anyan before he got in the driver's seat, Daoud sitting shotgun.

Anyan took Capitola aside to tell her everything we'd discovered in Rhode Island, and I took that moment to approach the 'doctor's' window. I stared inside until she belligerently raised her eyes to meet my own. She looked scared, and desperate, despite trying to maintain a mutinous facade.

I studied the woman before me, but overwhelming even my anger was a feeling of profound disgust for someone who could break every possible covenant invented by any society, even Alfar, through her sadism, her contempt for life, and a selfishness so profound it would kill any morality or conscience she might once have possessed.

For once, I didn't loathe handing somebody over to Alfar 'justice'. And I refused to feel bad about that fact.

Chapter Eighteen

We were all staring at the good doctor's door as if contemplating . . . well, murder. Mostly because I think we were all, genuinely, contemplating murder.

That was part of the reason Ryu had gotten the three-bedroom suite. We'd all been worn out from the past few days *before* driving to Pittsburgh, so, after a brief discussion, we'd decided to bunk down in the city for a night. Nobody else knew where we were or what we were doing besides Morrigan, as Ryu had immediately let her know because he was a good little investigator.

With our frayed nerves and our exhausted bodies, I don't know if Dr Death would have survived the car ride back to the Territory. She still might not survive our overnighting in Pittsburgh, but as long as none of could see her she was, if not safe, saf*er*.

So we'd rented a big suite in a big hotel, asking for a room that was very far up off the ground. We'd stuck our prisoner in one of the bedrooms and sealed the door behind her. Then we'd tried to act like she wasn't there, so that we didn't kill her. That said, I caught even our equable satyr, Caleb, staring at the door with fire in his eyes.

When Ryu suggested cards, I think everyone was relieved except for me, as I sucked at card games. So I turned on the television to pretend I was watching Paula Deen add butter to sour cream, while the boys started playing. Julian also eschewed the game, coming to sit by me, instead. I watched him as he sat down. He'd been so quiet since joining us to retrieve our captive – very contemplative and dour. In fact, if I was reading him correctly, he looked a little lost.

So after a few minutes, I decided to take action, Jane-style. Sliding to Julian's side of the couch, I cuddled against him, my cheek against his sternum. It wasn't sexual, obviously: he wasn't into lady bits. But I also knew he needed comfort, and I had a feeling I knew what was bothering him. Julian had caught a glimpse of another way to live as a halfling, but now he was back to his 'normal' life. I knew the others on his team loved Julian, and they didn't think of him as less than them because he was a halfling. But other people in the Territory undoubtedly made up for his cohorts' acceptance by degrading his mixed blood, and I knew from my own experience how silent persecution could be just as painful and ostracizing as shouts and curses.

He stiffened when I first snuggled up against him, but after a few moments he dropped a kiss on the top of my head, and he let his arm fall around me to give me an admittedly rather awkward pat. Finally he relaxed, for what must have been the first time since I'd clapped eyes on him upon his return. We sat like that for about five minutes, before I sat up, leaving my warmth pressed up against him so that he knew I was still there, but no longer smothering him in selkie-halfling.

Unfortunately, while I'm glad I could make Julian feel a bit better, he was definitely the only one in the room who felt that way. Within fifteen minutes of sitting down to play cards, Anyan and Ryu were snipping at each other, while

Daoud and Caleb rolled their eyes. Meanwhile, I was spending more time watching that door than I spent watching the Food Network's fatfest unfold before me. I couldn't stop thinking of our captive, and what she might or might not have done.

What if she was one of the ones who killed my mother? I thought. *Or Iris?*

My focus at that point was so riveted on the door, my hands clenching into fists, that when I felt a hand wrap around my hair and tug, I nearly leaped out of my skin.

'C'mon, starey-pants. Let's go outside.'

Anyan's rough voice instantly calmed me, as did the heavy weight of his hand in my hair. I hadn't realized how tense I'd gotten until that moment. Of course, I realized I was tense because my body melted like a pat of butter on one of Paula Deen's hush puppies at his touch, much to my embarrassment.

'Yes. Outside,' I agreed a little breathlessly.

The barghest smiled as the tip of his nose twitched. 'We can work on your quick-draw mage balls, Jesse James.'

I couldn't help but grin as I unfolded myself from the uncomfortable little couch I'd nestled into. Ryu watched our progress to the door from where he sat, still playing cards with Daoud and Caleb. Ryu's expression was dark, but he didn't put down his hand.

When we got out of the hotel I took a long, deep breath of the still-chilly, wet spring air, feeling my lungs fill and then release with a grateful sigh. It was a gross day out, to be honest: damp and dreary. But the water around me, and the storm brewing above, also made my water-magics tingle with the power in the surrounding air.

Anyan smiled at me, then nodded toward the little park that was across from our hotel.

'Let's go over there. Work on some combat moves.'

After we'd wandered over to the park, we both boosted our shields and raised mage balls. I watched the swirling green energy of Anyan's power, feeling how his combined air and water felt so different from my own water-based power. The orb I raised to match his was iron-gray, swirling with white like waves foaming over the sea.

My power is the same color as his eyes, I thought, just as the object of my affection lobbed a missile in my direction. My shields absorbed the impact without hesitation, and, with a sigh, I lobbed my own mage ball back at Anyan.

This one went wide since, once again, my instincts had overridden my training and I'd chucked it at him. Anyan shook his curly haired head in response.

'*Send* it, Jane. Don't throw it.'

I nodded, then did as he'd said. This time, my mage ball connected squarely with his shields right where I'd been aiming: about crotch level.

I winked when he looked up, startled, and sent a bunch more mage balls zinging his way. I laughed at the expression on his face, then swore as he returned his own barrage and I had to quickly beef up my shields. We stood there, lobbing power at each other for a while, eventually making a game of trying to hit each other's mage balls in midair with our own. Anyan and I both laughed as two of our balls collided in midair and, for some reason, didn't dissipate, but clung to each other, finally sinking to the wet spring earth where they sat smoking before melting back into the ground.

I watched the barghest watching the mage balls disappear, a smile still curling his wide mouth. Wanting more than anything to kiss those lips, and knowing I couldn't, I fell back on playground tactics and sent a mage ball zinging at him.

His eyes, suddenly predatory, snapped up to meet mine and his smile turned into something other than humor.

He raised another lovely green orb in his hand, but this time he strode forward rather than zinging it at me.

I started to backpedal, launching my own missiles at him, but he just kept striding forward. With a squawk, I turned tail to run, fleeing down the nicely manicured path on my right.

I'd spent so much time the last week sitting in cars, or on planes, that running felt *good*. Granted, I was never going to be mistaken for a Kenyan, but I was really going for it, enjoying the ache in my muscles and the expansion of my lungs.

And I was also getting nowhere fast compared to my pursuer. I could see a shadow in the very back of my peripheral vision. More to the point, I *felt* the barghest immediately behind me.

'Faster, Jane,' he breathed right behind my ear, causing me to squeal like a stuck pig and pump my little legs as if he really was the Big Bad Wolf.

Maybe if you stop running, he'll eat you, my libido, ever libidinous, suggested.

My legs actually slowed down a little bit at that thought, before I cursed myself roundly and picked my pace back up.

I could hear Anyan chuckling behind me. I was starting to get winded, but this was the equivalent of a country stroll for him.

Damned tall people with their long legs, I thought, irritated.

With those marvelous thighs, the libido added. I couldn't even get annoyed at that thought.

They are magnificent thighs, I admitted. *Now get yours working . . .*

That last thought was precipitated by the fact Anyan's hot breath was again stroking the back of my neck. I wanted to melt, truth be told. Unfortunately, the barghest wasn't chasing me to catch me, he was chasing to chase me.

But you could *really use a good catching*, my libido

reminded me, right before Anyan spoke again, tickling the shell of my ear with his breath.

'Use your power, Jane. Use it to run . . .'

My mind went blank at his words, then started roaring. What if I could do what he said? What if I could use my power to run just like I used it to swim?

Move over, Kenyans, I thought, as I tentatively started applying my powers to running.

It took me a bit to get the hang of it, and it wasn't anywhere near as effective as what I did in the ocean. In the ocean, I could literally cut through the water like a scythe. On land, I was still five foot one with short legs, and my lungs still ached and my legs still hurt. That said, I was much, much faster than I had been. So fast that while trees weren't blurring around me *Twilight*-style, they were definitely passing ever faster and, for a second or two, I pulled away from the barghest.

Laughing wildly, and then nearly passing out from the lack of oxygen, I kept following the trail as it looped back to the little meadow where Anyan and I had originally been practicing. For the first time since I'd learned of my mother's murder, I felt nearly whole again. There was still an ache, deep in my heart, that I suspected would always be there. But I felt my own life at that moment so deeply that all I could do was revel in my body and blood and breath.

With a shout I pulled up from my run, feeling power reverberate through me with a slightly painful backlash. But it only made my already engorged, sensitized nerve endings tingle even more. Feeling cocky, I did a rather anemic little cartwheel, before attempting a round-off. Keep in mind that I haven't successfully completed a round-off since I was in the sixth grade, so I was very proud of myself for the neat twist I did mid-cartwheel that had me landing solidly on both feet, facing Anyan. Until I completely lost my balance and, wide eyes latched on to the barghest's laughing visage, I windmilled, teetering, only to land on my butt with a thud.

'Oof,' I announced, feeling my keister protest the rough handling.

'Indeed.' Anyan laughed, coming forward to help me up. He stretched out a big hand, which I took, marveling at how small my own fingers were in his, before he pulled me to my feet.

Only to spin me about to pin me, my back to his chest, with a heavy arm around my waist, muscular biceps across my breasts, and one huge hand wrapped around my throat.

'Word to the wise, honey,' he said in my ear. 'When you're running away from someone, don't attempt gymnastics and then fall on your ass.'

I'd stopped breathing when Anyan had grabbed me, my second mistake after falling down. After running all that way, power-driven or not, I was panting like a spaniel when I'd entered the meadow. So when I finally remembered I needed oxygen to live, I drew in a huge, shuddering breath that necessarily lodged the barghest's rigid arm tighter against my breasts. An act that, equally necessarily, set off a whole other set of reactions in my already heaving bosoms.

If my nipples get any harder, I'm gonna bore a hole into his arm. Even my libido was panicking at that thought.

'You've been captured, Jane. Now what do you do?'

The barghest's voice rumbled from his chest into mine, and I forced myself not to shiver.

This is work to him, Jane. He's in 'training Jane' mode. So get out of 'fondling Anyan' mode before you make a tit of yourself.

Not that my breasts weren't already making a tit of me by practically sitting up and begging for attention . . .

'C'mon, now. You'd already be dead if this were real. But I'm not letting you go until you free yourself. Think, Jane.'

I stared blindly across the park, toward the hotel we'd just vacated, trying to clear my mind.

Ohmigod, get it together or no more cookies for you, ever, I scolded myself. Then I thought, hard, till I came up with an excellent plan.

And it *was* an excellent plan. I realized I could do a sort of thin-edge-of-the-wedge thing between us just as I'd done before, with Phaedra's Alfar net. I could do it with my shields, then force us apart. Maybe stomp on Anyan's big foot at the same time, my revenge for his unmerited sexual torture.

Unfortunately, that's not what I did. Oh no. Because I'm Jane, and I like to humiliate myself for fun.

Granted, what happened next wasn't entirely my fault. Anyan shifted, causing his torso to rub against me, and his arms to move back and forth right over the very places I was most aching.

So I responded instinctually. I was, after all, in the arms of a man I wanted very, very badly to boff. He had his arms around me. I was right where I wanted to be . . . and then he shifted . . .

And then I shimmied.

My ass.

Into his crotch.

Don't get me wrong: I didn't dry-hump him or start grinding against him like some hoochie dancer in a rap video. But I definitely *shimmied* my *ass* into his *crotch*. Well, I'm so damned short and he's so damned tall I mostly just rubbed my buttocks on his knees, but whatever. There was my ass, on him, and I thought I would die.

Anyan froze behind me, and all my blood rushed to my head. I knew I was beet-red, and I honestly thought I would keel over from shame (or an aneurysm) when holy hell broke loose.

At first I had no idea what had happened. Suddenly Anyan

swore and sprang away from me. Luckily, he pointed almost immediately to the top of the hotel, or I would have died of humiliation thinking he was swearing at my actions.

Instead he was swearing 'cause tonight, much like in the Dropkick Murphys' song, there was a jailbreak.

Two elegant, winged figures were at the window that had to be our hotel suite. They were far away, and very far up, but I had no doubt who those slenderly androgynous figures were.

Fucking Phaedra's fucking harpies, I thought.

Anyan had already whipped out his phone and was calling Ryu. Unfortunately, just at that moment, I spotted Ryu strolling casually across the street toward us.

'I just came out to check on you,' the baobhan sith said as he pulled out his ringing phone, first frowning at it, then frowning at Anyan.

Anyan swore, flipped shut his phone, then opened it to dial again.

'Caleb, Kaya and Kaori are at the window . . .'

I heard a shout from Anyan's phone, then we were running across the street to underneath where the harpies were busting out our prisoner. Ryu squealed up in his rented SUV just as the harpies took off, another figure dangling between them.

We plunged into Ryu's car, me in back and Anyan in the passenger-side seat. Soon, however, they'd shoved me up through the sunroof so I could guide them. They might not have thought that was such a good idea had they seen I was holding my hands in front of me to make one L and one backward L, as I sometimes had trouble telling my left from my right.

'Left, hard left, *now!*' I shouted, holding on to the sides of the sunroof for dear life as Anyan's arms snaked around my waist to keep me standing.

'Right, they're turning right! Now keep straight . . . they're still going straight . . . wait, they're going sort of . . . I think left? Yes, go left! Now right! They're over that building . . . Haul ass, then go right!

'Wait . . . they're coming down, I think . . . they're lower . . .'

'Can you squeeze off a shot?' Anyan barked from below me.

'Umm . . . I think so . . . if they get a little . . .'

I raised my hand, mage ball at the ready, not sure if I could throw that far.

It's not throwing, Jane. Just send the friggin' thing . . . Distance shouldn't matter.

I narrowed my eyes on the dun wings of one of my most hated enemies, not caring if it was Kaya or Kaori. I just wanted them *down* and our prisoner *back* . . . With that thought, my magic pushed through me like a wave as I zeroed in on my target with both my magic and my will.

The flying figures were still far enough away that I couldn't actually see my mage ball go through the air, but I saw one figure buckle, then weave, then begin to fall out of the sky, dragging the other two with her.

'I think I hit one!' I shouted exultantly, forgetting I wasn't just the artillery, I was the navigator. 'And go left! Left! Shit!' I yelled, pounding on the roof of the car.

Ryu turned on a dime, just as I saw our harpies, with our prisoner, fall into an alley. Unfortunately, the turn was so hard that I, too, was falling, but not before I yelled:

'Right! Into that alley! Right! Oooof.'

The 'oof' was due to my whacking my head on the sunroof as I went down to land in a heap, partially on the barghest.

Stop landing on Anyan, I thought wearily. At this point, I myself wasn't sure if I was truly clumsy or just sexually harassing him. I couldn't begin to imagine what he must have thought.

We'd peeled into a through-alley just as our prey disappeared out the other end. Ryu gunned the engine as Anyan shoved me, surprisingly gently, back into my seat, both hands firmly on my bottom to do so.

I coulda swore he squeezed just as he sat me down, but I have no doubt it was my lurid imagination working overtime.

We raced around the far corner of the alley to come out into a wide, but empty, street. It was a Saturday, and we were in the business district of Pittsburgh so we could have been in a ghost town.

Unfortunately, the street wasn't near as ghostly as I'd have liked it. For sitting at the end of the block, parked rakishly across the intersection, was a familiar Escalade.

'Fucking Phaedra,' Anyan growled, just as we all threw up shields around our vehicle.

But it was too late. Phaedra had sent a wave of power surging over the ground that blew out our tires before our shields made it that far. The SUV bucked, swerved, then came to a halt as Ryu efficiently applied the brakes.

We bailed out of the SUV just as Phaedra exited the Escalade. The tiny, bald Alfar was wearing her leather biker gear, the hilts of various edged weapons bristling from her so she resembled a rabid, red-eyed porcupine. Kaya (or Kaori) was dragging Kaori (or Kaya) up the street with the help of our former prisoner, and they'd made it just about halfway to the Alfar.

Which meant we had about thirty seconds to take our Dr Death back alive.

Chapter Nineteen

I wasn't very good at math, but I didn't think our odds were *too* bad. Granted, Phaedra was Alfar, but I knew she was pretty low on the Alfar power-scale to be the sort of lackey that she was. Plus, one of the harpies was obviously hurting, they had a noncombatant to keep alive, and Anyan had been more than a match for way more powerful Alfar in the past, right?

We may just do this, I thought as I wove my water-power through Anyan's earth and air, feeling our shields further boosted by Ryu's own essence-charged magic.

Striding forward, we watched as Kaya and Kaori neared their mistress. As soon as they could, the healthy harpy shoved our doctor toward Phaedra and immediately hustled her sister off, presumably to heal her.

I could hear the doctor yelling, 'Help me!' to Phaedra, who held out her arms.

Harpies are out, I thought, watching Kaya (or Kaori) bundle her wounded sister into the SUV.

And Phaedra's about to have her hands full with a sadistic halfling-doctor to protect, my brain purred with satisfaction.

Unfortunately, things never go to plan, do they? For the minute our prisoner neared Phaedra, the Alfar was suddenly holding a knife.

Phaedra smiled at us from around our former captive, just as the evil little woman sank her blade deep. Dr Death jerked once, then again, then crumpled at Phaedra's feet.

So much for plan A, I thought, just as plan B went all to shit as well.

For one second we were alone on the street; the next a little sports car raced around the corner. Like a circus freak emerging from a clown car, Fugwat Spriggan unfurled himself from the passenger's side. I watched in trepidation as the driver himself was revealed: Graeme the rapist incubus, whose nasty, pain-infused juju immediately starting beating against our combined shield in waves.

'I was going to keep her alive,' Phaedra intoned, her voice Alfar-flat yet somehow betraying her pleasure in the scene. 'Let Graeme play with her. See just how much rats like her know, so that we would know who knew too much. But you three just keep getting in the way,' she said as she drove a wave of power straight at us.

Graeme and Fugwat moved to join her, and I finally got a full-frontal view of the rapist incubus. A victim of Graeme's sadistic cruelty, Conleth had applied his formidable power to melting Graeme's face when given the opportunity. And while I knew magic could heal, what Con had done to Graeme was a whole new level of the old ultraviolence.

Sure enough, Graeme's face was . . . off. Not like a human burn victim's, but almost as if his once beautiful (if cruel) features had been replaced by bizarrely healthy-looking, fleshy wax. He looked repellent, and I couldn't help but smile.

His exterior finally matches his interior, I thought as his eyes sought out mine and burned into me with their rage.

And here we have another pureblood who won't be joining the Jane True Fan Club, I surmised, trying to swallow the fear that welled up in me at seeing the hate in Graeme's eyes.

'Three against three.' The little Alfar smiled as she let loose another blast of her mixed-elemental force.

We didn't buckle under the onslaught, precisely. But we did back up a step as our shields were shoved as if by the sweep of a giant's arm.

I think we might be fucked, I thought, reevaluating my earlier optimism.

Luckily, however, I heard another car squeal to a stop behind us, as Anyan's rented SUV pulled up with Daoud, Caleb, and Julian. Relief washed through me, although I wasn't sure if, even with our reinforcements, we'd be able to take the Alfar.

'Fan out,' Anyan yelled, and we did. Or at least I tried to, for Ryu pulled me next to him, leaving a big hole in our line – just the sort of slipup Phaedra'd been waiting for.

With an evil smirk the Alfar lobbed something that looked like a mage ball but exploded like a grenade when it landed between Caleb and where I stood trying to extricate myself from Ryu's grasp.

The impact caught the edges of my defenses, which I'd solidified to keep all the flying asphalt from hitting me. This was not the wisest move, however, as it also meant that the blast caught my shields, flinging me a few feet behind where I'd originally been standing. I skidded to a halt, sitting on my butt, my palms all scraped to hell.

And that's when everything went supernova. Ryu and Julian engaged Graeme as Anyan sprang forward, concentrating his attack on Phaedra. Mage balls, and mage grenades, and mage-I-don't-even-know-whats were zinging through the air, which was saturated with power and cries. I shivered as the barghest's distinctive force roared out from him with its untamed, raw edge that almost matched the controlled hits of the Alfar in its ferocity.

Meanwhile, Daoud and Caleb were matching force with the spriggan. The satyr was lobbing power at Fugwat, while Daoud snuck around behind him, his hands in his waistband. If it had been anyone else, I would have wondered at the necessity of fondling yourself during a battle. But Daoud's power, as a djinn, was that he could pull anything he understood, down to its molecular composition, out of his pants. Sure enough, after a moment or two of rooting around with a rather pained expression on his face, the djinn pulled out a handful of crazy bling. Huge ropes of shiny beads and jewels sparkled in the sun: diamonds, pearls, rubies, and emeralds. Light danced across Fugwat's face as he stared like an addict confronted with an eight ball. I remembered Ryu once telling me that spriggans were like magpies, but we were in the middle of a battle. Surely he couldn't be *that* obsessed with shiny things . . .

Just call him Shirley, I thought, marveling as Fugwat stared, openmouthed, at the jewelry hanging from Daoud's hand, which the djinn waved back and forth like a metronome. I felt the spriggan's formidable defensive magics slowly falter, then fade. Meanwhile, as Daoud wove his spell with the jewels, Caleb had been pawing the earth with his hooves, and as soon as Fugwat was undefended physically and magically, the satyr struck. Rushing forward at ramming speed, head down, Caleb hit Fugwat with a combination of brute force and his earth's power backing up his formidable horns. The spriggan arced up, up, up into the air, before landing about fifteen feet away with a resounding *thud*.

Once Fugwat was down, Daoud and Caleb were on him; holding him in place with magic and their own bodies, till he was secured. Leaving Daoud to keep the spriggan contained, Caleb then went to help Ryu with Graeme. Julian, unfortunately, was sitting well away from the action, woozily weaving back and forth. My fellow halfling – never much of a fighter – had a pretty awful gash across his forehead, which oozed blood into his eyes.

And is that his thighbone jutting out of his jeans? my brain mused, forcing me to quash a wave of nausea in order to focus on the here and now. A broken bone would heal in minutes; there were bigger fish to fry.

Like a big-ass piranha named Phaedra, I thought, turning to where Anyan and the Alfar were duking it out.

Or you can just run away, the cowardly, scared-shitless part of my brain whispered.

Not an option, I thought grimly as I scampered closer to where Anyan had made his stand. *Go, go, Gadget True . . .*

The barghest was holding his own, but Phaedra's relentless onslaught was slowly driving him back. He wove to the left, and I waited till he'd started his own barrage on Phaedra – stilling hers as she shielded – to sprint over to him. He saw me coming and let me into the circle of his defenses, which I immediately bolstered with my own power.

'What should I do?' I yelled.

'We need to get out of the open with her; she'll just keep blasting away till we're exhausted. We need to get her in one of these alleys, figure out a way to get around her shields and attack her physically . . .'

Anyan grunted as Phaedra really went at us, her eyes narrowed on me. Killing me would be the ultimate way for her to gain favor with Jarl, so my coming to Anyan's side was a little like dangling a carrot in the ass's face.

Maybe we can use that, I realized as I felt Anyan grab my hand and tug me farther to the left.

'Anyan, I am to Phaedra as sparklies are to Fugwat!' I shouted at him over the din, finally using my SAT-analogy skills in the real world. 'You can use that! Just dangle me in front of her, and she'll do something stupid!'

Anyan looked at me like I was suggesting he trample babies, and I rolled my eyes at him. He was so damned protective, but we needed whatever advantage we could scrape up.

Before the barghest could respond to my suggestion, however, we were distracted by the sight of Daoud flying through the air as Fugwat finally shook the jewelry's spell and broke free.

Caleb immediately pivoted neatly, running back to take on the spriggan and scoop up the djinn on the way. Daoud looked dazed but unhurt, and he was already reaching into his pants for some more bling.

Which left Ryu once again battling Graeme by himself. Unsatisfied with their inability to beat the shit out of each other with mage balls, Ryu had conjured a sword of flaming blue light. Graeme, meanwhile, had armed himself with a tire iron from the SUV; his power arcing up the steel with a dull red flare.

Watching the two dueling was like enjoying a scene from *Star Wars*, and I mentally added the appropriate sound effects each time their weapon of choice whizzed through the air.

Meanwhile, Anyan and I were still creeping toward the alley to our left, holding our shields as tight and strong as we could against Phaedra's onslaught. She wasn't tiring at all and, if anything, had stepped up her barrage. I understood what Anyan meant about getting out of the open with her; she was gonna wear us out then take us down.

Luckily, we were close to some cover, and we had just

started to back our way into the alley when I saw Kaya (or Kaori) – whichever one was uninjured – get out of the van.

Fuck, I thought. *I hope whichever one that is, it's not Graeme's girlfriend.*

Unfortunately, the harpy hustled immediately over to where the incubus was now definitively getting his sexual-sadist ass kicked by Ryu, effectively turning the tables on our baobhan sith. Caleb and Daoud were still dealing with the spriggan, who was covering for his own weakness by keeping his eyes covered with one meaty hand, as he used his other arm to karate-chop through the air. While randomly hitting in front of you isn't a particularly effective strategy, the waves of buffeting power he sent in front of him were.

Fugwat may be dumb and rather ham-handed, but he's strong.

More important, the big brute was keeping his two attackers busy. Without the lure of the bling, Caleb and Daoud couldn't penetrate those ridiculously strong shields. And while they weren't in any danger and still had him effectively pinned, blind and in one spot, neither of them could slip away to help Ryu.

'Ryu needs help!' I yelled at Anyan, watching as Ryu gave up the sword fighting and backed away to duel his two foes with mage balls. In real life, unfortunately, our enemies didn't come at us one at a time, or stand in a circle waiting their turn for us to kick their ass. They came all at once, full on. They wanted to kill us, not pad out an action scene.

'So do we!' the barghest growled. He was right, of course, but I couldn't stop watching Ryu. He might be a rat fink at times, but that didn't mean I didn't still care about him.

I was trying to figure out a way to help – I was thinking I could do something to help take down Fugwat, so that Caleb or Daoud would be freed to aid Ryu – when Anyan pulled me fully into the cluttered, stinking alley. He was peering about, trying to find some advantage we could use in our fight, when I saw my former lover fall.

He'd been holding his own against his two attackers, when the other harpy – her wing held awkwardly behind her – made a surprise appearance behind him. I never saw her leave the car, but then again, I was rather distracted. She got close enough to cut him with one of Phaedra's cursed machetes. The pain broke Ryu's concentration, and his shields faltered. The other sister and Graeme, seeing their opportunity, blasted at Ryu with a simultaneous bolt of energy that sent him flying through the air to hit what I think was the Escalade – we were blinded by the alley's walls, but I could hear it – with a resounding crash.

Despite everything that had happened between us, seeing Ryu fly through the air like that nearly made my heart stop. I might not be able to see a future with him as a couple, but the gods know I never contemplated a world without Ryu in it.

Goddammit, Jarl will not be responsible for killing another person close to me, I thought as rage blossomed through me and I really *pulled* with my power.

This time I went on the offensive. I was still pretty juiced from the last time I swam, and there were spring showers tingling in the air that I pulled from. I battered at Phaedra with everything I had in me, taking a moment to yell at Anyan:

'Figure something out while I hold her! Sneak around the back way or something!'

For a second he responded just by looking at me, and I knew he didn't want to leave me.

'Go!' I roared. 'Now!'

So I blasted and I blasted, my libido noting with a small

harrumph that the barghest was shedding his clothing beside me. Alfar attacks do not make for good ogling conditions, however, so I couldn't spare any attention to the blur of tanned man-flesh on display in my peripheral vision.

Then Anyan was off and I was on my own. Against an Alfar. Who smiled at me like she was Garfield and I was a trayful of lasagna.

'Alone at last,' she purred, her red eyes almost glowing with power.

Fuck, I hate you, Phaedra, I thought as I pulled from the air around me, reaching all the way up to the rain clouds above, through the tiny droplets of moisture connecting us.

I let all that emotion come blasting out of me with my power. I knew the Alfar preached that emotions had to be shunted away in order to allow control, but I knew firsthand that was only one way of doing things. It was safer, as you were less likely to lose yourself to the power, but sometimes 'safe' wasn't the best option.

My enemy's eyes widened, almost imperceptibly, at the force I was unleashing. That said, and despite my bravado, I did recognize I was skating a thin line. With nearly disastrous results, I'd given myself over to the Atlantic all those months ago, when I'd connected myself to her in order to escape Phaedra's trap. The storm clouds above me were definitely different from the ocean, but equally strong in their own way . . . and equally tempestuous.

Keep your eyes on the prize, I reminded myself, forcing more power out of me in waves. *Need to keep her distracted.* So I pushed down my concern for Ryu and for Anyan, who was even now probably sneaking up on Phaedra, trying to focus on keeping the evil Alfar focused on *me*.

Luckily, I did annoying very well. Still concentrating on my power, I managed to pull my arms up, lodge my thumbs in my ears to make antlers, and then stick my tongue out at the little woman in front of me. Phaedra's only response was to narrow her eyes, but translated from the Alfar that was like a normal person yelling bloody murder.

We were blasting so hard at each other at this point that my own shields were almost entirely based at my front.

If someone were to sneak up on me now . . . But just then, as if to relieve some of my worry, Ryu came stumbling, half supported by Caleb, across the mouth of my smelly alley, the satyr and the baobhan sith engaged in a fierce battle with both harpies and Graeme.

Momentarily distracted by the kerfuffle directly behind her, Phaedra's attention faltered ever so slightly, and I used my chance to reach, reach, *reach* into the clouds and pull down a slug of power out of the sky. To my surprise, a lightning bolt came with it, which nearly hit me till I unconsciously redirected it at the Alfar. It sliced right through her shields, giving her quite a shock and spinning her like a top . . .

. . . directly into Anyan's ambush. I had been expecting him to go *around* the building, but somehow, he'd managed to go *up* it and had leaped down all four flights (cushioned by his earth magics) to land on top of the Alfar.

Well, theoretically to land on top of the Alfar. Because she'd spun about, she was looking right at him as he fell. The lightning bolt had fucked her up for sure, but not enough that she couldn't counter a direct attack.

With a pained expression Phaedra unleashed a burst of wild magic that flung Anyan aside. He hit the wall with a crack, his doggie-form sliding down to land in a sickening heap at the bottom. I heard myself crying out, panic and rage rushing through my system.

All I could think was that I had to get to Anyan, had to

make sure he was all right, had to heal him, *had to had to had to*, so I *reached* . . .

For a second, I felt like I was in that opening scene from *The Matrix*, with all the computer code streaming at me. Only instead of code, it was water droplets, attaching me through their atoms to every other bead of water on the planet. In that ever-so-brief moment of time, I saw that we were all connected and that we *were* indeed, as Gus the stone spirit had said not long ago, 'ugly bags of water'.

If I just reach, I thought, seeing how all the threads could come together if I pulled . . .

Only to have what felt like a bell jar drop over me, neatly cutting me off from all those pretty beads of water. I shook physically as all the power roared back into me and I felt just how far I'd extended myself.

'Never that, girlie,' came a woman's voice next to me. 'That will be the end of you.'

I pivoted around, aware that Phaedra was somehow contained behind a wall of power that stretched neatly in front of me and where Anyan still lay crumpled on the ground. More than anything, my legs wanted to carry me to him, but I had to know who was behind me.

Blondie, I realized as my eyes latched on to the overly skinny woman from the ice-cream shop.

She was wearing a man's white wifebeater, her tattooed arms and torso glimmering fiercely in the light created from Phaedra's attacks striking her shield wall behind us. Her jeans were huge and low-slung, showing off sharp, tattooed hipbones.

'We all have our limitations,' she intoned, patting my cheek gently. I was so in shock at seeing her again, I didn't even pull at my power, but feeling the force that emanated from her, I knew it was pointless if I did. Blondie would squish me flat as the medieval earth.

'Now go to your friend,' she said, flicking her fingers negligently at Anyan. I felt a burst of power fly through the air at him, and suddenly I didn't care that I could die.

'Don't you hit him!' I hollered, raising probably the wussiest mage ball of my life.

She smiled. 'It was healing magic, babydoll. Now go. I'll take care of that one.'

And Blondie walked away from me, opening her shield as she did so. Without even thinking I lunged over to Anyan, physically covering him with my body in case Phaedra chose that moment to hit. But Blondie was already taking care of the Alfar.

Standing just inside the alley so no one else could see her, Blondie lifted Phaedra off the ground. At the same time, my rescuer did the same thing to Phaedra she'd done to me, and neatly blockaded the Alfar's power in the same way I'd trap a fly in my cupped hands.

Then Blondie threw Phaedra, and I don't mean tossed her away. I mean she *flung* her, using more power than I'd ever felt. And Blondie didn't even bat an eyelash. But there was Phaedra, flying through the night sky like the catapulted cow in Monty Python's *Search for the Holy Grail*. She arced over the nearest building and away.

I saw the still-healthy harpy flying after her a split second later, even as Anyan's power shimmered beneath me. And now I was lying on top of all that naked man-flesh I'd been wanting to ogle just a little while before.

'What happened?' he moaned, putting his arms around me so he could pull himself up into a sitting position. It took every ounce of self-control I had not to snuggle close and breathe in his warm, healthy, healed, not-hurt-anymore skin. Instead, I pulled back, again keeping my eyes off the prize below.

I looked up to call Blondie over so she could explain herself, but she was gone.

This will be fun, I thought grimly, even as I crawled the short distance to where Anyan had dropped his clothes. After tossing them over to him, I stood shakily and headed toward the mouth of the alley. Caleb was healing both Ryu and Daoud, despite a cut on his own head that was bleeding like crazy.

Miraculously, everyone was alive. Except for the crumpled body of our doctor, lying dead in the center of the road.

And with her, our only chance of getting at Jarl.

Chapter Twenty

'Love you, too, Dad,' I said, before saying goodbye and closing my cell phone. I was in our new suite's bedroom – since
the old one now had a rather expansive hole in the outer wall
– taking a moment to make sure everyone was safe back at the
homestead.

I lay back on my bed for just a moment, feeling exhausted.
We'd been traveling all over, following so many leads, and
we'd put together so much information. Yet for all intents
and purposes, we had *nothing*. Losing that doctor had put us
back at square one.

My mother and Iris were still dead; labs were still oper-
ating; and we were no closer to nailing Jarl then we'd been
before we'd left Rockabill. Meanwhile, all I wanted, more
than anything, was to go *home*.

Instead, I joined the others in the main room of our suite.

'Everyone's fine,' I reported. 'Still crashed out at my place.
My dad thinks I'm now touring the Andes.'

I folded myself onto a free, out-of-the-way love seat, as
far away from everyone as I could get, and combed through
my wet hair. Anyan had taken me swimming, so I could

recharge and so he could question me about Blondie. The barghest was freaking out over who she could be. Even now, he was standing at the window, staring out with an expression similar to what I imagined Miss Marple's would be as she knitted and put together clues.

Then I thought of Anyan's big, clever hands busy knitting, and wished with all my heart we were in a different time and place.

Ryu, meanwhile, was in his own bedroom, talking to his king and queen. Caleb and Daoud were watching CNN, although Daoud looked so sleepy I was pretty sure he'd be watching the inside of his eyelids in a few minutes. Julian was working on his laptop, ordering some equipment he wanted for the investigation.

All of which left me to brood on my love seat; so brood I did. Until Anyan turned around and walked over to me.

Part of me couldn't help but enjoy him wedging his big frame beside me into the little two-seater sofa. But the other part of me knew what he wanted.

'Are you sure you couldn't recognize her power?'

I sighed. Rather unsurprisingly, the barghest was like a dog with a bone about this subject: worrying away at it so that he could get to the marrow.

'Anyan, I told you: no. It sort of felt elemental, but it was just so strong.'

'Hmph,' he said, his long nose twitching furiously as he thought.

'And she wasn't antagonistic?'

'Nope, she was really friendly. Called me "babydoll", and healed you. Then saved me from Phaedra. She was just . . . nice.'

'Nice,' Anyan grunted.

I nodded. *Yes.*

'Hmph. Maybe she's a renegade Alfar,' he hazarded after a few minutes.

'If I didn't think they were legend, I'd wonder if she was an Original,' Caleb said from where he sat on the couch. Anyan's face darkened in thought.

'An Original?' I asked. I'd never heard of the term.

'They're a myth,' Daoud said groggily, not bothering to open his eyes.

'Well, a myth of what?'

Anyan answered my question finally. 'The Originals are like the humans' missing link. They're supposed to be the very first generation of Alfar, before they were even really Alfar.'

'Well, how are they different from Alfar?'

'The legend is that they had *all* of our supernatural powers, even that of shape-shifting. So take every single faction, no matter how obscure, and combine them to make the Originals. They could fire up, like ifrits; shift shape, like nahuals; take power from any element, like the Alfar; and even harvest essence, like baobhan sith.'

'Wow,' I said. 'That's a lot of mojo.'

'Yeah, but they're myths,' Daoud mumbled again. 'Fairy tales we use to scare children.'

Thinking about what I'd just been told, I thought hard. 'She didn't do anything that wasn't . . . normal. I mean, nothing she did was *normal*, but it wasn't anything an Alfar with a lot of power couldn't do.'

'Yes,' said Caleb. 'No doubt she's a renegade Alfar.'

I shrugged my shoulders. I had no idea what she was, but 'renegade Alfar' was as good a guess as any.

'Maybe she senses discord in the Territory, thinks she can take advantage of it,' the barghest continued, unable to drop that bone.

I just looked at him.

'So you're *sure* you didn't recognize her power?'

Groaning, I buried my head in my hands, just as Ryu came back into the room.

'Well, according to Wally, Jarl's being extra-present around the Compound. Showing up for every meal, every event . . . making sure everyone knows he never leaves.'

'Making sure everyone thinks he can't be involved,' Daoud muttered, his eyes still at half-mast.

'Yup,' Ryu said, sitting down across from Anyan and me. 'Plus, he's called Phaedra, Graeme, and Fugwat home, announced publicly that they've been risking their lives running spying missions into the Borderlands and that they've brought him all sorts of important information.'

'And since Jarl is the spymaster, he can make up whatever "information" he likes to support his claim,' Anyan added. 'What about the harpies?'

'They're still unaccounted for. Jane did a real number on Kaya. Or did she hit Kaori? Anyway, whichever one she hurt, they're probably holed up somewhere, nursing wounds. But I'm sure they'll be back to spying on us once they're both at full strength.'

'So what are we going to do?' I asked glumly.

Ryu frowned, but Anyan spoke.

'Wait. Make calls. Contact more people. We'll get another lead.'

'I'm sick of waiting,' I said, knowing I sounded petulant but not caring anymore.

'I know,' Anyan soothed. 'We all are.'

Ryu had been watching our exchange, his frown deepening. He was about to speak, when we felt a familiar tingle in the air: First Magic.

Terk popped in a few seconds later on the carpet in front

of Anyan and me. Instead of his usual dramatic entrance, however, this time he stumbled and fell. Partly because he was holding another large envelope, but I also remembered Capitola saying he was worn out from the last raid.

With a worried little cry, I sprang forward to help the brownie to his feet. He grasped my fingers so I could pull him upright, but he looked up at me with such sad sets of eyes that I went ahead and picked him up for a cuddle. He nestled against me, cooing gently, as I walked back to the couch to hand the envelope to Anyan.

As the barghest opened Capitola's missive, he looked at me skeptically.

'Jane,' he began, 'you really might not want to— Shit.'

Whatever he'd been about to say was cut off as he glanced down at the papers in his hands.

He got up and strode out of the room, pulling his cell phone out of his back pocket as he went.

I smiled down at the fuzzy little creature in my arms, and Terk smiled back, blinking all six black eyes at me so that he showed off his long lashes. I laughed, and he chittered something at me in what the supes called 'old tongue', the ancient language spoken by those of the First Magics.

'Can I get you anything?' I asked. 'Are you thirsty?'

Terk chittered away, waving one of his little hands in front of my chest and nodding.

'Um, I'll take that as a yes . . . Would you like water? Or soda?'

Terk chittered again, still waving his little hand.

'Umm . . . I'll bring you some water and I have some Coke . . . I'll bring both.'

Gently, I set the little brownie down at my feet then went to fetch him a drink. I could hear Anyan swearing from his bedroom, and I wondered what was going on. Just as I'd walked back to the couch, and knelt down to place the two glasses I'd filled by Terk, the barghest reentered the room, snapping shut his cell phone.

'Shit's hit the fan in the Borderlands,' he said. 'Cap is concerned we have a leak; that's why she sent Terk. Because something has caused a panic among the enemy. The couple of remaining labs that different groups have been surveilling and preparing to raid went ahead and self-destructed last night. Everyone dead: patients, "doctors", everybody.'

I flipped through the pages Anyan had handed me: grainy faxed pictures of rooms with bodies strewn about, a map of the Borderlands with a smattering of little red Xs indicating the locations of labs, and a note from Capitola that read, 'Someone's getting paranoid. Have you discovered more? And has someone shared with your suspect? Call me if your line is safe.'

Rage began to burn in me, and I looked up at Anyan.

'He's getting rid of the evidence. He knows he's close to getting caught, so he's getting rid of the evidence. He'll just burn everything to the ground, kill everyone he doesn't trust, and it'll be like none of this ever happened, for him.'

The room was silent, everyone watching Anyan and me.

'We can't let him get away with this, Anyan,' I said, my voice deepening with passion. 'He needs to pay for what he's done . . .'

The barghest's eyes stared into mine, his glowing with understanding and compassion. Then his eyes dropped to about knee level on me, and I realized everyone else was also staring right behind me.

'What the fuck,' I said irritably as I arched my back to peer over my shoulder behind me.

Nothing there. So I looked down.

To find the 'adorable' little brownie thrusting his pelvis at me and making spanking motions, one hand behind his head in maximum porn-star imitation.

'You little *shit*,' I swore, turning around to confront Terk. For his part, he blinked up at me, smiling roguishly. With a wink and a kiss blown from one of his tiny hands, he apparated with a *poof*.

I stood there, staring at where the brownie had just been, so many feelings flooding my system I couldn't even begin to separate them.

'Oh. My. God,' I said, clenching my fists. 'Is there anyone else who wants to take a potshot at Jane? Anybody? Anybody?'

I turned back around to face the room, where the boys were staring at me like I was a live hand grenade. Hell, I *felt* like a live hand grenade.

Because I could *see* it, see it all already. Just like what had happened after my first visit to the Compound, Jarl was going to wreak havoc in people's lives – killing, kidnapping, maiming – and then he was going to let a bunch of his cronies take the blame, or the bullet, and *nothing would happen to him*. He'd continue in his position of power, in his cushy life at the Compound, with a few people suspecting something but nobody acting.

Meanwhile, my mother was dead, Iris was dead, all those other women were dead. Or sitting in hospital rooms, victims of atrocities, not knowing if they'd ever get their magic back.

And it's not like this setback was going to stop him. Jarl had lived centuries. He'd just wait for everyone to forget this latest kerfuffle – or die off – and then he'd be back at it once again. Or he'd concoct another half-baked, crazy scheme that involved other people's pain and suffering.

'We have to do something,' I ground out, surprised at the pain in my own voice. I'd been keeping it together pretty well up until now. Trying to keep my eye on the prize: catching

Jarl. Now that I saw that all of this might be in vain, cracks were spidering my veneer. I didn't know how much longer I could hold.

Both Ryu and Anyan stepped forward, but I was tired of comforting words, placating gestures. So I took a step back from both of them.

'No,' I said, my voice stronger. 'We have to *do* something.'

Both men looked at me, then at each other, then back at me.

'Jane,' Ryu said, but I shook my head.

'No, Ryu. No excuses. We have to figure out what we can do.'

'And we will,' Anyan said. 'We just need a little more time. We're all exhausted, especially you . . .'

That's when I realized they were never going to do anything. Everyone in that room except for me, even Anyan, was such a part of the power structure that no one here would ever *do* anything. Attacking an Alfar like Jarl was, for them, like attacking the Pentagon, and they couldn't even see that fact.

They think they're doing something, but the fact is that they're giving up the moment things look difficult, because they can't imagine really rocking the boat . . .

Standing there, I had a sudden moment of clarity. Or at least I thought it was clarity at the time. Looking back, I realized it was the sort of 'clarity' that is really the hangover effects of that potent cocktail comprising a lack of sleep, grief, stress, and overwhelming anxiety.

I am going to have to do it myself, I realized. *I am going to have to take on Jarl.*

With that thought came a curious sense of calm. I'm an English lit nerd, as everyone knows, and one of my favorite authors is James Joyce. It took me forever to understand what he was all about when I first read his book of short stories, *Dubliners*. They're the coolest short stories that all end with their protagonist having an epiphany: one of those lightbulb moments when everything becomes clear. But in some of the short stories, like 'Araby', the epiphany was definitely important to the character, but I could also see that his 'epiphany' was really a shortsighted reaction to an event, and one that would get the character into trouble in the long term.

Then I read Joyce's *Portrait of the Artist as a Young Man*. That book is five chapters, and each chapter ends with this great big epiphany that totally changes Stephen Dedalus's perception of the world and his place in it. He has this transcendent moment and then *bang*: the next chapter starts with him living through the issues, problems, and backlash of whatever choice his epiphany led him to make in the preceding chapter. I finally realized that Joyce's epiphanies weren't wrong or right; they just *were*. The epiphanies brought a kind of momentary clarity that would soon be dispelled, but in that moment they were all-encompassing.

And that's the sort of calm I felt right at that moment. I felt as if I'd realized something so fundamental that, for me, it was as important as realizing the earth orbited the sun. Granted, I should have known to distrust such emotions from reading my Joyce, but whatever. The power of the epiphany is that you don't realize it's slightly batshit till *after* you've acted on it.

It's all up to me, was my epiphany, my moment of clarity. I also realized I couldn't let anyone know what I'd realized.

They'll try to stop you, I told myself. I wasn't sure yet what they'd try to stop, but I knew something was cooking in my overwrought brainpan. *So act normal.*

And normal I acted. I apologized, then sat down and watched TV with Daoud and Caleb. Ryu and Anyan talked strategy for a while, then both went to make some phone calls. Anyan tried to get me to go train with him, but I begged off, claiming exhaustion. I went to my room early, saying I wanted to shower and hit the hay. And I did take a shower, but I also packed up my bag with what I thought would be good sneaking-away items.

I waited, listening, till everyone had gone to bed. Then I crept out of my room. I tiptoed through the silent common area, only realizing when I was halfway through that Daoud was snoring away through his big hawk-nose where he'd fallen asleep on the couch.

Taking a deep breath and trying to still my pounding heart, I grabbed the keys to one of our rental cars, Ryu's Garmin, and a box of Clif bars (a girl has to eat, even when she's on the lam), then snuck out the main room into the hallway. Trying to be as quiet as I could, I very, very slowly and carefully closed the door behind me, where it settled with the softest of *snicks*. Standing there, listening to hear if Ryu or Anyan came bursting out of their bedrooms, I nearly realized how stupid I was being. But I was, in fact, being stupid, so that moment was short-lived.

Soon enough, there I was: waiting for the elevator, my old duffel slung half empty over my shoulder. It felt strange to be waiting for an elevator when I was embarking on what was going to be, one way or another, the climax of my vengeance quest, but I suppose that even the baddest badass sometimes has to wait for transportation.

Then I was in the parking garage, pressing the unlock button on the keys to figure out which of our rental cars I had the pleasure of stealing. When I saw lights flash from the SUV to my left, I went to throw my bag in the passenger's seat. And nearly pissed in my pants when I heard someone clear his throat behind me.

Clutching my racing heart, I turned around, ready to be yelled at by either Ryu or Anyan. Instead, watching me quietly and cleaning his glasses, stood Julian.

'Off to get captured?' he asked mildly before putting his glasses back on.

'No.' I frowned. 'I'm off to seek revenge!'

My voice echoed hollowly around the nearly empty parking garage as Julian and I blinked at each other. Then started giggling.

When we were finished laughing at me, and I'd retrieved my duffel from the passenger's seat, Julian and I sat on the rear bumper of the car so we could talk.

'Nothing's going to happen, Jules. Can I call you Jules?'

'Only if I can slap you each and every time you do.'

'Hmmm. Fair enough. Seriously, though, nothing's going to happen. Jarl's gonna walk away from all this chaos, again.'

'I know.'

'We have to *do* something.'

'We do. And, believe it or not, I think you have the right idea.'

'What?' I asked, blinking at him. Now that I'd been stopped, I realized just how patently ridiculous my 'plan' had been.

'You're Jane. And Jane does rash, stupid things that get her captured. You're our weak link, or so everyone thinks. No offense.'

'None taken?' I replied drily.

'Seriously, think about it. Everyone's always talked about using you as bait, about how you need to be watched, and guarded, etcetera. I think, even more than revenge, that's why Jarl's going after people close to you. I mean, I know he does hate you, but Jarl hasn't gotten to where he is today because he can't control himself.'

I blinked at Julian's words. I was used to thinking of Jarl

as out to get me, but even I had to admit that what Julian was saying made sense.

'Jarl thinks if he can get to you and flush you out, you'll be easy pickings. You are strong, and what you did to Ryu and Anyan proves your strength. But your greatest asset is that people can't help but underestimate you. Even people who should know better, like Ryu, can't help but think you're vulnerable. It's like you channel some baby seal aura that makes everyone want to coo over you. We can use that to our advantage.'

I giggled, knowing that what Julian said was true. And the thought of using something that had always driven me crazy – people's perception of me as weak – thrilled me.

'So what do we do?' I asked.

'We go rogue. You and I: Team Halfling.'

'But what do we *do*? Besides order vanity T-shirts?'

'We do what the others won't. We use you as bait. But we have a plan; we don't just send you out into the night with some Clif bars.'

'Clif bars are very sustaining. And delicious.'

Julian laughed. 'Only you would pack snacks for revenge.'

'Be nice. So what are you thinking of?'

'I'm thinking we figure out a way to track you. With current technologies, that should be pretty straightforward. Then we wait till we know the harpies are watching and we do a repeat of tonight's escape. Only smart and strategic, instead of cockamamie.'

'Did you take your sassy pills tonight, Jules?'

'Seriously, Jane. I will cut a bitch.'

'Where did you even learn that expression? Have you been watching *RuPaul's Drag Race* again?'

We laughed at each other, a laugh full of not only humor but also anticipation. I felt good about this – about having a plan and working with Julian.

'I think this might just work,' I said after a few moments.

'Yeah,' Julian said, meeting my black eyes with his sea-green. 'I do, too.'

At that moment, I remembered talking with Iris. It felt like years but was only a few weeks ago when she'd said, 'Your plans always suck, Jane.' And she was right. My plans *did* suck. But we could use that fact to our advantage, by backing up people's perception of me as a bit of a fuckwit with Julian's cool head for strategy. In other words, Team Halfling could use all that prejudice against halflings to our advantage, setting it against the worst perpetrators of that prejudice.

The only thing I enjoyed more than karma was chocolate cake. Oh, and cheese. And oysters. Oh, and . . . Anyway, my point is that I *liked* the idea of Team Halfling, on every level.

Chapter Twenty-One

Over the next week, Julian and I lay low. I made a show of sulking for a day or two, then slowly getting back on board with the investigation. Julian, meanwhile, did what Julian always did: he ordered gadgets, did computer research, and blinked owlishly at all of us from behind his glasses.

In reality, however, he was planning what we'd dubbed Team Halfling's Debut du Shenanigans. We were feeling international when we named our mission, as we'd been drinking Chimay. It happens.

Reports from the Borderlands and throughout the Territory, meanwhile, remained grim. Labs were still cropping up, burned out, with everyone in them slaughtered. Ryu would diligently travel to each place, looking for clues, but never turning up any.

The only good news we received in this time was that the powers of Ula Kappa and the other rescued females had begun to regenerate. She'd be able to return to the ocean soon, which I was very happy to hear. Otherwise we sat, and we waited. And whenever I started to lose my nerve, another report would come in, screwing my courage to the sticking-place. We needed a break in this case, and I was determined to be that break.

That said, I'd begun to lose faith we'd ever get our chance, when Caleb came into our suite one day carrying coffee.

'Harpies are back,' he declared. 'Caught a glimpse of one of our foul-feathered foes on the roof.'

I felt my face flush and forced myself not to look at Julian.

'Well, we knew they were probably around somewhere at this point,' Anyan sighed. 'Now we just have confirmation. Their presence changes nothing.'

Little does he know, I thought, then felt an uncomfortable flush of betrayal. The barghest and I had been training every day, laughing and enjoying each other's company. I felt horrible holding anything back from him, but I knew he would never agree to the scheme Julian and I had cooked up. And if I had to ruin my chances with Anyan long-term to get the evidence we needed against Jarl, so be it.

Idiot! my libido hissed at me, and if I were honest I had to agree. I hated the idea of betraying Anyan's trust. But some things were bigger than me and my own desires.

That night, I went to bed early and I did actually doze off for a few hours before there was a gentle knock on my door, at around three in the morning.

'They're all asleep,' Julian whispered, sidling into my room after I cracked the door open and closing it behind him. 'And Ryu's out feeding. This is our moment.'

It was testament to my nervousness that I didn't flinch at Julian's saying Ryu was out feeding.

'Let's do this quickly. I've tested the device – taped it inside Daoud's iPod arm-holster before he went jogging. Knew where he was every step of the time. Which reminds me, I'm not sure stopping at Dunkin' Donuts is really part of a serious fitness regimen, but it's his body.'

I giggled, only to have my giggle turn to a gulp as Julian pulled out a massive syringe.

'What the fuck?' I asked, wide-eyed.

'It's the only way to implant the device quickly,' he explained, his voice very reasonable for someone holding what looked like an elephant tranquilizer. 'This syringe is loaded with a tiny GPS tracker, about the size of a grain of rice. We need to insert it under your skin, and this is the best way.'

I blinked at Julian, then at the syringe, then back to Julian.

'C'mon, Jane. With this device, I know exactly where you are, every second you're gone. This is not negotiable.'

I gritted my teeth, nodding once sharply.

'Fine. Let's do it. Where do you want to stick it?'

'Somewhere squidgy. Your belly, maybe?'

'I can't believe you called my belly "squidgy". It's not squidgy, it's *pillowy*. And sexy!'

'I'm sure it's very sexy. Shirt up.'

'Can I lie on the bed?'

'Go for it.'

I lay down, pulling the bottom of my long-sleeved black tee up a little ways, screwing my eyes shut as Julian advanced on me with his horrible syringe.

At the end of the day, I've experienced much worse things than getting chipped, but not many. When Julian was done, he swiped an alcohol swatch over the pain. Then he helped me sit up, keeping his hand in mine as he stared into my eyes.

'We'll do a test lap around the hotel before you go, but that should do it.'

I gulped. Now that the Debut du Shenanigans was upon us, I was scared shitless.

'You ready for this, Jane?'

'No,' I replied.

'Good. I'll be, quite literally, one step behind you the entire time.'

He placed a Bluetooth device in his ear and opened his laptop as I grabbed my duffel, which was freshly packed with a change of clothes, Ryu's GPS I'd swiped earlier, and my Clif bars.

'I'll stay in here. Go down, get the car, and call me. When I give you the go-ahead, drive toward the Compound. I'll let you know right away if the chip isn't working, and you head back immediately. Got that?'

I nodded. 'Got it.'

'Ready?'

'As I'll ever be.'

We stared at each other from across the room: him sitting on my bed with his laptop, me by the door with my duffel.

'Go Team Halfling,' I said, grinning over my fear.

'Go Team Halfling,' he agreed, returning my smile. 'I'll keep you safe, Jane.'

I nodded. I already knew he would.

I idled on the empty night street in front of the hotel, lowering my head under cover of searching my purse. 'Can you hear me?' I whispered into the empty air. Hoping I was being watched by prying eyes, I needed to hide my lips and my own Bluetooth device with my long hair.

'Loud and clear,' came Julian's reply. 'And I'm tracking you fine so far. You ready?'

'Sure thing,' I replied before looking up. I scrolled through Ryu's Garmin till I found what I wanted: Compound. I pressed Go, and then I went where it told me to go.

'I'll let you know if the chip fails for some reason. But you're fine for right now. Keep your earpiece in as long as you can, okay?'

I mmm-hmmmed in response, as I had to keep my head up and my eyes on the road to drive.

'Good, thanks. I'll stop talking now, in case someone wakes up.'

I grimaced, envisioning what would happen when Anyan and Ryu woke up to find me missing, Julian propped up in my bed watching my progress on his laptop.

They better not kill him, I thought. Then, more nervously, *I hope they don't kill him . . .*

I shook my head, focusing on the here and now. They weren't going to kill Julian, and, in the meantime, I had to concentrate on making our plan a success.

Speaking of mission, I also couldn't help but think about my own, botched attempt at revenge last week. Now that I'd embarked upon a *real* mission, I couldn't help but shudder thinking about how stupid I'd been.

So many things could have gone wrong, I thought, horrifying visions sweeping through my brain like waves in a storm. *And even if you'd been successful and reached the Compound, what the hell were you going to do? Kill a man in cold blood? Are you really capable of such an act?*

I hated Jarl with every bone in my body. I loathed him; I thought he was a blight on the planet, a tumor to be excised. And yet, if I were honest, I knew I would never have been capable of doling out such justice myself.

Besides, what were you going to kill him with? Choke him with a Clif bar? You don't even have any physical weapons, let alone know how to handle one.

I remembered Conleth's face when he'd stuck that knife through my palm. He'd been a cold-blooded murderer, but lobbing fire or mage balls at someone from a distance was a fuck of a lot different than sticking a knife in someone's back.

Good Lord, I thought. *What would I have to do to become a real killer?*

I mused on that while driving through the dark night, my head full of even darker thoughts.

I'd been driving about two hours when my phone rang. It was Julian's name that popped up on my screen so, under cover of a cheek scratch, I accepted the call.

'Your signal's still coming in loud and clear,' Julian said. 'And everyone's still asleep. Any sign of the harpies?'

I was in a very wooded, very deserted stretch of highway somewhere. I was having trouble reading the GPS, as far as figuring out where I actually was. But as long as it kept telling me where to go next, I didn't really care. I looked around again, stretching my neck out as I peered into the darkness.

'Mmm-hmm,' I mumbled, not moving my lips.

''Kay,' he said. 'Don't forget to call me the second you think they're coming. In case the chip goes out, we need to know where you were when you were taken so we can track you on the ground. All right?'

I murmured my assent, and he was just saying goodbye when I hissed.

'Wait.'

I wasn't sure if I was seeing things, but I could swear that I'd seen a shadow moving strangely in the rearview.

'I think this is it,' I said as I finally went under one of the highway's sparse streetlights and, just as I'd expected, my SUV's shadow had suddenly grown just a little bit wider. And wingier.

'Game on,' I murmured. 'If this isn't it, I'll call back. Otherwise, expect me to have been kidnapped. Hanging up now,' I said. 'Don't lose me.'

'I won't, Jane. Good luck.'

'Thanks,' I said, then canceled the call from the earpiece, unclipping it deftly and stashing it under my seat.

This is really it, I thought, trying to buck up my courage.

Despite my attempts at preparing myself, I still felt a bizarre admixture of fear, adrenaline, and expectancy when something landed on the top of the SUV. And when a fist slammed through the window to my right, I remembered only at the last minute that I wasn't supposed to *want* to be captured, and threw up a shield.

From either side – one at each window – two upside-down sets of beady harpy eyes peered at me from above their small, hawk-like beaks.

The good news was that all of Phaedra's crew had been absent when I managed to extricate all of us from the Alfar's magical net all those months ago in Boston. So no one besides my allies knew exactly how much power I had. And, because I was a halfling, most assumed it was very little. In order to seal their assumptions, I threw a few weak mage balls at the harpies' heads, which they batted away contemptuously, motioning for me to pull off the road.

Feigning terror (hey, it was mostly feigned, really), I did as they bade me, forcing myself to maintain my shields at their weakest level as if that was all I could produce. I slowed the vehicle as I pulled off to my right, then stopped with my hands on the wheel.

'Kaya,' I said, my voice neutral as the dun-feathered harpy on my left side dropped to the ground and opened my door. 'Or Kaori,' I amended, having no idea which one she was.

The other harpy came around to join her sister, only *her* eyes were glowing with rage.

Graeme's girlfriend, I thought.

The less-desirous-of-my-death harpy jerked her head to the side, indicating she wanted me out of the car. I did as she asked me, my knees nearly buckling when I finally slid to a halt.

Then, with a little giggle that sounded more than a little crazy, even to my own ears, I held up both my hands.

'Take me to your leader,' I intoned, just as the angry harpy lunged toward me, fist extended.

Then I saw stars . . .

And then I saw nothing.

Chapter Twenty-Two

I woke up in a moving vehicle, with a sore jaw and unable to see. Luckily, the blindness wasn't an aftereffect of the punching; I'd been hooded with a rough sacking that chafed my nose. My wrists had also been tied behind me, leaving me lying on my right arm. The harpies must have pushed the backseat forward to lay me out. There was quiet whispering in front of me, and the car was cold and very windy. I put together that the harpies had just bundled me into my own vehicle.

I wasn't sure how long I'd been out, but I was really stiff – the arm I was lying on completely asleep – and it tasted like something had died in my mouth. So it must have been quite a while.

When the last of the muzziness had left my head and I was able to scootch around a bit to take some of the pressure off my dead arm, I tried listening to what the harpy twins were saying. I was also curious as I'd never heard them speak. Their voices were whispery and strange, with a lot of clacking from their beaks.

'. . . just kill her now. Phaedra will want to keep her. I want her dead.'

And that must be Graeme's girlfriend, I realized.

'Phaedra will kill *us* if we kill her. Be patient.'

'But I want her dead,' Kaya (or Kaori) whined.

And I wish I hadn't moved, I realized, as the burning, sword-sized cousins of pins and needles crept up my now-very-much-awake arm.

I gritted my teeth against the pain, trying to eavesdrop. Unfortunately, it was mostly about how, not if, I would die a terrible death. The one sister was demanding the horrible death *now*, while the other sister assured her twin that the horrible death would be *even more horrible* if only they waited till I was in 'his' hands.

Curiously, I was as yet unfazed by their discussion. In my discombobulated state, I clung to the idea that this was all part of the plan, that Julian knew where I was and that Anyan would crush heads when he came for me. On that note, I shifted about even more so the side of my belly that had the chip was pointed to the ceiling, beaming out its data for all and sundry to collect. The position was extremely painful, and I knew I didn't have to do so, that I was being silly. But as I became more conscious, I could feel an edge of panic start to flood over me . . .

Not least because, at the thought of the chip came other memories: those of the women we'd talked to in Rhode Island. I felt the panic creeping faster, and I prayed not to be implanted with any extraneous body parts before Anyan got to me.

Anyan, I thought, focusing on the barghest. I thought of his strength, his resolution, his fierce protectiveness.

He will find me, he will find me, he will find me . . .

Repeating this mantra to myself while envisioning the barghest's solid-black doggie-form, I rolled over till I was flat on my stomach and no longer squishing anything. Then I went ahead and pushed myself into my hospital-honed hypnagogic state, knowing I was going to need my wits about me whenever we arrived where we were going.

A long while later, I was jolted to full awareness by somebody opening the hatchback at my feet and pulling me out roughly by the ankles. My hood was dragged up as I came out and, for a split second, my light-dazzled eyes made out a few fuzzy black shapes. But then the hood was pulled down and all was black again.

I was breathing hard, fear flooding my system. Now that I'd rested a bit and had time to absorb what I'd just done, our 'brilliant' plan was showing its flaws.

What if somebody just shoots you in the head, moron? But I shook myself, unwilling to believe that would happen.

Julian and I have thought this through. I've gotta be worth something to somebody. At least to keep alive until somebody who really wants to kill me can come down and do it themselves . . . And worth even more as bait for the others.

So I stilled my trembling and forced myself to breathe, hearing people shuffle around me. I was led forward roughly, then dragged up a few steps, which of course I tripped and nearly fell over.

Whatever caught me before I could face-plant had very strong hands tipped with very, very sharp claws. Those hands raised me up, with disquieting gentleness, until I was standing solidly again on my own two feet.

Then the hands raised to my neck, the sharp claws grazing my jugular, as the hood was pulled from my head and discarded.

I stood there, blinking and willing my eyes to adjust. Finally, the black shape in front of me focused, revealing the identity of my captor.

The Healer, I realized, for the being in front of me could only be that infamous goblin-halfling.

We were standing in the bright sunshine on a low stoop in front of a grand old house. There was absolutely nothing else around that I could see, although my freedom to look around was hampered by both my stiff neck and the fact I was being held so close to my captor.

As for the Healer, human eyes stared at me from a neat, bland human face. Except the human flesh ended right along his jaw, up in front of his ears, and at his hairline. From there on he was all goblin: green scales, pointy ears, and so on. Except that his scales started tapering off again right along his forearms, which became pale, slightly freckled human flesh. On the tip of each otherwise human finger gleamed thick, black, wickedly sharp claws.

'Jane True. It's a pleasure to make your acquaintance,' the Healer murmured in an incongruously lovely Scottish accent.

I nodded my head, trying to appear unfazed.

'So many people wanting to get their hands on such a wee lass. Makes me wonder what all the fuss is about. Still, we must take precautions . . . Avery?'

With that, another goblin stepped close, only this one was a pureblood. And unlike the Healer, who was wearing a button-up dress shirt and slacks under a lab coat, Avery was wearing medical scrubs.

'Dr Avery here is going to give you a little shot. I'm afraid it does sting a bit.'

The Healer's hands pulled down on my forearms, holding them against my sides even as he held me still. I realized, then, what was about to happen . . .

They're going to give me that shot that takes away magic.

For a second I nearly panicked. The thought of being powerless, stripped of my only weapon, horrified me.

Easy, girl, I reminded myself. *You've had magic for about eight minutes of your life. And it's* not *your only weapon. You*

*survived a hell of a lot before you learned about your powers;
don't underestimate yourself.*

So again I stilled my body, calling on every calming tech-
nique I'd learned during my stay in the mental hospital. I
stared into the Healer's average brown eyes as the goblin,
Avery, raised a needle to my neck. After a moment, I felt a
sharp pain right near my collarbone.

When Avery pressed down on the plunger, it felt like he
was shooting fire into me. The pain was so sharp that I did
cry out then, jerking away even as the goblin withdrew the
syringe, causing my skin to tear around the exit wound. Blood
ran down my neck and into my shirt as the Healer *tsked*.
Pulling a pristine white handkerchief out of his pocket, he
pressed it against my neck.

'Such delicate skin . . . we don't want to mar it, Miss True.
Not yet, anyway.'

The Healer smirked, and his otherwise normal brown eyes
met mine. What I saw buried in them was so evil that, finally,
I lost control and struggled. He laughed, clamping his arms
about me along with his magic. Reflexively, I tried to raise
my own shields and do what I'd thought about doing to Anyan
in the park: use my defenses as a wall to force the goblin-
halfling away. But nothing happened; it was like reaching
into an abyss.

My magic is gone, I realized. With that final defeat I stopped
struggling.

'Aye, that's it. Good lass,' the Healer said, running the back
side of his claws down my cheek. 'You're ours now, hen. No
point in fighting it. Now, come inside, where it's warm.'

Is he going to offer me a cup of tea? I wondered, marveling
at how such a monster could be so very . . . British.

When we walked inside the beautiful, sprawling mansion,
it was like walking through a door to another dimension.

One minute everything was all manicured lawns, lovely orna-
mental trim, and clean white wood. The next minute we were
in some medical lab from Auschwitz.

The windows had been covered in heavy black material,
and what had no doubt once been chandeliers had been replaced
with caged fluorescent track lighting so that everything was
cast in an overly bright, eerie glow. The room to our left, which
might once have been a formal dining room, now contained a
blood-spattered gurney to which was strapped the remains
of . . . something. Whatever had been lying there was now just
a flagellated bundle of limbs. That sight was bad enough, but
when the limbs moved and I realized that whatever was lying
there was still alive, my gorge rose and I nearly vomited.

To the right of the once grand entryway was another large
room, now serving as some sort of break room. Various supes
in medical gear sat or stood about, chatting as if they were
in a hospital cafeteria rather than a factory of death.

I was hustled through another series of stately rooms, all
stocked with instruments of torture posing as medical devices.
Here and there I saw victims in various states of disrepair.
In one room, tied to a chair, sat a naked woman whose gaping
eye sockets stared blindly at me, crying wordlessly from a
mouth that no longer held a tongue. Two young boys – both
apparently human, although it was hard to tell – whose hands
had been amputated and their limbs sewn together at the
wrist, stared at me with exhausted eyes from the doorway of
one of the rooms we walked through. As we passed I could
smell the rot in their wounds so strongly I again nearly
vomited. In what had been a huge kitchen, a stack of heads
sat next to a stockpot bubbling on an expensive stove, and
the opened refrigerator held arms packed into it like cordwood –
their fingers sticking out like obscene sticks. The freezer
contained a similar stack of amputated legs.

Through the kitchen was a door, next to which sat a table. On the table lay a woman's body, spread-eagled and naked from the waist down. Her throat had been cut.

The kitchen is what did, finally, make me puke. Pulling away from where the Healer held me on my right, I leaned over to my left and heaved my guts out. At the same time, the Healer pulled up on my arms so that pain whizzed through me, causing tears to form in my eyes as I retched.

'It's hardly good form to vomit on the floor of your host,' the goblin-halfling said with a sigh, as if I had disappointed him deeply.

He held me there, my arms singing with pain, until I was done throwing up, then turned me around to face him. Pulling out another clean handkerchief from his other pocket, he wiped my mouth fussily.

'Really thought you'd be fiercer than that, hen,' he said. 'After all the trouble you've caused, I find out you're just another weak female . . .' He frowned at me, as if assessing me. 'But you are a pretty little thing. When we get the go-ahead to begin your treatment, my boys will enjoy you. And it is part of my job to keep my boys' morale boosted.'

Nodding to himself, he opened the door in front of me then pulled me down the stairs. If I thought I'd been horrified walking through the house, I should have known it could only get worse the farther one descended. Hell is under the earth for a reason, after all.

The first thing that hit me, going down those stairs, was the stench. Vomit, piss, shit, blood, sweat, and fear all battled with one another for supremacy within my nostrils. Layout-wise, it was a typical old-house basement, times about a thousand, with the same low ceilings as my basement in Maine, but this one sprawled out like a rabbit warren in every possible direction. Meanwhile, all I could see around me were cells. Many were empty, but they were so numerous that room was left for dozens of prisoners. Mostly the cells contained females, although I saw a few males here and there. Dirty faces with anguished eyes stared up at me as we passed individual cells, and I realized just how big the operation was here. And how crazy.

They're suffering a population crisis, yet they're destroying their own kind like children stepping on anthills. It's nuts . . . which is the point, I guess. Jarl and his cronies are nuts. And if they've convinced themselves that they can end the fertility crisis, they must also be able to convince themselves that a few sacrifices now are worth being able to breed freely later.

Plus, I realized, the victims were people like my mother, and Iris, who had given birth to halflings.

The enemy, according to Jarl.

I was led farther and farther back, until we came to another set of low doors. Before pushing through them, we acquired another guard, who followed us with curiosity etched all over his face. He had the same weird bendiness of the dryad maid Elspeth who'd served me at the Compound, and I assumed he was of her faction. When all four of us entered the white-tiled space behind the new doors, we were standing in a much smaller room full of cells. These cells were also much cleaner, with real cots instead of shabby blankets on the floor, and proper toilets and sinks.

Taking me to the first of the cells, the Healer opened the door with a large set of keys and pushed me through. I backed to the far corner as the guard who'd followed tried to enter the cell as well, his hands at the crotch of his pants. But the goblin-halfling stopped him.

'No, son. Not her; at least not yet. We've got plans for that one.'

The guard backed up, casting one last feverish glance over

my body before turning to leave the little room. The Healer shook his head as Avery stepped forward.

'Avery, you're in charge of her for the now. Don't touch; as I said, she's not yet for use. Most likely this little one will be bait. She has some powerful friends who have been a burr in our sides these many months. Apparently she's very valuable to the other side, for some reason, and the chief thinks they'll do just about anything to get her back. After they're dead, she can take her place in our experiments.' The Healer smiled at me, then Avery. 'Let her rest, but don't forget to give her a follow-up shot this evening. Oh, and remember to organize our other little surprise.'

With that, the Healer clapped Avery on the shoulder, very much like a father sending his favorite son off to play in the homecoming game, before he turned to leave.

'Oh, where are my manners,' he said, pausing mid-stride. 'Ta, Miss True. Enjoy your stay here at our humble abode. We'll take very good care of you, I can assure you.' And with that he smiled at me so pleasantly that I was nearly sick again. This time, when he turned to walk away, he didn't stop.

Avery stood at my cell door, studying me. His yolk-yellow goblin eyes were impossible to read, and his face was impassive. Not knowing what he was thinking, but assuming it was something foul, I put all my hatred and my pride in the look I sent back at him.

He just kept staring until he, too, walked out of the white-tiled room. Leaving me to sit, shaky-legged, on my cot, wondering what the hell we'd been thinking when Julian and I cooked up our little scheme.

The next hours were hell. I don't know how long I lay there, staring at the ceiling, but it was a long time. When there was finally a clattering at the main door, I leaped off my cot, ready to face whoever came at me.

It was Avery, his tall, slender goblin frame holding a syringe in one hand and a small plate with a sandwich and an apple in the other. Placing the plate on a small table near the door to the room, he used his now empty hand to retrieve a single-serving bottle of water from his pocket, which he also set down on the table. He came toward my cell, syringe in hand, when the door clattered open to reveal the overly eager guard from that afternoon.

'Need help?' the dryad asked Avery, and I saw the goblin frown before he blanked his expression and turned toward his cohort.

'Now, Derek, why would I need help with a little halfling-female?'

The guard blinked.

'Why don't you go play with someone else. Or better yet, clean out some of the other cages. It's fucking disgusting out there.'

Derek grunted, looking at the ground.

'Well?' Avery intoned, sounding increasingly miffed.

'Well, *he* says I'm supposed to watch. Make sure she gets her second dose.'

The goblin before me blinked at the dryad, his face speaking volumes in its coldness.

'Fine. Just . . . stay out of my way.'

'Yes, sir,' Derek said, shuffling his feet awkwardly.

Avery unlocked the door to my cell, then stepped through, carefully pocketing his syringe as he did so. I knew I had no chance in hell of escaping that place; not with all the guards milling about. But the thought of him giving me that second shot, which was obviously important, terrified me so much that I reacted reflexively. Striking out at Avery, I tried to make a break for it, only to be caught in the viselike grip of the goblin doctor.

'Stay there, Derek,' Avery barked as he used his goblin's terrific strength to manhandle me to my cot and sit me down. Then he positioned himself so that his back was to the door, turning me so that I had one butt cheek teetering on the cot with my own back to the walled corner of my cell.

What he did next was entirely unexpected. Leaning down, he placed his scaley green lips against my ear.

'Yell for me,' he whispered. 'As you know, it's supposed to hurt.'

And then he raised the needle to my neck, only to go right past it to squirt the contents of the syringe under my shirt and down my spine. Partly because he'd commanded, and partly because the fluid was cold, I groaned, then added another whimper for safety's sake.

Then I looked into his yellow eyes, cocking my head inquiringly. He lowered his lips to my ear one more time.

'I want out of this hellhole . . .' he whispered.

'And you, little halfling, are my Get Out of Jail Free card.'

Chapter Twenty-Three

I slept fitfully that evening, and was almost relieved when Avery the goblin came bright and early to give me breakfast and another shot. Just like last night, he squirted this one harmlessly behind me.

'Just don't use your magic at all,' he repeated sotto voce. 'Or the jig is up.'

I nodded, still completely unsure whether to trust this guy. On the one hand, I could understand somebody wanting to get out of this prison, even if he was one of the guards. On the other hand, these people obviously made a hobby out of sadism, so convincing me that I had an ally and then crushing my dreams of freedom might simply be an example from page 198 of their *Idiot's Guide to Torture*.

But why risk leaving me my powers? I thought. Then I frowned.

You don't actually know if your powers have reappeared, because if you use them, you're screwed. So you have to assume they're there . . . because the enemy doctor who is helping you for no obvious reason says they are.

I glared at the doctor kneeling before me, trying to figure out why the hell he would help me, but I couldn't read anything in those yellow eyes. When he rose to leave, I lay back down on my cot, planning to spend the day in the hypnagogic doze I'd mastered all those years ago when I'd been committed.

It had only been a short time – maybe an hour – when I heard the main door open once again. I liked to think I was ready for whatever they were going to spring on me, but I wasn't at all ready for what came through that door.

'Iris!' I shouted with a combination of joy and horror: joy to see my friend alive, horror at the condition she was in.

Her once-gorgeous blonde hair was lank and matted; her body emaciated and clad in only a too-short dirty T-shirt. But it was the haunted look in her eyes that almost destroyed me.

'Iris, Iris, Iris,' I chanted, *willing* her to look at me, *willing* her to show me that there was still a little of my friend behind that blank, shattered mask. She never once looked up as she was led to the cell opposite me.

The guard leading her – a small, wiry satyr – shoved her roughly inside, stopping once he'd shut the door to shake his head at her.

'She was such fun when she was brought in. But they just don't take proper care of themselves,' he told me conversationally. Like the Healer, he also had a British accent. But his was a posh one, like Wooster's in *Jeeves and Wooster*. The satyr's manners, however, were hardly elegant, as he let his eyes wander over my body. 'They come in so lovely, but after we get to play, they wind up looking like mangled dolls at a boot sale.'

What the fuck is a boot sale? I'll give him a boot, I thought, staring at him with fury beating through me. He was barely shielded. I could catch him unaware with a mage ball, right now, and there'd be one less monster lurking in the dark . . .

And that would kill your chances of getting Iris out of here, completely. So keep a lid on it.

I let hate fill my expression, but managed to hold in check both my temper and my magic. The satyr watched me with careful eyes, and only then did I realize he was assessing me.

This was a test, I thought. *And I passed. They wanted to make sure the goblin did his job, and they wanted to torture me with Iris's condition, no doubt. But in the meantime, they think I've been neutered.*

For the first time since the goblin had squirted that shot down my back, I started to believe he was on the up-and-up; that we were going to get out of here.

The satyr was still watching me quietly, waiting to feel something from me, but I kept my power contained. Having lived as a human for so long, I found it relatively easy to slip back into no-magic mode. After a few more minutes, he nodded and turned on his heel to stalk out. As soon as he was gone, I turned to my friend.

'Iris, honey, look at me . . .'

She kept staring at the ground in front of her, not registering my existence in any way that I could see.

'Iris. Iris? Honey, I'm here . . .' I kept on like that for a few minutes. Finally, and imperceptibly, she shook her head.

'Yes,' I said, starting to choke up. 'Yes, hon. I'm here.' Her only response was to keep shaking her head no.

Why? Why isn't she saying anything? My own brain spasmed with shock and pain at my friend's sudden reappearance, her condition, and her refusal to acknowledge me. Then I thought of my own reaction to the goblin doctor's help; my apprehension about trusting anyone or anything in this place.

She probably thinks I'm some illusion, here to torture her . . . So I switched tactics, and instead of telling Iris I was there, I started to talk about home.

'Remember the first time we met, Iris? When I was with

Ryu, and we were investigating Jakes's murder? I thought you were so intimidating. So put together and beautiful. I think I was a little scared of you.' Blinking back tears that cropped up as I thought of that shining woman and compared her with the broken body in front of me, I forged on. 'Ryu and I were just starting to see one another, and I was just learning about your world. I was so excited, but so scared. Remember?'

Iris still wasn't acknowledging my words, but she had stopped shaking her head.

She's listening, I told myself, praying I was right.

'Remember how you dressed me in all those crazy outfits? That big red belt, right under my boobs? Those pants? I'd only ever worn jeans and T-shirts up to then. I couldn't even figure out how to get into most of those clothes. I would have tied the sash on that kimono dress over my hair, like a head-band, if you hadn't helped me.'

Iris's head had cocked almost imperceptibly. If I hadn't been studying her like my life depended on it, I wouldn't have caught it. But it was there . . . just the tiniest crook to her neck.

She is *listening*, I thought exultantly.

'And those shoes. I nearly broke my neck about four times in all those heels. Remember how I told you about falling in the Compound? We were in the Pig Sty; it was only the second or third time we went out together. I'd been afraid to tell you at first, not wanting you to think I was criticizing your fashion choices. But then we drank a little too much, and I told you about how I fell, and you snorted vodka martini out of your nose into the pretzels, and it burned so badly your eyes watered and made your mascara run and I told you that you looked like a raccoon.'

Silence.

'Well, you got back at me when I forgot and ate the freaking pretzels. Then you said, "And you just ate my nose juice." We laughed for like twenty minutes.'

Silence. I was getting desperate.

'Anyway, I told you all about falling at the Compound. But at least I did it in Jimmy Choos, right? And I guess falling means that everyone got to see the red soles . . .'

'Louboutin,' came a hoarse whisper from across the way. I froze. 'Sorry?'

'Not Choos. They were Louboutins.'

'Oh, right.' I was thrilled to get a reaction, any reaction, but I knew Iris wasn't yet sold I was the real deal.

'They were Louboutins, weren't they, Iris? And you know the funniest part?' This time I didn't keep talking. I waited till she acknowledged my question. Eventually she did so, just the barest flick of her eyes in my direction: up, then back down at the floor.

'At the time, I freaked out because Ryu bought me all that stuff. I never liked him buying me things, but it felt really weird then since we barely knew each other. And I knew everything was expensive, but here's the funny part: I thought shoes like that cost around a hundred dollars.' I forced myself to laugh, just like we were sitting across from each other at the Sty rather than trapped in hell. 'A hundred dollars! For Louboutins! Can you believe it? And even then I felt so guilty . . .'

'Jane?' Iris whispered. My heart lurched and I forgot to breathe.

'Yes, Iris. It's really me.'

Then she started to cry. Wrenching sobs broke from her tortured body, and I reacted like a panicked mother hen. I jumped up, flapping my arms wildly.

'Oh, Iris, no, don't cry! It's okay! I'm here!'

'I don't want you here,' she said as she sobbed. 'They're going to hurt you . . . the things they do . . .' Her voice was no longer full of honeyed anything, but empty, aching.

'Shhh, Iris. Shhh. We're going to get out of here. Trust me . . . Shhh . . .'

But she obviously didn't trust me, because she sobbed until she'd cried herself out. Then she drank from the little sink in her cell, I guess to refill, and cried some more. The whole time I kept telling her how much I loved her, and that it was going to be okay. Eventually, however, I'd had enough. Under normal circumstances I'd let her cry till she shriveled up like a raisin if that's what she needed to do, but we had bigger fish to fry.

'Iris? Iris? You gotta stop crying . . . I need you to talk to me. Iris? I really need you to talk to me.' After I'd said that about four hundred times, she finally looked up.

'Iris, I need you to tell me about this place. Tell me about what goes on, and when, and about what you've seen of the layout . . .'

She was hesitant at first, scared to talk too much. I think she still half expected my form to shift into that of one of the guards, or the Healer, and she'd discover that she'd been duped. Or maybe to disappear altogether – just a mirage. But as she talked, and I listened without commenting, she grew in confidence until words were streaming out of her.

I shouldn't have been surprised at how much she knew; Iris was a consumate gossip, soaking up everything around her. She wasn't always able to perceive what was most important, or focus during the moment, but she heard everything. And everything is what she told me: the history of the house as she'd picked it up from hearing the idle talk of guards; the problems with the security; how they were stretched a bit thin at the moment, guard-wise . . .

Apparently, the mansion we were in had been used as about a thousand different things over the years. Most recently, and briefly, it was a luxury hotel that went bankrupt. All of the mansion's various incarnations meant that it was ideal, in some ways, as a place of torture: lots of separate rooms upstairs for barracking guards and doctors and keeping prisoners, large reception rooms downstairs for labs, etcetera. But it also meant that it was a total hodgepodge of additions that had all been brought up to snuff in terms of our modern fire code. So the mansion was a mess, architecturally: lots of staircases, lots of mazelike rooms, and lots of exits. All of which translated into its being a pain to keep under lock and key at the best of times, but with a shortage of guards it was especially difficult. No one here was sure why the guard supply was low, as they weren't party to knowledge of the rate at which Jarl and his minions were liquidating labs on the outside. But I knew damned well that explained why his force was stretched thin at the moment.

I listened to Iris pour out everything she knew, had seen, or had heard. The worst was about the food: the kitchen wasn't filled with body parts just as macabre decoration. Apparently, nothing broke a person down like knowing they were eating Former Cellmate Stew.

I was very glad my sandwich yesterday had appeared to be ham. At least, I hoped it was ham.

Putting that thought firmly to the side, I kept one ear tuned to Iris while I started sorting through the information she'd given me.

The key is gonna be this basement, I thought. It was understandable why they'd put their cells down here: the basement was gross, relatively out of the way; the short ceilings made installing cells easy, and it left the (much nicer) rest of the house for the guards and doctors. But the basement was also, apparently, a rabbit warren of weird little rooms; staircases leading to various floors installed for numerous generations of servants, staff, and fire regs, many with exits to the outside world.

We were in a room with no exit, but apparently it was one of the only ones thus lacking. Iris had noticed that a lot of the other exits had been bricked in, but that didn't mean they were closed off to someone whose power was still intact . . . someone like me.

Hopefully, I reminded myself, still cautious.

'So when are the others coming?' Iris whispered, jerking my train of thought up short.

'Pardon?'

'You said we're getting out. When are the others coming?'

I pursed my lips, trying to figure out what to do. I desperately wanted to tell Iris that this was all a clever ruse cooked up by Team Halfling – that Operation Debut du Shenanigans was in full effect. But I also knew I couldn't . . . I couldn't risk alerting any listening ears to our plans or to their own imminent demise.

So instead of bolstering my friend's crushed confidence, I made an embarrassed face, hating myself the whole time.

'Well, um, I don't really know when they're coming. I'm sure they will come . . . but we have to bust out as soon as possible.'

Iris looked at me, and my heart nearly broke when I saw her face fall.

'You mean the others aren't, like, right outside? Just waiting for you to signal?'

'Um . . . no. Not really. I sort of . . . ran away. And was captured,' I lied.

Huge tears once again rolled down Iris's face. 'Jane! No! They're going to kill you! First they're going to torture you, then they're going to kill you. We're never going to escape . . .'

At that moment I really, really wanted to spill the beans – to tell her that wasn't going to happen. That I still had my power, that I was chipped, and that we had, maybe, an ally on the inside that was going to help us. But I didn't trust our environment and, if I was honest, I still didn't even trust Iris . . . I'd been reminding myself that she thought I was some sort of plant put there just to torture her.

But the same goes for her.

So instead of comforting her with the truth, I comforted her with the sort of nonsense our captors would want to hear, just in case they were listening, or Iris wasn't really Iris, or she was so broken she would spy for them. I told her Anyan would find me, that Anyan would come for us . . . At that she looked up sharply.

'Not Ryu?'

'Well, yeah. He'll come, too. Ryu will be with Anyan.'

'But you said *Anyan* would rescue you. Not Ryu. What happened between you two?'

I paused, unable to believe that now, despite everything, she really *did* want to gossip like we were sitting at the Pig Sty.

Okay, I acknowledged. *She really is Iris.*

'Um . . .' I responded. 'It's . . . complicated?'

Iris smiled then, and my heart nearly broke. It was a tiny, fractured, hesitant smile, and it lasted maybe a millisecond. But it was a smile. And it was truly Iris's.

Despite everything, she smiled, I thought, marveling at the resilience of these abused women, even as tears welled up in my eyes. But I blinked them back fiercely. Iris didn't need more grief; she needed to get out of here.

'Yeah, well, you know me . . . it's *always* complicated . . .'

Iris was about to reply when we had a visitor. As Avery rushed in, she scuttled backward into a corner of her cell and huddled there. He ignored her.

'Your friends have been spotted. They're close, really close. No one saw them coming; I don't know how they got here so quickly. This is our chance.'

I nodded, standing. 'I have an idea,' I told him as he opened my cell and walked briskly back to the main door.

'Good. So do I. Let's go.'

I stopped at the door to my cell, realizing that he intended to free only me.

'I'm not leaving without Iris.'

The doctor's yellow eyes flicked at my friend, huddled in the corner of her cell.

'Not an option. She's a liability.'

That's when I just about snapped. I still kept a cap on my magic, *just* in case, but my voice was so barbed I'm surprised it didn't cut the good doctor.

'She is *not* a liability. She is my friend. And a person. And you might be able to treat people like the sadistic fuck you are, but I am not leaving Iris behind!'

The goblin looked at me, then looked at Iris. Finally, he visibly gritted his teeth and headed toward her cell.

'Fine. She comes with. But do not judge me; you have no idea what I've been through. I never wanted any of this.' I stared at him mutinously, not believing he was making excuses for his actions.

'You are a part of this. Nothing you do now will ever wipe that stain away.' Realistically, I probably shouldn't have been condemning the only thing standing between us and freedom, but I was not about to hear how *he* was a victim.

He stared down at me, his eyes blinking furiously. 'You know nothing, halfling. Nothing about my family, about me,

or about our politics. I prepare the serum. That is all. I've
never touched these women otherwise. I made myself too
valuable to kill by learning the one thing nobody else knew,
and then I disobeyed every direct order except administering
those shots.'

'The shots that made your captives vulnerable to everything
else that happened to them.'

He flinched. I'd struck home.

'You are right, halfling. And I will have to live with myself.
But I also have saved whom I could. Like your friend here . . .
It was my idea to keep her alive, in case you were captured.
I came up with putting a fake file on her in all of our remaining
labs, just in case. I argued that would hurt you, but nothing
would break you like torturing her in front of you.'

I blinked, unable to process. 'So I'm supposed to thank
you for coming up with a plot that involved torturing my
friend in front of me.'

He nodded vehemently. 'I thought you'd never be captured!
Between that investigator and Anyan Barghest, you were so
well protected. I saved her life, dammit.'

I looked between the 'doctor' and my friend, her battered,
abused figure huddled in the corner of her cell.

'Sorry, but I wouldn't wait around for a thank-you note.
Look what they've *done* to her!'

He frowned. 'But she's alive.'

'That she is. And I intend to keep her that way. So get her
out of there. I'm thinking, between the two of us, we can
open one of the exits they've bricked up down here. It's on
you to take us to one that's in a relatively unguarded part of
the house.'

He blinked at me. I was being very no-nonsense, and even
I was impressed by Sergeant Jane.

'Let her out, and let's go,' I concluded. He nodded and

opened Iris's cell. It took me a bit to coax her out, but she was finally standing next to me, avoiding looking at our captor-turned-liberator.

'We'll act like I'm taking you upstairs. For treatment,' he amended, his voice guilty. I nodded at his plan. I'd been about to suggest it myself.

'Yes. Oh, and I'd like to add that if you betray us, or try to hurt Iris, I will make sure that my very last act on this earth is to castrate you. Come hell or high water, I will separate you from your man-business. I don't care how, or if you kill me. If it means me, dead, holding your junk, I'll take your junk. Got that?'

He nodded, and I could swear I saw his Adam's apple bob under his scaley green skin.

I just made a man gulp with fear, I realized proudly, not stopping to analyze the fact that I was completely serious about the castration thing.

Knowing Iris depended on me meant just one thing . . .

Jane True means business.

Chapter Twenty-Four

'I'm taking them upstairs,' the goblin said to the guard posted a few feet away from the white room where we'd been held. I made myself look as small and scared as possible, which wasn't difficult. Despite all my bravado, I *was* small and scared. Iris, meanwhile, was equally convincing, clinging to me as she was.

After a few seconds, the guard responded with a nod and let us through. We walked to near the end of the block of stinking cells I'd come through on my way in, but instead of leaving through the stairs up to the kitchen, the goblin turned us left and we walked down a narrow walkway between two cells. At the end of the walkway sat another guard, who appeared to be dozing on the stool he'd set near a wall he could lean against. He waved us through the doorway he was ostensibly protecting, barely bothering to open his eyes.

We walked and walked after that, going on a confusing path through random small rooms, some stocked with scrubs, some with disused medical equipment, some empty but for plumbing and water heaters and the like. The goblin led the way, muttering to himself. I wanted to reiterate my castration threat, but I figured that continually repeating your intention to chop off someone's goolies was a bit like crying wolf.

We passed only two other guards, and both times the goblin put a hand on our napes as if he were leading us, and said something about taking us up 'the back way'. Which led to an absolutely laugh-a-minute series of anal-rape jokes from one particularly clever guard.

Can we castrate him, too? my libido whined, offended to its very core at the idea of using sex as a threat.

Yes, I soothed. *Once Iris is free, I will bring back the troops and there can be castration for all.*

My libido purred happily, while a small part of me did go ahead and wonder when I'd become so bloodthirsty.

You do realize you're completely serious, that small part of my brain reminded me. I was too busy enjoying my libido's rundown of possible emasculation techniques to care. In fact, I was so distracted that I nearly ran into the goblin when he suddenly stopped.

We were in a room that was empty except for gardening equipment. To my relief, I saw that the room had windows and a door that had obviously been bricked in.

'This door used to lead out to the far side of the garage, near the kitchen gardens. It's the farthest possible exit from the main part of the house and our best chance of escape. But we're going to have to blow it.'

'No problem.'

'Are you sure?'

I cocked my head at the door, then at him. 'Yeah, it's no problem. We can just use our shields like a battering ram . . . back it up with our mojo. No sweat.'

'Yes, well, you are going to have to do that,' Avery said.

'Sorry?'

'You are going to have to do that. Such things are . . . beyond my skill.'

'Really?'

'Yes, really. That's not a normal skill, halfling. It takes a lot of power to solidify shields.'

'Umm . . . everybody that I know . . .'

'Everyone you know is a warrior of some sort. Investigators, soldiers, spies . . . the majority of us can't do these things. I was useless until I discovered science and the Healer discovered me.'

I thought about what the goblin was saying. It had always seemed to me that *everyone* was so powerful, compared to me. But then I really examined my memories. Yes, it was true that Ryu, his deputies, Nell, and the like were all very strong. And when the nagas had attacked at the Compound all those many months ago, there *had* been a lot of fighting and a lot of beings *had* joined in the fray with gusto. But a lot had run around looking scared, and quite a few had also died that night.

And that would explain why people keep saying you're strong. That thought hit me like a hammer. I'd heard various beings, including Anyan, mention the fact I had a lot of power. But I'd never believed them, partly because I was always comparing myself to supes like the barghest and Ryu.

I'd always thought those creatures like Iris, who I knew was relatively weak, were the exception. The idea that she, and her abilities, were the norm floored me.

I am wicked hard-core, I thought. *Or something.*

'Um, all right,' I said. 'If you can just step back . . . And I'll be throwing around a lot of force. Can you shield yourself? And Iris?'

The goblin nodded. 'That much I'm capable of,' he said drily. He moved Iris away from me, causing her to whimper and reach out. I smiled at my friend, trying to look as reassuring as possible.

'It's okay, Iris. I'm going to blast through this door so

we can escape. The goblin will shield you. It'll just take a second.'

I waited till they were out of the way, and defended, before reaching. For a second nothing happened, and I thought I was, indeed, gonna do some castratin' before the day was through. But then it was like a dam burst and my power flooded through me, sharp and eager from being contained for so long.

I had one false start, where I hit the bricked-in door and it merely buckled.

'Oops,' I said sheepishly, and I tried again. This time I not only blew the bricks out of the doorway, but I took a bit of the doorframe as well.

I smiled at my handiwork before I walked forward – mage ball in hand and shields up – to peer out my impromptu exit and into the dusk.

'Coast is clear,' I called after a minute. 'Let's head ooooooooouuuuaaah!'

My words trailed off and ended in a shout as there was a tremendous blast that rocked the foundations of the house.

The cavalry has arrived, I thought as a heady cocktail of fear, pride, and excitement washed through me. I was proud of my friends for finding me, and excited they were rescuing us (even if I was already taking care of that myself), but terrified of what Anyan was going to do when he saw me.

Maybe a spanking? my libido volunteered unhelpfully.

'Okay, let's get out of here,' I started to say, right as the door we'd barred behind us flung open, a guard powering through on a wave of magic and adrenaline.

And then he was down, taken out by the mage ball I sent zinging at his face. He was shielded at the back, not expecting an attack from the front.

As he fell, he was trampled by a small cluster of guards

that stampeded through after him. They took one look at me, another mage ball ready to fly, and they all fell, quivering, to the floor.

'Don't kill me!' one guard shouted.

'Call off your Alfar!' another cried.

The other two just whimpered.

'Um, yes!' I said. 'Stay there! Or I will . . . summon my Alfar!'

My Alfar? I thought. *How the fuck did we get a . . . Moo!* I realized suddenly. The halflings of Tryptich had come to rescue me. I nearly started dancing at that idea, but I didn't think it would be too intimidating to the men at my feet if their captor started gamboling about like an idiot.

I kept my own mage balls at the ready, prepared to remove the cock-'n'-balls off any male that moved a muscle. We listened, all together, as another series of blasts rocked the mansion, followed by all sorts of unpleasant screams and noises. Eventually, there was trampling from the room above us, and the sound of fighting, as every corner of the mansion was cleaned of filth.

It was like hearing the Liberty Bell strike when voices came shouting from inside the basement. There were a few angry screams from guards who were quickly silenced, and then the sound of footsteps coming slow but steady through the rabbit warren of rooms before us.

'Hello?' I shouted. 'We're here!'

And then I saw him.

Anyan, I thought, my whole being trembling at the sight of his big body. He was striding forward, one large hand cupping a mage ball, the other holding an assault rifle. Then he saw me, too. The mage ball disappeared, the rifle was passed behind him, to Capitola. As for the expression on his face . . .

Dude, he looks pissed . . .

The rest of that thought was cut off as the barghest practically flew into the room, grabbed my elbow, and started to haul me out of the gap I'd made in the wall. I protested, needing to stay with Iris, till I saw Capitola take her in hand. Wrapping a long arm around my friend, the only other person I would have trusted with Iris's safety besides myself or Anyan called for a medic and led Iris to sit down on an overturned bucket. Knowing my friend was in good hands, I let myself be dragged.

'Um, Anyan,' I said, trying to catch his attention as he pulled me forward. It was almost fully evening now and I was stumbling in the dark, but he just kept dragging me toward a shed on the outskirts of the little garden.

He is *going to spank us*, my libido purred.

Or kill us, you idiot, came my virtue's dry rejoinder.

'Anyan, can we please talk about—'

'No,' he growled, hauling me about to face him. We were behind the shed now, hidden from view, although I could still hear an occasional random explosion from behind us.

'Fuck you, Jane! Do you have any idea what you put me through? What the fuck were you thinking?' Shocked, I stared at the barghest's red, angry face. His hands were clamped on my forearms as he shook me roughly and randomly. His grip hurt, but not as much as the look of fury on his face.

He's really yelling *at me*, I thought, suddenly scared.

'Were you even thinking? At all? About anyone besides yourself? What would I have told your father if you'd died! What would I have done, Jane? What would I have done!'

Between Anyan shouting, his mention of my father, and hearing the slightest hitch in his voice when he said that second 'What would I have done,' I did what any self-respecting warrior woman did after getting kidnapped, rescuing herself and her friend, and single-handedly capturing her first coterie of bad guys.

I started crying.

Hard.

With that, Anyan stopped yelling. Then, to my surprise, he dropped to his knees in front of me. Wrapping his arms around my hips, he drew me forward to bury his head in my breasts. But there was nothing sexual in the gesture; it was simply one of comfort. After a shocked few seconds, I realized he was reassuring himself as much as, or more than, he was me.

Tentatively, I reached down and stroked my hand over his rough curls, only to find that they indeed felt pretty rough. But they were Anyan's curls, and they were beautiful.

My fist clenched in his hair, and my free arm snaked around his head, pulling him tighter against me. I could feel wetness at my breasts, and unless some errant god had intervened and I'd begun lactating, such wetness could mean only one thing: Anyan was crying. Which only set me off again.

'I'm so sorry,' I crooned. 'So sorry . . . so sorry . . .' His only response was to mumble something inarticulate, over and over, that eventually revealed itself to be, 'Never again.'

'Never what, baby?' I whispered. 'Never what?'

'Never letting you leave the house again,' he replied, his voice taking on a stubborn edge.

If you're going to make a go of things with the barghest, you'll have to work on his social skills, my brain commented drily.

Naked tutorials! my libido suggested, unable to believe that the barghest was pressed against my breasts and there were still clothes between us.

'Definitely never gonna let you leave Rockabill,' Anyan

finally conceded, pulling away from me. He gave one mighty sniffle, lifted his T-shirt to scrub his face (revealing his thick, deliciously furry torso), and then sat back on his heels, staring up at me.

'You scared the shit out of me, Jane. I haven't been that scared since . . . since forever,' he finished, his voice still strained.

'I'm sorry,' I said. 'But I had to do something.'

'Just never like *that* ever again. Not the running. I nearly had a fucking heart attack when I realized you were gone. Plus, I seriously nearly killed Julian,' he admitted, the tip of his nose twitching with emotion.

'Is Julian still alive?'

'Yes. Barely, but yes.'

'Good,' I murmured, and then, without thinking, I raised my hand to soothe away his anger before pausing.

Do I get to touch him now? I thought. *Is it as easy as all that?*

As if realizing what made me pause, Anyan reached forward, took my hand, and laid it against his cheek, inclining his head so that his long nose nuzzled the inside of my wrist.

I'll give him something to nuzzle! chimed in my incorrigible libido. My virtue, for once, didn't interject with anything serious, or pessimistic, or snarky.

If touching was that easy, it suggested, to the shock of my libido, *what about a kiss?*

I stepped forward. Anyan, sensing my intention, helped by pulling me toward him, his big thumb caressing the scars that traced my wrists.

My knees suddenly weak, I was in front of him . . . I was leaning forward, so slowly, so nervously, I was . . .

Watching as Ryu raced around the corner of the shed, skidding to a halt as he saw me with Anyan. His face went from exultation at seeing me alive, to confusion, and then to anger.

'Oh, fuck,' I said, causing Anyan's eyes – which had snapped shut like those of a virgin schoolgirl about to be kissed by her beau for the first time – to fly open.

'Huh?' he asked, twisting around to see Ryu as I extricated myself from the barghest's grip.

'Ryu!' I called, swearing again as he bolted. 'Fuck. I gotta go . . . explain . . .'

Anyan's face was pained, but he released me. 'It's not . . . It's . . . Shit,' I said articulately before fleeing after the baobhan sith.

'Ryu,' I shouted when I'd cleared the shed, watching him stride angrily across the field. 'Ryu!'

He stopped then, but kept his back to me as I caught up.

Why, exactly, are we chasing after him, again? my libido questioned, horrified that I'd just run away from Anyan to chase after Ryu. For the second time that evening, my virtue was in agreement.

'Cause I owe him more than that, I scolded. *I owe him . . . closure.*

It was only then that I realized exactly why I had chased after Ryu.

'Ryu,' I said as I panted up to him.

'Jane,' he replied, his voice laced with ice.

'Look,' I said. 'I'm sorry, I really am, but . . .'

'Save it. I can fill in the blanks.'

'It's not like I intended this—'

Ryu held up his hand, angrily cutting me off. His hazel eyes glinted in the falling dusk and his fangs were extended – and not with lust – when he finally spoke again.

'Why, Jane? Why? I would have given you the *world*.'

My heart clenched convulsively as he put into words what I'd had such difficulty articulating.

'That's the whole problem, Ryu. I don't *want* the world. I never have.'

He stared into my face, uncomprehending. He would never understand; or, if he did, it wouldn't be for a very long time.

Then Ryu turned on his heel and strode into the darkness, alone.

And that's all she wrote, I thought, reconfirming that Ryu and Jane were done. Watching his shape grow dim, then disappear in the gathering darkness, I was unaccountably sad for something that I knew had to end.

Then I saw a huge bubble of power float through the air, containing a writhing mass of living bodies, most dressed in scrubs. Underneath it strode Moo, her arms aloft as she played with her sphere containing doctors and guards, shaking it like a rapist-filled maraca.

Beside her Shar cavorted, howling with laughter, cheering and pumping her fists in the air exultantly. When I saw her white teeth flash in her dark face, I realized Moo was smiling as well, despite her Alfar calm.

At least someone is having a good time tonight, I thought as I went to look for Anyan Barghest, another man who was undoubtedly rather miffed at me right about now.

Chapter Twenty-Five

'Thank you so much,' I murmured into Moo's side. After a moment, I felt her slender arms hug me back as she patted me awkwardly on the shoulder.

'It was my pleasure, Jane,' the Alfar-halfling intoned. And I knew she was telling the truth: she'd liberated the prisoners held at that mansion with even more gusto than she'd rounded up the guards. 'I'm just sorry we did not catch the Healer.'

I drew back from her and nodded. 'Damned getaway harpies . . . But we'll catch up with him eventually.'

She smiled at me then. A bloodthirsty little smile that both thrilled and chilled me.

'My turn! My turn!' Shar cooed, practically launching herself on top of me. I laughed, hugging her back, jumping when she grabbed my ass. 'Soooo yummy,' the succubus-halfling said, pulling away from me with a sigh.

I couldn't help but giggle. 'I think you're yummy, too, Shar,' I said before turning to Capitola.

'And thank you,' I said, going to give the tall woman her own hug.

'You're welcome, Jane. Really, it was our pleasure. That felt . . . substantive.'

I grinned up at her. 'It did, didn't it?'

Cappie laughed, patting my head. 'It's not over, though. You know that, right?'

'Of course,' I said. 'It's only begun.'

'What are your plans?'

'All of the prisoners will eventually be transported to the Compound, but Anyan and I are taking the goblin doctor back now. He can finger Jarl. More important, the goblin's father, who got him involved in all of this in the first place, is one of the oldest and most powerful of the goblins, and a total minion of Jarl's. If we can get him to squeal, even Orin and Morrigan will have to listen.'

The tall woman frowned. 'Is it safe?'

I shrugged. 'Who knows? But none of us are safe right now anyway. Something has to be done.'

That was one fact with which everyone was in agreement, even the most cautious of the supes who had been involved in raiding the mansion. Seeing the extent of the operations in that place drove home to everyone how badly this needed to be stopped.

'Well, be careful. Both of you. I'd give my eyeteeth to go with you, but we can't . . .'

'No, you can't take that risk,' I said. 'I'm sure the Alfar would love to get their hands on you, to find out more about the Borderlands. In fact, you should get out of here soon, before somebody puts two and two together . . .'

Cappie nodded, then leaned down for another hug. 'You're a great gal, Jane. Come visit when all this is over. And be careful.'

The tall woman straightened, then looked around. 'I'll just say goodbye to Anyan . . . Oh, and Jane?'

'Yeah?'

'Be patient with that one. He can be a bit slow sometimes. Better yet, be bold.'

'Bold?'

'Bold.'

'Um . . . Okay. I'll try.'

Capitola laughed, patted my cheek again, and then wandered away to say goodbye to Anyan.

Be bold? I thought. *With Anyan?* Even my libido was rather nervous about that idea.

I watched as the barghest said goodbye to Cappie, incapable of not comparing myself to the beautiful halfling.

That's who he should be with . . . somebody fierce, like him . . .

Anyan looked up and caught my eye, giving me a tight smile in response. He'd mostly been avoiding me since the scene behind the shed. That whole, crazy moment had obviously been a product of adrenaline, stress, and profound irritation (his for me), and I knew I needed to forget whatever had happened between us.

Anyan obviously has, my brain intoned sadly.

I watched as Tryptich said their goodbyes and made ready to stride off into the forest. They'd call Terk, and he'd apparate them back home. If any lingering purebloods felt the brownie's First Magics, they'd probably think they were crazy.

But before they left, they had one last surprise.

'Julian?' Capitola called. 'You ready?'

My fellow halfling was standing among his Boston crew, but when Capitola called for him he stepped away from them.

'Julian, what the fuck?' Ryu snarled, staring at his deputy as if Julian were tap-dancing naked.

'I'm sorry, sir. But I'm giving you my notice. I'm leaving.'

Ryu looked apoplectic, and I took a step backward even as Tryptich and Anyan took a step forward.

'How could you betray your people like this?' Ryu snarled, his fangs elongated in rage.

The look Julian gave Ryu in return was both proud and sad.

'You have always treated me well, sir. As have you, Caleb, and you, Daoud. You have all treated me like an equal. But as long as I live in the Territory, I'm not an equal. I'll always be just a halfling. One with a good power and one that people want around, but never an equal.'

Ryu looked like he was going to argue, but Caleb stopped Ryu by placing a hand on his shoulder.

'I've loved working for you, and I've been happy in the bubble we created in Boston. But it was just that: a bubble. The minute I left I was put back in my place. You've seen it happen, sir.'

Ryu's fangs had slowly retracted, his shoulders slumping in defeat.

'I have,' he said finally, grudgingly.

'I'm tired,' Julian whispered, so quietly we had to strain to hear him. 'And I want to feel at home.'

'And you felt at home, with them?' Ryu said, jerking his head toward Capitola and her friends.

'Yes.'

Ryu sighed, scrubbing a hand over his tired face, through his now longish, brassy hair.

'Then go. Keep in touch if you can,' he added resignedly.

'Thank you, sir. Please tell my mother . . . tell her I love her. That I'll see her again. That I'll finally be free, and so will she. She's looked out for me for so long . . . she has to be tired, too.'

Ryu nodded once sharply. 'I'll tell her. Goodbye, Julian. It's been a pleasure to work with you.'

He stepped forward, his hand extended, and took Julian's own proffered palm. After they'd shaken hands, Ryu backed away. He gave me a hard look before striding off toward where his car was parked. Then he drove away, leaving his deputies with us.

I had no idea where he was headed.

I felt someone nudge my elbow and saw that Anyan was beside me, holding out a red-paisley handkerchief. It was only then I realized that I was crying like a baby over Julian's defection.

'It's clean,' he murmured. 'Ish.'

I took it delicately, making sure I wasn't about to mop my face with barghest snot, before using it to wipe away my tears. Then I blew my own nose into it noisily.

Julian came and hugged me, told me he'd call me. Then he shook everyone else's hands and went off into the forest with Capitola, Moo, and Shar. I was so happy for him. And even happier I now had a good excuse to keep in contact with the fabulous ladies of Tryptich.

'About ready to go?' came that rough voice from behind me. I turned to face the barghest.

'Yup.' I nodded, wiping the last of my tears away and giving my nose one last, thorough blow. Then I looked pointedly from the barghest to his handkerchief.

'You can keep that one, too.' He grinned, and I couldn't help but return his infectious smile.

'What about the doctor?'

'He's ready. Not happy at all about the idea of confronting his father or Jarl, but he's gonna do it.'

'Like he's got a choice.' I smiled, remembering my threats of castration.

'He does have a lot to atone for . . .'

'What are they gonna do with the rest of the prisoners?'

'Transport them. We're rounding up some buses now.'

'What about the victims?'

'They'll be sent to clinics like the one you saw, all over

the Territory. Our healers are gonna be busy for a while. Did Iris leave already?'

I nodded glumly. That had been the hardest thing to do: say goodbye to Iris. The succubus hadn't wanted to leave my side, and I hadn't wanted her to leave. But she needed medical attention, and safety, not a crazy, possibly suicidal mission to attempt bearding Jarl in his own den.

So I'd hugged her, again and again, then watched as she got into a car with one of the local investigators. Dressed now in scrubs, rather than that horrible, filthy T-shirt, she looked so lost and vulnerable it had taken everything I had in me not to wrench her out of that car and take her home to Rockabill.

That would have been shortsighted, however. For this was going to be wrapped up, one way or another. We had an opportunity to grab Jarl by the short hairs, and we needed to act on it. Now was the time to end the Alfar second's reign of terror.

So right before saying goodbye to the girls, I'd waved goodbye to my Iris, knowing she needed to be safe. After which I loaded our goblin doctor into a borrowed SUV, so we'd be ready to take off as soon as Tryptich made their getaway. The rental car I'd stolen was out of commission, so we'd acquisitioned new vehicles from local investigators. Daoud and Caleb were in one car; Anyan, the goblin, and I in the other. Ryu might have buggered off, but his deputies were seeing our mission through to its bloody end. Soon enough, however, they shot ahead of us, on their way to Boston where they'd pick up Camille and another vehicle. Then they'd meet us in Montreal, at which point we'd have three cars in our convoy.

But no more Team Halfling, I thought, both happy for Julian and sad he wouldn't be here to see the mission come to its end. *Oh well, he was rubbish in a fight anyway.*

When we were all ready to go, Anyan took the driver's seat and I settled myself next to him, on the passenger side, the goblin doctor in back. We were finally headed off to end it all at the place where it had begun: the Territory's Compound outside Quebec, where we'd confront Jarl and his minions.

But first we were going to get some rest.

The mansion turned out to be a forlorn vestige of Pennsylvania's industrial past, right outside Allentown. I never even thought to ask where we were until I saw a sign on the highway. As soon as we came across something relatively decent, we rented rooms in a hotel – one for me, one for Anyan and the goblin. First I took a long, very hot shower – trying to scrub away the filth of that place. I lay down warily, frightened of the dreams my sleeping brain would plague me with after all the horrors I'd seen in the past twenty-four hours. But to my surprise, I was out like a light as soon as my head hit the pillow, and I slept heavily and dreamlessly until very early the next morning.

After a quick breakfast and another superhot shower for me, we were off. The trip to Montreal was a bit surreal. I wasn't all too comfortable in front of our captive, and Anyan didn't seem to want to talk. So most of the time we were all silent, except for an occasional request for a pit stop or a short debate on which roadside restaurant to choose for lunch.

I kept telling myself it was just the presence of Avery that kept Anyan and me from talking to each other, but I knew it was more than that. He was barely even looking at me, and I could feel the tension between us.

Why is he so distant? my libido questioned plaintively. After what had happened behind the shed, it was convinced we'd be making out by now. Instead, we were barely speaking.

He never meant to react that way, I told myself, trying to batten down the surge of sadness I felt. *And now he doesn't know how to take it back. He doesn't want to hurt me, but he doesn't really feel the way he acted. We were all just stressed . . .*

So I did what I normally do when someone doesn't seem all that impressed with me: I pretended to sleep. It wasn't hard, mostly because I think I did fall asleep. After all my recent shenanigans, I was exhausted. I also really needed a swim.

That evening found us in Montreal, at a swank hotel, waiting for our backup to arrive. Anyan still wasn't really talking, and I was getting increasingly pissed off. I got it that he regretted his actions, but they were *his* actions. He didn't have to be a dick to me just because he didn't like his own behavior.

'Do you want dinner?' Anyan asked, trying to hand me the room service menu.

'Whatever,' I said, not taking it.

'Well, are you hungry?'

'Doesn't matter to me,' I said. But my stomach betrayed my passive-aggression routine by yowling like a bobcat.

'You're hungry. We'll eat,' the barghest said, dropping the menu in my lap.

'Whatever,' was my petulant reply to his back as I angrily rubbed my disloyal belly.

We ordered and ate, all in silence. Even the goblin – trapped in his own funk of fear and guilt – seemed to notice something was up between Anyan and me, since he kept glancing between the two of us.

It wasn't until the others arrived that we talked freely.

'Camille,' I greeted Ryu's baobhan sith second with trepidation, as she was also Julian's mother.

'Jane,' Camille said, smiling. 'How are you?'

'I'm fine,' I responded. 'But how are you? About Julian, and everything?'

She smiled. It was a sad smile, but it was a smile. 'I'm happy for my son. And I know I'll see him soon. In the meantime, he's already e-mailed me. Not even our borders can stop e-mail,' she said, winking at me.

'Good,' I said, so happy to see she was doing okay with her son's defection.

'Now, let's take you swimming. You look like you could fall over, and I know the perfect place . . .'

Camille took me to one of the many enormous lakes surrounding Montreal, where I swam for a good two hours. Thoroughly charged, I felt like a million bucks when we returned to the hotel. Then, after a short strategy session, we all dispersed to our various bedrooms. We'd rented two suites, each of which had two bedrooms and a foldout couch in the lounge, so after a bit of shuffling we were all installed in a bed somewhere. Caleb ended up bunking with the goblin on the foldout sofa in the main room. After losing one prisoner, we weren't taking any chances.

But another night passed peacefully, and between the two solid nights of rest and my swim, I felt almost like myself again. I was still pissed about Anyan's treatment of me, but whatever. I kept telling myself that it was better to learn the barghest was an emotional fucktard *now*, rather than later. Not that it helped really. For every time I remembered the feel of his arms around me it was like somebody punched me in the gut.

And my guts were already roiling, needless to say, since we kept creeping ever closer to confronting Jarl. Surprisingly, I found myself only slightly panicked about the whole thing. For a large part of me felt that this was simply right; it was inevitable. We'd captured too many people who knew too much; now was the time for Jarl to get his comeuppance.

We were only about four and a half hours from the

Compound when we stopped in Quebec for lunch and to assess. We hadn't run into any opposition yet, but that couldn't last. From the beginning we'd figured that an ambush, if it came, would happen close to the Compound. Jarl had to know what had happened, since the harpies had escaped with the Healer, and the last of his most trusted force were with him at court.

No doubt they would be watching and waiting for us to arrive.

So we loaded ourselves into our cars, planning to drive, bunched together, until we got off the main highway that led to the Compound. Once on that final, two-lane road that quickly narrowed down to a one-lane dirt road, we'd be vulnerable. So we had to be ready.

I was still riding with Anyan. I'd rather have ridden with one of the others, but I didn't want to make a big deal of swapping with someone. So Anyan and I kept up our silence as we turned off the highway and onto the two-lane road. We had about a half hour till it became dirt, and we could expect an attack at any time.

Ridiculously, the goblin was asleep. He'd looked exhausted since before we'd left Pennsylvania, and apparently he hadn't really slept either night we'd stopped. So now that danger was imminent, he went ahead and crashed, sprawled out on our backseat.

How he can sleep right now is beyond me, I thought, for I was wound tight as the spring on a mousetrap. Which is why I nearly jumped out of my seat when Anyan finally spoke.

'Well, this appears to be about over, Jane.'

'Yup,' I said, unsure where he was going.

'And I think we're going to be successful. I think this is going to work . . . between the sleeping beauty and his father, there should be more than enough evidence against Jarl. Not even considering everyone else we captured, some of whom have to know something . . .' His voice trailed off, and I nodded.

'Yeah. We did a good job. Thank you for your help.'

Anyan frowned at me. 'Don't thank me, Jane. It was something I had to do as much as you did.'

I didn't know what to say to that one, unsure how to interpret his words.

'And pretty soon you can get back to your old life. Get back to work—'

'Thank the gods,' I interrupted. 'Before I get fired.'

'And to your dad,' Anyan said.

I nodded, but the barghest wasn't done.

'And to Ryu.'

'To Ryu?' I said, startled.

'Yeah,' he said with a twitch of his nose. 'To Ryu.'

'Um, yeah. Well, that's not going to happen. Ryu and I broke up.'

Both of Anyan's hands were on the wheel now, showing a little white-knuckle resolve.

'Broke up? But the way you chased after him the other night . . .'

'Well, yeah. I had to chase after him . . . I mean, I felt I had to. Because we'd fought and everything, but we hadn't really ended it. For real. I mean, we did really care for one another at one point,' I said, watching as Anyan's nose twitched again. 'And so there were things that needed to be said, to make things official. And stuff.'

The barghest paused, pursing his lips as if considering his choice of words.

'So *were* things made official? And stuff?'

I couldn't help but smile. 'Yeah, wicked official. And stuff.'

'Hmph,' he grunted as I turned back to stare in front of me.

Is that *why he's been such a pissy little cunt this whole time?* I marveled. *'Cause he thought I'd made up with Ryu or something?*

I watched the barghest out the corner of my eye. He was sort of pawing at the steering wheel with his right hand, indecisively, before he moved it to hover over the gear shift . . . then moved to hover over my knee . . . then it descended, slowly, till his palm was resting against my jeans.

'Jane, I—' he started to say, looking over at me from the driver's side.

'Don't say it,' I interrupted breathlessly, my eyes once again on the road in front of us. 'Don't say *anything*.'

'What? Why not? Jane . . .'

'Phaedra, twelve o'clock,' came the goblin's voice from the backseat as his bony, green-scaled finger shot between us to point at the road.

'Exactly,' I said, patting Anyan's hand. 'Phaedra, twelve o'clock.'

Anyan removed his hand from my knee even as we both raised strong shields around our vehicle. He also braked, hard, so we had a lot of wiggle room to stop before the little, leather-clad woman standing, apparently alone, in the middle of the dirt road.

Fucking Phaedra . . .

Chapter Twenty-Six

We idled in the middle of the dirt road, while Camille and Caleb pulled up their respective vehicles alongside ours. It was a tight squeeze on the small road, trees butting up close on either side, but we made it happen.

Phaedra just stood there, impassively watching as we conferenced.

'Stand and fight?' Camille suggested, as if she were suggesting a restaurant for dinner.

'Every time we do that,' Anyan responded, 'we lose our witness.'

The goblin sucked in his breath behind me.

'You three need to get to the Compound. Let us stay and keep Phaedra busy,' Daoud said from Caleb's passenger seat.

'But how do we get past her?' I asked. I'd figured out that while Phaedra was nowhere close to being the most powerful Alfar out there, she was still packing some major mojo.

'Big shield,' grunted Anyan. 'Lay on the gas.'

'And Jane can do that thing she does with her water force,' Camille called from her car.

'What thing?' I asked, confused.

'How you sort of shore up our shield cracks with your

own power,' Anyan said. 'None of us have ever seen that before.'

'Really?' I asked, suddenly wanting to preen.

Anyan smiled. 'Yes, Jane. Really. You do stuff all the time that none of us have ever seen. We've all been trained; you just do things.'

'And the shield thing is hot,' Daoud called to me, with a naughty little wink.

I blushed. 'Thanks, guys. But we should do this. Phaedra looks bored.'

We all looked forward to where the bald-pated little woman had begun tapping her toe in the dirt, a petulant little moue distorting her usually calm face.

Fucking Phaedra, I thought again, suddenly eager to get this over with.

'Lock and load,' I murmured as Anyan's power burst forth, to be joined by everyone else's. I felt a bit self-conscious then as I used my own power like a caulking device: making our shield seamless and strong. I had never realized what I did was weird; it had always felt so natural.

Water flows, after all, I philosophized as Anyan smiled at me. Encouraged by the barghest's attentions, I tried something different then, and added another coating of my power *behind* our shields . . .

Like two-ply toilet paper, I thought with an internal giggle. *With which we are gonna wipe some Alfar ass . . .*

'Nice,' Anyan murmured as he revved the engine.

'Vroom vroom,' I replied, waggling my eyebrows at him before turning to the backseat. 'Ya might want to fasten yourself in,' I told the goblin. 'We are going for a ride.'

And with that, we were off. We kept pace with one another, three abreast, as we pumped power into our magical battering ram.

Immediately I could feel pressure emanating from Phaedra. It was strong enough that our rental cars were bucking a bit, and I rammed more force into our defenses, trying to make them as offensive as possible.

We were picking up the pace, using the kinetic energy of our lurching vehicles to enhance our own shields and give us some momentum, but Phaedra's power was stifling. All three cars were grinding down, engines churning but the vehicles slowing until, finally, we were barely moving forward. I started to sweat, both with effort and with fear . . . We were so close! The thought of not making it to the Compound, when we'd come so far and seen so much, nearly destroyed me.

But then, like a rock star parting some groupie's thighs, there was an opening in Phaedra's force. It was just large enough for our car to fit through, and it looked like an obvious trap. Except for one thing . . .

'That's not Alfar power,' Anyan said, his nose twitching once, hard.

'Nope. *That's* what Blondie's power feels like,' I told the barghest. He frowned, but for some reason I wasn't surprised. This wasn't the first time she'd popped up when we needed her. She obviously had some stake in our mission; I just wish she'd tell us what that stake was.

'Do we trust it?' he asked.

'I don't see why not,' I said. 'She could have killed me, and you, at least twice. But she didn't. Plus, I get a good vibe from her.'

'You get a good vibe?' the barghest asked drily.

'Oh, c'mon, big boy.' I grinned. 'Trust me.'

Anyan cocked one thick eyebrow at me, and I couldn't help it.

'C'mon, puppy, trust me . . . and I'll be sure to give you a treat later.'

The look that Anyan gave me then was hot, and fierce, and made my whole body tingle. My libido nearly passed out as my virtue held up its hands in defeat.

And then he pressed on the gas, shooting our SUV through the narrow tunnel in Phaedra's barrier made by Blondie's own weird force.

I held my breath until we were through, when I let out a triumphant shout. Phaedra was standing there, looking equally confused and pissed off, while our friends had stopped their cars and bailed out, ready to keep Phaedra busy while we got away.

And there, on the side of the road, just past where Phaedra had made her stand, was Blondie. She was wearing the wife-beater and big jeans again, although her hair was spiked up in an outrageous blonde Mohawk, tipped with fuchsia.

She gave me a thumbs-up then turned back toward Phaedra, a spring in her step as she approached the Alfar.

I grinned and shooed Anyan forward as he started to slow down.

'We should stop, find out what she is,' he complained.

'Not now. Later. Now we have a Jarl-fish to fry.'

My voice was adamant, and Blondie had already walked off. So, with a last backward glance and a sigh, the barghest obeyed.

Such a good puppy, I thought, my hands itching to touch him. But touching him still seemed like such a dream come true that I didn't trust my freedom to take such liberties.

So we drove, and drove, and soon enough we were parked outside the Compound.

The first bullet nearly took off my ear, it was so close. I sat there, confused – I'd never been shot at in my life – until Anyan pulled me down to huddle in the SUV's wheel well.

'Shields, Jane . . . and manifest them.'

So that's what we did, the barghest and I: manifested a solid, bullet-stopping shield around our car that absorbed the next spray of bullets. They hung there in midair, a more frightening sight in their snub-nosed physicality than any of the magics I'd ever seen.

I hate guns, I thought wearily as Anyan finally pointed to a clump of decorative bushes.

'Graeme!' he shouted, and then his strong air magics blew past us, carrying a pulse that set the bushes on fire. The wax-faced incubus came hopping out from behind the bushes, only to be greeted by my own little show of force.

If I can merge my magic with our shields to strengthen them, I thought, *what would happen if I did the same to Graeme's?*

So I tried it, and the results were magnificent. Where my power could thread between cracks in our force to help us form a tight defensive barrier, I used it like a molasses trap for flies when I threaded it through Graeme's shields. Inspired a bit by his mistress Phaedra's powerful Alfar web she'd used against us in Boston all those months ago, I wove my power through his, manifested it, and then pulled it tight. The incubus froze, unable to move, and I smiled like a little girl on Christmas morning.

'Impressive,' Anyan grunted. 'How long will it hold?'

'Not long. We should get inside. Ready, Avery?'

The goblin nodded from the backseat then turned to rootle around in the very back of the SUV. Pulling out a tire iron, he smiled. 'Now I'm ready.'

We bailed out of the car and started up the Compound's wide steps. We pushed through the doors, and I felt that same strange feeling of being watched that I'd felt the first time I'd come here. This time, however, I recognized it for what it was: a magical probe that assessed us as friend or foe.

The magic drifted off, quickly enough, having determined we were friends. It did linger a bit on me, as if unsure what to make of my halfling composition. But pretty soon it let up, and we were free to move forward.

Except for the irate spriggan blocking our path.

'Bloody hell, Fugwat,' Anyan swore. 'Won't you just *go away.*'

I thought that was an awfully polite way to greet someone who wanted to kill us, but I didn't chide Anyan. After all, it was always a good idea to show a strong collective front when facing either children or sworn enemies.

'Yes, won't you just go away!' I echoed, sounding rather silly.

Anyan shot me an annoyed look just as Fugwat sprang. He didn't get very far, however, for Avery the goblin calmly walloped him, with tremendous force, over the head with his tire iron, causing the spriggan to collapse in a heap.

'Well done,' I said, giving the goblin an admiring glance.

He shrugged, his yolk-yellow eyes impassive. 'We are physically the strongest of all the factions,' he intoned, using a lecturing voice.

'Still,' I murmured as we crept past the spriggan's prone form.

'Quite,' he said drily.

Soon enough we were inside the Compound, walking through the white room with the elemental mosaics I'd so admired my first time here. And then we were pushing through the main doors, into the grand hall of the court.

It was dinnertime, and it seemed we were interrupting a gala shindig. Many of the beings at the Compound suffered from the boredom of an immortality spent in servitude, and so the Alfar were always throwing parties. I'd been so impressed by all the finery, and so eager to please, the first time I had been here. But now? It looked pathetic: everyone all gussied up to sit at the same table with the same people they'd sat next to for generations of human lives.

We'd entered quietly enough, but just walking down that central aisle brought us so much attention you'd think we were doing a naked tango.

And we must have made quite the incongruous picture. Amid all the splendor of the Alfar court, Anyan looked like a wayward biker, while I trotted next to him, looking like some college student he'd kidnapped from the library where she was studying for finals.

'Avery?' came a voice in front of us as a goblin pushed through the crowd.

'Father,' came the droll voice of our 'doctor'.

'What are you doing? Why are you here?' Avery's father looked panicked, his yellow eyes round as saucers and his black-clawed hands twitching nervously.

'It has to end, Father,' was the son's only response. 'You are my father. I loved you and trusted you. I followed you into hell and I've become someone I hate. Your beliefs, Father, are *wrong*. And they're like an infection – rotting, spreading. It has to end, and we're here to end it.'

Avery's father grimaced, and then he started forward as if he would try to confront his son. But Anyan stared him down, and he soon backed away. Then he was running, straight out of the hall and, I presumed, out of the Compound itself. I really hoped somebody stopped him, as we might need the father to back up the son's testimony.

'Anyan Barghest!' called the court herald as we neared the dais. 'Avery Goblin! And Jane True!'

The Alfar monarchs watched us pace toward them with impassive faces. Only Jarl, my enemy, betrayed his emotion with eyes so full of hate and rage they practically burned me.

But I could burn right back, and so I did; all the enmity I felt for the pureblood fanaticist exuding from my every pore.

'To what do we owe this pleasure, Anyan Barghest?' intoned Morrigan in her sleepy Alfar voice.

The barghest dropped to one knee before his king and queen. I gave it a hard thought, and stayed standing. Morrigan's eyes flickered toward me, but all she did was smile.

'As you know, my queen,' said Anyan from where he knelt, 'I have been investigating the recent spate of kidnappings in our Territory, as per your orders.'

The queen nodded, while her husband sat beside her like a statue. I wondered whether he even knew what was happening around him.

'And you have news?' Morrigan asked. 'Have there been developments?'

'Yes, my lady. May I stand?'

Morrigan nodded, and Anyan rose.

'We've raided the laboratory that we think was the base of operations, and we've brought back a witness. One of the so-called "doctors".'

'A laboratory? Doctors?' Orin's voice creaked out of his still form, as if he weren't used to speaking.

'Yes, my liege. The kidnappings that have plagued our Territory were committed in order to harvest test subjects. They were pureblooded females, and sometimes males, who had been successfully fertile with humans.'

'Test subjects?' the king repeated. No doubt he found the words unfamiliar.

'Yes, test subjects. These laboratories were built under the auspices of attempting to cure our fertility problems with what is purported to be human science. What actually occurred, however, was simply torture. Atrocities were committed on the victims: horrific abuse, beatings, rape—'

'Murder most foul,' I interrupted.

'And murder,' the barghest agreed.

'Science,' Orin mused, obviously stuck on that one idea.

'Yes, science. Or pseudoscience, to be accurate. And these attacks were not limited to our Territory, sir. Using a special chemical serum, purebloods have had their magic muted. Stripped of power, they were taken into the Borderlands, where many of the laboratories were set up under the charge of halflings promised pureblood mates.'

'These charges are quite serious, Anyan Barghest. And yet no specific accusations have been made. Do you know who is responsible for these treasonous acts?' Morrigan's voice was calm, but there was tension underneath her words.

I loved that Anyan had told her people had been raped, tortured, and murdered, and all Morrigan could see in such monstrous acts was the fact 'treason' had been committed.

Anyan paused, no doubt unsure how best to implicate Jarl, when Avery stepped forward.

'As one of the designers of the serum used to inhibit magic, I have met with the leader of these operations personally. I can testify to his identity.'

I would never be able to forgive Avery his role in everything, but I had to admit he was brave, stepping forward the way he did. This was his world; these were his leaders. And yet he had the guts to make an accusation that could get him killed, even as he admitted to crimes that had just been defined as treasonous.

'Avery,' hissed Jarl from behind Morrigan, a world of threat in his voice.

'No, Jarl. It's finished. I never wanted this, any of this, and now I'm done. After what I've seen, what I've helped to enact, there is nothing but death that will bring me peace. So any threats you may make are idle.'

At this exchange, everyone started peering around at everyone else, trying to make sense of what was happening.

'My king, my queen. I regret to inform you that the being responsible for the laboratories, the kidnappings, and the testing, is none other than your second: Jarl.'

Avery's voice was strong and clear, and rang out within a perfectly silent hall. His words echoed, as if to ensure that everybody heard. That's when chaos erupted.

Beings were shoving one another around, repeating what had been said and jostling either to cram closer to the dais to see what happened or to flee from the room in an expectation of violence. I hoped my gentle dryad maid, Elspeth, was one of the latter.

Jarl leaped forward, his face a mask of rage. He would probably have killed Avery right then if Orin hadn't stopped him with a simple gesture of his hand, combined with a pulse of magic so pure and powerful Jarl jerked to a halt like he was on a leash.

That's why Orin is king, I thought, *and his older brother is his servant.*

The king set a bubble of power around his sibling, holding him still mere inches from where our goblin witness stood.

'These are serious accusations,' Orin intoned, his voice calm despite learning of his brother's treachery. Meanwhile, his queen sat, as impassive as ever, beside him. 'Have you any proof other than your own testimony?'

'My father worked closely with Jarl. You may question him,' said Avery.

Shit, I swore. *Dad took off* . . .

Only to see motion behind me as Ryu strode forward, frog-marching Avery's father before him. Ryu glanced at me as he went past, but it wasn't a lovey-dovey look. If anything, I think Ryu was telling me that he wasn't here for me.

Orin's heavy gaze moved toward the captured goblin.

'Winston Goblin, your son has made serious accusations against my second. He also claims you can testify on this matter. What do you have to say?'

Avery's father had his jaw clamped shut, mutinously staring away from his king. Orin's only response was another negligible flick of his fingers; a spell to loosen Winston's tongue and another to make him tell nothing but the truth.

And loosen it did: everything, and I mean *everything*, poured forth from the goblin. How Jarl had come to be obsessed with the idea of human science after discovering Conleth in his lab; how he'd sent out his nagas to bring back halfling bodies for experiments; how Conleth's escape had led to Jarl's collecting his own living subjects. Everything was there, out in the open. If the nagas, and later Phaedra and her gang, had been Jarl's muscle, Winston Goblin was obviously his right-hand man when it came to strategy and execution.

The whole court was silent throughout Winston's frenetic, magic-fueled testimony. Most creatures looked shocked; some looked guilty; others looked like they couldn't believe what they were hearing. It did sound crazy: the schemes of lunatics whose unlimited power allowed them to bear their wackiest fantasies to fruition.

Indeed, I was almost enjoying watching everyone's faces, till it was my turn to go pale and slack jawed.

'And then we accidentally kidnapped and killed the halfling's mother,' Winston babbled, as my heart dropped into my shoes.

'We knew the selkie had halfling children, but didn't realize she was Jane True's mother until after she was dead. We realized our mistake – there was no way Anyan Barghest would give up once his halfling pet was involved. So we kidnapped her succubus friend, another human-lover, hoping to scare them off. Then my son suggested we use the succubus as leverage instead . . .'

My mind had gone blank as the goblin's words washed over me.

Accident? I thought. *My mother's death was just an* accident *to these bastards?*

And children? Plural? Do I have other brothers and sisters?

My face heated up as my blood rushed to my head. I swayed on my feet, feeling faint, as if the goblin's words were attacking my nervous system.

A calloused hand gripped mine, squeezing gently. I looked up at Anyan beseechingly, and his dark-gray eyes locked on my black. He squeezed my fingers again, harder this time.

Get a grip, I told myself, heeding his silent warning. Now was not the time to lose it. I could lose it all I wanted, later, but the Alfar Compound was far too dangerous a place for me to fall apart. So I steeled myself, and refocused on Winston Goblin's testimony.

When he was done, the goblin collapsed, kneeling on the floor and gasping for breath. At some point during Winston's testimony, Orin had risen, leaving his queen still sitting on her throne. At that moment, the way Orin stood there, as if incapable of movement, was the closest thing to emotion I'd seen from the king. He'd always acted with complete, un-wavering resolve. He'd sentenced Jarl's nagas to death without batting an eyelash, but Orin stood before his brother as if incapable of proceeding. Eventually, however, he spoke.

'Jarl, my brother. The testimony laid out before me, from one whom I have ensured cannot lie, is damning. Have you anything to say in your defense?'

Orin's magic let up on Jarl just enough so that his brother could speak.

'What I did I did for our kind, *brother*,' Jarl practically spat. 'Your negligence would see us all wiped out, eliminated through attrition. You are no king; you are the figurehead of all that has led to our current predicament. All-powerful, and yet powerless: you squat upon your throne of lies.'

Someone's been watching Elf, I thought, as Orin's face grew even whiter at his second's admissions.

'My brother,' the king whispered, before his voice grew strong again. 'My brother, you leave me no choice. It is with regret that I accuse you of treason. Kneel and accept your punishment.'

I couldn't believe what I was seeing. After everything we'd been through, everything that happened, this was going to be it? Jarl would be gone, and I'd finally be free to live my life?

As if sensing my confusion, Anyan reached down and took my hand in his huge paw, squeezing gently to let me know he was there. I moved in closer to the big man, unsure whether I could watch anyone – even Jarl – executed in front of my eyes.

Orin's power surged, forcing Jarl to his knees. Morrigan was still sitting and I noticed she was clutching the arms of her throne with both hands.

This has to be a shock for her, too. I mean, she suspected her brother-in-law, but still... I thought, watching as Morrigan rose from her chair and approached her husband from behind.

What happened next will always be a blur in my memory. One minute Orin was standing, his hand raised to smite his own flesh and blood; the next he was gasping. Then the Alfar monarch was on his knees, and then he was lying prone, facedown, the sudden absence of his tremendous power leaving a tangible void in the room.

There was a lovely, ornamentally hilted knife sticking straight up out of his back, from where it had slid in between the king's ribs to pierce his heart.

And then the king's wife, and murderer, held out her hand to her husband's brother. Jarl stood and took Morrigan's fingers, bending gracefully from the waist to plant a fervid kiss to her knuckles.

Right about then, holy hell broke loose, allowing Lord and Lady Macbeth to flee, together, through a door hidden by the tapestry behind them.

Never saw that one coming, my brain commented, awed, before retreating behind a fog of pure adrenaline.

Chapter Twenty-Seven

The first time I was involved in a fight at the Alfar Compound, I'd been defenseless. I'd crept about, and hidden, and tried to stay out of the way.

This time, things were different.

Making sure their master and mistress had time to get away were a coterie of minions, mostly relatively weak Alfar, who had taken the dais to make their stand. Orin's body had been unceremoniously kicked aside and lay awkwardly on its back, propped up at a weird angle by the hilt of the knife that had killed him.

Anyan led the attack, Ryu at his side, both men battling as ferociously as lions. Their differences put aside, they were an intimidating team. They were backed up by other powerful beings. The remaining force wasn't going to last long, although I knew Jarl would have a good getaway plan.

So I did what I was best at: I guarded a group of Compound servants, surrounding them with one of my expansive barriers so nobody got killed. Slowly but surely, they added their own power and, however weak those individual shields may have been, I stitched them together with my water force so that our defenses were soon well nigh invulnerable.

Meanwhile, my well-guarded corner of the main hall offered me a good view of the battle, and Morrigan wasn't the only being to surprise me.

For example, the person who appeared the most poleaxed by the queen's treachery was Nyx. Over and over I'd been told that Nyx was in Morrigan's pocket, that she was Morrigan's Jarl. So I'd totally expected her to be part of the force covering Jarl and Morrigan's retreat. After all, the female baobhan sith loved a fight and she certainly loved her monarch. But she didn't move once throughout the whole brawl. She just stood, staring at where Morrigan had once sat, as if by willing her queen back she'd reappear.

The master manipulator was manipulated, I realized. But I then admitted I shouldn't be so hard on Nyx.

Morrigan was gooooood, I thought, remembering all the Alfar queen's kind words, and all her control. While there had always seemed to be a lot more simmering under that superficial calm, I'd thought it was so easy to interpret that simmering, just as Morrigan had undoubtedly intended. I remembered walking with her through the Compound on my first visit, listening to her talking about their fertility problem. The way she'd introduced the issue, but then seemed so resolved in her assertion that all would end well, had made me believe that she was surrounded by *other* people who worried her about the subject. But it must have been her own feelings all the time, elegantly masked.

And her apparent mistrust of Jarl? The Alfar queen was practicing the lesson first learned around third grade but honed by master adulterers worldwide: act like you dislike the object of your affection.

I watched the battle unfold, occasionally flicking a mage ball at whoever wandered too close without making their intentions known. Most creatures were other servants wanting to take shelter behind my shield, but there were a few beings who must have been Jarl's flunkies who thought I would be easy pickings. A glowering goblin nearly got close enough to me to do some damage physically, but instead I watched, wincing, as he was neatly beheaded. A grinning fat man was revealed by the goblin's falling body, until my rescuer stood uncovered before me, clad only in loose pantaloons and curly toed shoes.

Wally, I salute you, I thought, raising my fingers to my forehead to complete the gesture. The djinn, Daoud's uncle, grinned even broader in response and gave me an air smooch before turning back to join the fray.

After about a half hour of intense fighting, Jarl's remaining force was either dead or overpowered. But not until Anyan came over – bloody, bruised, and grim – to retrieve me, did I let my shields drop.

'You all right?' he asked.

'Yup. You?'

He nodded, and we stood facing each other awkwardly. I was pretty jacked up by the adrenaline of tonight's events, and I knew Anyan must be, too. But what to do about that fact?

Be bold, whispered Capitola's voice. So I tried.

Stepping forward, I leaned into Anyan, wanting to know, for real, that he was solid, and whole, and healthy. He was so tall, my forehead was basically resting against the top of his flat stomach, but it would do.

His long arms wrapped around me and he held me gently. We stood like that for what felt like an hour, but could have been only a minute or two. Finally, I looked up to meet his eyes.

'What's gonna happen now?'

'Chaos. Jarl was Orin's heir. There's no one to replace

him; no Alfar, that is. Most of the court Alfar have run off with Jarl or just been killed. Of the innocent remaining, we've got a scholar, a historian, a bard, and a wannabe stand-up comedian. So none of our remaining Alfar are exactly leadership material.'

'Is that going to be a problem?'

The barghest's nose twitched. 'We're not exactly a democratic society, Jane. And we've only ever been led by Alfar. So yeah, there's going to be a lot of sorting out to do.'

'You'll be busy,' I said mournfully. I figured I would lose the barghest to this mess. He was, after all, one of the supernatural community's strongest and most respected leaders.

A big hand stroked through my hair and I shivered. 'Yup,' he said. 'I'll be busy.'

I frowned. 'How long will you have to stay?'

'We'll be out of here by tomorrow night.'

'We?' I asked, figuring he meant me and whomever he sent me home with as my guard.

'Maybe earlier if everything goes quickly. I want to get you home as soon as possible and start your real training. Jarl's not gonna stop gunning for you, and we have to be ready . . .'

'We?' I asked again, my voice small and hopeful.

'Yes, Jane, *we*. You didn't think I'd let you out of my sight with Jarl running free, did you?'

'We?' was my oh-so-clever response.

Anyan laughed and crouched down. He took my hands in both of his, then gave me a serious look.

'War is coming, Jane. I don't know what form that war will take yet. But war will come. This Territory is now undefended and leaderless. Not to mention there's the little matter of Jarl and Morrigan. Despite their actions, after a few months many people will think they're our most obvious leaders. It wouldn't be the first time an Alfar monarch has arisen to take a throne he or she first bathed in blood.'

I shuddered at the thought.

'So we must be ready. But we're relatively safe in Rockabill. There we can plan, and there we can prepare. And I'm not leaving you. Not again.'

'Why?' I squeaked, unable to believe Anyan would give up his chance to lead to be with me.

'I don't want any part of the political clusterfuck that's gonna be the next few months,' Anyan growled. 'And I told you once about my loyalties. I care for few creatures here, Jane. My loyalties are elsewhere.'

With that he sat back on his heels, looking up into my face. I behaved with my usual dignity and grace.

I shuffled and hemmed and hawed as I turned beet-red. I didn't know how to respond to his declarations. He was *Anyan*, fercrissakes. I felt like Johnny Depp had stepped out of the pages of a magazine to declare that he'd been admiring me right back.

'Mine, too,' I mumbled eventually, feeling my face get even hotter. But I squeezed his hands in mine, and he responded by stroking a thumb over my knuckles.

He stood then, and was about to say something more when I was attacked from behind by a weeping dryad.

'Elspeth,' I cried, throwing my arms around my former lady's maid. She was hysterical, but I was just glad to find her alive after all the kerfuffle. Before he walked away to attend to business, Anyan gave me a smile that was full of promise. Then I watched him stride off into the hall, toward where Ryu, Wally, Nyx, and a few other of the more powerful members of court were conferencing.

The next twenty-four hours were a blur. I comforted Elspeth and tried to stay out of the way while the supes sorted out what to do in terms of a leader. It was Anyan who suggested that they vote, like humans. Everyone stared at him for a bit, and then tried to vote for him. But he refused their nomination.

And so the power fell to the next two most obvious candidates. Unable to choose between them, both were elected interim leaders. I watched as Ryu and Nyx shook hands, agreeing to share power and defend the Territory until a proper leader could be found. Ryu's face was flushed, and he almost glowed with pride. I was happy for him. But I was even happier I didn't have to be at his side.

Anyan and I left quietly the following evening without telling anyone but Caleb. He'd keep our leaving secret till we were back in Rockabill. He also promised Anyan to inform him of everything that occurred when we were gone.

The barghest and I drove to the local airfield that was, unknown to the tiny local human population, entirely staffed by supes loyal to the Compound. We chartered Orin and Morrigan's private jet – as neither of them would be using it anytime soon – to fly to Eastport where Anyan's motorcycle was waiting, safe in one of the hangars.

The plane was a Gulfstream six-seater thingie, so Anyan and I sat across the aisle from each other. My libido kept urging me to sit on his lap, but my virtue was glad of the slight reprieve. It was going to take me quite some time to adjust to the idea that Anyan and I might just be a possibility.

Besides, we had a lot to talk about.

'Wanna talk?' the barghest asked, echoing my thoughts as he turned so that he was squished up on his right arm, his right cheek laid against the headrest. He looked sleepy.

'About what?' I asked, imitating his body position so that we lay almost as if we were girls at a sleepover, separated by the length of our sleeping bags.

'About how you feel, now that everything is over. About your mom. And Jarl.'

I thought about what Anyan was asking. As usual, of course, he was right; I did have a lot to think about. When all of this had started, I knew that part of the reason I wanted to be involved in the investigation was because it allowed me to run away from reality. But reality was like an annoying houseguest and couldn't be ignored for long.

'Up until what that goblin said at the Compound, I had been feeling better. I hadn't been thinking through everything consciously, but I think that I was chewing through it on some unconscious level. Letting everything simmer in the back of my brain, I guess.'

'And?'

'Well, I think the hardest thing was letting go of the fantasy that someday I'd meet her again. But part of me always knew that *was* a fantasy. So that part of me is being practical and reminding me that nothing has changed. I said goodbye to my mother a long time ago; now I can know it's final.'

'But?' Anyan asked.

'There's always a but, isn't there?' I asked. The barghest smiled in response.

'Well, it still hurts. And I hate *how* she died. That makes me very angry. The fact that my mother was just kidnapped and disposed of "accidentally" bothers me. I know it shouldn't; I know it's completely illogical that the idea of her dying by "accident" really bothers me, but it does. I know I would be just as upset, maybe more, if Jarl *had* kidnapped my mother on purpose, to get at me. But still . . . that word, "accident", really sticks in my craw.' I realized then how good it felt to talk to Anyan about my mom. It felt right.

'How do you feel about what Winston said about your mother having other children?' Anyan asked gently.

'Did you know?' I countered, both hoping he had known, so he could tell me about them, but also fearing he'd kept something so big from me.

'Nope. I only knew Mari when she moved into Rockabill. Sea-folk keep to themselves, otherwise.'

I felt relief wash through me: relief tinged with an edge of disappointment that I now had one more mystery hanging over my head.

'Maybe when everything is over, and Jarl is caught, I can start thinking about the fact I may have half-brothers or -sisters running around,' I said, answering Anyan's original question. 'But right now, my biggest worry is that I need to tell my dad that Mom's dead, but I don't know how.'

The barghest nodded thoughtfully. 'My advice would be to tell him as much of the truth as you can. Tell him that part of the reason you left on this trip was you thought you had a lead on your mother. That you investigated and discovered she was dead. You stayed to help put her affairs in order. He doesn't need the gory details.'

I thought about that. 'That makes sense.'

'But?'

It was my turn to smile. 'But what do I tell him about *why* she left?'

'Well,' the barghest said, his nose twitching in thought. 'You can tell him the truth about that as well. That you know there was a reason she *had* to leave, but despite that fact she still loved both of you very much.'

'That makes it sound like she was a crack addict, Anyan.'

'The ocean is sort of like crack, for selkies,' he added, shrugging.

I sat up and stretched, then looked out the window. We weren't that far from Eastport, I figured, after looking at the time on my phone. Finally, I turned back to the big man next to me. His eyes were shut, and I noticed the shadows under his eyes.

I know the perfect way to send him to sleep, my libido purred. But I ignored the ensuing lewd suggestions, concentrating instead on studying the craggy face in front of me.

'What?' he rumbled after a few minutes, startling me.

'Um,' I fumbled. 'Just thinking about what you said.'

'And?'

'And it's a good idea. *But*,' I said, a split second before he did, causing his wide mouth to curve in a smile as his eyes twitched open to meet mine, 'will you be there with me when I tell him?' I didn't know why I said that, but I meant it. And it suddenly became very important to me that Anyan said yes.

'Of course,' the barghest answered without hesitation. Then he shut his eyes again and went to sleep, for the rest of the flight.

Just an hour later, we were on the ground and ready to leave.

'Almost home,' Anyan said as he handed me his spare helmet. 'Glad?'

'Yeah,' I said, watching him with appreciative eyes as he straddled his bike. We were still being careful with each other, unsure of exactly how to proceed. But we were getting . . . somewhere. We were turning the slightest moment of proximity into an opportunity for a hesitant touch: getting off the plane, Anyan's hand had found my hip, solicitously. I'd let my hand rest on his when he'd passed me my duffel.

I didn't know what the fuck was going to happen between the two of us, but just then – knowing I was about to clamber on the back of his motorcycle so that we could drive home, together – it felt like the possibilities were endless.

Grinning goofily, but not caring, I let him help me up

behind him. Then we were off, roaring down the dark highway toward Rockabill. It was too loud to chat, but we were both enjoying being together and the ride too much to care.

Less than an hour later, we glided onto the exit that would shortly lead to the center of our town. Soon enough we were on Main Street, nearing the central square.

With greedy eyes I feasted on the sight of my home, so safe and quiet. Everything was just as I'd left it; just as it had always been. Read It and Weep was still standing; as was the Trough, and the hardware store, and our little bakery. Despite everything being closed up for the night, the empty town center didn't appear desolate. It just seemed asleep, ready to wake up for a new day tomorrow.

'Home sweet home,' I murmured. One of Anyan's hands fell on top of my own, clasped together over his waist. He stroked my knuckles gently, and I felt a strong desire to let my hands drift downward, to where his body met the bike . . .

But before I could go ahead and be bold, the barghest swore and braked hard, swerving into a skidding stop that had us both looking to our right.

There, lit up underneath one of our lovely antique streetlamps as if she were on a stage, stood Blondie.

She was naked again, her entirely tattooed, beringed body glowing with power. She started to move then, and after a startled second I realized she was doing a soft-shoe tap dance on the sidewalk. Every few seconds she'd do a toe tap, one leg bent behind her, arms extended behind her in a 'ta-da!' pose. Only, instead of saying 'ta-da!' she'd do a bit of magic. Pulling on that strong, fully elemental power that felt both familiar and yet somehow foreign, she'd shoot off mage balls that exploded like fireworks above her head; or she'd make everything go black and surround us with her psychedelic vines.

They were all powerful, all beautiful, but all *normal* tricks for an incredibly powerful Alfar. Until she did something abnormal.

One minute she was giving us the jazz hands, the next minute she straightened, threw wide her arms, and transformed. Standing before us, tall and elegant, was a gorgeous white doe, sporting silver hoops in her elegantly pointed ears.

I remembered Anyan's words from all those days ago, about how Alfar could do everything except shift. Which meant only one thing . . .

'You're an Original, aren't you?' the barghest's deep voice rolled through the night air. The doe cocked her head, lowered her neck, and extended one foreleg to rub out an itch on her muzzle; then a second later the deer disappeared in a burst of magic, returning to her tattooed, human skin.

'You're an Original,' Anyan repeated. And this time, he got an answer. Blondie put one finger to the side of her nose and winked. *Spot on*, the gesture agreed.

I let out a low whistle as Anyan started barking off questions.

'What do you want? Why are you here? Why are you helping us?'

Blondie merely smiled, raising her arms as her body rolled up like a window shade, leaving behind a white hawk floating in midair. And then the bird flew away.

We sat there, staring at the spot Blondie had vacated, both Anyan and I entirely speechless as we tried to figure out what the hell had just happened.

I knew Blondie was powerful; one of the most powerful beings I'd ever met. I knew she was also an Original, although I had little clue what this actually implied. I did know, however, that she was here for me.

I only wished I knew what it was she wanted.

Acknowledgments

As always, huge thanks to my family and friends. I love you and thank you for your unfailing support.

My students and colleagues at LSUS have been an inspiration, especially considering the upset of the current budget crisis. Thanks for being so excited about my work and so understanding about my propensity to stare off into space and mutter.

To my Alpha Team of beta readers – James Clawson, Mary Lois White, Christie Ko – you're amazing and I adore you. Thanks for keeping Jane on her toes.

Same goes to my fabulous critique partner, Diana Rowland, whose Demon series rocks my socks. You're a fantastic influence and friend, and I thank you.

To everyone at the League of Reluctant Adults for inviting me in, letting me get comfortable, and never once making me comb my hair. I adore you all and am so grateful to you.

And to my teams at McIntosh and Otis and at Orbit Books, thank you! Rebecca and Ian, you're beautiful. We've accomplished so much and I have you to blame. At Orbit, thanks to Jack and Alex for making things fly. To Lauren, as always, for making such beautiful covers with the talented Sharon

Tancredi (Thank you, Sharon!). Thanks to Jennifer for greasing the wheels, to Devi for keeping me honest, and to Tim for signing my contracts.

Finally, thank you to my fans. Those of you who really 'get' Jane and understand what I'm trying to do in these books have made this process such a pleasure. Thanks for writing and sharing your own stories and for being so warm and encouraging. Because of your support, Jane's adventures – and my own – have only just begun.

extras

www.orbitbooks.net

about the author

Nicole D. Peeler resides in Pittsburgh and is a Creative Writing professor for Seton Hill's MFA in Popular Fiction. Yes, folks, she mentors students in writing urban fantasy. Or, as she likes to call it, 'infecting them with her madness'. Equally infectious is her love of life, food, travel and friends. Visit her website: www.nicolepeeler.com

Find about more about Nicole Peeler and other Orbit authors by registering for the free monthly newsletter at www.orbitbooks.net

if you enjoyed
TEMPEST'S LEGACY

look out for

DEATH MOST DEFINITE

book one of the Death Works novels

by

Trent Jamieson

1

I know something's wrong the moment I see the dead girl standing in the Wintergarden food court. She shouldn't be here. Or I shouldn't. But no one else is working this. I'd sense them if they were. My phone's hardly helpful. There are no calls from Number Four, and that's a serious worry. I should have had a heads-up about this: a missed call, a text, or a new schedule. But there's nothing. Even a Stirrer would be less peculiar than what I have before me. Christ, all I want is my coffee and a burger. Then our eyes meet and I'm not hungry anymore. A whole food court's worth of shoppers swarm between us, but from that instant of eye contact, it's just me and her, and that indefinable something. A bit of *déjà vu*. A bit of lightning. Her eyes burn into mine, and there's a gentle, mocking curl to her lips that is gorgeous; it hits me in the chest. This shouldn't be. The dead don't seek you out unless there is no one (or no thing) working their case: and that just doesn't happen. Not these days. And certainly not in the heart of Brisbane's CBD. She shouldn't be here.

This isn't my gig. This most definitely will not end well. The girl is dead; our relationship has to be strictly professional.

She has serious style.

I'm not sure I can pinpoint what it is, but it's there, and it's unique. The dead project an image of themselves, normally in something comfortable like a tracksuit, or jeans and a shirt. But this girl, her hair shoulder length with a ragged cut, is in a black, long-sleeved blouse, and a skirt, also black. Her legs are sheathed in black stockings. She's into silver jewellery, and what I assume are ironic brooches of Disney characters. Yeah, serious style, and a strong self-image.

And her eyes.

Oh, her eyes. They're remarkable, green, but flecked with grey. And those eyes are wide, because she's dead – newly dead – and I don't think she's come to terms with that yet. Takes a while: sometimes it takes a long while.

I yank pale ear buds from my ears, releasing a tinny splash of 'London Calling' into the air around me.

The dead girl, her skin glowing with a bluish pallor, comes towards me, and the crowd between us parts swiftly and unconsciously. They may not be able to see her but they can *feel* her, even if it lacks the intensity of my own experience. Electricity crackles up my spine – and something else, something bleak and looming like a premonition. She's so close now I could touch her. My heart's accelerating, even before she opens her mouth, which I've already decided, ridiculously, impossibly, that I want to kiss. I can't make up my mind whether that means I'm exceedingly shallow or prescient. I don't know what I'm thinking because this is such unfamiliar territory: total here-be-dragons kind of stuff.

She blinks that dead person blink, looks at me as though I'm some puzzle to be solved. Doesn't she realise it's the other way around? She blinks again, and whispers in my ear, 'Run.'

And then someone starts shooting at me.

Not what I was expecting.

Bullets crack into the nearest marble-topped tables. One. Two. Three. Shards of stone sting my cheek.

The food court surges with desperate motion. People

scream, throwing themselves to the ground, scrambling for cover. But not me. She said run, and I run: zigging and zagging. Bent down, because I'm tall, easily a head taller than most of the people here, and far more than that now that the majority are on the floor. The shooter's after me; well, that's how I'm taking it. Lying down is only going to give them a motionless target.

Now, I'm in OK shape. I'm running, and a gun at your back gives you a good head of steam. Hell, I'm sprinting, hurdling tables, my long legs knocking lunches flying, my hands sticky with someone's spilt Coke. The dead girl's keeping up in that effortless way dead people have: skimming like a drop of water over a glowing hot plate.

We're out of the food court and down Elizabeth Street. In the open, traffic rumbling past, the Brisbane sun a hard light overhead. The dead girl's still here with me, throwing glances over her shoulder. Where the light hits her she's almost translucent. Sunlight and shadow keep revealing and concealing at random; a hand, the edge of a cheekbone, the curve of a calf.

The gunshots coming from inside haven't disturbed anyone's consciousness out here.

Shootings aren't exactly a common event in Brisbane. They happen, but not often enough for people to react as you might expect. All they suspect is that someone needs to service their car more regularly, and that there's a lanky bearded guy, possibly late for something, his jacket bunched into one fist, running like a madman down Elizabeth Street. I turn left into Edward, the nearest intersecting street, and then left again into the pedestrian-crammed space of Queen Street Mall.

I slow down in the crowded walkway panting and moving with the flow of people; trying to appear casual. I realise that my phone's been ringing. I look at it, at arm's length, like the monkey holding the bone in *2001: A Space Odyssey*. All I've got on the screen is Missed Call, and Private Number.

Probably someone from the local DVD shop calling to tell me I have an overdue rental, which, come to think of it, I do – I always do.

'You're a target,' the dead girl says.

'No shit!' I'm thinking about overdue DVDs, which is crazy. I'm thinking about kissing her, which is crazier still, and impossible. I haven't kissed anyone in a long time. If I smoked this would be the time to light up, look into the middle distance and say something like: 'I've seen trouble, but in the Wintergarden, on a Tuesday at lunchtime, c'mon!' But if I smoked I'd be even more out of breath and gasping out questions instead, and there's some (well, most) types of cool that I just can't pull off.

So I don't say anything. I wipe my Coke-sticky hands on my tie, admiring all that *je ne sais quoi* stuff she's got going on and feeling as guilty as all hell about it, because she's dead and I'm being so unprofessional. At least no one else was hurt in the food court: I'd feel it otherwise. Things aren't *that* out of whack. The sound of sirens builds in the distant streets. I can hear them, even above my pounding heart.

'This is so hard.' Her face is the picture of frustration. 'I didn't realise it would be so hard. There's a lot you need—' She flickers like her signal's hit static, and that's a bad sign: who knows where she could end up. 'If you could get in—'

I reach towards her. Stupid, yeah, but I want to comfort her. She looks so pained. But she pulls back, as though she knows what would happen if I touch her. She shouldn't be acting this way. She's dead; she shouldn't care. If anything, she should want the opposite. She flickers again, swells and contracts, grows snowy. Whatever there is of her here is fracturing. I take a step towards her. 'Stop,' I yell. 'I need to—'

Need to? I don't exactly know what I need. But it doesn't matter because she's gone, and I'm yelling at nothing. And I didn't pomp her.

She's just gone.

2

That's not how it's meant to happen. Unprofessional. So unprofessional. I'm supposed to be the one in control.

After all, I'm a Psychopomp: a Pomp. Death is my business, has been in my family for a good couple of hundred years. Without me, and the other staff at Mortmax Industries, the world would be crowded with souls, and worse. Like Dad says, pomp is a verb and a noun. Pomps pomp the dead, we draw them through us to the Underworld and the One Tree. And we stall the Stirrers, those things that so desperately desire to come the other way. Every day I'm doing this – well, five days a week. It's a living, and quite a lucrative one at that.

I'm good at what I do. Though this girl's got me wondering.

I wave my hand through the spot where, moments ago, she stood. Nothing. Nothing at all. No residual electrical force. My skin doesn't tingle. My mouth doesn't go dry. She may as well have never been there.

The back of my neck prickles. I turn a swift circle. Can't see anyone, but there are eyes on me, from somewhere. Who's watching me?

Then the sensation passes, all at once, a distant scratching pressure released, and I'm certain (well, pretty certain) that

I'm alone – but for the usual Brisbane crowds pushing past me through the mall. Before, when the dead girl had stood here, they'd have done anything to keep away from her and me. Now I'm merely an annoying idiot blocking the flow of foot traffic. I find some cover: a little alcove between two shops where I'm out of almost everyone's line of sight.

I get on the phone, and call Dad's direct number at Mortmax. Maybe I should be calling Morrigan, or Mr D (though word is the Regional Manager's gone fishing), but I need to talk to Dad first. I need to get this straight in my head.

I could walk around to Number Four, Mortmax's office space in Brisbane. It's on George Street, four blocks from where I'm standing, but I'm feeling too exposed and, besides, I'd probably run into Derek. While the bit of me jittery with adrenalin itches for a fight, the rest is hungry for answers. I'm more likely to get those if I keep away. Derek's been in a foul mood and I need to get through him before I can see anyone else. Derek runs the office with efficiency and attention to detail, and he doesn't like me at all. The way I'm feeling, that's only going to end in harsh words. Ah, work politics. Besides, I've got the afternoon and tomorrow off. First rule of this gig is: if you don't want extra hours keep a low profile. I've mastered that one to the point that it's almost second nature.

Dad's line must be busy because he doesn't pick up. Someone else does, though. Looks like I might get a fight after all.

'Yes,' Derek says. You could chill beer with that tone.

'This is Steven de Selby.' I can't hide the grin in my voice. Now is not the time to mess with me, even if you're Morrigan's assistant and, technically, my immediate superior.

'I know who it is.'

'I need to talk to Dad.'

There are a couple of moments of uncomfortable silence, then a few more. 'I'm surprised we haven't got you rostered on.'

'I just got back from a funeral. Logan City. I'm done for the day.'

Derek clicks his tongue. 'Do you have any idea how busy we are?'

Absolutely, or I'd be talking to Dad. I wait a while: let the silence stretch out. He's not the only one who can play at that. 'No,' I say at last, when even I'm starting to feel uncomfortable. 'Would you like to discuss it with me? I'm in the city. How about we have a coffee?' I resist the urge to ask him what he's wearing.

Derek sighs, doesn't bother with a response, and transfers me to Dad's phone.

'Steve,' Dad says, and he sounds a little harried. So maybe Derek wasn't just putting it on for my benefit.

'Dad, well, ah . . .' I hesitate, then settle for the obvious. 'I've just been shot at.'

'What? Oh, Christ. You sure it wasn't a car backfiring?' he asks somewhat hopefully.

'Dad . . . do cars normally backfire rounds into the Wintergarden food court?'

'That was you?' Now he's sounding worried. 'I thought you were in Logan.'

'Yeah, I was. I went in for some lunch and someone started shooting.'

'Are you OK?'

'Not bleeding, if that's what you mean.'

'Good.'

'Dad, I wouldn't be talking to you if someone hadn't warned me. Someone not living.'

'Now that shouldn't be,' he says. He sounds almost offended. 'There are no punters on the schedule.' He taps on the keyboard. I could be in for a wait. 'Even factoring in the variables, there's no chance of a Pomp being required in the Wintergarden until next month: elderly gentleman, heart attack. There shouldn't be any activity there at all.'

I clench my jaw. 'There was, Dad. I'm not making it up. I was there. And, no, I haven't been drinking.'

I tell him about the dead girl, and am surprised at how vivid the details are. I hadn't realised that I'd retained them. The rest of it is blurring, what with all the shooting and the sprinting, but I can see her face so clearly, and those eyes.

'Who was she?'

'I don't know. She looked familiar: didn't stay around long enough for me to ask her anything. But Dad, I didn't pomp her. She just disappeared.'

'Loose cannon, eh? I'll look into it, talk to Morrigan for you.'

'I'd appreciate that. Maybe I was just in the wrong place at the wrong time, but it doesn't feel like that. She was trying to save me, and when do the dead ever try and look after Pomps?'

Dad chuckles at that. There's nothing more self-involved than a dead person. Talking of self-involved . . . 'Derek says you're busy.'

'We're having trouble with our phone line. Another one of Morrigan's "improvements",' Dad says; I can hear the inverted commas around improvements. 'Though . . . that seems to be in the process of being fixed.' He pauses. 'I *think* that's what's happening, there's a half-dozen people here pulling wiring out of the wall.' I can hear them in the background, drills whining; there's even a little hammering. 'Oh, and there's the Death Moot in December. Two months until everything's crazy and the city's crowded with Regional Managers. Think of it, the entire Orcus here, all thirteen RMs.' He groans.

'Not to mention the bloody Stirrers. They keep getting worse. A couple of staffers have needed stitches.'

I rub the scarred surface of the palm of my free hand. Cicatrix City as we call it, an occupational hazard of stalling stirs, but the least of them when it came to Stirrers. A Pomp's blood is enough to exorcise a Stirrer from a newly dead body, but the blood needs to be fresh. Morrigan is researching ways around this, but has come up with nothing as of yet. Dad calls it time-wastery. I for one would be happy if I didn't have to slash open my palm every time a corpse came crashing up into unlife.

A stir is always a bad thing. Unsettling, dangerous and bloody. Stirrers, in essence, do the same thing as Pomps, but without discretion: they hunger to take the living and the dead. They despise life, they drain it away like plugholes to the Underworld, and they're not at all fond of me and mine. Yeah, they hate us.

'Well, I didn't see or sense one in Logan. Just a body, and a lot of people mourning.'

'Hmm, you got lucky. Your mother had two.' Dad sighs. 'And here I am stuck in the office.'

I make a mental note to call Mum. 'So Derek wasn't lying.'

'You've got to stop giving Derek so much crap, Steve. He'll be Ankou one day; Morrigan isn't going to be around forever.'

'I don't like the guy, and you can't tell me that the feeling isn't mutual.'

'Steven, he's your boss. Try not to piss him off too much,' Dad says and, by the tone of his voice, I know we're about to slip into the same old argument. Let me list the ways: my lack of ambition. How I could have had Derek's job, if I'd really cared. How there's more Black Sheep in me than is really healthy for a Pomp. That Robyn left me three years ago. Well, I don't want to go there today.

'OK,' I say. 'If you could just explain why the girl was there and, maybe, who she was. She understood the process, Dad. She wouldn't let me pomp her.' There's silence down the end of the line. 'You do that, and I'll try and suck up to Derek.'

'I'm serious,' Dad says. 'He's already got enough going on today. Melbourne's giving him the run-around. Not returning calls, you know, that sort of thing.'

Melbourne giving Derek the run-around isn't that surprising. Most people like to give Derek the run-around.

I don't know how he became Morrigan's assistant. Yeah, I know *why*, he's a hard worker, and ambitious, almost as ambitious as Morrigan – and Morrigan is Ankou, second only to Mr D. But Derek's hardly a people person. I can't think of anyone who Derek hasn't pissed off over the years: anyone *beneath* him, that is. He'd not dare with Morrigan, and only a madman would consider it with Mr D – you don't mess with Geoff Daly, the Australian Regional Manager. Mr D's too creepy, even for us.

'OK, I'll send some flowers,' I say. 'Gerberas, everyone likes gerberas, don't they?'

Dad grunts. He's been tapping away at his computer all this time. I'm not sure if it's the computer or me that frustrates him more.

'Can you see anything?'

A put-upon sigh, more tapping. 'Yeah . . . I'm . . . looking into . . . All right, let me just . . .' Dad's a one-finger typist. If glaciers had fingers they'd type faster than him. Morrigan gives him hell about it all the time; Dad's response requires only one finger as well. 'I can't see anything unusual in the records, Steve. I'd put it down to bad luck, or good luck. You didn't get shot after all. Maybe you should buy a scratchie, one of those $250,000 ones.'

'Why would I want to ruin my mood?'

Dad laughs. Another phone rings in the background; wouldn't put it past Derek to be on the other end. But then all the phones seem to be ringing.

'Dad, maybe I should come into the office. If you need a hand . . .'

'No, we're fine here,' Dad says, and I can tell he's trying to keep me away from Derek, which is probably a good thing. My Derek tolerance is definitely at a low today.

We say our goodbyes and I leave him to all those ringing phones, though my guilt stays with me.